The Quadroon
Adventures In The Far West

By

Captain Mayne Reid

The Quadroon
Adventures In The Far West
by Captain Mayne Reid

Copyright © 2024

All Rights reserved.

No part of this publication may be reproduced, stored in a retrieval system, or transmitted in any form or by any means, electronic, mechanical, photocopying or Otherwise, without the written permission of the publisher.
The author/editor asserts the moral right to be identified as the author/editor of this work.

ISBN: 978-93-61155-85-7

Published by

DOUBLE 9 BOOKS
2/13-B, Ansari Road
Daryaganj, New Delhi – 110002
info@double9books.com
www.double9books.com
Tel. 011-40042856

This book is under public domain

ABOUT THE AUTHOR

Thomas Mayne Reid, an Irish-American novelist, participated in the Mexican–American War. His numerous books on American life discuss colonial policy in the American colonies, the horrors of slave labor, and the lifestyles of American Indians. "Captain" Reid created adventure stories similar to those of Frederick Marryat and Robert Louis Stevenson. They were primarily situated in the American West, Mexico, South Africa, the Himalayas, and Jamaica. He admired Lord Byron. Dion Boucicault turned his anti-slavery novel Quadroon (1856) into a drama called The Octoroon (1859), which was staged in New York. Reid was born in Ballyroney, a hamlet near Katesbridge in County Down, Northern Ireland, as the son of Rev. Thomas Mayne Reid Sr., a senior clerk of the General Assembly of the Presbyterian Church in Ireland, and his wife. Reid's father intended him to become a Presbyterian pastor, so he enrolled at the Royal Belfast Academical Institution in September 1834. He stayed for four years, but lacked the ambition to finish his studies and graduate. He returned to Ballyroney to teach at a school.

CONTENTS

Chapter One
The Father of Waters 11

Chapter Two
Six Months in the Crescent City 15

Chapter Three
The "Belle of the West" 19

Chapter Four
The Rival Boats 22

Chapter Five
A Desirable Fellow-Passenger 25

Chapter Six
Antoine the Steward 28

Chapter Seven
The Starting 31

Chapter Eight
The "Coast" of the Mississippi 34

Chapter Nine
Eugénie Besançon 37

Chapter Ten
A New Mode of raising the Steam 41

Chapter Eleven
A Boat-Race upon the Mississippi 47

Chapter Twelve
The Life-Preserver 51

Chapter Thirteen
"Blessé" 54

Chapter Fourteen
Where am I? 58

Chapter Fifteen
"Ole Zip." 62

Chapter Sixteen
Monsieur Dominique Gayarre 67

Chapter Seventeen
"Aurore." 71

Chapter Eighteen
The Creole and Quadroon 76

Chapter Nineteen
A Louisian Landscape 80

Chapter Twenty
My Journal 85

Chapter Twenty One
A Change of Quarters 91

Chapter Twenty Two
Aurore loves me 96

Chapter Twenty Three
A Surprise 100

Chapter Twenty Four
A Rival 104

Chapter Twenty Five
An Hour of Bliss 109

Chapter Twenty Six
The "Nigger Quarter." 114

Chapter Twenty Seven
The Devil's Douche 118

Chapter Twenty Eight
Gayarre and "Bully Bill." 123

Chapter Twenty Nine
"Elle t'aime!" 127

Chapter Thirty
Thoughts 130

Chapter Thirty One
Dreams 134

Chapter Thirty Two
Stung by a Snake 137

Chapter Thirty Three
The Runaway 141

Chapter Thirty Four
Gabriel the Bambarra 145

Chapter Thirty Five
The Snake-Doctor 148

Chapter Thirty Six
Charming the Crotalus 152

Chapter Thirty Seven
Killing a Trail 157

Chapter Thirty Eight
The Pirogue 160

Chapter Thirty Nine
The Tree-Cavern 164

Chapter Forty
Hotel Gossip 167

Chapter Forty One
The Letter 173

Chapter Forty Two
The Wharf-Boat 177

Chapter Forty Three
The Norway Rat 181

Chapter Forty Four
The Houma 184

Chapter Forty Five
Jealousy 188

Chapter Forty Six
A Scientific Julep 193

Chapter Forty Seven
A Game of Whist 197

Chapter Forty Eight
The Game Interrupted 202

Chapter Forty Nine
The Sportsmen of the Mississippi 205

Chapter Fifty
The City 212

Chapter Fifty One
Vente Importante des Nègres 216

Chapter Fifty Two
Brown and Co 220

Chapter Fifty Three
Eugène d'Hauteville 224

Chapter Fifty Four
Pity for Love 227

Chapter Fifty Five
On Games and Gambling 232

Chapter Fifty Six
The Faro Bank 237

Chapter Fifty Seven
The Watch and Ring 241

Chapter Fifty Eight
My Forlorn Hope 246

Chapter Fifty Nine
The Rotundo 250

Chapter Sixty
The Slave-Mart 255

Chapter Sixty One
Bidding for my Betrothed 259

Chapter Sixty Two
The Hackney-Carriage 264

Chapter Sixty Three
To Bringiers 266

Chapter Sixty Four
Two Villains 270

Chapter Sixty Five
The Pawpaw Thicket 275

Chapter Sixty Six
The Elopement 279

Chapter Sixty Seven
The Lost Mustangs 283

Chapter Sixty Eight
A Night in the Woods 287

Chapter Sixty Nine
Love's Vengeance 291

Chapter Seventy
Hounds on our Trail...295

Chapter Seventy One
The Signal 298

Chapter Seventy Two
The Sleuth-Hounds 302

Chapter Seventy Three
The Man-Hunter 305

Chapter Seventy Four
Shot for Shot 308

Chapter Seventy Five
Love in the Hour of Peril 311

Chapter Seventy Six
A Terrible Fate 315

Chapter Seventy Seven
The Sentence of Judge Lynch 318

Chapter Seventy Eight
In the Hands of the Sheriff 321

Chapter Seventy Nine
The Crisis 324

Chapter One
The Father of Waters

Father of Waters! I worship thy mighty stream! As the Hindoo by the shores of his sacred river, I kneel upon thy banks, and pour forth my soul in wild adoration!

Far different are the springs of our devotion. To him, the waters of his yellow Ganges are the symbols of a superstitious awe, commingled with dark fears for the mystic future; to me, thy golden wares are the souvenirs of joy, binding the present to the known and happy past. Yes, mighty river! I worship thee in the past. My heart fills with joy at the very mention of thy name!

Father of Waters! I know thee well. In the land of a thousand lakes, on the summit of the *"Hauteur de terre,"* I have leaped thy tiny stream. Upon the bosom of the blue lakelet, the fountain of thy life, I have launched my birchen boat; and yielding to thy current, have floated softly southward. I have passed the meadows where the wild rice ripens on thy banks, where the white birch mirrors its silvery stem, and tall *coniferae* fling their pyramid shapes, on thy surface. I have seen the red Chippewa cleave thy crystal waters in his bark canoe—the giant moose lave his flanks in thy cooling flood—and the stately wapiti bound gracefully along thy banks. I have listened to the music of thy shores—the call of the cacawee, the laugh of the wa-wa goose, and the trumpet-note of the great northern swan. Yes, mighty river! Even in that far northern land, thy wilderness home, have I worshipped thee!

Onward through many parallels of latitude—through many degrees of the thermal line!

I stand upon thy banks where thou leapest the rocks of Saint Antoine, and with bold frothing current cleavest thy way to the south. Already I note a change in the aspect of thy shores. The *coniferae* have disappeared, and thou art draped with a deciduous foliage of livelier hue. Oaks, elms, and maples, mingle their frondage, and stretch their broad arms over thee. Though I still look upon woods that seem illimitable, I feel that the wilderness is past.

My eyes are greeted by the signs of civilisation—its sounds fall upon my ear. The hewn cabin—picturesque in its rudeness—stands among prostrate trunks; and the ring of the lumberer's axe is heard in the far depths of the forest. The silken blades of the maize wave in triumph over fallen trees, its golden tassels giving promise of a rich return. The spire of the church peers above the green spray of the woods, and the prayer of the Christian ascends to heaven sublimely mingling with the roar of thy waters!

I launch my boat once more on thy buoyant wave; and, with heart as buoyant, glide onward and southward. I pass between bold bluffs that hem thy surging waves, and trace with pleasant wonder their singular and varied outlines—now soaring abruptly upward, now carried in gentle undulations along the blue horizon. I behold the towering form of that noted landmark "*La montaigne qui trempe à l'eau,*" and the swelling cone on whose summit the soldier-traveller pitched his tent. I glide over the mirrored bosom of Pepin's lake, regarding with admiration its turreted shores. I gaze with deeper interest upon that precipitous escarpment, the "Lover's Leap," whose rocky wall has oft echoed back the joyous chaunt of the light-hearted voyageur, and once a sadder strain—the death-song of Wanona—beautiful Wanona, who sacrificed life to love!

Onward I glide, where the boundless prairies of the West impinge upon thy stream; and my eye wanders with delight over their fadeless green.

I linger a moment to gaze upon the painted warrior spurring his wild steed along thy banks—to gaze upon the Dacotah girls bathing their lithe limbs in thy crystal wave—then on again past the "Cornice Rocks"—the metalliferous shores of Galena and Dubuque—the aerial tomb of the adventurous miner.

I reach the point where the turbid Missouri rushes rudely upon thee, as though he would force thee from thy onward course. Poised in my light canoe, I watch the struggle. Fierce but short it is, for thou triumphest, and thy conquered rival is compelled to pay his golden tribute to thy flood that rolls majestically onward!

Upon thy victorious wave I am borne still southward. I behold huge green mounds—the sole monuments of an ancient people—who once trod thy shores. Near at hand I look upon the dwellings of a far different race. I behold tall spires soaring to the sky; domes, and cupolas glittering in the sun; palaces standing upon thy banks, and palaces floating upon thy wave. I behold a great city—a metropolis!

I linger not here. I long for the sunny South; and trusting myself once more to thy current I glide onward.

I pass the sea-like estuary of the Ohio, and the embouchure of another of thy mightiest tributaries, the famed river of the plains. How changed the aspect of thy shores! I no longer look upon bold bluffs and beetling cliffs. Thou hast broken from the hills that enchained thee, and now rollest far and free, cleaving a wide way through thine own alluvion. Thy very banks are the creation of thine own fancy—the slime thou hast flung from thee in thy moments of wanton play—and thou canst break through their barriers at will. Forests again fringe thee—forests of giant trees—the spreading *platanus*, the tall tulip-tree, and the yellow-green cotton-wood rising in terraced groves from the margin of thy waters. Forests stand upon thy banks, and the wreck of forests is borne upon thy bubbling bosom!

I pass thy last great affluent, whose crimson flood just tinges the hue of thy waters. Down thy delta I glide, amid scenes rendered classic by the sufferings of De Soto—by the adventurous daring of Iberville and La Salle.

And here my soul reaches the acmé of its admiration. Dead to beauty must be heart and eye that could behold thee here, in this thy southern land, without a thrill of sublimest emotion!

I gaze upon lovely landscapes ever changing, like scenes of enchantment, or the pictures of a panorama. They are the loveliest upon earth—for where are views to compare with thine? Not upon the Rhine, with its castled rocks—not upon the shores of that ancient inland sea—not among the Isles of the Ind. No. In no part of the world are scenes like these; nowhere is soft beauty blended so harmoniously with wild picturesqueness.

And yet not a mountain meets the eye—not even a hill—but the dark *cyprières*, draped with the silvery *tillandsia*, form a background to the picture with all the grandeur of the pyrogenous granite!

The forest no longer fringes thee here. It has long since fallen before the planter's axe; and the golden sugar-cane, the silvery rice, and the snowy cotton-plant, flourish in its stead. Forest enough has been left to adorn the picture. I behold vegetable forms of tropic aspect, with broad shining foliage—the *Sabal* palm, the anona, the water-loving tupelo, the catalpa with its large trumpet flowers, the melting *liquidambar*, and the wax-leaved mangolia. Blending their foliage with these fair *indigènes* are an hundred lovely exotics—the orange, lemon, and fig; the Indian-lilac and tamarind; olives, myrtles, and bromelias; while the Babylonian willow contrasts its drooping fronds with the erect reeds of the giant cane, or the lance-like blades of the *yucca gloriosa*.

Embowered amidst these beautiful forms I behold villas and mansions; of grand and varied aspect—varied as the races of men who dwell beneath their roofs. And varied are they; for the nations of the world dwell together upon thy banks—each having sent its tribute to adorn thee with the emblems of a glorious and universal civilisation. Father of Waters, farewell!

Though not born in this fair southern land, I have long lingered there; and I love it *even better than the land of my birth*. I have there spent the hours of bright youth, of adventurous manhood; and the retrospect of these hours is fraught with a thousand memories tinged with a romance that can never die. There my young heart yielded to the influence of Love—a first and virgin love. No wonder the spot should be to me the most hallowed on earth!

Reader! listen to the story of that love!

Chapter Two
Six Months in the Crescent City

Like other striplings escaped from college, I was no longer happy at home. The yearning for travel was upon me; and I longed to make acquaintance with that world, as yet only known to me through the medium of books.

My longing was soon to be gratified; and without a sigh I beheld the hills of my native land sink behind the black waves—not much caring whether I should ever see them again.

Though emerging from the walls of a classic college, I was far from being tinctured with classic sympathies. Ten years spent in pondering over the wild hyperbole of Homer, the mechanical verse-work of Virgil, and the dry indelicacies of Horatius Flaccus, had failed to imbue me with a perception of that classic beauty felt, or pretended to be felt, by the spectacled *savant*. My mind was not formed to live on the ideal, or dream over the past. I delight rather in the real, the positive, and the present. Don Quixotes may play the troubadour among ruined castles, and mincing misses cover the ground of the guide-books. For my part I have no belief in the romance of old-world life. In the modern Tell I behold a hireling, ready to barter his brawny limbs to the use of whatever tyrant; and the picturesque Mazzaroni, upon closer acquaintance, dwindles down to the standard of a hen-roost thief. Amid the crumbling walls of Athens and the ruins of Rome I encounter inhospitality and hunger. I am not a believer in the picturesqueness of poverty. I have no relish for the romance of rags.

And yet it was a yearning for the romantic that called me from home. I longed for the poetic and picturesque, for I was just at that age when the mind is imbued with its strongest faith in their reality. Ha! mine is not yet disabused of this belief. I am older now, but the hour of disenchantment has not yet come upon me—nor ever will. There is a romance in life, that is no illusion. It lives not in the effete forms and childish ceremonies of the fashionable drawing-room—it has no illustration in the tinsel trappings and gaudy puerilities of a Court. Stars, garters, and titles are its antidotes; red cloth and plush the upas-trees of its existence.

Its home is elsewhere, amid the grand and sublime scenes of Nature—though these are not necessary accompaniments. It is no more incidental to field and forest, rock, river, and mountain, than to the well-trodden ways of the trading-town. Its home is in human hearts—hearts that throb with high aspirations—bosoms that burn with the noble passions of Liberty and Love!

My steps then were not directed towards classic shores, but to lands of newer and more vigorous life. Westward went I in search of romance. I found it in its most attractive form under the glowing skies of Louisiana.

In the month of January, 18—, I set foot upon the soil of the New-World—upon a spot stained with English blood. The polite skipper, who had carried me across the Atlantic, landed me in his gig. I was curious to examine the field of this decisive action; for at that period of my life I had an inclination for martial affairs. But something more than mere curiosity prompted me to visit the battle-ground of New Orleans. I then held an opinion deemed heterodox—namely, that the *improvised* soldier is under certain circumstances quite equal to the professional hireling, and that long military drill is not essential to victory. The story of war, superficially studied, would seem to antagonise this theory, which conflicts also with the testimony of all military men. But the testimony of mere military men on such a matter is without value. Who ever heard of a military man who did not desire to have his art considered as mythical as possible? Moreover, the rulers of the world have spared no pains to imbue their people with false ideas upon this point. It is necessary to put forward some excuse for that terrible incubus upon the nations, the "standing army."

My desire to view the battle-ground upon the banks of the Mississippi had chiefly reference to this question. The action itself had been one of my strong arguments in favour of my belief; for upon this spot some six thousand men—who had never heard the absurd command, "Eyes right!"—out-generalled, "whipped," in fact nearly annihilated, a well-equipped and veteran army of twice their number!

Since standing upon that battle-ground I have carried a sword in more than one field of action. What I then held only as a theory, I have since proved as an experience. The "drill" is a delusion. The standing army a cheat.

In another hour I was wandering through the streets of the Crescent City, no longer thinking of military affairs. My reflections were turned into a far different channel. The social life of the New-World, with all its freshness and vigour, was moving before my eyes, like a panorama; and despite of my assumption of the *nil admirari*, I could not help *wondering as I went*.

And one of my earliest surprises—one that met me on the very threshold of Transatlantic existence—was the discovery of my own utter uselessness. I could point to my desk and say, "There lie the proofs of my erudition—the highest prizes of my college class." But of what use they? The dry theories I had been taught had no application to the purposes of real life. My logic was the prattle of the parrot. My classic lore lay upon my mind like lumber; and I was altogether about as well prepared to struggle with life—to benefit either my fellow-man or myself—as if I had graduated in Chinese mnemonics.

And oh! ye pale professors, who drilled me in syntax and scansion, ye would deem me ungrateful indeed were I to give utterance to the contempt and indignation which I then felt for ye—then, when I looked back upon ten years of wasted existence spent under your tutelage—then, when, after believing myself an educated man, the illusion vanished, and I awoke to the knowledge that I *knew nothing*!

With some money in my purse, and very little knowledge in my head, I wandered through the Streets of New Orleans, wondering as I went.

Six months later, and I was traversing the same streets, with very little money in my purse, but with my stock of knowledge vastly augmented. During this six months I had acquired an experience of the world more extensive, than in any six years of my previous life.

I had paid somewhat dearly for this experience. My travelling fund had melted away in the alembic of cafés, theatres, masquerades, and "quadroon" balls. Some of it had been deposited in that bank (faro) which returns neither principal nor interest!

I was almost afraid to "take stock" of my affairs. At length with an effort I did so; and found, after paying my hotel bills, a balance in my favour of exactly twenty-five dollars! Twenty-five dollars to live upon until I could write home, and receive an answer—a period of three months at the least—for I am talking of a time antecedent to the introduction of Atlantic steamers.

For six months I had been sinning bravely. I was now all repentance, and desirous of making amends. I was even willing to engage in some employment. But my cold classic training, that had not enabled me to protect my purse, was not likely to aid me in replenishing it; and in all that busy city I could find no office that I was fitted to fill!

Friendless—dispirited—a little disgusted—not a little anxious in regard to my immediate future, I sauntered about the streets. My acquaintances were becoming scarcer every day. I missed them from their usual haunts—the haunts of pleasure. "Whither had they gone?"

There was no mystery in their disappearance. It was now mid-June. The weather had become intensely hot, and every day the mercury mounted higher upon the scale. It was already dancing in the neighbourhood of 100 degrees of Fahrenheit. In a week or two might be expected that annual but unwelcome visitor known by the soubriquet of "Yellow Jack," whose presence is alike dreaded by young and old; and it was the terror inspired by him that was driving the fashionable world of New Orleans, like birds of passage, to a northern clime.

I am not more courageous than the rest of mankind.

I had no inclination to make the acquaintance of this dreaded demon of the swamps; and it occurred to me, that I, too, had better get out of his way. To do this, it was only necessary to step on board a steamboat, and be carried to one of the up-river towns, beyond the reach of that tropical malaria in which the *vomito* delights to dwell.

Saint Louis was at this time the place of most attractive name; and I resolved to go thither; though how I was to live there I could not tell—since my funds would just avail to land me on the spot.

Upon reflection, it could scarce be "out of the frying-pan into the fire," and my resolution to go to Saint Louis became fixed. So, packing up my *impedimenta*, I stepped on board the steamboat "Belle of the West," bound for the far "City of the Mounds."

Chapter Three
The "Belle of the West"

I was on board at the advertised time; but punctuality on a Mississippi steamboat must not be expected; and I found myself too early, by a couple of hours at least.

The time was not thrown away. I spent it to some profit in examining the peculiar craft in which I had embarked. I say, *peculiar*; for the steamers employed upon the Mississippi and its tributary waters are unlike those of any other country—even unlike those in use in the Atlantic or Eastern States.

They are strictly "river-boats," and could not live in anything like a rough sea; though the reckless owners of some of them have occasionally risked them along the coast from Mobile to Galveston, Texas!

The hull is built like that of a sea boat, but differs materially from the latter in depth of hold. So shallow is it, that there is but little stowage-room allowed; and the surface of the main deck is but a few inches above the water-line. Indeed, when the boat is heavily laden, the waves lip over the gunwales. Upon the deck is placed the machinery; and there rest the huge cast-iron boilers, and the grates or "furnaces," necessarily large, because the propelling power is produced from logs of wood. There, also, most of the freight is stowed, on account of the light capacity of the hold; and on every part, not occupied by the machinery and boilers, may be seen piles of cotton-bales, hogsheads of tobacco, or bags of corn, rising to the height of many feet. This is the freight of a down-river-boat. On the return trip, of course, the commodities are of a different character, and consist of boxes of Yankee furniture, farming implements, and "notions," brought round by ship from Boston; coffee in bags from the West Indies, rice, sugar, oranges, and other products of the tropical South.

On the after-part of this deck is a space allotted to the humbler class of travellers known as "deck passengers." These are never Americans. Some are labouring Irish—some poor German emigrants on their way to the far North-West; the rest are negroes—free, or more generally slaves.

I dismiss the hull by observing that there is a good reason why it is built with so little depth of hold. It is to allow the boats to pass the shoal water in many parts of the river, and particularly during the season of drought. For such purpose the lighter the draught, the greater the advantage; and a Mississippi captain, boasting of the capacity of his boat in this respect, declared, that all he wanted was *a heavy dew upon, the grass, to enable him to propel her across the prairies*!

If there is but little of a Mississippi steamboat under the water, the reverse is true of what may be seen above its surface. Fancy a two-story house some two hundred feet in length, built of plank, and painted to the whiteness of snow; fancy along the upper story a row of green-latticed windows, or rather doors, thickly set, and opening out upon a narrow balcony; fancy a flattish or slightly rounded roof covered with tarred canvas, and in the centre a range of sky-lights like glass forcing-pits; fancy, towering above all, two enormous black cylinders of sheet-iron, each ten feet in diameter, and nearly ten times as high, the "funnels" of the boat; a smaller cylinder to one side, the "'scape-pipe;" a tall flag-staff standing up from the extreme end of the bow, with the "star-spangled banner" flying from its peak;—fancy all these, and you may form some idea of the characteristic features of a steamboat on the Mississippi.

Enter the cabin, and for the first time you will be struck with the novelty of the scene. You will there observe a splendid saloon, perhaps a hundred feet in length, richly carpeted and adorned throughout. You will note the elegance of the furniture,—costly chairs, sofas, tables, and lounges; you will note the walls, richly gilded and adorned with appropriate designs; the crystal chandeliers suspended from the ceiling; the hundred doors that lead to the "state-rooms" on each side, and the immense folding-door of stained or ornamental glass, which shuts in the sacred precinct of the "ladies' saloon." In short, you will note all around you a style and luxuriance to which you, as a European traveller, have not been accustomed. You have only read of such a scene in some Oriental tale—in Mary Montagu, or the "Arabian Nights."

And yet all this magnificence is sometimes sadly at variance with the style of the company that occupies it—for this splendid saloon is as much the property of the coarse "rowdy" as of the refined gentleman. You are startled by the apparition of a rough horse-skin boot elevated along the edge of the shining mahogany; and a dash of brown nicotian juice may have somewhat altered the pattern of the carpet! But these things are exceptional—more exceptional now than in the times of which I write.

Having satisfied myself with examining the interior structure of the "Belle of the West," I sauntered out in front of the cabin. Here a large open space, usually known as the "awning," forms an excellent lounging-place for the male passengers. It is simply the continuation of the "cabin-deck," projected forward and supported by pillars that rest upon the main deck below. The roof, or "hurricane-deck," also carried forward to the same point, and resting on slight wooden props, screens this part from sun or rain, and a low guard-rail running around it renders it safe. Being open in front and at both sides, it affords the best view; and having the advantage of a cool breeze, brought about by the motion of the boat, is usually a favourite resort. A number of chairs are here placed to accommodate the passengers, and smoking is permitted.

He must take very little interest in the movements of human life, who cannot kill an hour by observing it upon the "Levee" of New Orleans; and having seated myself and lighted my cigar, I proceeded to spend an hour in that interesting occupation.

Chapter Four
The Rival Boats

The part of the "Levee" under my eyes was that known as the "Steamboat Landing." Some twenty or thirty boats lay along a series of wooden wharves that projected slightly into the river. Some had just arrived from up-river towns, and were discharging their freight and passengers, at this season a scanty list. Others, surrounded by a bustling swarm, were getting up steam; while still others appeared to be abandoned by both officers and crew—who were no doubt at the time enjoying themselves in the brilliant cafés and restaurants. Occasionally might be seen a jauntily-dressed clerk, with blue cottonade trowsers, white linen coat, costly Panama hat, shirt with cambric ruffles, and diamond studs. This stylish gentleman would appear for a few minutes by one of the deserted boats—perhaps transact a little business with some one—and then hurry off again to his more pleasant haunts in the city.

There were two points upon the Levee where the bustle of active life was more especially observable. These were the spaces in front of two large boats. One was that on which I had taken passage. The other, as I could read upon her wheel-house, was the "Magnolia." The latter was also upon the eve of starting, as I could tell by the movements of her people, by the red fires seen in her furnaces, and the hissing of steam, that every now and then screamed sharply from the direction of her boilers.

On the Levee directly in front of her "drays" were depositing their last loads, passengers were hurrying forward hat-box in hand, in fear they might be too late; trunks, boxes, bags, and barrels were being rudely pushed or rolled over the staging-planks; the gaily-dressed clerks, armed with book and pencil, were checking them off; and everything denoted the intention of a speedy departure. A scene exactly similar was being enacted in front of the "Belle of the West."

I had not been regarding these movements very long, before I observed that there was something unusual "in the wind." The boats lay at no great distance from each other, and their crews, by a slight elevation of voice, could converse. This they were freely doing; and from some expressions that reached me, coupled with a certain tone of defiance in which they were uttered, I could perceive that the "Magnolia" and the "Belle of the West" were "rival boats." I soon gathered the further information, that they were about to start at the same time, and that a "race" was in contemplation!

I knew that this was no unusual occurrence among what are termed "crack" boats, and both the "Belle" and her rival came under that category. Both were of the first-class in size and magnificence of fitting; both ran in the same "trade," that is, from New Orleans to Saint Louis; and both were commanded by well-known and popular river "captains." They could not be otherwise than rivals; and this feeling was shared in by the crews of both, from captain to cabin-slave.

As regards the owners and officers in such cases, there is a substantial *money motive* at the bottom of this rivalry. The boat that "whips" in one of these races, wins also the future patronage of the public. The "fast boat" becomes the fashionable boat, and is ever afterwards sure of a strong list of passengers at a high rate of fare—for there is this peculiarity among Americans: many of them will spend their last dollar to be able to say at the end of his journey that he came upon the fashionable boat, just as in England you find many people desirous of making it known that they travelled "first-class." Snobbery is peculiar to no country—it appears to be universal.

With regard to the contemplated trial of speed between the "Belle of the West" and the "Magnolia," the feeling of rivalry pervaded not only the crews of both boats, but I soon discovered that the passengers were affected with it. Most of these seemed as eager for the race as an English blackleg for the Derby. Some no doubt looked forward to the sport and excitement, but I soon perceived that the greater number were betting upon the result!

"The Belle's boun' to win!" cried a gold-studded vulgar-looking fellow at my shoulder. "I'll go twenty dollars on the Belle. Will you bet, stranger?"

"No," I replied, somewhat angrily, as the fellow had taken a liberty by laying his hand on my shoulder.

"Well," retorted he, "jest as you like 'bout that;" and addressing himself to some one else he continued, "the Belle's the conquering boat for twenty dollars! Twenty dollars on the Belle!"

I confess I had no very pleasant reflections at that moment. It was my first trip upon an American steamboat, and my memory was brimful of stories of "boiler burstings," "snaggings," "blowings up," and boats on fire. I had heard that these races not infrequently resulted in one or other of the above-named catastrophes, and I had reason to know that my information was correct.

Many of the passengers—the more sober and respectable ones—shared my feelings; and some talked of appealing to the Captain not to allow the race. But they knew they were in the minority, and held their peace.

I had made up my mind at least to ask the Captain "his intentions." I was prompted rather by curiosity than by any other motive.

I left my seat, therefore, and having crossed the staging, walked toward the top of the wharf, where this gentleman was standing.

Chapter Five
A Desirable Fellow-Passenger

Before I had entered into conversation with the Captain, I saw a barouche approaching on the opposite side, apparently coming from the French quarter of the city. It was a handsome equipage, driven by a well-clad and evidently well-fed black, and as it drew near, I could perceive that it was occupied by a young and elegantly-attired lady.

I cannot say why, but I felt a presentiment, accompanied perhaps by a silent wish, that the occupant of the barouche was about to be a fellow-passenger. It was not long before I learnt that such was her intention.

The barouche drew up on the crest of the Levee, and I saw the lady directing some inquiry to a bystander, who immediately pointed to our Captain. The latter, perceiving that he was the object inquired after, stepped up to the side of the carriage, and bowed to the lady. I was close to the spot, and every word reached me.

"Monsieur! are you the captain of the Belle of the West?"

The lady spoke in French, a smattering of which the Captain in his intercourse with the Creoles had picked up.

"Yes, madame," was the reply.

"I wish to take passage with you."

"I shall be most happy to accommodate you, madame. There is still one state-room disengaged, I believe, Mr Shirley?"

Here the Captain appealed to the clerk, in order to ascertain if such was the case.

"Never mind!" said the lady, interrupting him, "for the matter of a state-room it is of no importance! You will reach my plantation before midnight, and therefore I shall not require to sleep aboard."

The phrase, "my plantation," evidently had an effect upon the Captain. Naturally not a rude man, it seemed to render him still more attentive and polite. The proprietor of a Louisiana plantation is a somebody not to be treated with nonchalance; but, when that proprietor chances to be a young and charming lady, who could be otherwise than amiable? Not Captain B., commander of the "Belle of the West!" The very name of his boat negatived the presumption!

Smiling blandly, he inquired where he was to land his fair charge.

"At Bringiers," replied the lady. "My residence is a little below, but our landing is not a good one; besides, there is some freight which it would be better to put ashore at Bringiers."

Here the occupant of the barouche pointed to a train of drays, loaded with barrels and boxes, that had just driven up, and halted in the rear of the carriage.

The sight of the freight had a still further pleasant effect on the Captain, who was himself *part owner* of his boat. He became profuse in offers of service, and expressed his willingness to accommodate his new passenger in every way she might desire.

"Monsieur Capitaine," continued this handsome lady, still remaining seated in her carriage, and speaking in a tone of good-natured seriousness, "I must make one condition with you."

"Please to name it, madame."

"Well then! It is reported that your boat is likely to have a race with some other one. If that be so, I cannot become your passenger." The Captain looked somewhat disconcerted. "The fact is," continued she, "I had a narrow escape once before, and I am determined to run no such risk in future."

"Madame—," stammered the Captain—then hesitating—

"Oh, then!" interrupted the lady, "if you cannot give me the assurance that you will not race, I must wait for some other boat."

The Captain hung his head for some seconds. He was evidently reflecting upon his answer. To be thus denied the anticipated excitement and pleasure of the race—the victory which he confidently expected, and its grand consequences; to appear, as it were, afraid of trying the speed of his boat; afraid that she would be beaten; would give his rival a large opportunity for future bragging, and would place himself in no enviable light in the eyes of his crew and passengers—all of whom had already made up their minds for a race. On the other hand, to refuse the request of the lady—not very unreasonable when properly viewed—and still more reasonable when it was considered that that lady was the proprietress of several dray-loads of freight, and when still further considered that that lady was a rich *plantress* of the "French coast," and might see fit next fall to send several hundred casks of sugar and as many hogsheads of tobacco down on his (the Captain's) boat;—these considerations, I say, made the request quite reasonable. And so we suppose, upon reflection, it must have appeared to Captain B—, for after a little hesitation he granted it. Not with the best grace, however. It evidently cost him a struggle; but interest prevailed, and he granted it.

"I accept your conditions, madame. The boat shall *not* run. I give you my promise to that effect."

"*Assez*! thanks! Monsieur le Capitaine; I am greatly obliged to you. If you will be so good as to have my freight taken aboard. The carriage goes along. This gentleman is my steward. Here, Antoine! He will look to everything. And now pray, Capitaine, when do you contemplate starting?"

"In fifteen minutes, madame, at the latest."

"Are you sure of that, mon Capitaine?" she inquired, with a significant laugh, which told she was no stranger to the want of punctuality of the boats.

"Quite sure, madame," replied the Captain; "you may depend on the time."

"Ah! then, I shall go aboard at once!" And, so saying, she lightly tripped down the steps of the barouche, and giving her arm to the Captain, who had gallantly proffered himself, was conducted to the ladies' cabin, and of course for a time lost to the admiring eyes, not only of myself, but of a goodly number of others who had already been attracted to gaze upon this beautiful apparition.

Chapter Six
Antoine the Steward

I had been very much struck by the appearance of this dame. Not so much on account of her physical beauty—though that was of a rare kind—as by the air that characterised her. I should feel a difficulty in describing this, which consisted in a certain *braverie* that bespoke courage and self-possession. There was no coarseness of manner—only the levity of a heart gay as summer, and light as gossamer, but capable, when occasion required, of exhibiting a wonderful boldness and strength. She was a woman that would be termed beautiful in any country; but with her beauty there was combined elegance, both in dress and manner, that told you at once she was a lady accustomed to society and the world. And this, although still young—she certainly could not have been much over twenty. Louisiana has a precocious climate, however; and a Creole of twenty will count for an Englishwoman of ten years older.

Was she married? I could not bring myself to think so; besides the expressions, "my plantation" and "my steward," would scarcely have been used by a lady who had "somebody" at home, unless, indeed, that somebody were held in very low estimation—in short, considered a "nobody." A widow she might be—a very young widow—but even that did not seem to me probable. She had not the "cut" of a widow in my eyes, and there was not the semblance of a "weed" either about her dress or her looks. The Captain had styled her *Madame*, but he was evidently unacquainted with her, and also with the French idiom. In a doubtful case such as this, it should have been "Mademoiselle."

Inexperienced as I was at the time—"green," as the Americans have it—I was not without some curiosity in regard to women, especially when these chanced to be beautiful. My curiosity in the present case had been stimulated by several circumstances. First, by the attractive loveliness of the lady herself; second, by the style of her conversation and the facts it had revealed; third, by the circumstance that the lady was, or I fancied her to be, a "Creole."

I had as yet had but little intercourse with people of this peculiar race, and was somewhat curious to know more about them. I had found them by no means ready to open their doors to the Saxon stranger—especially the old "Creole *noblesse,"* who even to this hour regard their Anglo-American fellow-citizens somewhat in the light of invaders and usurpers! This feeling was at one time deeply rooted. With time, however, it is dying out.

A fourth spur to my curiosity was found in the fact, that the lady in passing had eyed me with a glance of more than ordinary inquisitiveness. Do not be too hasty in blaming me for this declaration. Hear me first. I did not for a moment fancy that that glance was one of admiration. I had no such thoughts. I was too young at the time to flatter myself with such fancies. Besides, at that precise moment I was far from being "in my zenith." With scarce five dollars in my purse, I felt rather forlorn; and how could I have fancied that a brilliant beauty such as she—a star of first magnitude—a rich proprietress—the owner of a plantation, a steward, and a host of slaves— would condescend to look admiringly on such a friendless wretch as I?

In truth, I did not flatter myself with such thoughts. I supposed that it was simple curiosity on her part—and no more. She saw that I was not of her own race. My complexion—the colour of my eyes—the cut of my garments—perhaps something *gauche* in my manner—told her I was a stranger to the soil, and that had excited her interest for a passing moment. A mere ethnological reflection—nothing more.

The act, however, had helped to pique my curiosity; and I felt desirous of knowing at least the name of this distinguished creature.

The "steward," thought I, may serve my purpose, and I turned towards that individual.

He was a tall, grey-haired, lathy, old Frenchman, well-dressed, and sufficiently respectable-looking to have passed for the lady's father. His aspect, too, was quite venerable, giving you the idea of long service and a very old family.

I saw, as I approached him, that my chances were but indifferent. I found him as "close as a clam." Our conversation was very brief; his answers laconic.

"Monsieur, may I ask who is your mistress?"

"A lady."

"True: any one may tell that who has the good fortune of looking at her. It was her name I asked for."

"It does not concern you to know it."

"Not if it be of so much importance to keep it a secret!"

"*Sacr-r-ré!*"

This exclamation, muttered, rather than spoken aloud, ended the dialogue; and the old fellow turned away on giving expression to it—no doubt cursing me in his heart as a meddling Yankee.

I applied myself to the sable Jehu of the barouche, but with no better success. He was getting his horses aboard, and not liking to give direct answers to my questions, he "dodged" them by dodging around his horses, and appearing to be very busy on the offside. Even the *name* I was unable to get out of him, and I also gave *him* up in despair.

The name, however, was furnished me shortly after from an unexpected source. I had returned to the boat, and had seated myself once more under the awning, watching the boatmen, with rolled-up red shirts, use their brawny arms in getting their freight aboard. I saw it was the same which had been delivered from the drays—the property of the lady. It consisted, for the most part, of barrels of pork and flour, with a quantity of dried hams, and some bags of coffee.

"Provisions for her large establishment," soliloquised I.

Just then some packages of a different character were pushed upon the staging. These were leathern trunks, travelling bags, rosewood cases, bonnet-boxes, and the like.

"Ha! her personal luggage," I again reflected, and continued to puff my cigar. Regarding the transfer of the trunks, my eye was suddenly attracted to some lettering that appeared upon one of the packages—a leathern portmanteau. I sprang from my seat, and as the article was carried up the gangway stair I met it halfway. I glanced my eye over the lettering, and read—

"*Mademoiselle Eugénie Besançon.*"

Chapter Seven
The Starting

The last bell rings—the "can't-get-away" folks rush ashore—the staging-plank is drawn in—some heedless wight has to jump for it—the cable is pulled aboard and coiled—the engineer's bell tinkles—the great wheels revolve, lashing the brown water into foam—the steam "whistles" and screams at the boilers, and booms from the 'scape-pipe in regular repetitions—neighbouring boats are pressed out of their places—their planks cringe and crackle—guards are broken, or the slight timbers of wheel-houses, causing a cross-fire of curses between the crews—and after some minutes of this pandemoniac confusion, the huge craft clears herself, and rides out upon the broad bosom of the river.

She heads up-stream; a few strokes of the revolving paddles and the current is mastered; and the noble boat yielding to the mighty propulsion, cleaves her liquid way, "walking the water like a thing of life!"

Perchance the boom of a cannon announces her departure; perchance it is animated by the harmonious swell of brazen instruments; or still more appropriate, some old "boatman's song," with its lively chorus, is heard issuing from the rude, though not unmusical throats of the "hands" below.

Lafayette and Carrolton are soon passed; the humbler roofs of stores and dwellings sink out of sight; and the noble dome of Saint Charles, the spires of churches, and the towers of the great cathedral, are all of the Crescent City that remain above the horizon. These, at length, go down; and the "floating palace" moves on in stately grandeur between the picturesque shores of the Mississippi.

I have said "picturesque." This word does not satisfy me, nor can I think of one that will delineate my idea. I must make use of a phrase, "picturesquely beautiful," to express my admiration of the scenery of those shores. I have no hesitation in pronouncing it the finest in the world.

I am not gazing upon it with a mere cold eye-glance. I cannot separate scenery from its associations—not its associations of the past, but with the present. I look upon the ruined castles of the Rhine, and their story impresses me with a feeling of disgust for what *has been*. I look upon its modern homes and their dwellers; I am equally filled with disgust for what *is*. In the Bay of Naples I experience a similar feeling, and roaming "around" the lordly parks of England, I see them through an enclosure of wretchedness and rags, till their loveliness seems an illusion!

Here alone, upon the banks of this majestic river, do I behold wealth widely diffused, intelligence broadcast, and comfort for all. Here, in almost every house, do I meet the refined taste of high civilisation—the hospitality of generous hearts combined with the power to dispense it. Here can I converse with men by thousands, whose souls are free—not politically alone, but free from vulgar error and fanatic superstition; here, in short, have I witnessed, not the perfectedness—for that belongs to a far future time—but the most advanced stage of civilisation yet reached upon the globe.

A dark shadow crosses my eye-glance, and my heart is stung with sudden pain. It is the shadow of a human being with a black skin. *He is a slave*!

For a moment or two the scene looks black! What is there to admire here—in these fields of golden sugar-cane, of waving maize, of snow-white cotton? What to admire in those grand mansions, with their orangeries, their flowery gardens, their drooping shade-trees, and their soft arbours? All this is but the sweat of the slave!

For a while I behold without admiring. The scene has lost its *couleur de rose*; and a gloomy wilderness is before me! I reflect. Slowly and gradually the cloud passes away, and the brightness returns. I reflect and compare.

True, he with the black skin is a slave—but not a *voluntary* slave. That is a difference in his favour at least.

In other lands—mine own among them—I see around me slaves as well, and far more numerous. Not the slaves of an individual, but of an association of individuals—a class—an oligarchy. Not slaves of the corvée—serfs of the feud—but victims of its modern representative the tax, which is simply its commutation, and equally baneful in its effects.

On my soul, I hold that the slavery of the Louisiana black is less degrading than that of the white pleb of England. The poor, woolly-headed helot is the victim of conquest, and may claim to place himself in the honourable category of a prisoner of war. He has not willed his own bondage; while you, my grocer, and butcher, and baker—ay, and you, my fine city merchant, who fondly fancy yourself a freeman—ye are voluntary in your serfdom; ye are loyal to a political juggle that annually robs ye of half your year's industry; that annually requires some hundred thousands of your class to be sloughed off into exile, lest your whole body should gangrene and die. And all this without even a protest. Nay, worse—you are ever ready to cry "crucify" to him who would attempt to counteract this condition—ever ready to glorify the man and the motion that would fix another rivet in your fetters!

Even while I write, the man who loves you least; he who for forty years—for all his life, in fact—has been your systematic enemy, is the most popular of your rulers! Even while I write the Roman wheel is revolving before your eyes, squibs and crackers sound sweetly in your ears, and you are screaming forth your rejoicings over the acts of a convention that had for its sole object the strengthening of your chains! But a short twelve months ago, you were just as enthusiastic for a war that was equally antagonistic to your interests, equally hostile to the liberties of your kind! Miserable delusion!

I repeat what I have uttered with a feeling of solemnity. On my soul, I hold that the slavery of the Louisiana black is less degrading than that of the white pleb of England.

True, this black man is a *slave,* and there are three millions of his race in the same condition. Painful thought! but less painful when accompanied by the reflection that the same broad land is trodden by *twenty millions of free and sovereign men.* Three millions of slaves to twenty millions of masters! In mine own land the proportion is exactly reversed!

The truth may be obscure. For all that, I dare say there are some who will understand it.

Ah! how pleasant to turn from these heart-stirring but painful thoughts to the calmer contemplation of themes furnished by science and nature. How sweet was it to study the many novel forms that presented themselves to my eyes on the shores of that magnificent stream! There is a pleasaunce even in the retrospect; and as I now sit dreaming over them far away—perhaps never more to behold them with mortal eye—I am consoled by a fond and faithful memory, whose magic power enables me to recall them before the eye of my mind in all their vivid colouring of green and gold!

Chapter Eight
The "Coast" of the Mississippi

As soon as we had fairly started, I ascended to the "hurricane-deck," in order to obtain a better view of the scenery through which we were passing. In this place I was alone; for the silent pilot, boxed up in his little tower of glass, could hardly be called a companion.

I make the following observations:

The breadth of the Mississippi river has been much exaggerated. It is here about half a mile wide. Sometimes more, occasionally less. (This average width it preserves for more than a thousand miles from its mouth.) Its waters run at the rate of three or four miles to the hour, and are of a yellowish cast, with a slight tincture of "red." The yellow colour it derives from the Missouri, while the deeper tint is obtained by the influx of the "Red."

Driftwood floats thickly upon its surface; here in single logs, there in raft-like clusters. To run a boat against one of these is attended with danger, and the pilot avoids them. Sometimes one swimming below the surface escapes his eye; and then a heavy bumping against the bows shakes the boat, and startles the equanimity of the less experienced passengers. The "snag" is most dreaded. That is a dead tree with heavy roots still adhering. These, from their weight, have settled upon the bottom, and the *débris* gathering around holds them firmly imbedded. The lighter top, riven of its branches, rises towards the surface; but the pressure of the current prevents it from attaining to the perpendicular, and it is held in a slanting position. When its top rises above the water, the danger is but trifling—unless in a very dark night—it is when the top is hidden a foot or two below the surface that the snag is feared. Then a boat running upon it up-stream, is lost to a certainty. The roots firmly imbedded in the bottom mud, prevent the pile from yielding; and the top, usually a spiky one, penetrates the bow timbers of the boat, sinking her almost instantly. A boat properly "snagged" will go down in a few minutes.

The "sawyer" is a log fixed in the water similarly to the snag, but kept bobbing up and down by the current, thus suggesting the idea of a sawyer engaged at his work—hence the name. A boat getting aground upon a sunken log *crosswise,* is sometimes snagged upon its branches, and sometimes broken into two pieces by the pressure of her own weight.

Among the drift, I notice odd matters that interest me. Stalks of sugar-cane that have been crushed in the press-mill (a hundred miles farther up I should not meet these), leaves and stems of the maize plant, corn-cobs, pieces of broken gourd-shell, tufts of raw cotton, split fence-rails, now and then the carcase of some animal, with a buzzard or black vulture (*Cathartes aura* and *atratus*) perched upon it, or hovering above.

I am within the geographical range of the alligator but here the great Saurian is seldom seen. He prefers the more sluggish *bayous,* or the streams whose shores are still wild. In the rapid current of the Mississippi, and along its well-cultivated banks, he is but rarely observed by the passing traveller.

Alternately the boat approaches both shores of the river ("coasts" they are called). The land is an alluvion of no very ancient formation. It is a mere strip of *terra firma,* varying in breadth from a few hundred yards to several miles, and gradually declining from the banks, so that the river is actually running along the top of a ridge! Beyond this strip commences the "Swamp," a tract that is annually inundated, and consists of a series of lagoons and marshes covered with coarse grass and reeds. This extends in some places for a score of miles, or even farther—a complete wilderness of morass. Some portions of this—where the inundation is only annual— are covered with dark and almost impenetrable forests. Between the cultivated strip on the immediate bank of the river, and the "Swamp" in the rear, runs a belt of this forest, which forms a kind of background to the picture, answering to the mountain-ranges in other lands. It is a high, dark forest, principally composed of cypress-trees (*Cupressus disticka*). But there are other kinds peculiar to this soil, such as the sweet-gum (*Liquidambar styraciflua*), the live-oak (*Quercus vivens*), the tupelo (*Nyssa aquatica*), the water-locust (*Gleditschia aquatica*), the cotton-wood (*Populus angulata*), with *carya, celtis,* and various species of *acer, cornus, juglans, magnolia,* and oaks. Here an underwood of palmettoes (*Sabal* palms), *smilax, llianes,* and various species of *vitis;* there thick brakes of cane (*Arundo gigantea*), grow among the trees; while from their branches is suspended in long festoons that singular parasite, the "Spanish moss" (*Tillandsia usneoides*), imparting a sombre character to the forest.

Between this dank forest and the river-banks lie the cultivated fields. The river current is often several feet above their level; but they are protected by the "Levee," an artificial embankment which has been formed on both sides of the river, to a distance of several hundred miles from its mouth.

In these fields I observe the culture of the sugar-cane, of the rice-plant, of tobacco and cotton, of indigo and maize. I see the "gangs" of black slaves at their work, in their cotton dresses of striped and gaudy colours, in which sky-blue predominates. I see huge waggons drawn by mules or oxen returning from the cane-fields, or slowly toiling along the banks. I see the light-bodied Creole, in "cottonade" jacket and trousers of bright blue, mounted upon his small Spanish horse, and galloping along the Levee road. I see the grand mansion of the planter, with its orange-groves and gardens, its green Venetians, cool verandahs, and pretty palings. I see the huge sugar-house, or tobacco-shed, or cotton "pickery;" and there, too, are the neat "cabins," clustering together or running in a row, like the bathing-boxes at a fashionable watering-place.

Now we are passing a plantation where they are making merry—a *fête champêtre*. Many horses stand under the trees, "hitched" in the shade with saddles on, not a few of which are "ladies' saddles." In the verandah, the lawn, and through the orange shrubbery, may be seen moving about gentlemen and ladies richly attired. Music is heard, and there is dancing in the open air. One cannot help envying these happy Creoles the enjoyment of their Arcadian life.

Scenes varied and lovely were passing panorama-like before my eyes. Lost in admiration of them, I had for the moment forgotten *Eugénie Besançon*.

Chapter Nine
Eugénie Besançon

No, Eugénie Besançon was not forgotten. Every now and then her sylph-like form flitted before my imagination, and I could not help associating it with the scenery through which we were passing, and amidst which, no doubt, she was born and nurtured—its fair *indigène*. The glimpse of the *fête champêtre*, where several Creole-like girls were conspicuous, brought her more forcibly into my thoughts; and, descending from the hurricane-deck, I entered the cabin with some curiosity, once more to look upon this interesting lady.

For some time I dreaded disappointment. The great glass folding-door of the ladies' cabin was closed; and although there were several ladies outside in the main saloon, the Creole was not among the number. The ladies' cabin, which occupies the after-part of the boat, is a sacred precinct, into which bachelors are admitted only when they enjoy the privilege of having a friend inside—then only at certain hours.

I was not one of the privileged. Out of the hundred and odd passengers on board, I did not know a soul, male or female; and I had the happiness or misfortune of being equally unknown to them. Under these circumstances my entry into the ladies' cabin would have been deemed an intrusion; and I sat down in the main saloon, and occupied myself in studying the physiognomy and noting the movements of my fellow-passengers.

They were a mixed throng. Some were wealthy merchants, bankers, money or commission brokers from New Orleans, with their wives and daughters, on their annual migration to the north, to escape from the yellow fever, and indulge in the more pleasant epidemic of life at a fashionable watering-place. There were corn and cotton-planters from the up-country, on their return home, and storekeepers from the up-river towns; boatmen who, in jean trousers and red flannel shirts, had pushed a "flat" two thousand miles down stream, and who were now making the back trip in shining broadcloth and snow-white linen. What "lions" would these be on getting back to their homes about the sources of Salt River, the Cumberland, the Licking, or the Miami! There were Creoles, too—old wine-merchants of the French quarter—and their families; the men distinguished by a superabundance of ruffles, plaited pantaloons, shining jewellery, and light-coloured cloth boots.

There was a sprinkling of jauntily-dressed clerks, privileged to leave New Orleans in the dull season; and there were some still more richly-dressed gentlemen, with the finest of cloth in their coats, the whitest of linen and raffles, the brightest of diamonds in their studs, and the most massive of finger-rings. These last were "sportsmen." They had already fathered around a table in the "smoking-saloon," and were fingering a span new pack of cards—the implements of their peculiar industry.

Among these I observed the fellow who had so loudly challenged me to bet upon the boat-race. He had passed me several times, regarding me with a glance that appeared anything but friendly.

Our close friend the steward was seated in the saloon. You must not suppose that his holding the office of steward, or overseer, disentitled him to the privileges of the first-class cabin. There is no "second saloon" on board an American steamer. Such a distinction is not known so far west as the Mississippi.

The overseers of plantations are usually men of rude and brutal dispositions. The very nature of their calling makes them so. This Frenchman, however, seemed to be an exception. He appeared a most respectable old gentleman. I rather liked his looks, and began to feel quite an interest in him, though he by no means appeared to reciprocate the feeling.

Some one complained of the mosquitoes, and suggested the opening of the folding-doors of the ladies' cabin. This suggestion was backed up by several others—ladies and gentlemen. The clerk of the boat is the man charged with such responsibilities. He was at length appealed to. The appeal was reasonable—it was successful; and the great gates of the steamboat Paradise were thrown open. The result was a current of air which swept through the long saloon from stem to stern; and in less than five minutes not a mosquito remained on board, except such as had escaped the blast by taking shelter in the state-rooms. This was certainly a great relief.

The folding-doors were permitted to remain open—an arrangement quite satisfactory to all, but particularly to a number of the gaily-dressed young clerks, who could now command a full view of the interior of the harem. Several of them might be observed taking advantage of the new arrangement—not staring broadly, as that would be accounted rude and noted against them. They only appealed to the sacred shrine by side-glances, or over books which they pretended to read, or pacing up and down approached the favoured limit, glancing in at intervals, as if undesignedly. Some appeared to have acquaintances inside, though not upon terms of sufficient familiarity to give them the right of entry. Others were in hopes of making acquaintances, should opportunity offer. I could detect expressive looks, and occasionally a smile that seemed to denote a mutual intelligence. Many a pleasant thought is conveyed without words. The tongue is often a sad disenchanter. I have known it to spoil many a nice love-plot silently conceived, and almost ripe for being carried out.

I was amused at this speechless pantomime, and sat for some minutes regarding it. My eyes wandered at intervals towards the interior of the ladies' saloon, guided thither partly by a common curiosity. I have an observant habit. Anything new interests me, and this cabin-life on an American steamboat was entirely new, and not a little *piquante*. I desired to study it. Perhaps I was somewhat interested in another way—desirous of having one more look at the young Creole, Besançon.

My desire, then, was gratified. I saw the lady at last. She had come out of her state-room, and was moving around the saloon, graceful and gay. She was now unbonneted, and her rich golden tresses were arranged *à la Chinoise*—a Creole fashion as well. The thick masses, coiled into a large "club" at the back of the head, denoted the luxuriance of her hair: and the style of coiffure, displaying her noble forehead and finely-formed neck, became her well. Fair hair with blonde complexion, although rare among the Creoles, is sometimes met with. Dark hair with a brunette skin is the rule, to which Eugénie Besançon was a remarkable exception.

Her features expressed gaiety, approaching to volatility; yet one could not help feeling that there was firmness of character *en perdu*. Her figure was beyond criticism; and the face, if not strikingly beautiful was one that you could not look upon without emotions of pleasure.

She appeared to know some of her fellow-passengers—at least she was conversing with them in a style of easy freedom. Women, however, rarely exhibit embarrassment among themselves; women of French race, never.

One thing I observed—her cabin companions appeared to regard her with deference. Perhaps they had already learnt that the handsome carriage and horses belonged to her. That was very, very likely!

I continued to gaze upon this interesting lady. Girl I cannot call her, for although young enough, she had the air of a woman—a woman of experience. She appeared quite at ease; seemed mistress of herself, and indeed of everything else.

"What an air of *insouciance*," thought I. "That woman is not in love!"

I cannot tell why I should have made these reflections, or why the thought pleased me; but certainly it did. Why? She was nothing to me—she was far above me. I dared scarce look upon her. I regarded her as some superior being, and with timid stolen glances, as I would regard beauty in a church. Ho! she was nothing to me. In another hour it would be night, and she was to land in the night; I should never see her again! I should think of her though for an hour or two, perhaps for a day—the longer that was now foolish enough to sit gazing upon her! I was weaving a net for myself—a little agony that might last for some time after she was gone.

I had formed a resolution to withdraw from the fascinating influence, and return to my meditation on the hurricane-deck. A last look at the fair Creole, and I should depart.

Just at that moment she flung herself into a chair.

It was of the kind known as a "rocking-chair," and its motions displayed the fine proportion and outlines of her form. As she now sat she was facing the door, and her eye for the first time rested upon me. By Heavens! she was gazing on me just as before! What meant that strange glance? those burning eyes?

Stedfast and fixed, they remained bent upon mine—and mine trembled to answer them!

Thus for some moments her eyes dwelt upon me, without motion or change of direction. I was too young at that time to understand the expression that was in them. I could translate such an one afterwards, but not then.

At length she rose from her seat with an air of uneasiness, as if displeased either with herself or me; and, turning away her head, she opened the latticed door and passed into her state-room.

Had I done anything to give offence? No! not by word, nor look, nor gesture. I had not spoken—I had not moved, and my timid glance could not have been construed into one of rudeness.

I was somewhat bewildered by the conduct of Mademoiselle Besançon; and, in the full belief that I should never see her again, I hurried away from the saloon, and once more climbed up to the hurricane-deck.

Chapter Ten
A New Mode of raising the Steam

It was near sunset—the fiery disc was going down behind the dark outline of cypress forest that belted the western horizon, and a yellow light fell upon the river. Promenading back and forward upon the canvas-covered roof, I was gazing upon the scene, wrapt in admiration of its glowing beauty.

My reverie was interrupted. On looking down the river I saw that a large boat was in our wake, and coming rapidly after us. The volume of smoke rolling up out of her tall funnels, and the red glowing of her fires, showed that she was moving under a full head of steam. Her size, as well as the loud reports of her 'scape-pipe, told that she was a boat of the first-class. She was the "Magnolia." She was moving with great velocity, and I had not watched her long, before I perceived that she was fast gaining upon us.

At this moment my ears were assailed by a variety of sounds coming from below. Loud voices in earnest tones, the stamping and pattering of feet, as of men rushing over the wooden decks and along the guard-ways. The voices of women, too, were mingled in the medley.

I surmised what all this meant. The approach of the rival boat was the cause of the excitement.

Up to this time the boat-race seemed to have been nearly forgotten. It had got abroad among both "hands" and passengers that the Captain did not intend to "run;" and although this backing-out had been loudly censured at first, the feeling of disappointment had partially subsided. The crew had been busy at their work of stowage—the firemen with their huge billets of cord-wood—the gamblers with their cards—and the passengers, in general, with their portmanteaus, or the journal of the day. The other boat not starting at the same time, had been out of sight until now, and the feeling of rivalry almost "out of mind."

The appearance of the rival produced a sudden change. The gamblers flung down the half-dealt pack, in hopes of having something more exciting to bet upon; the readers hastily closed their books, and tossed aside their newspapers; the rummagers of trunks banged down the lids; the fair occupants of rocking-chairs suddenly sprang to their feet; and all ran out of the cabins, and pressed towards the after-part of the boat.

My position on the hurricane-deck was the best possible for a good view of the rival boat, and I was soon joined by a number of my fellow-passengers. I wished, however, to witness the scene on the cabin-deck, and went below.

On reaching the main saloon, I found it quite forsaken. All the passengers, both male and female, had gone out upon the guard-way; and leaning against the guards were anxiously watching the approach of the Magnolia.

I found the Captain under the front-cabin awning. He was surrounded by a crowd of gentlemen-passengers, all of whom appeared to be in a high state of excitement. One after the other was proffering speech to him. They were urging him to "raise the steam."

The Captain, evidently wishing to escape from these importunities, kept passing from place to place. It was to no purpose. Wherever he went he was met or followed by a knot of individuals, all with the same request in their mouths—some even begging him for "God's sake" not to let the Magnolia pass him!

"Wal, Cap!" cried one, "if the Belle don't run, I guess she'll never be heerd of on these waters agin, she won't."

"You're right!" added another. "For my part the next trip I make I'll try the Magnolia."

"She's a fast boat that 'ere Magnolia!" remarked a third.

"She ain't anything else," rejoined the first speaker: "she's got her steam on a few, I reckon."

I walked out on the guard-way in the direction of the ladies' cabin. The inmates of the latter were clustered along the guards, and seemingly as much interested in the boat-race as the men. I could hear several of them expressing their wishes aloud that the boats would run. All idea of risk or fear of consequences had departed; and I believe that if the company had been "polled" at the moment in favour of the race, there would not have been three dissentient voices. I confess that I, myself, would have voted for running,—I had caught the infection, and no longer thought of "snags," "sawyers," or bursting boilers.

As the Magnolia drew near the excitement increased. It was evident that in a few minutes more she would be alongside, and then pass us. The idea was unsupportable to some of the passengers; and loud words could be heard, now and then interspersed with an angry oath. The poor Captain had to bear all this—for it was known that the rest of the officers were well disposed for a trial of speed. It was the Captain only who "showed the white feather."

The Magnolia was close in our wake; her head bearing a little to one side. She was evidently preparing to pass us!

Her officers and crew were moving actively about; both pilots were seen above at the wheel-house; the firemen were all at work upon the deck; the furnace-doors were glowing red-hot; and the bright blaze stood several feet above the tops of her tall funnels! One might have fancied she was on fire!

"They are burning bacon hams!" shouted a voice.

"They are by—!" exclaimed another. "See, yonder's a pile of them in front of the furnace!"

I turned my eyes in that direction. It was quite true. A pyramidal-shaped mass of dark-brown objects lay upon the deck in front of the fires. Their size, shape, and colour told what they were—dried hams of bacon. The firemen were seen taking them from the pile, and thrusting them one after another up the red tunnels of the furnace!

The Magnolia was still gaining upon us. Already her head was even with the wheel-house of the Belle. On the latter boat the excitement increased, and the noise along with it. An occasional taunt from the passengers of the rival boat added fuel to the flame; and the Captain was once more abjured to run. Men almost threatened him with violence!

The Magnolia continued to advance. She was now head for head with us. Another minute passed—a minute of deep silence—the crews and passengers of both boats watched their progress with hearts too full for utterance. Another minute, and the Magnolia had shot ahead!

A triumphant cheer rang along her decks, mingled with taunting shouts and expressions of insult.

"Throw us a line, and we'll tow you!" cried one.

"Whar's yer old ark now?" shouted another.

"Hurraw for the Magnolia! Three groans for the Belle of the West! Three groans for the old dugout!" vociferated a third, amidst jeers and shouts of laughter.

I can hardly describe the mortification felt by those on board the Belle. It was not confined to the officers and crew. The passengers, one and all, seemed to partake of the feeling. I shared it myself, more than I could have believed to be possible.

One dislikes to be among the conquered, even on any terms of association. Besides, one involuntarily catches the impulse of the moment. The sentiment that surrounds you—perhaps by physical laws which you cannot resist—for the moment becomes your own; and even when you know the object of exultation to be worthless or absurd, you are controlled by the electric current to join in the enthusiasm. I remember once being thus carried away, and mingled my voice with the rude throats that cheered the passing cortege of royalty. The moment it was past, however, my heart fell, abashed at its own meanness and wickedness.

Both his crew and passengers seemed to think our Captain imprudent in his prudence: and a general clamour, mingled with cries of "Shame!" was heard all over the boat.

The poor Captain! I had my eyes upon him all this while. I really pitied him. I was perhaps the only passenger on board, beside the fair Creole, who knew his secret; and I could not help admiring the chivalric fortitude with which he kept it to himself. I saw his cheek glow, and his eye sparkle with vexation; and I felt satisfied, that had he been called upon to make that promise then, he would not have done so for the privilege of carrying all the freight upon the river.

Just then, as if to escape the importunities that beset him, I saw him steal back and pass through the ladies' cabin. There he was at once recognised, and a general onset was made upon him by his fair passengers, who were almost as noisy in their petitions as the men. Several threatened him, laughingly, that they would never travel by his boat again; while others accused him of a want of gallantry. Surely it was impossible to resist such banterings; and I watched the Captain closely, expecting a crisis one way or the other. The crisis was at hand.

Drawing himself up in the midst of a knot of these importunates, he thus addressed them:—

"Ladies! Nothing would give me more pleasure than to gratify you, but before leaving New Orleans I gave my promise—in fact, passed my word of honour to a lady—" Here the gallant speech was interrupted by a young lady, who, rushing up from another part of the boat, cried out—

"Oh, Capitaine! cher Capitaine! do not let that wicked boat get ahead of us! do put on more steam, and pass her—that is a dear Captain!"

"Why, Mademoiselle!" replied the Captain, in astonishment, "it was to you I gave the promise not to run—it was—"

"Pardieu!" exclaimed Mademoiselle Besançon, for it was she. "So you did. I had quite forgotten it. Oh, cher Capitaine, I release you from that promise. *Hélas!* I hope it is not too late. For Heaven's sake, try to pass her! *Écoutez! les polissons!* how they taunt us!"

The Captain's face brightened up for a moment, and then suddenly resumed its vexed expression. He replied—

"Mademoiselle, although grateful to you, I regret to say that under the circumstances I cannot hope to run successfully against the Magnolia. We are not on equal terms. *She is burning bacon hams,* of which she has a large supply. I should have had the same, but after promising you not to run, I, of course, did not take any on board. It would be useless to attempt a race with only common cord-wood—unless indeed the Belle be much the faster boat, which we do not yet know, as we have never tried her speed."

Here appeared to be a dilemma, and some of the ladies regarded Mademoiselle Besançon with looks of displeasure.

"Bacon hams!" she exclaimed; "bacon hams did you say, cher Capitaine? How many would be enough? Would two hundred be enough?"

"Oh! less than that," replied the Captain.

"Here! Antoine! Antoine!" continued she, calling to the old steward. "How many bacon hams have you on board?"

"Ten barrels of them, Mademoiselle," answered the steward, bowing respectfully.

"Ten barrels! that will do, I suppose? Cher Capitaine, they are at your service!"

"Mademoiselle, I shall pay you for them," said the Captain, brightening up, and becoming imbued with the general enthusiasm.

"No—no—no! Let the expense be mine. I have hindered you. They were for my plantation people, but they are not in want. We shall send down for more. Go, Antoine! go to the firemen. Knock in the heads of the barrels! Use them as you please, but do not let us be beaten by that wicked Magnolia! Hark! how they cheer! Ha! we shall pass them yet."

So saying, the fiery Creole rushed back to the guard-way, followed by a group of admirers.

The Captain's "dander" was now fairly up; and the story of the bacon hams soon spreading over the boat, still further heightened the enthusiasm of both passengers and crew. Three loud cheers were given for the young lady, which seemed to mystify the Magnolians, who had now been for some time in the enjoyment of their triumph, and had forged a considerable distance ahead.

All hands went to work with a will—the barrels were rolled-up, their heads knocked in, and part of their contents "chucked" up the blazing furnace. The iron walls soon grew red—the steam rose—the boat trembled under the increased action of the engine—the bells of the engineers tinkled their signals—the wheels revolved more rapidly, and an increase of velocity was soon perceptible.

Hope had stifled clamour—comparative silence was restored. There was heard only an occasional utterance—the expression of an opinion upon the speed of the rival boats—the fixing the conditions of a bet—and now and then some allusion to the story of the bacon hams.

At intervals, all eyes were bent upon the water eagerly glancing along the line that separated the rival steamers.

Chapter Eleven
A Boat-Race upon the Mississippi

It had now become quite dark. There was no moon in the sky—not a speck of a star. A clear heaven over the lower region of the Mississippi, at night, is rather rare than otherwise. The film of the swamp too often obscures it.

There was light enough for the race. The yellow water shone clear. It was easily distinguishable from the land. The track was a wide one; and the pilots of both boats—old hands—knew every "shute" and sand-bar of the river.

The rival steamers were quite visible to one another. No lamps needed to be hung out, although the gaff over the bow of each boat carried its coloured signal. The cabin windows of both were full of light, and the blaze of the bacon fires flung a vermilion glare far over the water.

Upon each boat the spectators could be seen from the other in their state-room windows, or leaning against the guards, in attitudes that betokened their interest.

By the time the Belle had fairly got up steam, the Magnolia was a full half-mile in advance of her. This distance, though nothing where there is a large difference of speed, is not so easily overtaken where the swiftness of the boats approximates to anything like an equality. It was a long while, therefore, before the people of the Belle could be certain as to whether she was gaining upon her rival; for it is somewhat difficult to tell this when one vessel is running in the wake of the other. Questions were put by passengers to the various officials and to one another, and "guesses" were continually being made on this interesting point.

At length an assurance was derived from the Captain, that several hundred yards had been already taken up. This produced general joy, though not *universal*; for there were some "unpatriotic" individuals on board the Belle who had risked their dollars on the Magnolia.

In another hour, however, it was clear to all that our boat was fast gaining upon the Magnolia, as she was now within less than a quarter of a mile of her. A quarter of a mile on smooth water appears but a short distance, and the people of the two boats could hold converse at will. The opportunity was not neglected by those of the Belle to pay back the boasts of the Magnolians. Shouts of banter reached their ears, and their former taunts were now returned with interest.

"Have you any message for Saint Louis? We're going up there, and will be happy to carry it for you," shouted one from the Belle.

"Hurraw for the bully-boat Belle!" vociferated another.

"How are you off for bacon hams?" asked a third. "We can lend you a few, if you're out."

"Where shall we say we left you?" inquired a fourth. "In Shirt-tail Bend?" And loud peals of laughter followed this joking allusion to a point in the river well-known to the boatmen.

It had now approached the hour of midnight, and not a soul on either boat had thought of retiring to rest. The interest in the race precluded the idea of sleep, and both men and women stood outside the cabins, or glided out and in at short intervals to note the progress. The excitement had led to drinking, and I noticed that several of the passengers were already half intoxicated. The officers, too, led on by those, were indulging too freely, and even the Captain showed symptoms of a similar condition. No one thought of censure—prudence had fled from the boat.

It is near midnight, and amidst the growling and grinding of the machinery, the boats are moving on! There is deep darkness upon the water, but this is no impediment. The red fires glow; the blaze stands high above the tall funnels; steam booms from the iron pipes; the huge paddles lash the water into foam; the timbers creak and tremble under the fierce pressure, and the boats move on!

It is near midnight. A space of two hundred yards alone separates the steamers—the Belle is bounding upon the waves of the Magnolia. In less than ten minutes her head will overlap the stern of her rival. In less than twenty, and the cheer of victory rising from her deck will peal from shore to shore!

I was standing by the Captain of our boat, regarding him not without a feeling of solicitude. I regretted to see him pass so often to the "bar." He was drinking deeply.

He had returned to his station by the wheel-house, and was gazing ahead. Some straggling lights were gleaming on the right bank of the river, a mile farther up. The sight of these caused him to start, and utter a wild exclamation:—

"By Heavens! it is *Bringiers*!"

"Ye-e-s," drawled the pilot at his elbow. "We've reached it in quick time, I reckon."

"Great God! I must lose the race!"

"How?" said the other, not comprehending him; "what has that got to do with it?"

"I must land there. I must—I must—the lady who gave us the hams—I must land her!"

"Oh! *that*," replied the phlegmatic pilot; "a darned pity it is," he added; "but if you must, you must. Darn the luck! We'd a-beat them into shucks in another quarter, I reckon. Darn the luck!"

"We must give it up," said the Captain. "Turn her head in."

Saying this, he hurried below; and, observing his excited manner, I followed him.

A group of ladies stood upon the guard-way where the Captain descended over the wheel-house. The Creole was among them.

"Mademoiselle," said the Captain, addressing himself to this lady, "we must lose the race after all."

"Why?" asked she in surprise; "are there not enough? Antoine! have you delivered them all?"

"No, Mademoiselle," replied the Captain, "it is not that, thanks to your generosity. You see those lights?"

"Yes—well?"

"That is *Bringiers*."

"Oh! it is, is it?"

"Yes;—and of course you must be landed there."

"And that would lose you the race?"

"Certainly."

"Then, of course, I must *not* be landed there. What care I for a day? I am not so old but that I can spare one. Ha! ha! ha! You shall not lose your race, and the reputation of your fine boat, on my account. Think not of landing, cher Capitaine! Take me on to Baton Rouge. I can get back in the morning!"

A cheer rose from the auditory; and the Captain, rushing back to the pilot, countermanded his late order.

The Belle again stands in the wake of the Magnolia, and again scarce two hundred yards of the river lie between. The rumbling of their machinery—the booming of their steam—the plashing of their paddles—the creaking of their planks—the shouts of those on board, mingle in rude concert.

Up forges the Belle—up—up—gaining in spite of the throes of her antagonist. Up, nearer still—nearer, till her head laps upon the stern, then the wheel-house, then the foredeck of the Magnolia! Now the lights of both cross each other—their fires glow together upon the water—they are head and head!

Another foot is gained—the Captain waves his hat—and the cheer of triumph peals forth!

That cheer was never finished. Its first notes had scarce broke upon the midnight air, when it was interrupted by an explosion like the bursting of some vast magazine—an explosion that shook the air, the earth, and the water! Timbers crashed and flew upward—men shouted as their bodies were projected to the heavens—smoke and vapour filled the air—and one wild cry of agony arose upon the night!

Chapter Twelve
The Life-Preserver

The concussion, unlike anything I had ever heard, was, nevertheless, significant of the nature of the catastrophe. I felt an instantaneous conviction that the boilers had burst, and such in reality was the fact.

At the moment, I chanced to be on the balcony in rear of my state-room. I was holding by the guard-rail,—else the shock and the sudden lurch of the boat would have flung me headlong.

Scarce knowing what I did, I staggered into my state-room, and through the opposite door into the main saloon.

Here I paused and looked around me. The whole forward part of the boat was shrouded in steam and smoke, and already a portion of the hot scalding vapour floated through the cabin.

Dreading the contact of this, I rushed aft; but by a fortunate chance the lurch of the boat had brought her stern to windward, and the breeze blew the dangerous element away.

The engine was now silent—the wheels had ceased to move—the 'scape-pipe no longer gave out its booming notes; but instead of these sounds, others of terrible import fell upon the ear. The shouts of men, mingled with oaths—wild, awful imprecations—the more shrill piercing shrieks of women—the groans of rounded from the deck below—the agonised cry of those blown into the water and drowning—all rang upon the ear with terrible emphasis!

How changed the tones from those that, but a moment before, pealed from the self-same lips!

The smoky vapour was soon partially blown off, and I could catch a glimpse of the forward part of the boat. There a complete chaos met the eye. The smoking-saloon, the bar with its contents, the front awning, and part of the starboard wheel-house, were completely carried away—blown up as if a mine had been sprung beneath them—and the huge sheet-iron funnels had fallen forward upon the deck! At a glance I was convinced that captain, pilots, all who had been upon that part of the boat, must have perished!

Of course such reflections passed with the rapidity of thought itself, and occupied me not a moment of time. I felt that *I* was still unhurt, and my first natural thought was that of preserving my life. I had sufficient presence of mind to know there was no danger of a second explosion; but I perceived that the boat was badly injured, and already leaning to one side. How long would she swim?

I had hardly asked myself the question when it was answered by a voice that, in terrified accents, shouted out:—

"Good God! she is sinking! she is sinking!"

This announcement was almost simultaneous with the cry of "Fire!" and at the same moment flames were seen bursting forth and shooting up to the height of the hurricane-deck! Whether by burning up or going down, it was evident the wreck would afford us but short refuge.

The thoughts of the survivors were now turned to the Magnolia. I looked in the direction of that boat. I perceived that she was doing her best to back, and put round toward us; but she was still several hundred yards off! In consequence of the Belle having steered a while towards the Bringiers landing, the boats no longer ran in the same track; and, although they were head and head at the moment of the explosion, they were separated from each other by a wide stretch of the river. A full quarter of a mile distant appeared the Magnolia; and it was evident that a considerable time must elapse before she could get alongside. Would the wreck of the Belle keep afloat so long?

At a glance I was convinced it would not. I felt it settling down under my feet inch by inch; and the blaze already threatened the after-part of the boat, licking the light wood-work of the gaudy saloon as if it had been flax! Not a moment was to be lost: we must take voluntarily to the water, be drawn in by the sinking wreck, or driven to it by the fire. One of the three was inevitable!

You will fancy me to have been in a state of extreme terror at this moment. Such, however, was not the case. I had not the slightest fear for my own safety: not that I was redeemed from the common lot by any superior courage, but simply that I had confidence *in my resources*. Though sufficiently reckless in my temperament, I have never been a fatalist. I have saved my life more than once by acts of volition—by presence of mind and adroitness. The knowledge of this has freed me from the superstitions of fore-ordination and fatalism; and therefore, when not too indolent, I take precautions against danger.

I had done so on the occasion of which I am writing. In my portmanteau I carried—I do so habitually—a very simple contrivance, a life-preserver. I always carry it in such a position as to be ready to the hand. It is but the work of a moment to adjust this, and with it around my body I feel no fear of being plunged into the broadest river, or even a channel of the sea. It was the knowledge of this, and not any superior courage, that supported me.

I ran back to my state-room—the portmanteau was open—and in another moment I held the piece of quilted cork in my hands. In a few seconds its strap was over my head, and the strings securely knotted around my waist.

Thus accoutred, I stood *inside* the state-room, intending to remain there till the wreck should sink nearer the surface of the water. Settling rapidly as it was, I was convinced I should not have long to wait. I closed the inner door of the room, and turned the bolt. The outer one I held slightly ajar, my hand firmly clutching the handle.

I had my object in thus shutting myself up. I should be less exposed to the view of the terror-stricken wretches that ran to and fro like spectres—for any fear I now had was of *them*—not of the water. I knew that, should the life-preserver be discovered, I should have a crowd around me in a moment—in fact, that escape by such means would be hopeless. Dozens would follow me into the water—would cling to my limbs—would drag me, in their despairing grasp, to the bottom!

I knew this; and, clutching the Venetian door with firmer grasp, I stood peering through the apertures in stealthy silence.

Chapter Thirteen
"Blessé"

I had not been in this position more than a few seconds, when some figures appeared in front of the door, and voices fell upon my ear that I thought I recognised. Another glance revealed the speakers. They were the young Creole and her steward.

The conversation passing between them was not a dialogue, but a series of exclamations—the hurried language of terror. The old man had got together a few cabin chairs; and with trembling hands was endeavouring to bind them together, with the design of forming a raft. He had no other cord than a handkerchief, and some strips of silk, which his young mistress was tearing from her dress! It would have been but a feeble raft, had it been completed—not fit to have floated a cat. It was but the effort of the drowning man "catching at straws." I saw at a glance that it would afford to neither of them the respite of a minute's life. The chairs were of heavy rosewood; and, perchance, would have gone to the bottom of themselves!

The scene produced upon me an impression indescribably strange. I felt myself standing upon a crisis. I felt called upon to choose between self and self-sacrifice. Had the choice left no chance of saving my own life, I fear I should have obeyed the "first law of nature;" but, as already stated, of my own life I felt secure; the question was, whether it would be possible for me also to save the lady?

I reasoned rapidly, and as follows;—The life-preserver—a very small one—will not sustain us both! What if I fasten it upon her, and swim alongside? A little help from it now and then will be sufficient to keep me afloat. I am a good swimmer. How far is it to the shore?

I looked in that direction. The glare of the blazing boat lit up the water to a wide circumference. I could see the brown bank distinctly. It was full a quarter of a mile distant, with a sharp cross-current running between it and the wreck.

"Surely I can swim it?" thought I: "sink or swim, I shall make the attempt to save her!"

I will not deny that other reflections passed through my mind as I was forming this resolve. I will not deny that there was a little *French* gallantry mixed up with better motives. Instead of being young and lovely, had Mademoiselle Besançon been old and plain, I think—that is—I—I fear—she would have been left to Antoine and his raft of chairs! As it was, my resolve was made; and I had no time to reflect upon motives.

"Mademoiselle Besançon!" I called out of the door.

"Ha! Some one calls me;" said she, turning suddenly. "Mon Dieu! who is there?"

"One who, Mademoiselle—"

"*Peste!*" muttered the old steward, angrily, as his eyes fell upon my face. He was under the belief that I wished to share his raft.

"*Peste!*" he repeated; "'twill not carry two, monsieur."

"Nor one," I replied. "Mademoiselle," I continued, addressing myself to the lady; "those chairs will not serve,—they will rather be the means of drowning you,—here—take this! it will save your life."

As I spoke I had pulled off the preserver, and held it towards her.

"What is this?" she inquired hastily; and then, comprehending all, she continued, "No—no—no, Monsieur! Yourself—yourself!"

"I believe I can swim ashore without it. Take it, Mademoiselle! Quick! quick! there is no time to be lost. In three minutes the boat will go down. The other is not near yet: besides, she may fear to approach the fire! See the flames! they come this way! Quick! Permit me to fasten it for you?"

"My God!—my God! generous stranger—!"

"No words; now—now it is on! Now to the water! Have no fear! plunge in, and strike out from the wreck! fear not! I shall follow and guide you! Away!"

The girl, partly influenced by terror, and partly yielding to my remonstrances, sprang off into the water; and the next moment I saw her body afloat, distinguishable by the whitish drapery of her dress, that still kept above the surface.

At that instant I felt some one grasping me by the hand. I turned round. It was Antoine.

"Forgive me, noble youth! forgive me!" he cried, while the tears ran down his cheeks.

I would have replied, but at the moment I perceived a man rush forward to the guards, over which the girl had just passed. I could see that his eye was fixed upon her, and that he had marked the life-preserver! His intention was evident—he had mounted the guard-rail, and was just springing off as I reached the spot. I caught him by the collar, and drew him back. As I did so his face came under the blaze, and I recognised my betting bully. "Not so fast, Sir!" said I, still holding him. He uttered but one word in reply—and that was a fearful oath—but at the moment I saw in his uplifted hand the shining blade of a bowie-knife! So unexpectedly did this weapon appear, that I had no chance of evading the blow; and the next moment I felt the cold steel passing through my arm. It was not a fatal stab, however; and before the brute could repeat it, I had, in the phraseology of the ring, "planted" a blow upon his chin, that sent him sprawling over the chairs, while at the same time the knife flew out of his grasp. This I caught up, and hesitated for a moment whether to use it upon the ruffian; but my better feelings overcame my passion, and I flung the weapon into the river.

Almost instantaneously I plunged after. I had no time to tarry. The blaze had reached the wheel-house, close to which we were, and the heat was no longer to be borne. My last glance at the spot showed me Antoine and my antagonist struggling among the chairs!

The white drapery served me for a beacon, and I swam after it. The current had already carried it some distance from the boat, and directly down stream.

I had hurriedly divested myself of coat and boots, and as my other garments were of light material they did not impede me. After a few strokes I swam perfectly free; and, keeping the white dress before my eyes, I continued on down the river.

Now and then I raised my head above the surface and looked back. I still had fears that the ruffian might follow; and I had nerved myself for a struggle in the water!

In a few minutes I was alongside my *protegée*; and, after half-a-dozen hurried words of encouragement, I laid hold of her with one hand, and with the other endeavoured to direct our course towards the shore.

In this way the current carried us in a diagonal line, but we still floated down stream at a rapid rate. A long and weary swim it seemed to me. Had it been much longer I never should have reached the end of it.

At length we appeared to be near the bank; but as we approached it my strokes became feebler, and my left hand grasped my companion with a sort of convulsive effort.

I remember reaching land, however; I remember crawling up the bank with great difficulty, my companion assisting me! I remember seeing a large house directly in front of where we had come ashore; I remember hearing the words—

"*C'est drôle! c'est ma maison—ma maison veritable!*"

I remember staggering across a road, led by a soft hand, and entering a gate, and a garden where there were benches, and statues, and sweet-smelling flowers—I remember seeing servants come from the house with lights, and that my arms were red, and my sleeves dripping with blood! I remember from a female voice the cry—

"*Blessé!*" followed by a wild shriek; and of that scene I remember no more!

Chapter Fourteen
Where am I?

When I awoke to consciousness, it was day. A bright sun was pouring his yellow light across the floor of my chamber; and from the diagonal slanting of the beam, I could perceive that it was either very early in the morning, or near sunset.

But birds were singing without. It must be morning, reasoned I.

I perceived that I was upon a low couch of elegant construction—without curtains—but in their stead a mosquito-netting spread its gauzy meshes above and around me. The snow-white colour and fineness of the linen, the silken gloss of the counterpane, and the soft yielding mattress beneath, imparted to me the knowledge that I lay upon a luxurious bed. But for its extreme elegance and fineness, I might not have noticed this; for I awoke to a sense of severe bodily pain.

The incidents of the preceding night soon came into my memory, and passed rapidly one by one as they had occurred. Up to our reaching the bank of the river, and climbing out of the water, they were all clear enough. Beyond that time I could recall nothing distinctly. A house, a large gateway, a garden, trees, flowers, statues, lights, black servants, were all jumbled together on my memory.

There was an impression on my mind of having beheld amid this confusion a face of extraordinary beauty—the face of a lovely girl! Something angelic it seemed; but whether it had been a real face that I had seen, or only the vision of a dream, I could not now tell. And yet its lineaments were still before me, so plainly visible to the eye of my mind, so clearly outlined, that, had I been an artist, I could have portrayed them! The face alone I could remember nothing else. I remembered it as the opium-eater his dream, or as one remembers a beautiful face seen during an hour of intoxication, when all else is forgotten! Strange to say, I did not associate this face with my companion of the night; and my remembrance painted it not at all like that of Eugénie Besançon!

Was there any one besides—any one on board the boat that my dream resembled? No, not one—I could not think of one. There was none in whom I had taken even a momentary interest—with the exception of the Creole—

but the lineaments my fancy, or memory, now conjured up were entirely unlike to hers: in fact, of quite an opposite character!

Before my mind's eye hung masses of glossy black hair, waving along the brows and falling over the shoulders in curling clusters. Within this ebon framework were features to mock the sculptor's chisel. The mouth, with its delicate rose-coloured ellipse; the nose, with smooth straight outline, and small recurvant nostril; the arching brows of jet; the long fringes upon the eyelids; all were vividly before me, and all unlike the features of Eugénie Besançon. The colour of the skin, too—even that was different. It was not that Circassian white that characterised the complexion of the Creole, but a colour equally clear, though tinged with a blending of brown and olive, which gave to the red upon the cheeks a tint of crimson. The eye I fancied, or remembered well—better than aught else. It was large, rounded, and of dark-brown colour; but its peculiarity consisted in a certain expression, strange but lovely. Its brilliance was extreme, but it neither flashed nor sparkled. It was more like a gorgeous gem viewed by the spectator while at rest. Its light did not blaze—it seemed rather to burn.

Despite some pain which I felt, I lay for many minutes pondering over this lovely portrait, and wondering whether it was a memory or a dream. A singular reflection crossed my mind. I could not help thinking, that if such a face were real, I could forget Mademoiselle Besançon, despite the romantic incident that had attended our introduction!

The pain of my arm at length dissipated the beautiful vision, and recalled me to my present situation. On throwing back the counterpane, I observed with surprise that the wound had been dressed, and evidently by a surgeon! Satisfied on this head, I cast my eye abroad to make a reconnoissance of my quarters.

The room I occupied was small, but notwithstanding the obstruction of the mosquito bar, I could see that it was furnished with taste and elegance. The furniture was light—mostly cane-work—and the floor was covered with a matting of sea-grass finely woven, and stained into various colours. The windows were garnished with curtains of silk damask and muslin, corresponding to the colour of the wood-work. A table richly inlaid was near the centre of the floor, another, with *portefeuille*, pens, and ornamental ink stand, stood by the wall, and over this last was a collection of books ranged upon shelves of red cedar-wood. A handsome clock adorned the mantelpiece; and in the open fireplace was a pair of small "andirons," with silver knobs, cast after a fanciful device, and richly chased. Of course, there was no fire at that season of the year. Even the heat caused by the mosquito bar would have been annoying, but that the large glass-door on one side, and the window on the other, both standing open, gave passage to the breeze that penetrated through the nettings of my couch.

Along with this breeze came the most delicious fragrance—the essence of flowers. Through both door and window I could see their thousand clustering corollas—roses, red, pink, and white—the rare camelia—azaleas, and jessamines—the sweet-scented China-tree—and farther off a little I could distinguish the waxen leaves and huge lily-like blossoms of the great American laurel—the *Magnolia grandiflora*. I could hear the voices of many singing-birds, and a low monotonous hum that I supposed to be the noise of falling water. These were the only sounds that reached my ears.

Was I alone? I looked inquiringly around the chamber. It appeared so—no living thing met my glance.

I was struck with a peculiarity in the apartment I occupied. It appeared to stand by itself, and did not communicate with any other! The only door I could see, opened directly to the outside. So did the window, reaching door-like to the ground. Both appeared to lead into a garden filled with shrubs and flowers. Excepting the chimney, I could perceive no other inlet or outlet to the apartment!

This at first seemed odd; but a moment's reflection explained it. It is not uncommon upon American plantations to have a kind of office or summer-house apart from the main building, and often fitted up in a style of comfort and luxuriance. This becomes upon occasions the "stranger's room." Perhaps I was in such an apartment.

At all events, I was under an hospitable roof, and in good hands; that was evident. The manner in which I was encouched, along with certain preparations,—the signs of a projected *dejeuner* that appeared upon the table, attested this. But who was my host? or was it a hostess? Was it Eugénie Besançon? Did she not say something of her house—"*ma maison?*" or did I only dream it?

I lay guessing and reflecting over a mass of confused memories; but I could not from these arrive at any knowledge of whose guest I was. Nevertheless, I had a sort of belief that I was in the house of my last night's companion.

I became anxious, and in my weakness perhaps felt a little vexed at being left alone. I would have rung, but no bell was within reach. At that moment, however, I heard the sound of approaching footsteps.

Romantic miss! you will fancy that those footsteps were light and soft, made by a small satin slipper, scarcely discomposing the loosest, tiniest pebble—stealthily drawing near lest their sound might awake the sleeping invalid—and then, in the midst of bird-music, and humming waters, and the sweet perfume of flowers, a fair form appeared in the doorway, and I saw a gentle face, with a pair of soft, lovely eyes, in a timid inquiring glance, gazing upon me. You will fancy all this, no doubt; but your fancy is entirely at fault, and not at all like the reality.

The footsteps I heard were made by a pair of thick "brogans" of alligator leather, and full thirteen inches in length; which brogans the next moment rested upon the sill of the door directly before my eyes.

On raising my glance a little higher, I perceived a pair of legs, in wide copper-coloured "jeans," pantaloons; and carrying my eye still higher, I perceived a broad, heavy chest, covered with a striped cotton shirt; a pair of massive arms and huge shoulders, surmounted by the shining face and woolly head of a jet black negro!

The face and head came under my observation last; but on these my eyes dwelt longest, scanning them over and over, until I at length, despite the pain I was suffering, burst out into a sonorous laugh! If I had been dying, I could not have helped it; there was something so comic, so irresistibly ludicrous, in the physiognomy of this sable intruder.

He was a full-grown and rather large negro, as black as charcoal, with a splendid tier of "ivories;" and with eyeballs, pupil and irides excepted, as white as his teeth. But it was not these that had tickled my fancy. It was the peculiar contour of his head, and the set and size of his ears. The former was as round as a globe, and thickly covered with small kinky curlets of black wool, so closely set that they seemed to root at both ends, and form a "nap!" From the sides of this sable sphere stood out a pair of enormous ears, suggesting the idea of wings, and giving to the head a singularly ludicrous appearance.

It was this peculiarity that had set me laughing; and, indecorous though it was, for the life of me I could not help it.

My visitor, however, did not seem to take it amiss. On the contrary, he at once opened his thick lips, and displaying the splendid armature of his mouth in a broad and good-natured grin, began laughing as loudly as myself!

Good-natured was he. His bat-like ears had infused nothing of the vampire into his character. No—the very type of jollity and fun was the broad black face of "Scipio Besançon," for such was the cognomen of my visitor.

Chapter Fifteen
"Ole Zip."

Scipio opened the dialogue:—

"Gollies, young mass'r! Ole Zip 'joiced to see um well 'gain—daat he be."

"Scipio is it?"

"Ye', mass'r—daat same ole nigger. Doctor told um to nuss de white genl'um. Won't young missa be glad haself!—white folks, black folks—all be glad, Wugh!"

The finishing exclamation was one of those thoracic efforts peculiar to the American negro, and bearing a strong resemblance to the snort of a hippopotamus. Its utterance signified that my companion had finished his sentence, and waited for me to speak.

"And who is 'young missa'?" I inquired.

"Gorramighty! don't mass'r know? Why, de young lady you fotch from de boat, when twar all ober a blaze. Lor! what a swum you make—half cross de riber! Wugh!"

"And am I in her house?"

"Ob sartin, mass'r—daat ar in de summer-house—for de big house am on oder side ob de garden—all de same, mass'r."

"And how did I get here?"

"Golly! don't mass'r 'member how? Why, ole Zip carried 'im in yar in dese berry arms. Mass'r an young missa come 'shore on de Lebee, down dar jes by de gate. Missa shout—black folks come out an find um—white genl'um all blood—he faint, an missa have him carried in yar."

"And after?"

"Zip he mount fastest hoss—ole White Fox—an gallop for de doctor—gallop like de debil, too. Ob course de doctor he come back along and dress up mass'r's arm."

"But," continued Scipio, turning upon me an inquiring look, "how'd young mass'r come by de big ugly cut? Dat's jes wha de Doc wanted to know, an dat's jes wha young missa didn't know nuffin 'tall 'bout."

For certain reasons I forbore satisfying the curiosity of my sable nurse, but lay for a moment reflecting. True, the lady knew nothing of my encounter with the bully. Ha! Antoine—then. Had he not come ashore? Was he—? Scipio anticipated the question I was about to put. His face became sad as he recommenced speaking.

"Ah! young mass'r, Mamselle 'Génie be in great 'stress dis mornin—all de folks be in great 'stress. Mass'r Toney! Poor Mass'r Toney."

"The steward, Antoine? What of him? Tell me, has he not come home?"

"No, mass'r—I'se afeerd he nebber, nebber will—ebberybody 'feerd he be drownded—folks a been to de village—up an down de Lebee—ebery wha. No Toney. Captain ob de boat blowed clar into de sky, an fifty passengers gone to de bottom. Oder boat save some; some, like young mass'r, swam 'shore: but no Toney—no Mass'r Toney!"

"Do you know if he could swim?" I asked.

"No, mass'r, ne'er a stroke. I knows daat, 'kase he once fell into de bayou, and Ole Zip pull 'im out. No—he nebber swim—nebber."

"Then I fear he is lost indeed."

I remembered that the wreck went down before the Magnolia had got close alongside. I had noticed this on looking around. Those who could not swim, therefore, must have perished.

"Poor Pierre, too. We hab lost Pierre."

"Pierre? Who was he?"

"De coachman, mass'r, he war."

"Oh! I remember. You think he is drowned, also?"

"I'se afeerd so, mass'r. Ole Zip sorry, too, for Pierre. A good nigger war daat Pierre. But, Mass'r Toney, Mass'r Toney, ebberybody sorry for Mass'r Toney."

"He was a favourite among you?"

"Ebberybody like 'im—black folks, white folks, all lub 'im. Missa 'Génie lub 'im. He live wi' ole Mass'r Sançon all him life. I believe war one ob Missy 'Génie gardiums, or whatever you call 'em. Gorramighty! what will young Missa do now? She hab no friends leff; and daat ole fox Gayarre—he no good—"

Here the speaker suddenly interrupted himself, as if he feared that his tongue was going too freely.

The name he had pronounced and the expression by which it was qualified, at once awakened my curiosity—the name more than the qualification.

"If it be the same," thought I, "Scipio has characterised him not otherwise than justly. Can it be the same?"

"You mean Monsieur Dominique Gayarre, the *avocat*?" I asked, after a pause.

Scipio's great white eyeballs rolled about with an expression of mingled surprise and apprehension, and rather stammeringly he replied:—

"Daat am de genl'um's name. Know 'im, young mass'r?"

"Only very slightly," I answered, and this answer seemed to set my companion at his ease again.

The truth is, I had no *personal* acquaintance with the individual mentioned; but during my stay in New Orleans, accident had brought me in contact with the name. A little adventure had befallen me, in which the bearer of it figured—not to advantage. On the contrary, I had conceived a strong dislike for the man, who, as already stated, was a lawyer, or *avocat* of the New Orleans bar. Scipio's man was no doubt the same. The name was too rare a one to be borne by two individuals; besides, I had heard that he was owner of a plantation somewhere up the coast—at Bringiers, I remembered. The probabilities were it was he. If so, and Mademoiselle Besançon had no other friend, then, indeed, had Scipio spoken truly when he said, "She hab no friends leff."

Scipio's observation had not only roused my curiosity, but had imparted to me a vague feeling of uneasiness. It is needless to say that I was now deeply interested in this young Creole. A man who has saved a life—the life of a beautiful woman—and under such peculiar circumstances, could not well be indifferent to the after-fate of her he has rescued.

Was it a lover's interest that had been awakened within me?

My heart answered, No! To my own astonishment, it gave this answer. On the boat I had fancied myself half in love with this young lady; and now, after a romantic incident—one that might appear a very provocative to the sublime passion—I lay on my couch contemplating the whole affair with a coolness that surprised even myself! I felt that I had lost much blood—had my incipient passion flowed out of my veins at the same time?

I endeavoured to find some explanation for this rare psychological fact; but at that time I was but an indifferent student of the mind. The land of love was to me a *terre inconnue*.

One thing was odd enough. Whenever I essayed to recall the features of the Creole, the dream-face rose up before me more palpable than ever!

"Strange!" thought I, "this lovely vision! this dream of my diseased brain! Oh! what would I not give to embody this fair spectral form!"

I had no longer a doubt about it. I was certain I did not love Mademoiselle Besançon, and yet I was far from feeling indifferent towards her. Friendship was the feeling that now actuated me. The interest, I felt for her was that of a friend. Strong enough was it to render me anxious on her account—to make me desirous of knowing more both of herself and her affairs.

Scipio was not of secretive habit; and in less than half an hour I was the confidant of all he knew.

Eugénie Besançon was the daughter and only child of a Creole planter, who had died some two years before, as some thought wealthy, while others believed that his affairs were embarrassed. Monsieur Dominique Gayarre had been left joint-administrator of the estate with the steward Antoine, both being "guardiums" (sic Scipio) of the young lady. Gayarre had been the lawyer of Besançon, and Antoine his faithful servitor. Hence the trust reposed in the old steward, who in latter years stood in the relation of friend and companion rather than of servant to Besançon himself.

In a few months mademoiselle would be of age; but whether her inheritance was large, Scipio could not tell. He only knew that since her father's death, Monsieur Dominique, the principal executor, had furnished her with ample funds whenever called upon; that she had not been restricted in any way; that she was generous; that she was profuse in her expenditure, or, as Scipio described it, "berry wasteful, an flung about de shinin dollars as ef dey war *donicks*!"

The black gave some glowing details of many a grand ball and *fête champètre* that had taken place on the plantation, and hinted at the expensive life which "young missa" led while in the city, where she usually resided during most part of the winter. All this I could easily credit. From what had occurred on the boat, and other circumstances, I was impressed with the belief that Eugénie Besançon was just the person to answer to the description of Scipio. Ardent of soul—full of warm impulses—generous to a fault—reckless in expenditure—living altogether in the present—and not caring to make any calculation for the future. Just such an heiress as would exactly suit the purposes of an unprincipled administrator.

I could see that poor Scipio had a great regard for his young mistress; but, even ignorant as he was, he had some suspicion that all this profuse outlay boded no good. He shook his head as he talked of these matters, adding—

"I'se afeerd, young mass'r, it'll nebber, nebber last. De Planters' bank hisseff would be broke by such a constant drawin ob money."

When Scipio came to speak of Gayarre he shook his head still more significantly. He had evidently some strange suspicions about this individual, though he was unwilling, just then, to declare them.

I learnt enough to identify Monsieur Dominique Gayarre with my *avocat* of the Rue —, New Orleans. No doubt remained on my mind that it was the same. A lawyer by profession, but more of a speculator in stocks—a money-lender, in other words, usurer. In the country a planter, owning the plantation adjoining that of Besançon, with more than a hundred slaves, whom he treats with the utmost severity. All this is in correspondence with the calling and character of my Monsieur Dominique. They are the same.

Scipio gives me some additional details of him. He was the law adviser and the companion of Monsieur Besançon—Scipio says, "Too often for ole mass'r's good," and believes that the latter suffered much from his acquaintance: or, as Scipio phrases it, "Mass'r Gayarre humbug ole mass'r; he cheat 'im many an many a time, I'se certain."

Furthermore, I learn from my attendant, that Gayarre resides upon his plantation during the summer months; that he is a daily visitor at the "big house"—the residence of Mademoiselle Besançon—where he makes himself quite at home; acting, says Scipio, "as ef de place 'longed to him, and he war de boss ob de plantation."

I fancied Scipio knew something more about this man—some definite matter that he did not like to talk about. It was natural enough, considering our recent acquaintance. I could see that he had a strong dislike towards Gayarre. Did he found it on some actual knowledge of the latter, or was it instinct—a principle strongly developed in these poor slaves, who are not permitted to *reason*?

His information, however, comprised too many facts to be the product of mere instinct: it savoured of actual knowledge. He must have learnt these things from some quarter. Where could he have gathered them?

"Who told you all this, Scipio?"

"Aurore, mass'r."

"Aurore!"

Chapter Sixteen
Monsieur Dominique Gayarre

I felt a sudden desire, amounting almost to anxiety, to learn who was "Aurore." Why? Was it the singularity and beauty of the name,—for novel and beautiful it sounded in my Saxon ears? No. Was it the mere euphony of the word; its mythic associations; its less ideal application to the rosy hours of the Orient, or the shining phosphorescence of the North? Was it any of these associate thoughts that awoke within me this mysterious interest in the name "Aurore?"

I was not allowed time to reflect, or question Scipio farther. At that moment the door was darkened by the entrance of two men; who, without saying a word, stepped inside the apartment.

"Da doctor, mass'r," whispered Scipio, falling back, and permitting the gentlemen to approach.

Of the two it was not difficult to tell which was the "doctor." The professional face was unmistakeable: and I knew that the tall pale man, who regarded me with interrogative glance, was a disciple of Esculapius, as certainly as if he had carried his diploma in one hand and his door-plate in the other.

He was a man of forty, not ill-featured, though the face was not one that would be termed handsome. It was, however, interesting, from a quiet intellectuality that characterised it, as well as an habitual expression of kind feeling. It had been a German face some two or three generations before, but an American climate,—political, I mean,—had tamed down the rude lines produced by ages of European despotism, and had almost restored it to its primitive nobility of feature. Afterwards, when better acquainted with American types, I should have known it as a Pennsylvanian face, and such in reality it was. I saw before me a graduate of one of the great medical schools of Philadelphia, Dr Edward Reigart. The name confirmed my suspicion of German origin.

Altogether my medical attendant made a pleasing impression upon me at first sight.

How different was that I received on glancing toward his companion—antagonism, hatred, contempt, disgust! A face purely French;—not that noble French face we see in the Duguesclins, the Jean Barts, and among many of the old Huguenot heroes; and in modern days in a Rollin, a Hugo, an Arago, or a Pyat;—but such an one as you may see any day by hundreds sneaking around the Bourse or the *coulisses* of the Opera, or in thousands scowling from under a shako in the ranks of a ruffian soldiery. A countenance that I cannot describe better than by saying that its features forcibly reminded me of those of a fox. I am not in jest. I observed this resemblance plainly. I observed the same obliquity of eyes, the same sharp quick glance that betokened the presence of deep dissimulation, of utter selfishness, of cruel inhumanity.

In the Doctor's companion I beheld a type of this face,—the fox in human form, and with all the attributes of this animal highly developed.

My instincts chimed with Scipio's, for I had not the slightest doubt that before me stood Monsieur Dominique Gayarre. It was he.

A man of small stature he was, and thinly built, but evidently one who could endure a great deal before parting with life. He had all the subtle wiry look of the *carnivora*, as well as their disposition. The eyes, as already observed, obliqued strongly downwards. The balls were not globe-shaped, but rather obtuse cones, of which the pupil was the apex. Both pupils and irides were black, and glistened like the eyes of a weasel. They seemed to sparkle in a sort of habitual smile; but this smile was purely cynical and deceptive. If any one knew themselves guilty of a weakness or a crime they felt certain that Dominique Gayarre knew it, and it was at this he was laughing. When a case of misfortune did really present itself to his knowledge, his smile became more intensely satirical, and his small prominent eyes sparkled with evident delight. He was a lover of himself and a hater of his kind.

For the rest, he had black hair, thin and limp—shaggy dark brows, set obliquely—face without beard, of pale cadaverous hue, and surmounted by a parrot-beak nose of large dimensions. His dress had somewhat of a professional cut, and consisted of dark broadcloth, with vest of black satin; and around his neck, instead of cravat, he wore a broad black ribbon. In age he looked fifty.

The doctor felt my pulse, asked me how I had slept, looked at my tongue, felt my pulse a second time, and then in a kindly way desired me to keep myself "as quiet as possible." As an inducement to do so he told me I was still very weak, that I had lost a good deal of blood, but hoped that a few days would restore me to my strength. Scipio was charged with my diet, and was ordered to prepare tea, toast, and broiled chicken, for my breakfast.

The doctor did not inquire how I came by my wound. This I thought somewhat strange, but ascribed it to his desire that I should remain quiet. He fancied, no doubt, that any allusion to the circumstances of the preceding night might cause me unnecessary excitement. I was too anxious about Antoine to remain silent, and inquired the news. Nothing more had been heard of him. He was certainly lost.

I recounted the circumstances under which I had parted with him, and of course described my encounter with the bully, and how I had received the wound. I could not help remarking a strange expression that marked the features of Gayarre as I spoke. He was all attention, and when I told of the raft of chairs, and expressed my conviction that they would not support the steward a single moment, I fancied I saw the dark eyes of the *avocat* flashing with delight! There certainly was an expression in them of ill-concealed satisfaction that was hideous to behold. I might not have noticed this, or at all events not have understood it, but for what Scipio had already told me. Now its meaning was unmistakeable, and notwithstanding the "poor Monsieur Antoine!" to which the hypocrite repeatedly gave utterance, I saw plainly that he was secretly delighted at the idea of the old steward's having gone to the bottom!

When I had finished my narrative, Gayarre drew the doctor aside; and the two conversed for some moments in a low tone. I could hear part of what passed between them. The doctor seemed not to care whether I overheard him, while the other appeared equally anxious that their conversation should not reach me. From the replies of the doctor I could make out that the wily lawyer wished to have me removed from my present quarters, and taken to an hotel in the village. He urged the peculiar position in which the young lady (Mademoiselle Besançon) would be placed—alone in her house with a stranger—a young man, etcetera, etcetera.

The doctor did not see the necessity of my removal on such grounds. The lady herself did not wish it—in fact, would not hear of it; he pooh-poohed the "peculiarity" of the "situation," good Doctor Reigart!—the accommodation of the hotel was none of the best; besides, it was already crowded with other sufferers; and here the speaker's voice sank so low I could only catch odd phrases, as "stranger,", "not an American," "lost everything," "friends far away," "the hotel no place for a man without money." Gayarre's reply to this last objection was that *he* would be responsible for my hotel bill.

This was intentionally spoken loud enough for me to hear it; and I should have felt grateful for such an offer, had I not suspected some sinister motive for the lawyer's generosity. The doctor met the proposal with still further objections.

"Impossible," said he; "bring on fever," "great risk," "would not take the responsibility," "bad wound," "much loss of blood," "must remain where he is for the present at least," "might be taken to the hotel in a day or two when stronger."

The promise of my removal in a day or two appeared to satisfy the weasel Gayarre, or rather he became satisfied that such was the only course that could be taken with me, and the consultation ended.

Gayarre now approached the bed to take leave, and I could trace that ironical expression playing in the pupils of his little eyes as he pronounced some pretended phrases of consolation. He little knew to whom he was speaking. Had I uttered my name it would perhaps have brought the colour to his pale cheek, and caused him to make an abrupt exit. Prudence prevented me from declaring it; and when the doctor requested to know upon whom he had the honour of attending, I adopted the pardonable strategy, in use among distinguished travellers, of giving a *nom du voyage*. I assumed my maternal patronymic of Rutherford,—Edward Rutherford.

Recommending me to keep myself quiet, not to attempt leaving my bed, to take certain prescriptions at certain hours, etcetera, etcetera, the doctor took his leave; Gayarre having already gone out before him.

Chapter Seventeen
"Aurore."

I was for the moment alone, Scipio having betaken himself to the kitchen in search of the tea, toast, and chicken "fixings." I lay reflecting upon the interview just ended, and especially upon the conversation between the doctor and Gayarre, in which had occurred several points that suggested singular ideas. The conduct of the doctor was natural enough, indeed betokened the true gentleman; but for the other there was a sinister design—I could not doubt it.

Why the desire—an anxiety, in fact—to have me removed to the hotel? Evidently there was some strong motive, since he proposed to pay the expenses; for from my slight knowledge of the man I knew him to be the very opposite to generous!

"What can be his motive for my removal?" I asked myself.

"Ha! I have it—I have the explanation! I see through his designs clearly! This fox, this cunning *avocat*, this guardian, is no doubt in love with his own ward! She is young, rich, beautiful, a belle, and he old, ugly, mean, and contemptible; but what of that? He does not think himself either one or the other; and she—bah!—he may even hope: far less reasonable hopes have been crowned with success. He knows the world; he is a lawyer; he knows at least her world. He is her solicitor; holds her affairs entirely in his hands; he is guardian, executor, agent—all; has perfect and complete control. With such advantages, what can he not effect? All that he may desire—her marriage, or her ruin. Poor lady! I pity her!"

Strange to say, it was only *pity*. That it was not another feeling was a mystery I could not comprehend.

The entrance of Scipio interrupted my reflections. A young girl assisted him with the plates and dishes. This was "Chloe," his daughter, a child of thirteen, or thereabouts, but not black like the father! She was a "yellow girl," with rather handsome features. Scipio explained this. The mother of his "leettle Chlo," as he called her, was a mulatta, and "'Chlo' hab taken arter de ole 'oman. Hya! hya!"

The tone of Scipio's laugh showed that he was more than satisfied—proud, in fact—of being the father of so light-skinned and pretty a little creature as Chloe!

Chloe, like all her kind, was brimful of curiosity, and in rolling about the whites of her eyes to get a peep at the buckra stranger who had saved her mistress' life, she came near breaking cups, plates, and dishes; for which negligence Scipio would have boxed her ears, but for my intercession. The odd expressions and gestures, the novel behaviour of both father and daughter, the peculiarity of this slave-life, interested me.

I had a keen appetite, notwithstanding my weakness. I had eaten nothing on the boat; in the excitement of the race, supper had been forgotten by most of the passengers, myself among the number. Scipio's preparations now put my palate in tune, and I did ample justice to the skill of Chloe's mother, who, as Scipio informed me, was "de boss in de kitchen." The tea strengthened me; the chicken, delicately fricasséed and garnished upon rice, seemed to refill my veins with fresh blood. With the exception of the slight pain of my wound, I already felt quite restored.

My attendants removed the breakfast things, and after a while Scipio returned to remain in the room with me, for such were his orders.

"And now, Scipio," I said, as soon as we were alone, "tell me of Aurore!"

"'Rore, mass'r!"

"Yes—Who is Aurore?"

"Poor slave, mass'r; jes like Ole Zip heamseff."

The vague interest I had begun to feel in "Aurore" vanished at once.

"A slave!" repeated I, involuntarily, and in a tone of disappointment.

"She Missa 'Génie's maid," continued Scipio; "dress missa's hair—wait on her—sit wi' her—read to her—do ebbery ting—"

"Read to her! what!—a slave?"

My interest in Aurore began to return.

"Ye, mass'r—daat do 'Rore. But I 'splain to you. Ole Mass'r 'Sançon berry good to de coloured people—teach many ob um read de books—'specially 'Rore. 'Rore he 'struck read, write, many, many tings, and young Missa 'Génie she teach her de music. 'Rore she 'complish gal—berry 'complish gal. Know many ting; jes like de white folks. Plays on de peany—plays on de guitar—guitar jes like banjo, an Ole Zip play on daat heamseff—he do. Wugh!"

"And withal, Aurore is a poor slave just like the rest of you, Scipio?"

"Oh! no, mass'r; she be berry different from de rest. She lib different life from de other nigga—she no hard work—she berry vallyble—she fetch two thousand dollar!"

"Fetch two thousand dollars!"

"Ye, mass'r, ebbery cent—ebbery cent ob daat."

"How know you?"

"'Case daat much war bid for her. Mass'r Marigny want buy 'Rore, an Mass'r Crozat, and de American Colonel on de oder side ob ribber—dey all bid two thousand dollar—ole mass'r he only larf at um, and say he won't sell de gal for no money."

"This was in old master's time?"

"Ye—ye—but one bid since—one boss ob ribber-boat—he say he want 'Rore for de lady cabin. He talk rough to her. Missa she angry—tell 'im go. Mass'r Toney he angry, tell 'im go; and de boat captain he go angry like de rest. Hya! hya! hya!"

"And why should Aurore command such a price?"

"Oh! she berry good gal—berry good gal—but—"

Scipio hesitated a moment—"but—"

"Well?"

"I don't b'lieve, mass'r, daat's de reason."

"What, then?"

"Why, mass'r, to tell de troof, I b'lieve dar all bad men daat wanted to buy de gal."

Delicately as it was conveyed, I understood the insinuation.

"Ho! Aurore must be beautiful, then? Is it so, friend Scipio?"

"Mass'r, 'taint for dis ole nigger to judge 'bout daat; but folks dey say—bof white folks an black folks—daat she am de best-lookin' an hansomest quaderoom in all Loozyanna."

"Ha! a *quadroon*?"

"Daat are a fact, mass'r, daat same—she be a gal ob colour—nebber mind—she white as young missa herself. Missa larf and say so many, many time, but fr'all daat dar am great difference—one rich lady—t'other poor slave—jes like Ole Zip—ay, jes like Ole Zip—buy 'em, sell 'em, all de same."

"Could you describe Aurore, Scipio?"

It was not idle curiosity that prompted me to put this question. A stronger motive impelled me. The dream-face still haunted me—those features of strange type—its strangely-beautiful expression, not Caucasian, not Indian, not Asiatic. Was it possible—probable—

"Could you describe her, Scipio?" I repeated.

"'Scribe her, mass'r; daat what you mean? ye—yes."

I had no hope of a very lucid painting, but perhaps a few "points" would serve to identify the likeness of my vision. In my mind the portrait was as plainly drawn as if the real face were before my eyes. I should easily tell if Aurore and my dream were one. I began to think it was no dream, but a reality.

"Well, mass'r, some folks says she am proud, case de common niggers envy ob her—daat's de troof. She nebber proud to Ole Zip, daat I knows—she talk to 'im, an tell 'im many tings—she help teach Ole Zip read, and de ole Chloe, and de leettle Chloe, an she—"

"It is a description of her person I ask for, Scipio."

"Oh! a 'scription ob her person—ye—daat is, what am she like?"

"So. What sort of hair, for instance? What colour is it?"

"Brack, mass'r; brack as a boot."

"Is it straight hair?"

"No, mass'r—ob course not—Aurore am a quaderoom."

"It curls?"

"Well, not dzactly like this hyar;" here Scipio pointed to his own kinky head-covering; "but for all daat, mass'r, it curls—what folks call de wave."

"I understand; it falls down to her shoulders?"

"Daat it do, mass'r, down to de berry small ob her back."

"Luxuriant?"

"What am dat, mass'r?"

"Thick—bushy."

"Golly! it am as bushy as de ole coon's tail."

"Now the eyes?"

Scipio's description of the quadroon's eyes was rather a confused one. He was happy in a simile, however, which I felt satisfied with: "Dey am big an round—dey shine like de eyes of a deer." The nose puzzled him, but after some elaborate questioning, I could make out that it was straight and small. The eyebrows—the teeth—the complexion—were all faithfully pictured—that of the cheeks by a simile, "like de red ob a Georgium peach."

Comic as was the description given, I had no inclination to be amused with it. I was too much interested in the result, and listened to every detail with an anxiety I could not account for.

The portrait was finished at length, and I felt certain it must be that of the lovely apparition. When Scipio had ended speaking, I lay upon my couch burning with an intense desire to see this fair—this priceless quadroon. Just then a bell rang from the house.

"Scipio wanted, mass'r—daat him bell—be back, 'gain in a minute, mass'r."

So saying, the negro left me, and ran towards the house.

I lay reflecting on the singular—somewhat romantic—situation in which circumstances had suddenly placed me. But yesterday—but the night before—a traveller, without a dollar in my purse, and not knowing what roof would next shelter me—to-day the guest of a lady, young, rich, unmarried—the invalid guest—laid up for an indefinite period; well cared for and well attended.

These thoughts soon gave way to others. The dream-face drove them out of my mind, and I found myself comparing it with Scipio's picture of the quadroon. The more I did so, the more I was struck with their correspondence. How could I have dreamt a thing so palpable? Scarce probable. Surely I must have seen it? Why not? Forms and faces were around me when I fainted and was carried in; why not hers among the rest? This was, indeed, probable, and would explain all. But was she among them? I should ask Scipio on his return.

The long conversation I had held with my attendant had wearied me, weak and exhausted as I was. The bright sun shining across my chamber did not prevent me from feeling drowsy; and after a few minutes I sank back upon my pillow, and fell asleep.

Chapter Eighteen
The Creole and Quadroon

I slept for perhaps an hour soundly. Then something awoke me, and I lay for some moments only half sensible to outward impressions.

Pleasant impressions they were. Sweet perfumes floated around me; and I could distinguish a soft, silky rustling, such as betokens the presence of well-dressed women.

"He wakes, ma'amselle!" half whispered a sweet voice.

My eyes, now open, rested upon the speaker. For some moments I thought it was but the continuation of my dream. There was the dream-face, the black profuse hair, the brilliant orbs, the arching brows, the small, curving lips, the damask cheek—all before me!

"Is it a dream? No—she breathes; she moves; she speaks!"

"See! ma'amselle—he looks at us! Surely he is awake!"

"It is no dream, then—no vision; it is she—it is Aurore!"

Up to this moment I was still but half conscious. The thought had passed from my lips; but, perhaps, only the last phrase was uttered loud enough to be heard. An ejaculation that followed fully awoke me, and I now saw two female forms close by the side of my couch. They stood regarding each other with looks of surprise. One was Eugénie; beyond doubt the other was Aurore!

"Your name!" said the astonished mistress.

"My name!" repeated the equally astonished slave.

"But how?—he knows your name—how?"

"I cannot tell, ma'amselle."

"Have you been here before?"

"No; not till this moment."

"'Tis very strange!" said the young lady, turning towards me with an inquiring glance.

I was now awake, and in full possession of my senses—enough to perceive that I had been talking too loud. My knowledge of the quadroon's name would require an explanation, and for the life of me I knew not what to say. To tell what I had been thinking—to account for the expressions I had uttered—would have placed me in a very absurd position; and yet to maintain silence might leave Ma'amselle Besançon busy with some strange thoughts. Something must be said—a little deceit was absolutely necessary.

In hopes she would speak first, and, perchance, give me a key to what I should say, I remained for some moments without opening my lips. I pretended to feel pain from my wound, and turned uneasily on the bed. She seemed not to notice this, but remained in her attitude of surprise, simply repeating the words—

"'Tis very strange he should know your name!"

My imprudent speech had made an impression. I could remain silent no longer; and, turning my face once more, I pretended now for the first time to be aware of Mademoiselle's presence, at the same time offering my congratulations, and expressing my joy at seeing her.

After one or two anxious inquiries in relation to my wound, she asked—

"But how came you to name Aurore?"

"Aurore!" I replied. "Oh! you think it strange that I should know her name? Thanks to Scipio's faithful portraiture, I knew at the first glance that this was Aurore."

I pointed to the quadroon, who had retired a pace or two, and stood silent and evidently astonished.

"Oh! Scipio has been speaking of her?"

"Yes, ma'amselle. He and I have had a busy morning of it. I have drawn largely on Scipio's knowledge of plantation affairs. I am already acquainted with Aunt Chloe, and little Chloe, and a whole host of your people. These things interest me who am strange to your Louisiana life."

"Monsieur," replied the lady, seemingly satisfied with my explanation, "I am glad you are so well. The doctor has given me the assurance you will soon recover. Noble stranger! I have heard how you received your wound. For me it was—in my defence. Oh! how shall I ever repay you?—how thank you for my life?"

"No thanks, ma'amselle, are necessary. It was the fulfilment of a simple duty on my part. I ran no great risk in saving you."

"No risk, monsieur! Every risk—from the knife of an assassin—from the waves. No risk! But, monsieur, I can assure you my gratitude shall be in proportion to your generous gallantry. My heart tells me so;—alas, poor heart! it is filled at once with gratitude and grief."

"Yes, ma'amselle, I understand you have much to lament, in the loss of a faithful servant."

"Faithful servant, monsieur, say, rather, friend. Faithful, indeed! Since my poor father's death, he has been my father. All my cares were his; all my affairs in his hands. I knew not trouble. But now, alas! I know not what is before me."

Suddenly changing her manner, she eagerly inquired—

"When you last saw him, monsieur, you say he was struggling with the ruffian who wounded you?"

"He was.—It was the last I saw of either. There is no hope—none—the boat went down a few moments after. Poor Antoine! poor Antoine!"

Again she burst into tears, for she had evidently been weeping before. I could offer no consolation. I did not attempt it. It was better she should weep. Tears alone could relieve her.

"The coachman, Pierre, too—one of the most devoted of my people— he, too, is lost. I grieve for him as well; but Antoine was my father's friend— he was mine—Oh! the loss—the loss;—friendless; and yet, perhaps, I *may soon need friends. Pauvre Antoine!*"

She wept as she uttered these phrases. Aurore was also in tears. I could not restrain myself—the eyes of childhood returned, and I too wept.

This solemn scene was at length brought to a termination by Eugénie, who appearing suddenly to gain the mastery over her grief, approached the bedside.

"Monsieur," said she, "I fear for some time you will find in me a sad host. I cannot easily forget my friend, but I know you will pardon me for thus indulging in a moment of sorrow. For the present, adieu! I shall return soon, and see that you are properly waited upon. I have lodged you in this little place, that you might be out of reach of noises that would disturb you. Indeed I am to blame for this present intrusion. The doctor has ordered you not to be visited, but—I—I could not rest till I had seen the preserver of my life, and offered him my thanks. Adieu, adieu! Come, Aurore!"

I was left alone, and lay reflecting upon the interview. It had impressed me with a profound feeling of friendship for Eugénie Besançon;—more than friendship—sympathy: for I could not resist the belief that, somehow or other, she was in peril—that over that young heart, late so light and gay, a cloud was gathering.

I felt for her regard, friendship, sympathy,—nothing more. And why nothing more? Why did I not love her, young, rich, beautiful? Why?

Because I loved another—*I loved Aurore*!

Chapter Nineteen
A Louisian Landscape

Life in the chamber of an invalid—who cares to listen to its details? They can interest no one—scarce the invalid himself. Mine was a daily routine of trifling acts, and consequent reflections—a monotony, broken, however, at intervals, by the life-giving presence of the being I loved. At such moments I was no longer *ennuyé*; my spirit escaped from its death-like lassitude; and the sick chamber for the time seemed an Elysium.

Alas! these scenes were but of a few minutes' duration, while the intervals between them were hours—long hours—so long, I fancied them days. Twice every day I was visited by my fair host and her companion. Neither ever came alone!

There was constraint on my part, often bordering upon perplexity. My conversation was with the *Creole*, my thoughts dwelt upon the *Quadroon*. With the latter I dare but exchange glances. Etiquette restrained the tongue, though all the conventionalities of the world could not hinder the eyes from speaking in their own silent but expressive language.

Even in this there was constraint. My love-glances were given by stealth. They were guided by a double dread. On one hand, the fear that their expression should not be understood and reciprocated by the Quadroon. On the other, that they might be too well understood by the Creole, who would regard me with scorn and contempt. I never dreamt that they might awaken jealousy—I thought not of such a thing. Eugénie was sad, grateful, and friendly, but in her calm demeanour and firm tone of voice there was no sign of love. Indeed the terrible shock occasioned by the tragic occurrence, appeared to have produced a complete change in her character. The sylph-like elasticity of her mind, formerly a characteristic, seemed to have quite forsaken her. From a gay girl she had all at once become a serious woman. She was not the less beautiful, but her beauty impressed me only as that of the statue. It failed to enter my heart, already filled with beauty of a still rarer and more glowing kind. The Creole loved me not; and, strange to say, the reflection, instead of piquing my vanity, rather gratified me!

How different when my thoughts dwelt upon the Quadroon! Did *she* love me? This was the question, for whose answer my heart yearned with fond eagerness. She always attended upon Mademoiselle during her visits; but not a word dare I exchange with *her*, although my heart was longing to yield up its secret. I even feared that my burning glances might betray me. Oh! if Mademoiselle but knew of my love, she would scorn and despise me. What! in love with a slave! her slave!

I understood this feeling well—this black crime of her nation. What was it to me? Why should I care for customs and conventionalities which I at heart despised, even outside the levelling influence of love? But under that influence, less did I care to respect them. In the eyes of Love, rank loses its fictitious charm—titles seem trivial things. For me, Beauty wears the crown.

So far as regarded my feelings, I would not have cared a straw if the whole world had known of my love—not a straw for its scorn. But there were other considerations—the courtesy due to hospitality—to friendship; and there were considerations of a less delicate but still graver nature—the promptings of *prudence*. The situation in which I was placed was most peculiar, and I knew it. I knew that my passion, even if reciprocated, must be secret and silent. Talk of making love to a young miss closely watched by governess or guardian—a ward in Chancery—an heiress of expectant thousands! It is but "child's play" to break through the *entourage* that surrounds one of such. To scribble sonnets and scale walls is but an easy task, compared with the bold effrontery that challenges the passions and prejudices of a people!

My wooing promised to be anything but easy; my love-path was likely to be a rugged one.

Notwithstanding the monotony of confinement to my chamber, the hours of my convalescence passed pleasantly enough. Everything was furnished me that could contribute to my comfort or recovery. Ices, delicious drinks, flowers, rare and costly fruits, were constantly supplied to me. For my dishes I was indebted to the skill of Scipio's helpmate, Chloe, and through her I became acquainted with the Creole delicacies of "gumbo," "fish chowder," fricasséed frogs, hot "waffles," stewed tomatoes, and many other dainties of the Louisiana *cuisine*. From the hands of Scipio himself I did not refuse a slice of "roasted 'possum," and went even so far as to taste a "'coon steak,"—but only once, and I regarded it as once too often. Scipio, however, had no scruples about eating this fox-like creature, and could demolish the greater part of one at a single sitting!

By degrees I became initiated into the little habitudes and customs of life upon a Louisiana plantation. "Ole Zip" was my instructor, as he continued to be my constant attendant. When Scipio's talk tired me, I had recourse to books, of which a good stock (mostly French authors,) filled the little book-case in my apartment. I found among them nearly every work that related to Louisiana—a proof of rare judgment on the part of whoever had made the collection. Among others, I read the graceful romance of Chateaubriand, and the history of Du Pratz. In the former I could not help remarking that want of *vraisemblance* which, in my opinion, forms the great charm of a novel; and which must ever be absent where an author attempts the painting of scenes or costumes not known to him by actual observation.

With regard to the historian, he indulges largely in those childish exaggerations so characteristic of the writers of the time. This remark applies, without exception, to all the old writers on American subjects—whether English, Spanish, or French—the chroniclers of two-headed snakes, crocodiles twenty yards long, and was big enough to swallow both horse and rider! Indeed, it is difficult to conceive how these old authors gained credence for their incongruous stories; but it must be remembered that science was not then sufficiently advanced "to audit their accounts."

More than in anything else was I interested in the adventures and melancholy fate of La Salle; and I could not help wondering that American writers have done so little to illustrate the life of the brave chevalier—surely the most picturesque passage in their early history—the story and the scene equally inviting.

"The scene! Ah! lovely indeed!"

With such an exclamation did I hail it, when, for the first time, I sat at my window and gazed out upon a Louisiana landscape.

The windows, as in all Creole houses, reached down to the floor; and seated in my lounge-chair, with the sashes wide open, with the beautiful French curtains thrown back, I commanded an extended view of the country.

A gorgeous picture it presented. The pencil of the painter could scarcely exaggerate its vivid colouring.

My window faces westward, and the great river rolls its yellow flood before my face, its ripples glittering like gold. On its farther shore I can see cultivated fields, where wave the tall graceful culms of the sugar-cane, easily distinguished from the tobacco-plant, of darker hue. Upon the bank of the river, and nearly opposite, stands a noble mansion, something in the style of an Italian villa, with green Venetians and verandah. It is embowered in groves of orange and lemon-trees, whose frondage of yellowish green glistens gaily in the distance. No mountains meet the view—there is not a mountain in all Louisiana; but the tall dark wall of cypress, rising against the western rim of the sky, produces an effect very similar to a mountain background.

On my own side of the river the view is more gardenesque, as it consists principally of the enclosed pleasure-ground of the plantation Besançon. Here I study objects more in detail, and am able to note the species of trees that form the shrubbery. I observe the *Magnolia*, with large white wax-like flowers, somewhat resembling the giant *nympha* of Guiana. Some of these have already disappeared, and in their stead are seen the coral-red seed-cones, scarce less ornamental than the flowers themselves.

Side by side with this western-forest queen, almost rivalling her in beauty and fragrance, and almost rivalling her in fame, is a lovely exotic, a native of Orient climes—though here long naturalised. Its large doubly-pinnate leaves of dark and lighter green,—for both shades are observed on the same tree; its lavender-coloured flowers hanging in axillary clusters from the extremities of the shoots; its yellow cherry-like fruits—some of which are already formed,—all point out its species. It is one of the *meliaceae*, or honey-trees,—the "Indian-lilac," or "Pride of China" (*Melia azedarach*). The nomenclature bestowed upon this fine tree by different nations indicates the estimation in which it is held. "Tree of Pre-eminence," lays the poetic Persian, of whose land it is a native; "Tree of Paradise" (*Arbor de Paraiso*), echoes the Spaniard, of whose land it is an exotic. Such are its titles.

Many other trees, both natives and exotics, meet my gaze. Among the former I behold the "catalpa," with its silvery bark and trumpet-shaped blossoms; the "Osage orange," with its dark shining leaves; and the red mulberry, with thick shady foliage, and long crimson calkin-like fruits. Of exotics I note the orange, the lime, the West Indian guava (*Psidium pyriferum*), and the guava of Florida, with its boxwood leaves; the tamarisk, with its spreading minute foliage, and splendid panicles of pale rose-coloured flowers; the pomegranate, symbol of democracy—"the queen who carries her crown upon her bosom"—and the legendary but flowerless fig-tree, here not supported against the wall, but rising as a standard to the height of thirty feet.

Scarcely exotic are the *yuccas*, with their spherical heads of sharp radiating blades; scarcely exotic the *cactacea*, of varied forms—for species of both are indigenous to the soil, and both are found among the flora of a not far-distant region.

The scene before my window is not one of still life. Over the shrubbery I can see the white-painted gates leading to the mansion, and outside of these runs the Levee road. Although the foliage hinders me from a full view of the road itself, I see at intervals the people passing along it. In the dress of the Creoles the sky-blue colour predominates, and the hats are usually palmetto, or "grass," or the costlier Panama, with broad sun-protecting brims. Now and then a negro gallops past, turbaned like a Turk; for the chequered Madras "toque" has much the appearance of the Turkish head-dress, but is lighter and even more picturesque. Now and then an open carriage rolls by, and I catch a glimpse of ladies in their gossamer summer-dresses. I hear their clear ringing laughter; and I know they are on their way to some gay festive scene. The travellers upon the road—the labourers in the distant cane-field, chanting their chorus songs—occasionally a boat booming past on the river—more frequently a flat silently floating downward—a "keel," or a raft with its red-shirted crew—are all before my eyes, emblems of active life.

Nearer still are the winged creatures that live and move around my window. The mock-bird (*Turdus polyglotta*) pipes from the top of the tallest magnolia; and his cousin, the red-breast (*Turdus migratorius*), half intoxicated with the berries of the *melia*, rivals him in his sweet song. The oriole hops among the orange-trees, and the bold red cardinal spreads his scarlet wings amidst the spray of the lower shrubbery.

Now and then I catch a glimpse of the "ruby-throat," coming and going like the sparkle of a gem. Its favourite haunt is among the red and scentless flowers of the buck-eye, or the large trumpet-shaped blossoms of the *bignonia*.

Such was the view from the window of my chamber. I thought I never beheld so fair a scene. Perhaps I was not looking upon it with an impartial eye. The love-light was in my glance, and that may have imparted to it a portion of its *couleur de rose*. I could not look upon the scene without thinking of that fair being, whose presence alone was wanted to make the picture perfect.

Chapter Twenty
My Journal

I varied the monotony of my invalid existence by keeping a journal. The journal of a sick chamber must naturally be barren of incident. Mine was a diary of reflections rather than acts. I transcribe a few passages from it—not on account of any remarkable interest which they possess—but because, dotted down at the time, they represent more faithfully some of the thoughts and incidents that occurred to me during the remainder of my stay on the plantation Besançon.

July 12th.—To-day I am able to sit up and write a little. The weather is intensely hot. It would be intolerable were it not for the breeze which sweeps across my apartment, charged with the delicious perfume of the flowers. This breeze blows from the Gulf of Mexico, by Lakes Borgne, Pontchartrain, and Maauepas. I am more than one hundred miles from the Gulf itself—that is, following the direction of the river—but these great inland seas deeply penetrate the delta of the Mississippi, and through them the tidal wave approaches within a few miles of New Orleans, and still farther to the north. Sea-water might be reached through the swamps at a short distance to the rear of Bringiers.

This sea-breeze is a great benefit to the inhabitants of Lower Louisiana. Without its cooling influence New Orleans during the summer months would hardly be habitable.

Scipio tells me that a new "overseer" has arrived on the plantation, and thinks that he has been appointed through the agency of Mass'r Dominick. He brought a letter from the *avocat*. It is therefore probable enough.

My attendant does not seem very favourably impressed with the new comer, whom he represents as a "poor white man from de norf, an a Yankee at daat."

Among the blacks I find existing an antipathy towards what they are pleased to call "poor white men"—individuals who do not possess slave or landed property. The phrase itself expresses this antipathy; and when applied by a negro to a white man is regarded by the latter as a dire insult, and usually procures for the imprudent black a scoring with the "cowskin," or a slight "rubbing down" with the "oil of hickory."

Among the slaves there is a general impression that their most tyrannical "overseers" are from the New England States, or "Yankees," as they are called in the South. This term, which foreigners apply contemptuously to all Americans, in the United States has a restricted meaning; and when used reproachfully it is only applied to natives of New England. At other times it is used jocularly in a patriotic spirit; and in this sense every American is proud to call himself a Yankee. Among the southern blacks, "Yankee" is a term of reproach, associated in their minds with poverty of fortune, meanness of spirit, wooden nutmegs, cypress hams, and such-like chicanes. Sad and strange to say, it is also associated with the whip, the shackle, and the cowhide. Strange, because these men are the natives of a land peculiarly distinguished for its Puritanism! A land where the purest religion and strictest morality are professed.

This would seem an anomaly, and yet perhaps it is not so much an anomaly after all. I had it explained to me by a Southerner, who spoke thus:—

"The countries where Puritan principles prevail are those which produce vice, and particularly the smaller vices, in greatest abundance. The villages of New England—the foci of blue laws and Puritanism.—furnish the greatest number of the *nymphes du pavé* of New York, Philadelphia, Baltimore, and New Orleans; and even furnish a large export of them to the Catholic capital of Cuba! From the same prolific soil spring most of the sharpers, quacks, and cheating traders, who disgrace the American name. This is not an anomaly. It is but the inexorable result of a pseudo-religion. Outward observance, worship, Sabbath-keeping, and the various forms, are engrafted in the mind; and thus, by complicating the true duties which man owes to his fellow-man, obscure or take precedence of them. The latter grow to be esteemed as only of secondary importance, and are consequently neglected."

The explanation was at least ingenious.

July 14th.—To-day, twice visited by Mademoiselle; who, as usual, was accompanied by Aurore.

Our conversation does not flow easily or freely, nor is it of long continuance. She (Mademoiselle) is still evidently suffering, and there is a tone of sadness in everything she says. At first I attributed this to her sorrow for Antoine, but it has now continued too long to be thus explained. Some other grief presses upon her spirit. I suffer from restraint. The presence of

Aurore restrains me; and I can ill give utterance to those common-places required in an ordinary conversation. She (Aurore) takes no part in the dialogue; but lingers by the door, or stands behind her mistress, respectfully listening. When I regard her steadfastly, her fringed eyelids droop, and shut out all communion with her soul. *Oh that I could make her understand me*!

July 15th. — Scipio is confirmed in his dislike for the new overseer. His first impressions were correct. From two or three little matters which I have heard about this gentleman, I am satisfied that he is a bad successor to the good Antoine.

A propos of poor Antoine, it was reported that his body had been washed up among some drift-timber below the plantation; but the report proved incorrect. A body *was* found, but not that of the steward. Some other unfortunate, who had met with a similar fate. I wonder if the wretch who wounded me is yet above water!

There are still many of the sufferers at Bringiers. Some have died of the injuries they received on board the boat. A terrible death is this scalding by steam. Many who fancied themselves scarce injured, are now in their last agonies. The doctor has given me some details that are horrifying.

One of the men, a "fireman," whose nose is nearly gone, and who is conscious that he has but a short while to live, requested to see his face in a looking-glass. Upon the request being granted, he broke into a diabolical laugh, crying out at the same time, in a loud voice, "What a damned ugly corpse I'll make."

This reckless indifference to life is a characteristic of these wild boatmen. The race of "Mike Fink" is not extinct: many true representatives of this demi-savage still navigate the great rivers of the West.

July 20th. Much better to-day. The doctor tells me that in a week I may leave my room. This is cheering; and yet a week seems a long while to one not used to being caged in this way. The books enable me to kill time famously. All honour to the men who make books!

July 21st. — Scipio's opinion of the new overseer is not improved. His name is "Larkin." Scipio says that he is well-known in the village as "Bully Bill Larkin" — a soubriquet which may serve as a key to his character. Several of the "field-hands" complain (to Scipio) of his severity, which they say is daily on the increase. He goes about constantly armed with a "cowhide," and has already, once or twice, made use of it in a barbarous manner.

To-day is Sunday, and I can tell from the "hum" that reaches me from the negro "quarters," that it is a day of rejoicing. I can see the blacks passing the Levee road, dressed in their gayest attire—the men in white *beaver* hats, blue long-tailed coats, and shirts with enormous ruffles; the women in gaudy patterns of cotton, and not a few in silks brilliant enough for a ball-room! Many carry silk parasols, of course of the brightest colours. One would almost be tempted to believe that in this slave-life there was no great hardship, after all; but the sight of Mr Larkin's cowhide must produce a very opposite impression.

July 24th.—I noticed to-day more than ever the melancholy that seems to press upon the spirit of Mademoiselle. I am now convinced that Antoine's death is not the cause of it. There is some *present* source of distraction, which renders her ill at ease. I have again observed that singular glance with which she at first regarded me; but it was so transitory, I could not read its meaning, and my heart and eyes were searching elsewhere. Aurore gazes upon me less timidly, and seems to be interested in my conversation, though it is not addressed to her. Would that it were! Converse with her would perhaps relieve my heart, which burns all the more fiercely under the restraint of silence.

July 25th.—Several of the "field-hands" indulged too freely on yesternight. They had "passes" to the town, and came back late. "Bully Bill" has flogged them all this morning, and very severely—so as to draw the blood from their backs. This is rough enough for a *new* overseer; but Scipio learns that he is an "old hand" at the business. Surely Mademoiselle does not know of these barbarities!

July 26th.—The doctor promises to let me out in three days. I have grown to esteem this man—particularly since I made the discovery that he is *not* a friend of Gayarre. He is not his medical attendant either. There is another *medico* in the village, who has charge of Monsieur Dominique and his blacks, as also the slaves of the Besançon plantation. The latter chanced to be out of the way, and so Reigart was called to me. Professional etiquette partly, and partly my own interference, forbade any change in this arrangement; and the latter continued to attend me. I have seen the other gentleman, who came once in Reigart's company, and he appears much more suited to be the friend of the *avocat*.

Reigart is a stranger in Bringiers, but seems to be rapidly rising in the esteem of the neighbouring planters. Indeed, many of these—the "grandees" among them—keep physicians of their own, and pay them handsomely, too! It would be an unprofitable speculation to neglect the health of the slave; and on this account it is better looked after than that of the "poor white folks" in many a European state.

I have endeavoured to draw from the doctor some facts, regarding the connexion existing between Gayarre and the family of Besançon. I could only make distant allusion to such a subject. I obtained no very satisfactory information. The doctor is what might be termed a "close man," and too much talking would not make one of his profession very popular in Louisiana. He either knows but little of their affairs, or affects not to know; and yet, from some expressions that dropped from him, I suspect the latter to be the more probable.

"Poor young lady!" said he; "quite alone in the world. I believe there is an aunt, or something of the kind, who lives in New Orleans, but she has no male relation to look after her affairs. Gayarre seems to have everything in his hands."

I gathered from the doctor that Eugénie's father had been much richer at one period—one of the most extensive planters on the coast; that he had kept a sort of "open house," and dispensed hospitality in princely style. "Fêtes" on a grand scale had been given, and this more particularly of late years. Even since his death profuse hospitality has been carried on, and Mademoiselle continues to receive her father's guests after her father's fashion. Suitors she has in plenty, but the doctor has heard of no one who is regarded in the light of a "lover."

Gayarre had been the intimate friend of Besançon. Why, no one could tell; for their natures were as opposite as the poles. It was thought by some that their friendship had a little of the character of that which usually exists between *debtor* and *creditor*.

The information thus imparted by the doctor confirms what Scipio has already told me. It confirms, too, my suspicions in regard to the young Creole, that there is a cloud upon the horizon of her future, darker than any that has shadowed her past—darker even than that produced by the memory of Antoine!

July 28th.—Gayarre has been here to-day—at the house, I mean. In fact, he visits Mademoiselle nearly every day; but Scipio tells me something new and strange. It appears that some of the slaves who had been flogged, complained of the overseer to their young mistress; and she in her turn spoke to Gayarre on the subject. His reply was that the "black rascals deserved all they had got, and more," and somewhat rudely upheld the ruffian Larkin, who is beyond a doubt his *protégé*. The lady was silent.

Scipio learns these facts from Aurore. There is something ominous in all this.

Poor Scipio has made me the confidant of another, and a private grief. He suspects that the overseer is looking too kindly upon "him kettle Chloe." The brute! if this be so!—My blood boils at the thought—oh! slavery!

August 2nd.—I hear of Gayarre again. He has been to the house, and made a longer stay with Mademoiselle than usual. What can he have to do with her? Can his society be agreeable to her? Surely that is impossible! And yet such frequent visits—such long conferences! If she marry such a man as this I pity her, poor victim!—for victim will she be. He must have some power over her to act as he is doing. He seems master of the plantation, says Scipio, and issues his orders to every one with the air of its owner. All fear him and his "nigger-driver," as the ruffian Larkin is called. The latter is more feared by Scipio, who has noticed some further rude conduct on the part of the overseer towards "him leettle Chloe." Poor fellow! he is greatly distressed; and no wonder, when even the law does not allow him to protect the honour of his own child!

I have promised to speak to Mademoiselle about the affair; but I fear, from what reaches my ears, that she is almost as powerless as Scipio himself!

August 3rd.—To-day, for the first time, I am able to go out of my room. I have taken a walk through the shrubbery and garden. I encountered Aurore among the orange-trees, gathering the golden fruit; but she was accompanied by little Chloe, who held the basket. What would I not have given to have found her alone! A word or two only was I able to exchange with her, and she was gone.

She expressed her pleasure at seeing me able to be abroad. She *seemed* pleased; I fancied she felt so, I never saw her look so lovely. The exercise of shaking down the oranges had brought out the rich crimson bloom upon her cheeks, and her large brown eyes were shining like sapphires. Her full bosom rose and fell with her excited breathing, and the light wrapper she wore enabled me to trace the noble outlines of her form.

I was struck with the gracefulness of her gait as she walked away. It exhibited an undulating motion, produced by a peculiarity of figure—a certain *embonpoint* characteristic of her race. She was large and womanly, yet of perfect proportion and fine delicate outlines. Her hands were small and slender, and her little feet seemed hardly to press upon the pebbles. My eyes followed her in a delirium of admiration. The fire in my heart burned fiercer as I returned to my solitary chamber.

Chapter Twenty One
A Change of Quarters

I was thinking over my short interview with Aurore—congratulating myself upon some expressions she had dropped—happy in the anticipation that such encounters would recur frequently, now that I was able to be abroad—when in the midst of my pleasant reverie the door of my apartment became darkened. I looked up, and beheld the hated face of Monsieur Dominique Gayarre.

It was his first visit since the morning after my arrival upon the plantation. What could *he* want with *me*?

I was not kept long in suspense, for my visitor, without even apologising for his intrusion, opened his business abruptly and at once.

"Monsieur," began he, "I have made arrangements for your removal to the hotel at Bringiers."

"You have?" said I, interrupting him in a tone as abrupt and something more indignant than his own. "And who, sir, may I ask, has commissioned *you* to take this trouble?"

"Ah—oh!" stammered he, somewhat tamed down by his brusque reception, "I beg pardon, Monsieur. Perhaps you are not aware that I am the agent—the friend—in fact, the guardian of Mademoiselle Besançon—and—and—"

"Is it Mademoiselle Besançon's wish that I go to Bringiers?"

"Well—the truth is—not exactly her wish; but you see, my dear sir, it is a delicate affair—your remaining here, now that you are almost quite recovered, upon which I congratulate you—and—and—"

"Go on, sir!"

"Your remaining here any longer—under the circumstances—would be—you can judge for yourself, sir—would be, in fact, a thing that would be talked about in the neighbourhood—in fact, considered highly improper."

"Hold, Monsieur Gayarre! I am old enough not to require lessons in etiquette from you, sir."

"I beg pardon, sir. I do not mean that but—I—you will observe—I, as the lawful guardian of the young lady—"

"Enough, sir. I understand you perfectly. For *your purposes, whatever they be,* you do not wish me to remain any longer on this plantation. Your desire shall be gratified. I shall leave the place, though certainly not with any intention of accommodating you. I shall go hence this very evening."

The words upon which I had placed emphasis, startled the coward like a galvanic shock. I saw him turn pale as they were uttered, and the wrinkles deepened about his eyes. I had touched a chord, which he deemed a secret one, and its music sounded harsh to him. Lawyer-like, however, he commanded himself, and without taking notice of my insinuation, replied in a tone of whining hypocrisy—

"My dear monsieur! I regret this necessity; but the fact is, you see—the world—the busy, meddling world—"

"Spare your homilies, sir! Your business, I fancy, is ended; at all events your company is no longer desired."

"Humph!" muttered he. "I regret you should take it in this way—I am sorry—"

And with a string of similar incoherent phrases he made his exit.

I stepped up to the door and looked after, to see which way he would take. He walked direct to the house! I saw him go in!

This visit and its object had taken me by surprise, though I had not been without some anticipation of such an event. The conversation I had overheard between him and the doctor rendered it probable that such would be the result; though I hardly expected being obliged to change my quarters so soon. For another week or two I had intended to stay where I was. When quite recovered, I should have moved to the hotel of my own accord.

I felt vexed, and for several reasons. It chagrined me to think that this wretch possessed such a controlling influence; for I did not believe that Mademoiselle Besançon had anything to do with my removal. Quite the contrary. She had visited me but a few hours before, and not a word had been said of the matter. Perhaps she might have thought of it, and did not desire to mention it? But no. This could hardly be. I noticed no change in her manner during the interview. The same kindness—the same interest in my recovery—the same solicitude about the little arrangements of my food and attendance, were shown by her up to the last moment. She evidently contemplated no change so sudden as that proposed by Gayarre. Reflection convinced me that the proposal had been made without any previous communication with *her*.

What must be the influence of this man, that he dare thus step between her and the rites of hospitality? It was a painful thought to me, to see this fair creature in the power of such a villain.

But another thought was still more painful—the thought of parting with Aurore. Though I did not fancy that parting was to be for ever. No! Had I believed that, I should not have yielded so easily. I should have put Monsieur Dominique to the necessity of a positive expulsion. Of course, I had no apprehension that by removing to the village I should be debarred from visiting the plantation as often as I felt inclined. Had that been the condition, my reflections would have been painful indeed.

After all, the change would signify little. I should return as a visitor, and in that character be more independent than as a guest—more free, perhaps, to approach the object of my love! I could come as often as I pleased. The same opportunities of seeing her would still be open to me. I wanted but one—one moment alone with Aurore—and then bliss or blighted hopes!

But there were other considerations that troubled me at this moment. How was I to live at the hotel? Would the proprietor believe in promises, and wait until my letters, already sent off, could be answered? Already I had been provided with suitable apparel, mysteriously indeed. I awoke one morning and found it by my bedside. I made no inquiry as to how it came there. That would be an after-consideration; but with regard to money, how was that to be obtained? Must I become *her* debtor? Or am I to be under obligations to Gayarre? Cruel dilemma!

At this juncture I thought of Reigart. His calm, kind face came up before me.

"An alternative!" soliloquised I; "he will help me!"

The thought seemed to have summoned him; for at that moment the good doctor entered the room, and became the confidant of my wishes.

I had not misjudged him. His purse lay open upon the table; and I became his debtor for as much of its contents as I stood in need of.

"Very strange!" said he, "this desire of hurrying you off on the part of Monsieur Gayarre. There is something more in it than solicitude for the character of the lady. Something more: what can it all mean?"

The doctor said this partly in soliloquy, and as if searching his own thoughts for an answer.

"I am almost a stranger to Mademoiselle Besançon," he continued, "else I should deem it my duty to know more of this matter. But Monsieur Gayarre is her guardian; and if he desire you to leave, it will perhaps be wiser to do so. *She may not be her own mistress entirely.* Poor thing! I fear there is debt at the bottom of the mystery; and if so, she will be more a slave than any of her own people. Poor young lady!"

Reigart was right. My remaining longer might add to her embarrassments. I felt satisfied of this.

"I am desirous to go at once, doctor."

"My barouche is at the gate, then. You can have a seat in it. I can set you down at the hotel."

"Thanks, thanks! the very thing I should have asked of you, and I accept your offer. I have but few preparations to make, and will be ready for you in a moment."

"Shall I step over to the house, and prepare Mademoiselle for your departure?"

"Be so kind. I believe Gayarre is now there?"

"No. I met him near the gate of his own plantation, returning home. I think she is alone. I shall see her and return for you."

The doctor left me, and walked over to the house. He was absent but a few minutes, when he returned to make his report. He was still further perplexed at what he had learnt.

Mademoiselle had heard from Gayarre, just an hour before, that *I had expressed my intention* of removing to the hotel! She had been surprised at this, as I had said nothing about it at our late interview. She would not hear of it at first, but Gayarre had used *arguments* to convince her of the policy of such a step; and the doctor, on my part, had also urged it. She had at length, though reluctantly, consented. Such was the report of the doctor, who further informed me that she was waiting to receive me.

Guided by Scipio, I made my way to the drawing-room. I found her seated; but upon my entrance she rose, and came forward to meet me with both hands extended. I saw that *she was in tears*!

"Is it true you intend leaving us, Monsieur?"

"Yes, Mademoiselle; I am now quite strong again. I have come to thank you for your kind hospitality, and say adieu."

"Hospitality!—ah, Monsieur, you have reason to think it cold hospitality since I permit you to leave us so soon. I would you had remained; but—"

Here she became embarrassed: "but—you are not to be a stranger, although you go to the hotel. Bringiers is near; promise that you will visit us often—in fact, every day?"

I need not say that the promise was freely and joyfully given.

"Now," said she, "since you have given that promise, with less regret I can say adieu!"

She extended her hand for a parting salute. I took her fingers in mine, and respectfully kissed them. I saw the tears freshly filling in her eyes, as she turned away to conceal them.

I was convinced she was acting under constraint, and against her inclination, else I should not have been allowed to depart. Hers was not the spirit to fear gossip or scandal. Some other *pressure* was upon her.

I was passing out through the hall, my eyes eagerly turning in every direction. Where was *she*? Was I not to have *even a parting word*!

At that moment a side-door was gently opened. My heart beat wildly as it turned upon its hinge. Aurore!

I dare not trust myself to speak aloud. It would have been overheard in the drawing-room. A look, a whisper, a silent pressure of the hand, and I hurried away; but the return of that pressure, slight and almost imperceptible as it was, fired my veins with delight; and I walked on towards the gate with the proud step of a conqueror.

Chapter Twenty Two
Aurore loves me

"Aurore loves me!"

The thought thus expressed was of younger date than the day of my removing to Bringiers from the plantation. A month had elapsed since that day.

The details of my life during that month would possess but little interest for you, reader; though to me every hour was fraught with hopes or fears that still hold a vivid place in my memory. When the heart is charged with love, every trifle connected with that love assumes the magnitude of an important matter; and thoughts or incidents that otherwise would soon be forgotten, hold a firm place in the memory. I could write a volume about my affairs of that month, every line of which would be deeply interesting to *me*, but not to *you*. Therefore I write it not; I shall not even present you with the journal that holds its history.

I continued to live in the hotel at Bringiers. I grew rapidly stronger. I spent most of my time in rambling through the fields and along the Levee — boating upon the river — fishing in the bayous — hunting through the cane-breaks and cypress-swamps, and occasionally killing time at a game of billiards, for every Louisiana village has its billiard salon.

The society of Reigart, whom I now called friend, I enjoyed — when his professional engagements permitted.

His books, too, were my friends; and from these I drew my first lessons in botany. I studied the *sylva* of the surrounding woods, till at a glance I could distinguish every tree and its kind — the giant cypress, emblem of sorrow, with tall shaft shooting out of the apex of its pyramidal base, and crowned with its full head of sad dark foliage, — sadder from its drapery of *tillandsia*; the "tupelo" (*Nyssa aquatica*), that nymph that loves the water, with long delicate leaves and olive-like fruit — the "persimmon," or "American lotus" (*Diospyros Virginiana*), with its beautiful green foliage and red date-plums — the gorgeous magnolia grandiflora, and its congener, the tall tulip-tree (*Liriodendron tulipifera*) — the water-locust (*Gleditschia monosperma*); and, of the same genus, the three-thorned honey-locust (*triacanthos*), whose light pinnated leaves scarce veil the sun—the sycamore (*platanus*), with its smooth trunk and wide-reaching limbs of silvery hue—the sweet-gum (*Liquidambar styraciflua*), exuding its golden drops—the aromatic but sanitary "sassafras" (*Laurus sassafras*)—the "red-bay" (*Laurus Caroliniensis*), of cinnamon-like aroma—the oaks of many species, at the head of which might be placed that majestic evergreen of the southern forests, the "live-oak" (*Quercus virens*)—the "red ash," with its hanging bunches of *samarce*—the shady nettle-tree (*Celtis crassifolia*), with its large cordate leaves and black drupes—and last, though not least interesting, the water-loving cotton-wood (*Populus angulata*). Such is the sylva that covers the alluvion of Louisiana.

It is a region beyond the limits of the true palm-tree; but this has its representative in the palmetto—"latanier" of the French—the *Sabal* palm of the botanist, of more than one species, forming in many places the underwood, and giving a tropical character to the forest.

I studied the parasites—the huge llianas, with branches like tree-trunks, black and gnarled; the cane-vines, with pretty star-like flowers; the muscadine grape-vines, with their dark purple clusters; the *bignonias*, with trumpet-shaped corollas; the *smilacae*, among which are conspicuous the *Smilax rotundifolia*, the thick bamboo-briar, and the balsamic sarsaparilla.

Not less interesting were the vegetable forms of cultivation—the "staples" from which are drawn the wealth of the land. These were the sugar-cane, the rice-reed, the maize and tobacco-plants, the cotton shrub, and the indigo. All were new to me, and I studied their propagation and culture with interest.

Though a month apparently passed in idleness, it was, perhaps, one of the most profitably employed of my life. In that short month I acquired more real knowledge than I had done during years of classic study.

But I had learnt one fact that I prized above all, and that was, that *I was beloved by Aurore*!

I learnt it not from her lips—no words had given me the assurance—and yet I was certain that it *was* so; certain as that I lived. Not all the knowledge in the world could have given me the pleasure of that one thought!

"*Aurora loves me!*"

This was my exclamation, as one morning I emerged from the village upon the road leading to the plantation. Three times a week—sometimes even more frequently—I had made this journey. Sometimes I encountered strangers at the house—friends of Mademoiselle. Sometimes I found her alone, or in company with Aurore. The latter I could never find alone! Oh! how I longed for that opportunity!

My visits, of course, were ostensibly to Mademoiselle. I dared not seek an interflow with the slave.

Eugénie still preserved the air of melancholy, that now appeared to have settled upon her. Sometimes she was even sad,—at no time cheerful. As I was not made the confidant of her sorrows, I could only guess at the cause. Gayarre, of course, I believed to be the fiend.

Of him I had learnt little. He shunned me on the road, or in the fields; and upon *his* grounds I never trespassed. I found that he was held in but little respect, except among those who worshipped his wealth. How he was prospering in his suit with Eugénie I knew not. The world talked of such a thing as among the "probabilities"—though one of the strange ones, it was deemed. I had sympathy for the young Creole, but I might have felt it more profoundly under other circumstances. As it was, my whole soul was under the influence of a stronger passion—my love for Aurore.

"Yes—Aurore loves me!" I repeated to myself as I passed out from the village, and faced down the Levee road.

I was mounted. Reigart, in his generous hospitality, had even made me master of a horse—a fine animal that rose buoyantly under me, as though he was also imbued by some noble passion.

My well-trained steed followed the path without need of guidance, and dropping the bridle upon his neck, I left him to go at will, and pursued the train of my reflections.

I loved this young girl—passionately and devotedly I loved her. She loved me. She had not declared it in words, but her looks; and now and then a slight incident—scarce more than a fleeting glance or gesture—had convinced me that it was so.

Love taught me its own language. I needed no interpreter—no tongue to tell I was beloved.

These reflections were pleasant, far more than pleasant; but others followed them of a very different nature.

With whom was I in love? A slave! True, a beautiful slave—but still a slave! How the world would laugh! how Louisiana would laugh—nay, scorn and persecute! The very proposal to make her my wife would subject me to derision and abuse. "What! marry a slave! 'Tis contrary to the laws of the land!" Dared I to marry her—even were she free?—she, a *quadroon*!—I should be hunted from the land, or shut up in one of its prisons!

All this I knew, but not one straw cared I for it. The world's obloquy in one scale, my love for Aurore in the other—the former weighed but a feather.

True, I had deep regret that Aurore was a slave, but it sprang not from that consideration. Far different was the reason of my regret. *How was I to obtain her freedom*? That was the question that troubled me.

Up to this time I had made light of the matter. Before I knew that I was beloved it seemed a sequence very remote. But it was now brought nearer, and all the faculties of my mind became concentrated on that one thought— "How was I to obtain her freedom?" Had she been an ordinary slave, the answer would have been easy enough; for though not rich, my fortune was still equal to the *price of a human being*!

In my eyes Aurore was priceless. Would she also appear so in the eyes of her young mistress? Was my bride for sale on any terms? But even if money should be deemed an equivalent, would Mademoiselle *sell* her to *me*? An odd proposal, that of buying *her* slave for my wife! What would Eugénie Besançon think of it?

The very idea of this proposal awed me; but the time to make it had not yet arrived.

I must first have an interview with Aurore, demand a confession of her love, and then, if she consent to become mine,—*my wife*,—the rest may be arranged. I see not clearly the way, but a love like mine will triumph over everything. My passion nerves me with power, with courage, with energy. Obstacles must yield; opposing wills be coaxed or crushed; everything must give way that stands between myself and my love! "Aurore! I come! I come!"

Chapter Twenty Three
A Surprise

My reflections were interrupted by the neighing of my horse. I glanced forward to ascertain the cause. I was opposite the plantation Besançon. A carriage was just wheeling out from the gate. The horses were headed down the Levee road, and going off at a trot, were soon lost behind the cloud of dust raised by the hoofs and wheels.

I recognised the carriage. It was the barouche of Mademoiselle Besançon. I could not tell who were its occupants, though, from the slight glimpse I had got of them, I saw there were ladies in it.

"Mademoiselle herself, accompanied by Aurore, no doubt."

I believed that they had not observed me, as the high fence concealed all but my head, and the carriage had turned abruptly on passing out of the gate.

I felt disappointed. I had had my ride for nothing, and might now ride back again to Bringiers.

I had drawn bridle with this intent, when it occurred to me I could still overtake the carriage and change words with its occupants. With *her*, even the interchange of a glance was worth such a gallop.

I laid the spur to the ribs of my horse and sprang him forward.

As I came opposite the house I saw Scipio by the gate. He was just closing it after the carriage.

"Oh!" thought I, "I may as well be sure as to whom I am galloping after."

With this idea I inclined my horse's head a little, and drew up in front of Scipio.

"Gollies! how young mass'r ride! Ef he don't do daat business jes up to de hub! Daat 'im do. Wugh!"

Without taking notice of his complimentary speech, I inquired hastily if Mademoiselle was at home.

"No, mass'r, she jes dis moment gone out—she drive to Mass'r Marigny."

"Alone?"

"Ye, mass'r."

"Of course Aurore is with her?"

"No, mass'r; she gone out by harseff. 'Rore, she 'tay at home."

If the negro had been observant he might have noticed the effect of this announcement upon me, for I am sure it must have been sufficiently apparent. I felt it in the instant upheaving of my heart, and the flushing that suddenly fevered my cheeks.

"Aurore at home, and alone!"

It was the first time during all the course of my wooing that such a "chance" had offered; and I almost gave expression to my agreeable surprise.

Fortunately I did not; for even the faithful Scipio was not to be trusted with such a secret.

With an effort I collected myself, and tamed down my horse, now chafing to continue his gallop. In doing so his head was turned in the direction of the village. Scipio thought I was going to ride back.

"Sure mass'r not go till he rest a bit? Missa 'Génie not home, but dar am 'Rore. 'Rore get mass'r glass ob claret; Ole Zip make um sangaree. Day berry, berry hot. Wugh!"

"You are about right, Scipio," I replied, pretending to yield to his persuasion. "Take my horse round to the stable. I shall rest a few minutes."

I dismounted, and, passing the bridle to Scipio, stepped inside the gate.

It was about a hundred paces to the house, by the direct walk that led from the gate to the front door. But there were two other paths, that wound around the sides of the shrubbery, through copses of low trees—laurels, myrtles, and oranges. A person approaching by either of these could not be seen from the house until close to the very windows. From each of these paths the low verandah could be reached without going by the front. There were steps leading into it—into the interior of the house as well—for the windows that fronted upon the verandah were, after the Creole fashion, glass folding-doors, that opened to the bottom, so that the floors of the rooms and verandah-platform were upon the same level.

On passing through the gate, I turned into one of these side-paths (for certain reasons giving it the preference), and walked silently on towards the house.

I had taken the longer way, and advanced slowly for the purpose of composing myself. I could hear the beating of my own heart, and feel its quick nervous throbs, quicker than my steps, as I approached the long-desired interview. I believe I should have been more collected in going up to the muzzle of an antagonist's pistol!

The long yearning for such an opportunity—the well-known difficulty of obtaining it—the anticipation of that sweetest pleasure on earth—the pleasure of being alone with her I loved—all blended in my thoughts. No wonder they were wild and somewhat bewildered.

I should now meet Aurore face to face alone, with but Love's god as a witness. I should speak unrestrainedly and free. I should hear *her* voice, listen to the soft confession that she loved me. I should fold her in my arms—against my bosom! I should drink love from her swimming eyes, taste it on her crimson cheek, her coral lips! Oh, I should speak love, and hear it spoken! I should listen to its delirious ravings!

A heaven of happiness was before me. No wonder my thoughts were wild—no wonder I vainly strove to calm them.

I reached the house, and mounted the two or three steps that led up into the verandah. The latter was carpeted with a mat of sea-grass, and my *chaussure* was light, so that my tread was as silent as that of a girl. It could scarce have been heard within the chamber whose windows I was passing.

I proceeded on toward the drawing-room, which opened to the front by two of the large door-windows already mentioned. I turned the angle, and the next moment would have passed the first of these windows, had a sound not reached me that caused me to arrest my steps. The sound was a voice that came from the drawing-room, whose windows stood open. I listened—it was the voice of Aurore!

"In conversation with some one! with whom? Perhaps little Chloe? her mother? some one of the domestics?"

I listened.

"By Heaven! it is the voice of a man! Who can he be? Scipio? No; Scipio cannot yet have left the stable. It cannot be he. Some other of the plantation people? Jules, the wood-chopper? the errand-boy, Baptiste? Ha! it is not a negro's voice. No, it is the voice of a white man! the overseer?"

As this idea came into my head, a pang at the same time shot through my heart—a pang, not of jealousy, but something like it. I was angry at *him* rather than jealous with *her*. As yet I had heard nothing to make me jealous. His being present with her, and in conversation, was no cause.

"So, my bold nigger-driver," thought I, "you have got over your predilection for the little Chloe. Not to be wondered at! Who would waste time gazing at stars when there is such a moon in the sky? Brute that you are, you are not blind. I see you, too, have an eye to opportunities, and know when to enter the drawing-room."

"Hush!"

Again I listened. When I had first halted, it was through motives of delicacy. I did not wish to appear too suddenly before the open window, which would have given me a full view of the interior of the apartment. I had paused, intending to herald my approach by some noise—a feigned cough, or a stroke of my foot against the floor. My motives had undergone a change. I now listened with a design. I could not help it.

Aurore was speaking.

I bent my ear close to the window. The voice was at too great a distance, or uttered too low, for me to hear what was said. I could hear the silvery tones, but could not distinguish the words. She must be at the further end of the room, thought I. *Perhaps, upon the sofa.* This conjecture led me to painful imaginings, till the throbbings of my heart drowned the murmur that was causing them.

At length Aurore's speech was ended. I waited for the reply. Perhaps I might gather from that what *she* had said. The tones of the male voice would be loud enough to enable me—

Hush! hark!

I listened—I caught the sound of a voice, but not the words. The sound was enough. It caused me to start as if stung by an adder. *It was the voice of Monsieur Dominique Gayarre!*

Chapter Twenty Four
A Rival

I cannot describe the effect produced upon me by this discovery. It was like a shock of paralysis. It nailed me to the spot, and for some moments I felt as rigid as a statue, and almost as senseless. Even had the words uttered by Gayarre been loud enough to reach me, I should scarce have heard them. My surprise for the moment had rendered me deaf.

The antagonism I had conceived towards the speaker, so long as I believed it to be the brute Larkin, was of a gentle character compared with that which agitated me now. Larkin might be young and handsome; by Scipio's account, the latter he certainly was *not*: but even so, I had little fear of *his* rivalry. I felt confident that I held the heart of Aurore, and I knew that the overseer had no power over *her person*. He was overseer of the field-hands, and other slaves of the plantation—their master, with full licence of tongue and lash; but with all that, I knew that he had no authority over Aurore. For reasons I could not fathom, the treatment of the quadroon was, and had always been, different from the other slaves of the plantation. It was not the whiteness of her skin—her beauty neither—that had gained her this distinction. These, it is true, often modify the hard lot of the female slave, sometimes detailing upon her a still more cruel fate; but in the case of Aurore, there was some very different reason for the kindness shown her, though *I* could only *guess* at it. She had been tenderly reared alongside her young mistress, had received almost as good an education, and, in fact, was treated rather as a *sister* than a *slave*. Except from Mademoiselle, she received no commands. The "nigger-driver" had nothing to do with her. I had therefore no dread of any unlawful influence on his part.

Far different were my suspicions when I found the voice belonged to Gayarre. *He* had power not only over the slave, but the mistress as well. Though suitor,—as I still believed him,—of Mademoiselle, he could not be blind to the superior charms of Aurore. Hideous wretch as I thought him, he might for all be sensible to love. The plainest may have a passion for the fairest. The Beast loved Beauty.

The hour he had chosen for his visit, too! that was suspicious of itself. Just as Mademoiselle had driven out! Had he been there before she went out and been left by her in the house? Not likely. Scipio know nothing of his being there, else he would have told me. The black was aware of my antipathy to Gayarre, and that I did not desire to meet him. He would certainly have told me.

"No doubt," thought I, "the visit is a stolen one—the lawyer has come the back way from his own plantation, has watched till the carriage drove off, and then skulked in for the very purpose of finding the quadroon alone!"

All this flashed upon my mind with the force of conviction, I no longer doubted that his presence there was the result of design, and not a mere accident. He was *after* Aurore. My thoughts took this homely shape.

When the first shock of my surprise had passed away, my senses returned, fuller and more vigorous than ever. My nerves seemed freshly strung, and my ears new set. I placed them as close to the open window as prudence would allow, and listened. It was not *honourable*, I own, but in dealing with this wretch I seemed to lose all sense of honour. By the peculiar circumstances of that moment I was tempted from the strict path, but it was the "eavesdropping" of a jealous lover, and I cry you mercy for the act.

I listened. With an effort I stifled the feverish throbbings of my heart, and listened.

And I heard every word that from that moment was said. The voices had become louder, or rather the speakers had approached nearer. They were but a few feet from the window! Gayarre was speaking.

"And does this young fellow dare to make love to your mistress?"

"Monsieur Dominique, how should I know? I am sure I never saw aught of the kind. He is very modest, and so Mademoiselle thinks him. I never knew him to speak one word of love,—not he."

I fancied I heard a sigh.

"If he dare," rejoined Gayarre in a tone of bravado; "if he dare hint at such a thing to Mademoiselle—ay, or *even to you*, Aurore—I shall make the place too hot for him. He shall visit here no more, the naked adventurer! On that I am resolved."

"Oh, Monsieur Gayarre! I'm sure that would vex Mademoiselle very much. Remember! he saved her life. She is full of gratitude to him. She continually talks of it, and it would grieve her if Monsieur Edouard was to come no more. I am sure it would grieve her."

There was an earnestness, a half-entreaty, in the tone of the speaker that sounded pleasant to my ears. It suggested the idea that *she, too, might be grieved* if Monsieur Edouard were to come no more.

A like thought seemed to occur to Gayarre, upon whom, however, it made a very different sort of impression. There was irony mixed with anger in his reply, which was half interrogative.

"Perhaps it would grieve *some one else*? Perhaps you? All, indeed! Is it so? You love him? *Sacr-r-r-r!*"

There was a hissing emphasis upon the concluding word, that expressed anger and pain,—the pain of bitter jealousy.

"Oh monsieur!" replied the quadroon, "how can you speak thus? *I* love! I,—a poor slave! Alas! alas!"

Neither the tone nor substance of this speech exactly pleased me. I felt a hope, however, that it was but one of the little stratagems of love: a species of deceit I could easily pardon. It seemed to produce a pleasant effect on Gayarre, for all at once his voice changed to a lighter and gayer tone.

"You a *slave*, beautiful Aurore! No, in my eyes you are a *queen*, Aurore. Slave! It is your fault if you remain so. You know who has the power to make you free: ay, and the will too,—the will,—Aurore!"

"Please not to talk thus, Monsieur Dominique! I have said before I cannot listen to such speech. I repeat I cannot, and *will* not!"

The firm tone was grateful to my ears.

"Nay, lovely Aurore!" replied Gayarre, entreatingly, "don't be angry with me! I cannot help it. I cannot help thinking of your welfare. You *shall* be free;—no longer the slave of a capricious mistress—"

"Monsieur Gayarre!" exclaimed the quadroon, interrupting him, "speak not so of Mademoiselle! You wrong her, Monsieur. She is not capricious. What if she heard—"

"*Peste!*" cried Gayarre, interrupting in his turn, and again assuming his tone of bravado. "What care I if she did? Think you I trouble my head about her? The world thinks so! ha! ha! ha! Let them!—the fools! ha! ha! One day they may find it different! ha! ha! They think my visits here are on *her* account! ha! ha! ha! No, Aurore,—lovely Aurore! it is not Mademoiselle I come to see, but *you*,—you, Aurore,—whom I *love*,—ay, love with all—"

"Monsieur Dominique! I repeat—"

"Dearest Aurore! say you will but love me; say but the word! Oh, speak it! you shall be no longer a slave,—you shall be free as your mistress is;—you shall have everything,—every pleasure,—dresses, jewels, at will; my house shall be under your control,—you shall command in it, *as if you were my wife.*"

"Enough, Monsieur! enough! Your insult—I hear no more!"

The voice was firm and indignant. Hurrah!

"Nay, dearest, loveliest Aurore! do not go yet,—hear me—"

"I hear no more, Sir,—Mademoiselle shall know—"

"A word, a word! one kiss, Aurore! on my knees, I beg—"

I heard the knocking of a pair of knees on the floor, followed by a struggling sound, and loud angry exclamations on the part of Aurore.

This I considered to be my cue, and three steps brought me within the room, and within as many feet of the kneeling gallant. The wretch was actually on his "marrow-bones," holding the girl by the wrist, and endeavouring to draw her towards him. She, on the contrary, was exerting all her women's strength to get away; which, not being so inconsiderable, resulted in the ludicrous spectacle of the kneeling suitor being dragged somewhat rapidly across the carpet!

His back was toward me as I entered, and the first intimation he had of my presence was a boisterous laugh, which for the life of me I could not restrain. It lasted until long after he had released his captive, and gathered his limbs into an upright position; and, indeed, so loud did it sound in my own ears, that I did not hear the threats of vengeance he was muttering in return.

"What business have *you* here, Sir?" was his first intelligible question.

"I need not ask the same of you, Monsieur Dominique Gayarre. *Your* business I can tell well enough ha! ha! ha!"

"I ask you, Sir," he repeated, in a still angrier tone, "what's your business here?"

"I did not come here on *business*, Monsieur," said I, still keeping up the tone of levity. "I did not come here on business, *any more than yourself.*"

The emphasis on the last words seemed to render him furious.

"The sooner you go the better, then," he shouted, with a bullying frown.

"For whom?" I inquired.

"For yourself, Sir," was the reply.

I had now also lost temper, though not altogether command of myself.

"Monsieur," said I, advancing and confronting him, "I have yet to learn that the house of Mademoiselle Besançon is the property of Monsieur Dominique Gayarre. If it were so, I would be less disposed to respect the sanctity of its roof. You, Sir, have not respected it. You have acted infamously towards this young girl—this young *lady*, for she merits the title as much as the best blood in your land. I have witnessed your dastardly conduct, and heard your insulting proposals—"

Here Gayarre started, but said nothing. I continued—

"You are not a gentleman, Sir; and therefore not worthy to stand before my pistol. The owner of this house is not at home. At present it is as much mine as yours; and I promise you, that if you are not out of it in ten seconds you shall have my whip laid with severity upon your shoulders."

I said all this in a tone sufficiently moderate, and in cool blood. Gayarre must have seen that I meant it, for I *did* mean it.

"You shall pay dearly for this," he hissed out. "You shall find that this is not the country for a *spy*."

"Go, Sir!"

"And you, my fine pattern of quadroon virtue," he added, bending a malicious glance upon Aurore, "there may come a day when you'll be less prudish: a day when you'll not find such a gallant protector."

"Another word, and—"

The uplifted whip would have fallen on his shoulders. He did not wait for that, but gliding through the door, shuffled off over the verandah.

I stopped outside to make sure that he was gone. Advancing to the end of the platform I looked over the paling. The chattering of the birds told me that some one was passing through the shrubbery.

I watched till I saw the gate open. I could just distinguish a head above the palings moving along the road. I easily recognised it as that of the disappointed seducer.

As I turned back, towards the drawing-room I forgot that such a creature existed!

Chapter Twenty Five
An Hour of Bliss

Sweet is gratitude under any circumstances; how much sweeter when expressed in the eyes and uttered by the lips of those we love!

I re-entered the room, my heart swelling with delightful emotions. Gratitude was poured forth in, lavish yet graceful expressions. Before I could utter a word, or stretch out a hand to hinder, the beautiful girl had glided across the room, and fallen into a kneeling posture at my feet! Her thanks came from her heart.

"Rise, lovely Aurore!" said I, taking her unresisting hand, and leading her to a seat. "What I have done is scarce worth thanks like thine. Who would have acted otherwise?"

"Ah, Monsieur!—many, many. You know not this land. There are few to protect the poor slave. The chivalry, so much boasted here, extends not to *us*. We, in whose veins runs the accursed blood, are beyond the pale both of honour and protection. Ah me, noble stranger! you know not for how much I am your debtor!"

"Call me not *stranger*, Aurore. It is true we have had but slight opportunity of conversing, but our acquaintance is old enough to render that title no longer applicable. I would you would speak to me by one more *endearing*."

"Endearing! Monsieur, I do not understand you!"

Her large brown eyes were fixed upon me in a gaze of wonder, but they also interrogated me.

"Yes, endearing—I mean, Aurore—that you will not shun me—that you will give me your confidence—that you will regard me as a friend—a—a—brother."

"You, Monsieur! you as my brother—a white—a gentleman, high-born and educated! I—I—oh Heavens! what am I? A slave—a slave—whom men love only to *ruin*. O God!—why is my destiny so hard? O God!"

"Aurore!" I cried, gathering courage from her agony, "Aurore, listen to me! to me, your friend, your—"

She removed her hands that had been clasped across her face, and looked up. Her swimming eyes were bent steadfastly upon mine, and regarded me with a look of interrogation.

At that moment a train of thought crossed my mind. In words it was thus: "How long may we be alone? We may be interrupted? So fair an opportunity may not offer again. There is no time to waste in idle converse. I must at once to the object of my visit."

"Aurore!" I said, "it is the first time we have met alone. I have longed for this interview. I have a word that can only be spoken to you alone."

"To me alone, Monsieur! What is it?"

"*Aurore, I love you!*"

"Love *me*! Oh, Monsieur, it is not possible!"

"Ah! more than possible—it is *true*. Listen, Aurore! From the first hour I beheld you—I might almost say before that hour, for you were in my heart before I was conscious of having seen you—from, that first hour I loved you—not with a villain's love, such as you have this moment spurned, but with a pure and honest passion. And passion I may well call it, for it absorbs every other feeling of my soul. Morning and night, Aurore, I think but of you. You are in my dreams, and equally the companion of my waking hours. Do not fancy my love so calm, because I am now speaking so calmly about it. Circumstances render me so. I have approached you with a determined purpose—one long resolved upon—and that, perhaps, gives me this firmness in declaring my love. I have said, Aurore, that I love you. I repeat it again—*with my heart and soul, I love you!*"

"Love *me*! poor girl!"

There was something so ambiguous in the utterance of the last phrase, that I paused a moment in my reply. It seemed as though the sympathetic interjection had been meant for some third person rather than herself!

"Aurore," I continued, after a pause, "I have told you all. I have been candid. I only ask equal candour in return. *Do you love me?*"

I should have put this question less calmly, but that I felt already half-assured of the answer.

We were seated on the sofa, and near each other. Before I had finished speaking, I felt her soft fingers touch mine—close upon them, and press them gently together. When the question was delivered, her head fell forward on my breast, and I heard murmuring from her lips the simple words—"*I too from the first hour!*"

My arms, hitherto restrained, were now twined around the yielding form, and for some moments neither uttered a word. Love's paroxysm is best enjoyed in silence. The wild intoxicating kiss, the deep mutual glance, the pressure of hands and arms and burning lips, all these need no tongue to make them intelligible. For long moments ejaculations of delight, phrases of tender endearment, were the only words that escaped us. We were too happy to converse. Our lips paid respect to the solemnity of our hearts.

It was neither the place nor time for Love to go blind, and prudence soon recalled me to myself. There was still much to be said, and many plans to be discussed before our new-sprung happiness should be secured to us. Both were aware of the abyss that still yawned between us. Both were aware that a thorny path must be trodden before we could reach the elysium of our hopes. Notwithstanding our present bliss, the future was dark and dangerous; and the thought of this soon startled us from our short sweet dream.

Aurora had no longer any *fear* of my love. She did not even wrong me with suspicion. She doubted not my purpose to make her my *wife*. Love and gratitude stifled every doubt, and we now conversed with a mutual confidence which years of friendship could scarce have established.

But we talked with hurried words. We knew not the moment we might be interrupted. We knew not when again we might meet alone. We had need to be brief.

I explained to her my circumstances—that in a few days I expected a sum of money—enough, I believed, for the purpose. What purpose? *The purchase of my bride*!

"Then," added I, "nothing remains but to get married, Aurore!"

"Alas!" replied she with a sigh, "even were I free, we could not be married *here*. Is it not a wicked law that persecutes us even when pretending to give us freedom?"

I assented.

"We could not get married," she continued, evidently suffering under painful emotion, "we could not unless you could swear there was African blood in your veins! Only think of such a law in a Christian land!"

"Think *not* of it, Aurore," said I, wishing to cheer her. "There shall be no difficulty about swearing that. I shall take this gold pin from your hair, open this beautiful blue vein in your arm, drink from it, and take the oath!"

The quadroon smiled, but the moment after her look of sadness returned.

"Come, dearest Aurore! chase away such thoughts! What care we to be married here? We shall go elsewhere. There are lands as fair as Louisiana, and churches as fine as Saint Gabriel to be married in. We shall go northward—to England—to France—anywhere. Let not that grieve you!"

"It is not that which grieves me."

"What then, dearest?"

"Oh! It is—I fear—"

"Tear not to tell me."

"That you will not be able—"

"Declare it, Aurore."

"To become *my master—to—to buy me*!"

Here the poor girl hung her head, as if ashamed to speak of such conditions. I saw the hot tears springing from her eyes.

"And why do you fear." I inquired.

"Others have tried. Large sums they offered—larger even than that you have named, and they could not. They failed in their intentions, and oh! how grateful was I to Mademoiselle! That was my only protection. She would not part with me. How glad was I then! but now—now how different!—the very opposite!"

"But I shall give more—my whole fortune. Surely that will suffice. The offers you speak of were infamous proposals, like that of Monsieur Gayarre. Mademoiselle knew it; she was too good to accept them."

"That is true, but she will equally refuse yours. I fear it, alas! alas!"

"Nay, I shall confess all to Mademoiselle. I shall declare to her my honourable design. I shall implore her consent. Surely she will not refuse. Surely she feels gratitude—"

"Oh, Monsieur!" cried Aurore, interrupting me, "she *is* grateful—you know not how grateful; but never, never will she—You know not all—alas! alas!"

With a fresh burst of tears filling her eyes, the beautiful girl sank down on the sofa, hiding her face under the folds of her luxuriant hair.

I was puzzled by these expressions, and about to ask for an explanation, when the noise of carriage-wheels fell upon my ear. I sprang forward to the open window, and looked over the tops of the orange-trees. I could just see the head of a man, whom I recognised as the coachman of Mademoiselle Besançon. The carriage was approaching the gate.

In the then tumult of my feelings I could not trust myself to meet the lady, and, bidding a hurried adieu to Aurore, I rushed from the apartment.

When outside I saw that, if I went by the front gate I should risk an encounter. I knew there was a small side-wicket that led to the stables, and a road ran thence to the woods. This would carry me to Bringiers by a back way, and stepping off from the verandah, I passed through the wicket, and directed myself towards the stables in the rear.

Chapter Twenty Six
The "Nigger Quarter."

I soon reached the stables, where I was welcomed by a low whimper from my horse. Scipio was not there.

"He is gone upon some other business," thought I; "perhaps to meet the carriage. No matter, I shall not summon him. The saddle is on, and I can bridle the steed myself—only poor Scipio loses his quarter-dollar."

I soon had my steed bitted and bridled; and, leading the animal outside, I sprang into the saddle, and rode off.

The path I was taking led past the "negro quarters," and then through some fields to the dark cypress and tupelo woods in the rear. From these led a cross-way that would bring me out again upon the Levee road. I had travelled this path many a time, and knew it well enough.

The "nigger quarter" was distant some two hundred yards from the "grande maison," or "big house," of the plantation. It consisted of some fifty or sixty little "cabins," neatly built, and standing in a double row, with a broad way between. Each cabin was a facsimile of its neighbour, and in front of each grew a magnolia or a beautiful China-tree, under the shade of whose green leaves and sweet-scented flowers little negroes might be seen all the livelong day, disporting their bodies in the dust. These, of all sizes, from the "piccaninny" to the "good-sized chunk of a boy," and of every shade of slave-colour, from the fair-skinned quadroon to the black Bambarra, on whom, by an American witticism of doubtful truthfulness; "charcoal would make a white mark!" Divesting them of dust, you would have no difficulty in determining their complexion. Their little plump bodies were nude, from the top of their woolly heads to their long projecting heels. There roll they, black and yellow urchins, all the day, playing with pieces of sugar-cane, or melon-rind, or corn-cobs—cheerful and happy as any little lords could be in their well-carpeted nurseries in the midst of the costliest toys of the German bazaar!

On entering the negro quarter, you cannot fail to observe tall papaw poles or cane-reeds stuck up in front of many of the cabins, and carrying upon their tops large, yellow gourd-shells, each perforated with a hole in the side.

These are the dwellings of the purple martin, (*Hirundo purpurea*)—the most beautiful of American swallows, and a great favourite among the simple negroes, as it had been, long before their time, among the red aborigines of the soil. You will notice, too, hanging in festoons along the walls of the cabins, strings of red and green pepper-pods (species of capsicum); and here and there a bunch of some dried herb of medicinal virtue, belonging to the negro *pharmacopoeia*. All these are the property of "aunt Phoebe," or "aunty Cleopatra," or "ole aunt Phillis;" and the delicious "pepper pot" that any one of those "aunts" can make out of the aforesaid green and red capsicums, assisted by a few other ingredients from the little garden "patch" in the rear of the cabin, would bring water to the teeth of an epicure.

Perhaps on the cabin walls you will see suspended representatives of the animal kingdom—perhaps the skin of a rabbit, a raccoon, an opossum, or the grey fox—perhaps also that of the musk-rat (*Fiber zibethicus*), or, rarer still, the swamp wild-cat (bay lynx—*Lynx rufus*). The owner of the cabin upon which hangs the lynx-skin will be the Nimrod of the hour, for the cat is among the rarest and noblest game of the Mississippi *fauna*. The skin of the panther (*cougar*) or deer you will not see, for although both inhabit the neighbouring forest, they are too high game for the negro hunter, who is not permitted the use of a gun. The smaller "varmints" already enumerated can be captured without such aid, and the pelts you see hanging upon the cabins are the produce of many a moonlight hunt undertaken by "Caesar," or "Scipio," or "Hannibal," or "Pompey." Judging by the nomenclature of the negro quarter, you might fancy yourself in ancient Rome or Carthage!

The great men above-named, however, are never trusted with such a dangerous weapon as a rifle. To their *skill* alone do they owe their success in the chase; and their weapons are only a stick, an axe, and a "'coon-dog" of mongrel race. Several of these last you may see rolling about in the dust among the "piccaninnies," and apparently as happy as they. But the hunting trophies that adorn the walls do not hang there as mere ornaments. No, they are spread out to dry, and will soon give place to others—for there is a constant export going on. When uncle Ceez, or Zip, or Hanny, or Pomp, get on their Sunday finery, and repair to the village, each carries with him his stock of small pelts. There the storekeeper has a talk with them, and a "pic" (picayune) for the "mussrat," a "bit" (Spanish real) for the "'coon," and a "quarter" for the fox or "cat," enable these four avuncular hunters to lay in a great variety of small luxuries for the four "aunties" at home; which little comforts are most likely excluded from the regular rice-and-pork rations of the plantation.

So much is a little bit of the domestic economy of the negro quarter.

On entering the little village,—for the negro quarter of a grand plantation merits the title,—you cannot fail to observe all of these little matters. They are the salient points of the picture.

You will observe, too, the house of the "overseer" standing apart; or, as in the case of the plantation Besançon, at the end of the double row, and fronting the main avenue. This, of course, is of a more pretentious style of architecture; can boast of Venetian blinds to the windows, two stories of height, and a "porch." It is enclosed with a paling to keep off the intrusion of the children, but the dread of the painted cowhide renders the paling almost superfluous.

As I approached the "quarter," I was struck with the peculiar character of the picture it presented,—the overseer's house towering above the humbler cabins, seeming to protect and watch over them, suggesting the similarity of a hen with her brood of chickens.

Here and there the great purple swallows boldly cleft the air, or, poised on wing by the entrance of their gourd-shell dwellings, uttered their cheerful "tweet—tweet—tweet;" while the fragrant odour of the China-trees and magnolias scented the atmosphere to a long distance around.

When nearer still, I could distinguish the hum of human voices—of men, women, and children—in that peculiar tone which characterises the voice of the African. I fancied the little community as I had before seen it—the men and women engaged in various occupations—some resting from their labour, (for it was now after field hours,) seated in front of their tent-like cabins, under the shade-tree, or standing in little groups gaily chatting with each other—some by the door mending their fishing-nets and tackle, by which they intended to capture the great "cat" and "buffalo fish" of the bayous—some "chopping" firewood at the common "wood-pile," which half-grown urchins were "toating," to the cabins, so that "aunty" might prepare the evening-meal.

I was musing on the patriarchal character of such a picture, half-inclined towards the "one-man power"—if not in the shape of a slaveholder, yet something after the style of Rapp and his "social economists."

"What a saving of state machinery," soliloquised I, "in this patriarchal form! How charmingly simple! and yet how complete and efficient!"

Just so, but I had overlooked one thing, and that was the imperfectness of human nature—the possibility—the probability—nay, the almost certainty, that the *patriarch* will pass into the *tyrant*.

Hark! a voice louder than common! It is a cry!

Of cheerful import? No—on the contrary, it sounds like the utterance of some one in pain. It is a cry of agony! The murmur of other voices, too, heard at short intervals, carries to my ear that deep portentous sound which accompanies some unnatural occurrence.

Again I hear the cry of agony—deeper and louder than before! It comes from the direction of the negro quarter. What is causing it?

I gave the spur to my horse, and galloped in the direction of the cabins.

Chapter Twenty Seven
The Devil's Douche

In a few seconds I entered the wide avenue between the cabins, and drawing bridle, sat glancing around me.

My patriarchal dreams vanished at the sight that met my eyes. Before me was a scene of tyranny, of torture—a scene from the tragedy of slave-life!

At the upper end of the quarter, and on one side of the overseer's house, was an enclosure. It was the enclosure of the sugar-mill—a large building which stood a little further back. Inside the fence was a tall pump, rising full ten feet in height, with the spout near its top. The purpose of this pump was to yield a stream of water, which was conducted to the sugar-house by means of a slender trough, that served as an aqueduct.

A platform was raised a few feet above the ground, so as to enable the person working the pump to reach its handle.

To this spot my attention was directed by seeing that the negroes of the quarter were grouped around it, while the women and children, clinging along the fence, had their eyes bent in the same direction.

The faces of all—men, women, and children—wore an ominous and gloomy expression; and the attitudes in which they stood betokened terror and alarm. Murmurs I could hear—now and then ejaculations—and sobs that bespoke sympathy with some one who suffered. I saw scowling brows, as if knit by thoughts of vengeance. But these last were few—the more general expression was one of terror and submission.

It was not difficult to tell that the cry I had heard proceeded from the neighbourhood of the pump, and a glance unfolded the cause. Some poor slave was undergoing punishment!

A group of negroes hid the unfortunate from my view, but over their heads I could see the slave Gabriel, his body naked to the breech, mounted upon the platform and working the pump with all his might.

This Gabriel was a Bambarra negro, of huge size and strength, branded on both shoulders with the *fleur-de-lis*. He was a man of fierce aspect, and, as I had heard, of fierce and brutal habit—feared not only by the other negroes, but by the whites with whom he came in contact. It was not he that was undergoing punishment. On the contrary, he was the instrument of torture.

And torture it was—I knew the punishment well.

The trough or aqueduct had been removed; and the victim was placed at the bottom of the pump, directly under the spout. He was fast bound in a species of stocks; and in such a position that he could not move his head, which *received the continuous jet in the very centre of the crown*!

Torture? No doubt, you are incredulous? You fancy there can be no great torture in that. A simple shock—a shower-bath—nothing more!

You are right. For the first half-minute or so it is but a shock, a shower-bath, but then—

Believe me when I declare to you—that a stream of molten lead—an axe continually crashing through the skull—would not be more painful than the falling of this cold-water jet! It is torture beyond endurance—agony indescribable. Well may it be called the "devil's douche."

Again the agonised cry came from the pump, almost curdling my blood.

As I have said, I could not see the sufferer at first. A row of bodies was interposed between him and me. The negroes, however, seeing me ride up, eagerly opened their ranks and fell back a pace, as if desiring I should be a witness to what was going forward. They all knew me, and all had some impression that I *sympathised* with their unfortunate race.

This opening gave me a full view of the horrid spectacle, disclosing a group that made me start in the saddle. Under the torture was the victim—a man of sable hue. Close by him, a large mulatto woman and a young girl of the same complexion—mother and daughter—stood folded in each other's arms, both weeping bitterly. I could hear their sobs and ejaculations, even at the distance of a score of yards, and above the plashing sound of the falling water. I recognised at a glance who these were—they were the little Chloe and her mother!

Quick as lightning my eyes were directed towards the sufferer. The water, as it bounded from his crown, spread into a glassy sheet, that completely concealed his head, but the huge, fin-like, projecting ears told me who was the victim. It was Scipio!

Again his cry of agony pealed upon my ears, deep and prolonged, as though it issued from the innermost recesses of his soul!

I did not wait till that cry was ended. A fence of six rails separated me from the sufferer; but what of that? I did not hesitate a moment, but winding my horse round to give him the run, I headed him at the leap, and with a touch of the spur lifted him into the inclosure. I did not even stay to dismount, but galloping up to the platform, laid my whip across the naked shoulders of the Bambarra with all the force that lay in my arm. The astonished savage dropped the pump-handle as if it had been iron at a white heat; and leaping from the platform, ran off howling to his cabin!

Exclamations and loud murmurings of applause followed; but my horse, brought so suddenly to this exciting work, snorted and plunged, and it was some time before I could quiet him. While thus engaged, I observed that the exclamations were suddenly discontinued; and the murmurs of applause were succeeded by a dead, ominous silence! I could hear several of the negroes nearest me muttering some words of caution, as though meant for me; among others the cry of—

"De oberseer! de oberseer! Look out, mass'r! Dar he kum!"

At that moment an abominable oath, uttered in a loud voice, reached my ears. I looked in the direction whence it came. As I anticipated, it was the overseer.

He was just issuing from the back-door of his house, from a window of which he had been all the while a spectator of Scipio's torture!

I had not come in contact with this person before; and I now saw approaching a man of fierce and brutal aspect, somewhat flashily dressed, and carrying in his hand a thick waggon-whip. I could see that his face was livid with rage, and that he was directing himself to attack me. I had no weapon but my riding-whip, and with this I prepared to receive his assault.

He came on at a run, all the while venting the most diabolical curses.

When he had got nearly up to my horse's head, he stopped a moment, and thundered out—

"Who the Hell are you, meddling with my affairs? Who the damn are—"

He suddenly paused in his speech, and stood staring in astonishment. I reciprocated that astonishment, for I had now recognised in the brutal overseer my antagonist of the boat! the hero of the bowie-knife! At the same instant he recognised me.

The pause which was the result of our mutual surprise, lasted but a moment.

"Hell and furies!" cried the ruffian, changing his former tone only into one more horribly furious—

"It's *you*, is it? Whip be damned! I've something else for *you*."

And as he said this he drew a pistol from his coat, and hastily cocking it, aimed it at my breast.

I was still on horseback and in motion, else he would no doubt have delivered his fire at once; but my horse reared up at the gleam of the pistol, and his body was thus interposed between mine and its muzzle.

As I have said, I had no weapon but the whip. Fortunately it was a stout hunting-whip, with loaded butt. I hastily turned it in my hand, and just as the hoofs of my horse came back to the earth, I drove the spur so deeply into his ribs that he sprang forward more than his own length. This placed me in the very spot I wanted to be—alongside my ruffian antagonist, who, taken aback by my sudden change of position, hesitated a moment before taking fresh aim. Before he could pull trigger, the butt of my whip descended upon his skull, and doubled him up in the dust! His pistol went off as he fell, and the bullet ploughed up the ground between my horse's hoofs, but fortunately hit no one. The weapon itself new out of his hand, and lay beside him where he had fallen.

It was a mere lucky hit—all owing to the spur being touched, and my horse having sprung forward in good time. Had I missed the blow, I should not likely have had a second chance. The pistol was double-barrelled, and on examination I found he carried another of a similar kind.

He was now lying as still as if asleep, and I began to fear I had killed him. This would have been a serious matter. Although perfectly justifiable in me to have done so, who was to show that? The evidence of those around me—the whole of them together—was not worth the asseveration of one white man; and under the circumstances not worth a straw. Indeed, considering what had immediately led to the rencontre, such testimony would have been more likely to *damage* my case than otherwise! I felt myself in an awkward situation.

I now dismounted, and approached the prostrate form, around which the blacks were congregating. They made way for me.

I knelt down and examined the head. It was cut and bleeding, but the skull was still sound!

The knowledge of this fact set my mind at rest, and before I rose to my feet I had the satisfaction to see that the fellow was coming to his senses, under the influence of a douche of cold-water. The butt of the second pistol came under my eye, as it stuck out from the breast of his coat. I drew it forth, and along with its fellow took them into my own keeping.

"Tell him," said I, "as soon as he comes to himself, that when he next attacks me, I shall have pistols as well as he!"

Having ordered him to be carried into the house, I now turned my attention to his victim. Poor Scipio! he had been most cruelly tortured, and it was some time before he recovered his faculties, so as to be able to tell me why he had been thus punished.

The relation he at length gave, and it made the blood boil afresh within my veins. He had surprised the overseer in some of the outbuildings with little Chloe in his arms, the child crying out and struggling to get free. Natural indignation on the part of the father led to a blow—an offence for which Scipio might have lost an arm; but the white wretch, knowing that he dare not, for his own sake, expose the motive, had commuted Scipio's legal punishment to a little private torture under the pump!

My first impulse on hearing this sad story was to return to the house, report what had occurred to Mademoiselle, and urge upon her the necessity of getting rid of this savage overseer at all risk.

After a little reflection I changed my mind. I purposed to return upon the morrow, on business of—to me—much greater importance. To-morrow it was my intention to *bid for Aurore*!

"I can then," thought I, "introduce the case of poor Scipio. Perhaps it may be an introduction to the 'graver theme?'"

Having promised this much to my old attendant, I mounted my horse, and rode off, amidst a shower of blessings.

As I passed through the avenue at a walk, women and half-grown girls hurried from their doors, and kissed my feet as they hung in the stirrups!

The burning love which so late filled my heart was for a moment unfelt. Its place was occupied by a calm, sweet happiness—the happiness that springs from benefaction!

Chapter Twenty Eight
Gayarre and "Bully Bill."

On riding out from the quarter I changed my intention of taking the back road. My visit would no doubt become known to Mademoiselle, and it differed not if I should now be seen from the house. My blood was up— so was that of my horse. A rail-fence was nothing to either of us now; so heading round, I cleared a couple of palings; and then striking across a cotton-field arrived once more on the Levee road.

After a while, as soon as I had cooled down my horse, I rode slowly, reflecting upon what had just happened.

It was evident that this ruffian had been put upon the plantation by Gayarre for some secret purpose. Whether he and the lawyer had had previous acquaintance I could not guess; but such men have a sort of instinctive knowledge of one another, and he might be only a waif that the latter had picked up since the night of the wreck. On the boat I had supposed him to be some rough gambler, by the propensity he exhibited for betting; and possibly he might have been playing that *rôle* of late. It was evident, however, that "negro-driving" was his trade; at all events it was not new to him.

Strange that he had been all this time on the plantation without knowing of me! But that could be easily accounted for. He had never seen me during my stay at the house. Moreover, he may have been ignorant that Mademoiselle was the lady with whom he intended to have shared the life-preserver. This last hypothesis was probable enough, for there were other ladies who escaped by means of rafts, and sofas, and life-preservers. I fancied he had not seen Mademoiselle until she was springing over the guards, and would therefore scarce recognise her again.

The cause of my being an invalid was only known to Mademoiselle, Aurore, and Scipio; and the latter had been charged not to carry this knowledge to the negro quarter. Then the fellow was but new on the plantation, and had but little intercourse with its mistress, as he received most of his orders from Gayarre; besides, he was but a dull brute after all.

It was just like enough that, up to the moment of our late encounter, he had no suspicion either that I was his former antagonist on the boat, or

Eugénie Besançon the lady who had escaped him. He must have known of my presence on the plantation, but only as one of the survivors of the wreck, badly wounded,—scalded, perhaps,—but there had been a number of others, picked up,—scarce a house for some distance along the coast but had given shelter to some wounded or half-drowned unfortunate. He had been busy with his own affairs; or rather, perhaps, those of Gayarre: for I had no doubt there was some conspiracy between them in which this fellow was to play a part. Dull as he was, he had something which his employer might regard of more value than intellect; something, too, which the latter himself lacked,—brute strength and brute courage. Gayarre no doubt had a use for him, else he would not have been there.

He knew me now, and was not likely soon to forget me. Would he seek revenge? Beyond doubt he would, but I fancied it would be by some base underhand means. I had no fear that he would again attack me openly, at least by himself. I felt quite sure that I had conquered, and encowardiced him. I had encountered his like before. I know that his courage was not of that character to outlive defeat. It was the courage of the bravo.

I had no fear of an open attack. All I had to apprehend was some, secret revenge, or perhaps the law!

You will wonder that any thought or dread of the latter should have occurred to me: but it did; and I had my reasons.

The knowledge of Gayarre's designs, the detection of his villainous purpose with Aurore, and my rencontre with Larkin, had brought matters to a crisis. I was filled with anxiety, and convinced of the necessity of a speedy interview with Mademoiselle, in relation to what was nearest to my heart, *the purchase of the quadroon*. There was no reason why a single hour should be wasted, now that Aurore and I understood each other, and had, in fact, *betrothed* ourselves.

I even thought of riding back at once, and had turned my horse for the purpose. I hesitated. My resolution wavered. I wheeled round again, and kept on to Bringiers, with the determination to return to the plantation at an early hour in the morning.

I entered the village and proceeded straight to the hotel. On my table I found a letter containing a cheque for two hundred pounds on the Bringiers bank. It was from my banking agent in New Orleans, who had received it from England. The letter also contained the information that five hundred more would reach me in a few days. The sum received was a pleasant relief, and would enable me to discharge my pecuniary obligations to Reigart; which in the next hour I had the pleasure of doing.

I passed a night of great anxiety,—almost a sleepless night. No wonder. To-morrow was to be a crisis. For me, happiness or misery was in the womb of to-morrow. A thousand hopes and fears hung suspended on the result of my interview with Eugénie Besançon. I actually looked forward to this interview with more anxiety than I had done but a few hours ago to that with Aurore! Perhaps, because I had less confidence in a favourable result.

As early as etiquette would allow of a morning visit, I was in the saddle, and heading towards the plantation Besançon.

As I rode out of the village I noticed that men regarded me with glances that bespoke an unusual interest.

"My affair with the overseer is already known," thought I. "No doubt the negroes have spread the report of it. Such matters soon become public."

I was unpleasantly impressed with an idea that the expression on people's faces was anything but a friendly one. Had I committed an unpopular act in protecting myself? Usually the conqueror in such an encounter is rather popular than otherwise, in the chivalric land of Louisiana. Why, then, did men look scowling upon me? What had I done to merit reproach? I had "whipped" a rude fellow, whom men esteemed a "bully;" and in self-defence had I acted. The act should have gained me applause, according to the code of the country. Why then,—ha! stay! I had interfered between *white* and *black*. I had *protected a slave from punishment*. Perhaps that might account for the disagreeable expression I had observed!

I could just guess at another cause, of a very different and somewhat ludicrous character. It had got rumoured abroad that I "was upon good terms with Mademoiselle Besançon," and that it was not unlikely that one of these fine days the adventurer, whom nobody knew anything about, would carry off the rich plantress!

There is no part of the world where such a *bonne fortune* is not regarded with envy. The United States is no exception to the rule; and I had reason to know that on account of this absurd rumour I was not very favourably regarded by some of the young planters and dandy storekeepers who loitered about the streets of Bringiers.

I rode on without heeding the "black looks" that were cast upon me, and indeed soon ceased thinking of them. My mind was too full of anxiety about the approaching interview to be impressed with minor cares.

Of course Eugénie would have heard all about the affair of yesterday. What would be her feelings in relation to it? I felt certain that this ruffian was forced upon, her by Gayarre. She would have no sympathy with *him*.

The question was, would she have the courage—nay, the *power* to discharge him from her service? Even on hearing *who* he was? It was doubtful enough!

I was overwhelmed with sympathy for this poor girl. I felt satisfied that Gayarre must be her creditor to a large amount, and in that way had her in his power. What he had said to Aurore convinced me that such was the case. Indeed, Reigart had heard some whisper that his debt had already been proved before the courts in New Orleans; that no opposition had been made; that he had obtained a verdict, and could seize upon her property, or as much of it as would satisfy his demands, at any moment! It was only the night before Reigart had told me this, and the information had rendered me all the more anxious to hasten my business in relation to Aurore.

I spurred into a gallop, and soon came in sight of the plantation. Having arrived at the gate, I dismounted. There was no one to hold my horse, but that is a slight matter in America, where a gate-post or a branch of a tree often serves as a groom.

Bethinking me of this ready expedient I tossed my rein over one of the palings, and walked toward the house.

Chapter Twenty Nine
"Elle t'aime!"

It was natural I should have thoughts about my yesterday's antagonist. Would I encounter him? Not likely. The butt of my whip had no doubt given him a headache that would confine him for some days to his quarters. But I was prepared for any event. Under my waistcoat were his own double-barrelled pistols, which I intended to use, if attacked. It was my first essay at carrying "concealed weapons," but it was the fashion of the country at the time—a fashion followed by nineteen out of every twenty persons you met—by planters, merchants, lawyers, doctors, and even divines! So prepared, I had no fear of an encounter with "Bully Bill." If my pulse beat quick and my step was nervous, it was on account of the anticipated interview with his mistress.

With all the coolness I could command, I entered the house.

I found Mademoiselle in the drawing-room. She received me without reserve or embarrassment. To my surprise as well as gratification she appeared more cheerful than usual. I could even detect a significant smile! I fancied she was pleased at what had occurred; for of course she was aware of it all. I could understand this well enough.

Aurore was not present. I was glad she was not. I hoped she would not come into the room—*at least for a time*. I was embarrassed. I scarce knew how to open the conversation, much less to break to Mademoiselle the matter that was nearest my heart. A few ordinary phrases passed between us, and then our conversation turned upon the affair of yesterday. I told her all—everything—except the scene with Aurore. That was omitted.

I hesitated for some time whether I should let her know *who* her overseer was. When she should ascertain that he was the fellow who had wounded me on the boat, and who but for me would have taken away her chances of safety, I felt certain she would insist upon getting rid of him at all risks.

For a moment I reflected upon the consequences. "She will never be safe," thought I, "with such a ruffian at her side. Better for her to make stand at once." Under this belief I boldly came out with the information.

She seemed astounded, and clasping her hands, remained for some moments in an attitude of mute agony. At length she cried out—

"Gayarre—Gayarre! it is you, Monsieur Gayarre! Oh! *mon Dieu! mon Dieu!* Where is my father? where is Antoine? God have mercy upon me!"

The expression of grief upon her lovely countenance went to my heart. She looked an angel of sorrow, sad but beautiful.

I interrupted her with consolatory phrases of the ordinary kind. Though I could only guess the nature of her sorrow, she listened to me patiently, and I fancied that what I said gave her pleasure.

Taking courage from this, I proceeded to inquire more particularly the cause of her grief. "Mademoiselle," said I, "you will pardon the liberty I am taking; but for some time I have observed, or fancied, that you have a cause of—of—unhappiness—"

She fixed her eyes upon me in a gaze of silent wonder. I hesitated a moment under this strange regard, and then continued—

"Pardon me, Mademoiselle, if I speak too boldly; I assure you my motive—"

"Speak on, Monsieur!" she said, in a calm sad voice.

"I noticed this the more, because when I first had the pleasure of seeing you, your manner was so very different—in fact, quite the reverse—"

A sigh and a sad smile were the only reply. These interrupted me for but a moment, and I proceeded:—

"When first observing this change, Mademoiselle, I attributed it to grief for the loss of your faithful servitor and friend."

Another melancholy smile.

"But the period of sorrowing for such a cause is surely past, and yet—"

"And yet you observe that I am still sad?"

"Just so, Mademoiselle."

"True, Monsieur; it is even so."

"I have ceased therefore to regard that as the cause of your melancholy; and have been forced to think of some other—"

The gaze of half surprise, half interrogation, that now met mine, caused me for a moment to suspend my speech. After a pause, I resumed it, determined to come at once to the point, "You will pardon me, Mademoiselle, for this free interest in your affairs—you will pardon me for asking. Do I not recognise in Monsieur Gayarre the cause of your unhappiness?"

She started at the question, and turned visibly paler. In a moment, however, she seemed to recover herself, and replied calmly, but with a look of strange significance:—

"Hélas! Monsieur, your suspicions are but *partially* correct. Hélas! Oh! God, support me!" she added, in a tone that sounded like despair. Then, as if by an effort, her manner seemed to undergo a sudden alteration, and she continued:—

"Please, Monsieur, let us change the subject? I owe you life and gratitude. Would I knew how to repay you for your generous gallantry— your—your—*friendship*. Perhaps some day you may know all. I would tell you now, but—but—Monsieur—there are—I cannot—"

"Mademoiselle Besançon, I entreat you, do not for a moment let the questions I have asked have any consideration. They were not put from idle curiosity. I need not tell you, Mademoiselle, that my motive was of a higher kind—"

"I know it, Monsieur—I know it; but no more of it now, I pray you—let us speak on some other subject."

Some other subject! I had no longer the choice of one. I had no longer control of my tongue. The subject which was nearest my heart sprang spontaneously to my lips; and in hurried words I declared my love for Aurore.

I detailed the whole course of my passion, from the hour of my dreamlike vision up to that when we had plighted our mutual troth.

My listener was seated upon the low ottoman directly before me; but from motives of bashfulness I had kept my eyes averted during the time I was speaking. She heard me without interruption, and I augured well from this silence.

I concluded at length, and with trembling heart was awaiting her reply; when a deep sigh, followed by a rustling sound, caused me suddenly to turn. *Eugénie had fallen upon the floor*!

With a glance I saw she had fainted. I flung my arms around her, and carried her to the sofa.

I was about to call for assistance when the door opened, and a form glided into the room. *It was Aurore*!

"Mon Dieu!" exclaimed the latter; "*vous l'avez faire mourir! Elle t'aime—Elle t'aime!*"

Chapter Thirty
Thoughts

That night I passed without repose. How was it with Eugénie? How with Aurore?

Mine was a night of reflections, in which pleasure and pain were singularly blended. The love of the quadroon was my source of pleasure; but, alas! pain predominated as my thoughts dwelt upon the Creole! That the latter loved me I no longer doubted; and this assurance, so far from giving me joy, filled me with keen regret. Accursed vanity, that can enjoy such a triumph,—vile heart, that can revel in a love it is unable to return! Mine did not: it grieved instead.

In thought I reviewed the short hours of intercourse that had passed between us—Eugénie Besançon and myself. I communed with my conscience, asking myself the question, Was I innocent? Had I done aught, either by word, or look, or gesture, to occasion this love?—to produce the first delicate impression, that upon a heart susceptible as hers soon becomes a fixed and vivid picture? Upon the boat? Or afterwards? I remembered that at first sight I had gazed upon her with admiring eyes. I remembered that in hers I had beheld that strange expression of interest which I had attributed to curiosity or some other cause—I knew not what. Vanity, of which no doubt I possess my share, had not interpreted those tender glances aright—had not even whispered me they were the flowers of love, easily ripened to its fruits. Had I been instrumental in nurturing those flowers of the heart?—had I done aught to beguile them to their fatal blooming?

I examined the whole course of my conduct, and pondered over all that had passed between us. I thought of all that had occurred during our passage upon the boat—during the tragic scene that followed. I could not remember aught, either of word, look, or gesture, by which I might condemn myself. I gave full play to my conscience, and it declared me innocent.

Afterwards—after that terrible night—after those burning eyes and that strange face had passed dreamlike before my disordered senses—after that moment I could not have been guilty of aught that was trivial. During the hours of my convalescence—during the whole period of my stay upon the plantation—I could remember nothing in my intercourse with Eugénie

Besançon to give me cause for regret. Towards her I had observed a studied respect—nothing more. Secretly I felt friendship and sympathy; more especially after I had noted the change in her manner, and feared that some cloud was shadowing her fortune. Alas, poor Eugénie! Little did I guess the nature of that cloud! Little did I dream how dark it was!

Notwithstanding my self-exculpation, I still felt pain. Had Eugénie Besançon been a woman of ordinary character I might have borne my reflections more lightly. But to a heart so highly attuned, so noble, so passionate, what would be the shock of an unrequited love? Terrible it must be; perhaps the more so at thus finding her rival in her own slave!

Strange confidante had I chosen for my secret! Strange ear into which I had poured the tale of my love! Oh that I had not made my confession! What suffering had I caused this fair, this unfortunate lady!

Such painful reflections coursed through my mind; but there were others equally bitter, and with bitterness springing from a far different source. What would be the effect of the disclosure? How would it affect our future—the future of myself and Aurore? How would Eugénie act? Towards me? towards Aurore—*her slave*?

My confession had received no response. The mute lips murmured neither reply nor adieu. I had gazed but a moment on the insensible form. Aurore had beckoned me away, and I had left the room in a state of embarrassment and confusion—I scarce remembered how.

What would be the result? I trembled to think. Bitterness, hostility, revenge?

Surely a soul so pure, so noble, could not harbour such passions as these?

"No," thought I; "Eugénie Besançon is too gentle, too womanly, to give way to them. Is there a hope that she may have pity on *me*, as I pity *her*? Or is there not? She is a Creole—she inherits the fiery passions of her race. Should these be aroused to jealousy, to revenge, her gratitude will soon pass away—her love be changed to scorn. *Her own slave!*"

Ah! I well understood the meaning of this relationship, though I cannot make it plain to you. You can ill comprehend the horrid feeling. Talk of a *mésalliance* of the aristocratic lord with the daughter of his peasant retainer, of the high-born dame with her plebeian groom—talk of the scandal and scorn to which such rare events give rise! All this is little—is mild, when compared with the positive disgust and horror felt for the "white" who would ally himself *in marriage* with a *slave*! No matter how white *she* be, no matter how beautiful—even lovely as Aurore—he who would make her his *wife* must bear her away from her native land, far from the scenes where she has hitherto been known! His *mistress*—all! that is another affair. An alliance of this nature is pardonable. The "society" of the South is satisfied with the *slave-mistress*; but the *slave-wife*—that is an impossibility, an incongruity not to be borne!

I knew that the gifted Eugénie was above the common prejudices of her class; but I should have expected too much to suppose that she was above this one. No; noble, indeed, must be the soul that could have thrown off this chain, coiled around it by education, by habit, by example, by every form of social life. Notwithstanding all—notwithstanding the relations that existed between herself and Aurore, I could not expect this much. Aurore was her companion, her friend; but still Aurore was *her slave*!

I trembled for the result. I trembled for our next interview. In the future I saw darkness and danger. I had but one hope, one joy—the love of Aurore!

I rose from my sleepless couch. I dressed and ate my breakfast hurriedly, mechanically.

That finished, I was at a loss what to do next. Should I return to the plantation, and seek another interview with Eugénie. No—not then. I had not the courage. It would be better, I reflected, to permit some time to pass—a day or two—before going back. Perhaps Mademoiselle would send for me?

Perhaps— At all events, it would be better to allow some days to elapse. Long days they would be to me!

I could not bear the society of any one. I shunned conversation; although I observed, as on the preceding day, that I was the object of scrutiny—the subject of comment among the loungers of the "bar," and my acquaintances of the billiard-room. To avoid them, I remained inside my room, and endeavoured to kill time by reading.

I soon grew tired of this chamber-life; and upon the third morning I seized my gun, and plunged into the depth of the forest.

I moved amidst the huge pyramidal trunks of the cypresses, whose thick umbellated foliage, meeting overhead, shut out both sun and sky. The very gloom occasioned by their shade was congenial to my thoughts; and I wandered on, my steps guided rather by accident than design.

I did not search for game. I was not thinking of sport. My gun rested idly in the hollow of my arm. The raccoon, which in the more open woods is nocturnal, is here abroad by day. I saw the creature plunging his food into the waters of the bayou, and skulking around the trunks of the cypresses.

I saw the opossum gliding along the fallen log, and the red squirrel, like a stream of fire, brushing up the bark of the tall tulip-tree. I saw the large "swamp-hare" leap from her form by the selvage of the cane-brake; and, still more tempting game, the fallow-deer twice bounded before me, roused from its covert in the shady thickets of the pawpaw-trees. The wild turkey, too, in all the glitter of his metallic plumage, crossed my path; and upon the bayou, whose bank I for some time followed, I had ample opportunity of discharging my piece at the blue heron or the egret, the summer duck or the snake-bird, the slender ibis or the stately crane. Even the king of winged creatures, the white-headed eagle, was more than once within range of my gun, screaming his maniac note among the tops of the tall taxodiums.

And still the brown tubes rested idly across my arm; nor did I once think of casting my eye along their sights. No ordinary game could have tempted me to interrupt the current, of my thoughts, that were dwelling upon a theme to me the most interesting in the world—Aurore the quadroon!

Chapter Thirty One
Dreams

Yielding up my soul to its sweet love-dream, I wandered on—where and how long I cannot tell, for I had taken no note either of distance or direction.

I was roused from my reverie by observing a brighter light gleaming before me; and soon after I emerged from the darker shadow of the forest. My steps, chance-directed, had guided me into a pretty glade, where the sun shone warmly, and the ground was gay with flowers. It was a little wild garden, enamelled by blossoms of many colours, among which, bignonias and the showy corollas of the cotton-rose were conspicuous. Even the forest that bordered and enclosed this little parterre was a forest of flowering-trees. They were magnolias of several kinds; on some of which the large liliaceous blossoms had given place to the scarcely less conspicuous seed-cones of glowing red, whose powerful but pleasant odour filled the atmosphere around. Other beautiful trees grew alongside, mingling their perfume with that of the magnolias. Scarce less interesting were the "honey-locusts" (*gleditschias*), with their pretty pinnate leaves, and long purple-brown legumes; the Virginian lotus, with its oval amber-coloured drupes, and the singular bow-wood tree (*madura*), with its large orange-like pericarps, reminding one of the *flora* of the tropics. The Autumn was just beginning to paint the forest, and already some touches from his glowing palette appeared among the leaves of the sassafras laurel, the sumach (*rhus*), the persimmon (*diospyros*), the nymph-named tupelo, and those other species of the American *sylva* that love to array themselves so gorgeously before parting with their deciduous foliage. Yellow, orange, scarlet, crimson, with many an intermediate tint, met the eye; and all these colours, flashing under the brilliant beams of a noonday sun, produced an indescribable *coup-d'oeil*. The scene resembled the gaudy picture-work of a theatre, more than the sober reality of a natural landscape.

I stood for some minutes wrapt in admiration. The dream of love in which I had been indulging became heightened in its effect; and I could not help thinking that if Aurore were but present to enjoy that lovely scene—to wander with me over that flowery glade—to sit by my side under the shade of the magnolia laurel—then, indeed, would my happiness be complete. Earth itself had no fairer scene than this. A very love-bower it appeared!

Nor was it unoccupied by lovers; for two pretty doves—birds emblematic of the tender passion—sat side by side upon the bough of a tulip-tree, their bronzed throats swelling at intervals with soft amorous notes.

Oh, how I envied those little creatures! How I should have rejoiced in a destiny like theirs! Thus mated and happy—amidst bright flowers and sweet perfumes, loving the livelong day—loving through all their lives!

They deemed me an intruder, and rose on whirring wing at my approach. Perchance they feared my glittering gun. They had not need. I had no intention of harming them. Far was it from my heart to spoil their perfect bliss.

But no—they feared me not—else their flight would have been more distant. They only flitted to the next tree; and there again, seated side by side, resumed their love-converse. Absorbed in mutual fondness, they had already forgotten my presence!

I followed to watch these pretty creatures—the types of gentleness and love. I flung me on the grass, and gazed upon thorn, tenderly kissing and cooing. I envied their delight.

My nerves, that for days had been dancing with more than ordinary excitement, were now experiencing the natural reaction, and I felt weary. There was a drowsiness in the air—a narcotic influence produced by the combined action of the sun's rays and the perfume of the flowers. It acted upon my spirit, and I fell asleep.

I slept only about an hour, but it was a sleep of dreams; and during that short period I passed through many scenes. Many a visionary tableau appeared before the eye of my slumbering soul, and then melted away. There were more or less characters in each; but in all of them two were constant, both well defined in form and features. They were Eugénie and Aurore.

Gayarre, too, was in my dreams; and the ruffian overseer, and Scipio, and the mild face of Reigart, and what I could remember of the good Antoine. Even the unfortunate Captain of the boat, the boat herself, the Magnolia, and the scene of the wreck—all were reproduced with a painful distinctness!

But my visions were not all of a painful character. Some were the very opposite—scenes of bliss. In company with Aurore, I was wandering through flowery glades, and exchanging the sweet converse of mutual love. The very spot where I lay—the scene around me—was pictured in the dream.

Strangest of all, I thought that Eugénie was with us, and that she, too, was happy; that she had consented to my marrying Aurore, and had even assisted us in bringing about this happy consummation!

In this vision Gayarre was the fiend; and I thought that after a while he endeavoured to drag Aurore from me. A struggle followed, and then the scene ended with confused abruptness.

A new tableau arose—a new vision. In this *Eugénie* played the part of the evil genius. I thought she had refused my requests—refused to *sell Aurore*. I fancied her jealous, hostile, vengeful. I thought she was loading me with imprecations, my betrothed with threats. Aurore was weeping. It was a painful vision.

The scene changed again. Aurore and I were happy—she was free—she was now mine, and we were married. But there was a cloud upon our happiness. *Eugénie was dead.*

Yes, dead. I thought I was bending over her, and had taken her hand. Suddenly her fingers closed upon mine, and held them with a firm pressure. I thought that the contact was disagreeable; and I endeavoured to withdraw my hand, but could not. My fingers remained bound within that cold clammy grasp; and with all my strength I was unable to release them! Suddenly I was stung; and at the same instant the chill hand relaxed its grasp, and set me free.

The stinging sensation, however, awoke me; and my eyes mechanically turned towards the hand, where I still felt pain.

Sure enough my wrist was punctured and bleeding!

A feeling of horror ran through my veins, as the "sker-r-rr" of the *crotalus* sounded in my ear; and, looking around, I saw the glittering body of the reptile extended along the grass, and gliding rapidly away!

Chapter Thirty Two
Stung by a Snake

The pain was not a dream; the blood upon my wrist was no illusion. Both were real. I was bitten by a *rattlesnake*!

Terror-stricken I sprang to my feet; and, with an action altogether mechanical, passed my hand over the wound, and wiped away the blood. It was but a trifling puncture, such as might have been made by the point of a lancet, and only a few drops of blood oozed from it.

Such a wound need not have terrified a child, so far as appearance went; but I, a man, *was* terrified, for I knew that that little incision had been made by a dread instrument—by the envenomed fang of a serpent—and *in one hour I might be dead*!

My first impulse was to pursue the snake and destroy it; but before I could act upon that impulse the reptile had escaped beyond my reach. A hollow log lay near—the trunk of a large tulip-tree, with the heart-wood decayed and gone. The snake had made for this—no doubt its haunt—and before I could come up with it, I saw the long slimy body, with its rhomboid spots, disappear within the dark cavity. Another "sker-r-rr" reached my ears as it glided out of sight. It seemed a note of triumph, as if uttered to tantalise me!

The reptile was now beyond my reach, but its destruction would not have availed me. Its death could not counteract the effect of its poison already in my veins. I knew that well enough, but for all I would have killed it, had it been in my power to do so. I felt angry and vengeful.

This was but my first impulse. It suddenly became changed to a feeling of terror. There was something so weird in the look of the reptile, something so strange in the manner of its attack and subsequent escape, that, on losing sight of it, I became suddenly impressed with a sort of supernatural awe—a belief that the creature was possessed of a fiendish intelligence!

Under this impression I remained for some moments in a state of bewilderment.

The sight of the blood, and the stinging sensation of the wound, soon brought me to my senses again, and admonished me of the necessity of taking immediate steps to procure an antidote to the poison. But what antidote?

What knew I of such things? I was but a classical scholar. True, I had lately given some attention to botanical studies; but my new knowledge extended only to the *trees* of the forest, and none of these with which I was acquainted possessed alexipharmic virtues. I knew nothing of the herbaceous plants, the milk-worts, and *aristolochias*, that would now have served me. The woods might have been filled with antidotal remedies, and I have died in their midst. Yes, I might have lain down upon a bed of Seneca root, and, amidst terrible convulsions, have breathed my last breath, without knowing that the rhizome of the humble plant crushed beneath my body would, in a few short hours, have expelled the venom from my veins, and given me life and health.

I lost no time in speculating upon such a means of safety. I had but one thought—and that was to reach Bringiers at the earliest possible moment. My hopes rested upon Reigart.

I hastily took up my gun; and, plunging once more under the dark shadows of the cypress-trees, I hurried on with nervous strides. I ran as fast as my limbs would carry me; but the shock of terror I had experienced seemed to have enfeebled my whole frame, and my knees knocked against each other as I went.

On I struggled, regardless of my weakness, regardless of everything but the thought of reaching Bringiers and Reigart. Over fallen trees, through dense cane-brakes, through clumps of palmettoes and pawpaw thickets, I passed, dashing the branches from my path, and lacerating my skin at every step. Onward, through sluggish rivulets of water, through tough miry mud, through slimy pools, filled with horrid newts, and the spawn of the huge *rana pipiens*, whose hoarse loud croak at every step sounded ominous in my ear. Onward!

"Ho! whither am I going? Where is the path? where the tracks of my former footsteps? Not here—not there. Good God! I have lost them!—lost! lost!"

Quick as lightning came these thoughts. I looked around with eager glances. On every side I scanned the ground. I saw no path, no tracks, but those I had just made. I saw no marks that I could remember. I had lost my way. Beyond a doubt I was lost!

A thrill of despair ran through me—the blood curdled cold in my veins at the thought of my peril.

No wonder. If lost in the forest, then was I lost indeed. A single hour might be enough. In that time the poison would do its work. I should be found only by the wolves and vultures. O God!

As if to make my horrid fate appear more certain, I now remembered to have heard that it was the very season of the year—the hot autumn—when the venom of the *crotalus* is most virulent, and does its work in the shortest period of time. Cases are recorded where in a single hour its bite has proved fatal.

"Merciful heaven!" thought I, "in another hour I shall be no more!" and the thought was followed by a groan.

The danger nerved me to renewed efforts. I turned back on my tracks. It seemed the best thing I could do; for in the gloomy circle around, there was no point that indicated my approach to the open ground of the plantations. Not a bit of sky could I discover,—that welcome beacon to the wood-ranger, denoting the proximity of the clearings. Even the heaven above was curtained from my view; and when I appealed to it in prayer, my eyes rested only upon the thick black foliage of the cypress-trees, with their mournful drapery of *tillandsia*.

I had no choice but to go back, and endeavour to find the path I had lost, or wander on trusting to mere chance.

I chose the former alternative. Again I broke through the cane-brakes and palmetto-thickets—again I forded sluggish bayous, and waded across muddy pools.

I had not proceeded more than a hundred yards on the back track, when that also became doubtful. I had passed over a reach of ground higher and drier than the rest. Here no footprints appeared, and I knew not which way I had taken. I tried in several directions, but could not discover my way. I became confused, and at length completely bewildered. Again was I lost!

To have been lost in the forest under ordinary circumstances would have mattered little,—an hour or two of wandering—perhaps a night spent under the shade of some tree, with the slight inconvenience of a hungry stomach. But how very different was my prospect then, with the fearful thoughts that were pressing upon me! The poison was fast inoculating my blood. I fancied I already felt it crawling through my veins!

One more struggle to find the clearings!

I rushed on, now guided by chance. I endeavoured to keep in a straight line, but to no purpose. The huge pyramidal buttresses of the trees, so characteristic of these *coniferae*, barred my way; and, in passing around them, I soon lost all knowledge of my direction.

I wandered on, now dragging wearily across the dull ditches, now floundering through tracts of swamp, or climbing over huge prostrate logs. In my passage I startled the thousand denizens of the dank forest, who greeted me with their cries. The qua-bird screamed; the swamp-owl hooted; the bullfrog uttered his trumpet-note; and the hideous alligator, horribly bellowing from his gaunt jaws, crawled sulkily out of my way, at times appearing as if he would turn and assail me!

"Ho! yonder is light!—the sky!"

It was but a small patch of the blue heaven—a disc, not larger than a dining-plate. But, oh! you cannot understand with what joy I greeted that bright spot. It was the lighthouse to the lost mariner.

It must be the clearings? Yes, I could see the sun shining through the trees, and the horizon open as I advanced. No doubt the plantations were before me. Once there I should soon cross the fields, and reach the town. I should yet be safe. Reigart would surely know how to extract the poison, or apply some antidote?

I kept on with bounding heart and straining eyes—on, for the bright meteor before me.

The blue spot grew larger—other pieces of sky appeared—the forest grew thinner as I advanced—I was drawing nearer to its verge.

The ground became firmer and drier at every step, and the timber of a lighter growth. The shapeless cypress "knees" no longer impeded my progress. I now passed among tulip-trees, dogwoods, and magnolias. Less densely grew the trunks, lighter and less shadowy became the foliage above; until at length I pushed through the last selvage of the underwood, and stood in the open sunshine.

A cry of agony rose upon my lips. It was wrung from me by despair. I had arrived at my point of starting—I was once more within the glade!

I sought not to go farther. Fatigue, disappointment, and chagrin, had for the moment paralysed my strength. I staggered forward to a prostrate trunk,—the very one which sheltered my reptile assassin!—and sat down in a state of irresolution and bewilderment.

It seemed as though I were destined to die in that lovely glade—amidst those bright flowers—in the midst of that scene I had so lately admired, and upon the very spot where I had received my fatal wound!

Chapter Thirty Three
The Runaway

Man rarely yields up his life without an extreme effort to preserve it. Despair is a strong feeling, but there are those whose spirit it cannot prostrate. In later life mine own would not have given way to such circumstances as surrounded me at that time; but I was then young, and little experienced in peril.

The paralysis of my thoughts did not continue long. My senses returned again; and I resolved to make a new effort for the salvation of my life.

I had conceived no plan, further than to endeavour once more to escape out of the labyrinth of woods and morass in which I had become entangled, and make as before for the village. I thought I knew the direction in which it lay, by observing the side at which I had first entered the glade. But, after all, there was no certainty in this. It was mere conjecture. I had entered the glade with negligent steps. I had strayed all around it before lying down to sleep. Perhaps I had gone around its sides before entering it—for I had been wandering all the morning.

While these reflections were passing rapidly through my mind, and despair once more taking possession of my spirits, I all at once remembered having heard that tobacco is a powerful antidote to snake-poison. Strange the idea had not occurred to me before. But, indeed, there was nothing wonderful that it did not, as up to that moment I had only thought of making my way to Bringiers. With no reliance upon my own knowledge, I had thought only of a doctor. It was only when I became apprehensive of not being able to get to *him*, that I began to think of what resources lay within my reach. I now remembered the tobacco.

Quick as the thought my cigar-case was in my fingers. To my joy one cigar still remained, and drawing it out I proceeded to macerate the tobacco by chewing. This I had heard was the mode of applying it to the snakebite.

Dry as was my mouth at first, the bitter weed soon supplied me with saliva, and in a few moments I had reduced the leaves to a pulp, though nauseated—almost poisoned by the powerful *nicotine*.

I laid the moistened mass upon my wrist, and at the same time rubbed it forcibly into the wound. I now perceived that my arm was sensibly swollen—even up to the elbow—and a singular pain began to be felt throughout its whole length! O God! the poison was spreading, surely and rapidly spreading! I fancied I could feel it like liquid fire crawling and filtering through my veins!

Though I had made application of the nicotine, I had but little faith in it. I had only heard it casually talked of as a remedy. It might, thought I, be one of the thousand fancies that people love to indulge in; and I had only used it as a "forlorn hope."

I bound the mass to my wrist—a torn sleeve serving for lint; and then, turning my face in the direction I intended to take, I started off afresh.

I had scarce made three strides when my steps were suddenly arrested. I stopped on observing a man on the edge of the glade, and directly in front of me.

He had just come out of the underwood, towards which I was advancing, and, on perceiving me, had suddenly halted—perhaps surprised at the sight of one of his own kind in such a wild place.

I hailed his appearance with a shout of joy. "A guide!—a deliverer!" thought I.

What was my astonishment—my chagrin—my indignation—when the man suddenly turned his back upon me; and, plunging into the bushes, disappeared from my sight!

I was astounded at this strange conduct. I had just caught a glimpse of the man's face as he turned away. I had seen that he was a negro, and I had noticed that he appeared to be frightened. But what was there about me to terrify him?

I called out to him to stop—to come back. I shouted in tones of entreaty— of command—of menace. In vain. He made neither stop nor stay. I heard the branches crackle as he broke through the thicket—each moment the noise appearing more distant.

It was my only chance for a guide. I must not lose it; and, bracing myself for a run, I started after him.

If I possess any physical accomplishment in which I have confidence it is my fleetness of foot. At that time an Indian runner could not have escaped me, much less a clumsy, long-heeled negro. I knew that if I could once more got my eyes upon the black, I would soon overhaul him; but therein lay the difficulty. In my hesitation I had given him a long start; and he was now out of sight in the depth of the thicket.

But I could hear him breaking through the bushes like a hog; and, guiding myself by the sound, I kept up the pursuit.

I was already somewhat jaded by my previous exertions; but the conviction that *my life depended on overtaking the negro* kindled my energies afresh, and I ran like a greyhound. Unfortunately it was not a question of simple speed, else the chase would soon have been brought to an end. It was in getting through the bushes, and dodging round the trunks of the trees, that the hindrance lay; and I had many a struggle among the branches, and many a zigzag turn to make, before I could get my eyes upon the object I was in pursuit of.

However, I at length succeeded in doing so. The underwood came to an end. The misshapen cypress trunks alone stood up out of the miry, black soil; and far off, down one of their dark aisles, I caught sight of the negro, still running at the top of his speed. Fortunately his garments were light-coloured, else under the sombre shadow I could not have made him out. As it was, I had only a glimpse of him, and at a good distance off.

But I had cleared the thicket, and could run freely. Swiftness had now everything to do with the race; and in less than five minutes after I was close upon the heels of the black, and calling to him to halt.

"Stop!" I shouted. "For God's sake, stop!"

No notice was taken of my appeals. The negro did not even turn his head, but ran on, floundering through the mud.

"Stop!" I repeated, as loudly as my exhausted breath would permit. "Stop, man! why do you run from me? I mean you no harm."

Neither did this speech produce any effect. No reply was given. If anything, I fancied that he increased his speed; or rather, perhaps, he had got through the quagmire, and was running upon firm ground while I was just entering upon the former.

I fancied that the distance between us was again widening; and began to fear he might still elude me. I felt that my life was on the result. Without him to guide me from the forest, I would miserably perish. He *must* guide me. Willing or unwilling, I should force him to the office.

"Stop," I again cried out; "halt, or I fire!"

I had raised my gun. Both barrels were loaded. I had spoken in all seriousness. I should in reality have fired—not to kill, but to detain him.

The shot might injure him, but I could not help it. I had no choice—no other means of saving my own life.

I repeated the awful summons:—

"Stop—or I fire!"

This time my tone was earnest. It left no doubt of my intention; and this seemed to be the impression it produced upon the black; for, suddenly halting in his tracks, he wheeled about, and stood facing me.

"Fire! and be dam!" cried he; "have a care, white man—don't you miss. By Gor-amighty! if ya do, your life's mine. See dis knife! fire now and be dam!"

As he spoke he stood full fronting me, his broad chest thrown out as if courageously to receive the shot, and in his uplifted hand I saw the shining blade of a knife!

A few steps brought me close up; and in the man that stood before me I recognised the form, and ferocious aspect of *Gabriel the Bambarra*!

Chapter Thirty Four
Gabriel the Bambarra

The huge stature of the black—his determined attitude—the sullen glare of his lurid bloodshot eyes, set in a look of desperate resolve—the white gleaming file-pointed teeth—rendered him a terrible object to behold. Under other circumstances I might have dreaded an encounter with such a hideous-looking adversary—for an *adversary* I deemed him. I remembered the flogging I had given him with my whip, and I had no doubt that *he* remembered it too. I had no doubt that he was now upon his errand of revenge instigated partly by the insult I had put upon him, and partly set on by his cowardly master. He had been dogging me through the forest—all the day, perhaps—waiting for an opportunity to execute his purpose.

But why had he run away from me? Was it because he feared to attack me openly. Certainly it was—he feared my double-barrelled gun!

But I had been asleep. He might have approached me then—he might have—Ha!

This ejaculation escaped my lips, as a singular thought flashed into my mind. The Bambarra was a "snake-charmer"—I had heard so—could handle the most venomous serpents at rail—could guide and direct them! Was it not he who had guided the *crotalus* to where I lay—who had caused me to be bitten?

Strange as it may appear, this supposition at that moment crossed my mind, and seemed probable; nay, more—I actually *believed it*. I remembered that I had been struck with a peculiarity about the reptile—its weird look—the superior cunning exhibited in its mode of escape—and not less peculiar the fact of its having stung me unprovoked—a rare thing for the rattlesnake to do! All these points rushing simultaneously into my mind, produced the conviction that for the fatal wound on my wrist I was indebted, not to chance, but to Gabriel the snake-charmer!

Not half the time I have been telling you of it—not the tenth nor the hundredth part of the time, was I in forming this horrid conviction. It was done with the rapidity of thought—the more rapid that every circumstance guiding to such a conclusion was fresh in my memory. In fact the black had not changed his attitude of menace, nor I mine of surprise at recognising him, until all these thoughts had passed through my mind!

Almost with equal rapidity was I disabused of the singular delusion. In another minute I became aware that my suspicions were unjust. I had been wronging the man who stood before me.

All at once his attitude changed. His uplifted arm fell by his side; the expression of fierce menace disappeared; and in as mild a tone as his rough voice was capable of giving utterance to, he said—

"Oh! you mass'—brack man's friend! Dam! thought 'twar da cussed Yankee driber!"

"And was that why you ran from me?"

"Ye, mass'; ob course it war."

"Then you are—"

"Am runaway; ye, mass', jes so—runaway. Don't mind tell you. Gabr'el truss you—He know you am poor nigga's friend. Look-ee-dar."

As he uttered this last phrase, he pulled off the scanty copper-coloured rag of a shirt that covered his shoulders, and bared his back before my eyes!

A horrid sight it was. Besides the *fleur-de-lis* and many other old brands, there were sears of more recent date. Long wales, purple-red and swollen, traversed the brown skin in every direction, forming perfect network. Here they were traceable by the darker colour of the extravasatod blood, while there the flesh itself lay bare, where it had been exposed to some prominent fold of the spirally-twisted cowskin. The old shirt itself was stained with black blotches that had once been red—the blood that had oozed out during the infliction! The sight sickened me, and called forth the involuntary utterance—

"Poor fellow!"

This expression of sympathy evidently touched the rude heart of the Bambarra.

"Ah, mass'!" he continued, "you flog me with hoss-whip—dat nuff'n! Gabr'l bress you for dat. He pump water on ole Zip *'gainst him will*—glad when young mass' druv im way from de pump."

"Ha! you were forced to it, then?"

"Ye, mass', forced by da Yankee driber. Try make me do so odder time. I 'fuse punish Zip odder time—dat's why you see dis yeer—dam!"

"You were flogged for refusing to punish Scipio?"

"Jes so, mass' Edwad; 'bused, as you see; but—" here the speaker hesitated, while his face resumed its fierce expression; "but," continued he, "I'se had rebenge on de Yankee—dam!"

"What?—revenge? What have you done to him?"

"Oh, not much, mass'. Knock im down; he drop like a beef to de axe. Dat's some rebenge to poor nigga. Beside, I'se a runaway, *an' dat's rebenge*! Ha! ha! Dey lose good nigga—good hand in de cotton-feel—good hand among de cane. Ha! ha!"

The hoarse laugh with which the "runaway" expressed his satisfaction sounded strangely on my ear.

"And you have run away from the plantation?"

"Jes so, mass' Edward—nebber go back." After a pause, he added, with increased emphasis, *"Nebber go back 'live!"*

As he uttered these words he raised his hand to his broad chest, at the same time throwing his body into an attitude of earnest determination.

I saw at once that I had mistaken the character of this man. I had had it from his enemies, the whites, who feared him. With all the ferocity of expression that characterised his features, there was evidently something noble in his heart. He had been flogged for refusing to flog a fellow-slave. He had resented the punishment, and struck down his brutal oppressor. By so doing he had risked a far more terrible punishment—even life itself!

It required courage to do all this. A spirit of liberty alone could have inspired him with that courage—the same spirit which impelled the Swiss patriot to strike down the cap of Gessler.

As the negro stood with his thick muscular fingers spread over his brawny chest, with form erect, with head thrown back, and eyes fixed in stern resolve, I was impressed with an air of grandeur about him, and could not help thinking that in the black form before me, scantily clad in coarse cotton, there was the soul and spirit of a man!

Chapter Thirty Five
The Snake-Doctor

With admiring eyes I looked for some moments on this bold black man—this slave-hero. I might have gazed longer, but the burning sensation in my arm reminded me of my perilous situation.

"You will guide me to Bringiers?" was my hurried interrogatory.

"Daren't, mass'."

"Daren't! Why?"

"Mass' forgot I'se a runaway. White folk cotch Gabr'l—cut off him arm."

"What? Cut off your arm?"

"Saten sure, mass'—dats da law of Loozyaney. White man strike nigga, folk laugh, folk cry out, 'Lap de dam nigga! lap him!' Nigga strike white man, cut off nigga's arm. Like berry much to 'bleege mass' Edwad, but daren't go to de clearins. White men after Gabr'l last two days. Cuss'd blood-dogs and nigga-hunters out on im track. Thought young mass' war one o' dem folks; dat's why um run."

"If you do not guide me, then I must die."

"Die!—die! why for mass' say dat?"

"Because I am lost. I cannot find my way out of the forest. If I do not reach the doctor in less than twenty minutes, there is no hope. O God!"

"Doctor!—mass' Edwad sick? What ail um? Tell Gabr'l. If dat's da case, him guide de brack man's friend at risk ob life. What young mass' ail?"

"See! I have been bitten by a rattlesnake."

I bared my arm, and showed the wound and the swelling.

"Ho! dat indeed! sure 'nuff—it are da bite ob de rattlesnake. Doctor no good for dat. Tobacc'-juice no good. Gabr'l best doctor for de rattlesnake. Come 'long, young mass'!"

"What! you are going to guide me, then?"

"I'se a gwine to *cure* you, mass'."

"You?"

"Ye, mass'! tell you doctor no good—know nuffin' 't all 'bout it—he kill you—truss Ole Gabe—he cure you. Come 'long, mass', no time t' be loss."

I had for the moment forgotten the peculiar reputation which the black enjoyed—that of a snake-charmer and snake-doctor as well, although I had so late been thinking of it. The remembrance of this fact now returned, accompanied by a very different train of reflections.

"No doubt," thought I, "he possesses the requisite knowledge—knows the antidote, and how to apply it. No doubt he is the very man. The doctor, as he says, may not understand how to treat me."

I had no very great confidence that the doctor could cure me. I was only running to him as a sort of *dernier ressort*.

"This Gabriel—this snake-charmer, is the very man. How fortunate I should have met with him!"

After a moment's hesitation—during the time these reflections were passing through my mind—I called out to the black—

"Lead on! I follow you!"

Whither did he intend to guide me? What was he going to do? Where was *he* to find an antidote? How was he to cure me?

To these questions, hurriedly put, I received no reply.

"You truss me, mass' Edward; you foller me!" were all the words the black would utter as he strode off among the trees.

I had no choice but to follow him.

After proceeding several hundred yards through the cypress swamp, I saw some spots of sky in front of us. This indicated an opening in the woods, and for that I saw my guide was heading. I was not surprised on reaching this opening to find that it was the glade—again the fatal glade!

To my eyes how changed its aspect! I could not bear the bright sun that gleamed into it. The sheen of its flowers wearied my sight—their perfume made me sick!

Maybe I only fancied this. I was sick, but from a very different cause. The poison was mingling with my blood. It was setting my veins on fire. I was tortured by a choking sensation of thirst, and already felt that spasmodic compression of the chest, and difficulty of breathing—the well-known symptoms experienced by the victims of snake-poison.

It may be that I only fancied most of this. I knew that a venomous serpent had bitten me; and that knowledge may have excited my imagination to an extreme susceptibility. Whether the symptoms did in reality exist, I suffered them all the same. My fancy had all the painfulness of reality!

My companion directed me to be seated. Moving about, he said, was not good. He desired me to be calm and patient, once more begging me to "truss Gabr'l."

I resolved to be quiet, though patient I could not be. My peril was too great.

Physically I obeyed him. I sat down upon a log—that same log of the liriodendron—and under the shade of a spreading dogwood-tree. With all the patience I could command, I sat awaiting the orders of the snake-doctor. He had gone off a little way, and was now wandering around the glade with eyes bent upon the ground. He appeared to be searching for something.

"Some plant," thought I, "he expects to find growing there."

I watched his movements with more than ordinary interest. I need hardly have said this. It would have been sufficient to say that I felt my life depended on the result of his search. His success or his failure were life or death to me.

How my heart leaped when I saw him bend forward, and then stoop still lower, as if clutching something upon the ground! An exclamation of joy that escaped his lips was echoed in a louder key from my own; and, forgetting his directions to remain quiet, I sprang up from the log, and ran towards him.

As I approached he was upon his knees, and with his knife-blade was digging around a plant, as if to raise it by the roots. It was a small herbaceous plant, with erect simple stem, oblong lanceolate leaves, and a terminal spike of not very conspicuous white flowers. Though I knew it not then, it was the famed "snake-root" (*Polygala senega*).

In a few moments he had removed the earth, and then, drawing out the plant, shook its roots free of the mould. I noticed that a mass of woody contorted rhizomes, somewhat thicker than those of the sarsaparilla briar, adhered to the stem. They were covered with ash-coloured bark, and quite inodorous. Amid the fibres of these roots lay the antidote to the snake-poison—in their sap was the saviour of my rife!

Not a moment was lost in preparing them. There were no hieroglyphics nor Latinic phraseology employed in the prescription of the snake-charmer. It was comprised in the phrase, "*Chaw it!*" and, along with this simple direction, a piece of the root scraped clear of the bark was put into my hand. I did as I was desired, and in a moment I had reduced the root to a pulp, and was swallowing its sanitary juices.

The taste was at first rather sweetish, and engendered a slight feeling of nausea; but, as I continued to chew, it became hot and pungent, producing a peculiar tingling sensation in the fauces and throat.

The black now ran to the nearest brook, filled one of his "brogans" with water, and, returning, washed my wrist until the tobacco juice was all removed from the wound. Having himself chewed a number of the leaves of the plant into a pulpy mass, he placed it directly upon the bitten part, and then bound up the wound as before.

Everything was now done that could be done. I was instructed to abide the result patiently and without fear.

In a very short time a profuse perspiration broke out over my whole body, and I began to expectorate freely. I felt, moreover, a strong inclination to vomit—which I should have done had I swallowed any more of the juice, for, taken in large doses, the seneca root is a powerful emetic.

But of the feelings I experienced at that moment, the most agreeable was the belief that *I was cured*!

Strange to say, this belief almost at once impressed my mind with the force of a conviction. I no longer doubted the skill of the snake-doctor.

Chapter Thirty Six
Charming the Crotalus

I was destined to witness still further proofs of the wonderful capabilities of my new acquaintance.

I felt the natural joy of one whose life has been, saved from destruction — singularly, almost miraculously saved. Like one who has escaped from drowning, from the field of slaughter, from the very jaws of death. The reaction was delightful. I felt gratitude, too, for him who had saved me. I could have embraced my sable companion, black and fierce as he was, like a brother.

We sat side by side upon the log, and chatted gaily;—gaily as men may whose future is dark and unsettled. Alas! it was so with both of us. Mine had been dark for days past; and his—what was his, poor helot?

But even in the gloom of sadness the mind has its moments of joy. Nature has not allowed that grief may be continuous, and at intervals the spirit must soar above its sorrows. Such an interval was upon me then. Joy and gratitude were in my heart. I had grown fond of this slave,—this runaway slave,—and was for the moment happy in his companionship.

It was natural our conversation should be of snakes and snake-roots, and many a strange fact he imparted to me relating to reptile life. A herpetologist might have envied me the hour I spent upon that log in the company of Gabriel the Bambarra.

In the midst of our conversation my companion abruptly asked the question, whether I had killed the snake that had bitten me.

"No," I replied. "It escaped."

"'Scaped, mass'! whar did um go?"

"It took shelter in a hollow log,—the very one on which we are seated."

The eyes of the negro sparkled with delight.

"Dam!" exclaimed he, starting to his feet; "mass' say snake in dis yeer log? Dam!" he repeated, "if do varmint yeer in dis log, Gabr'l soon fetch 'im out."

"What! you have no axe?"

"Dis nigga axe no want for dat."

"How, then, can you get at the snake? Do you intend to set fire to the log?"

"Ho! fire no good. Dat log burn whole month. Fire no good: smoke white men see,—b'lieve 'im runaway,—den come de blood-dogs. Dis nigga daren't make no fire."

"How, then?"

"Wait a bit, mass' Edwad, you see. Dis nigga fetch de rattlesnake right out ob 'im boots. Please, young mass', keep still; don't speak 'bove de breff: ole varmint, he hear ebbery word."

The black now talked in whispers, as he glided stealthily around the log. I followed his directions, and remained perfectly "still," watching every movement of my singular companion.

Some young reeds of the American bamboo (*Arundo gigantea*) were growing near. A number of these he cut down with his knife; and then, sharpening their lower ends, stuck them into the ground, near the end of the log. He arranged the reeds in such a manner that they stood side by side, like the strings of a harp, only closer together. He next chose a small sapling from the thicket, and trimmed it so that nothing remained but a straight wand with a forked end. With this in one hand, and a piece of split cane in the other, he placed himself flat along the log, in such a position that his face was directly over the entrance to the cavity. He was also close to the row of canes, so that with his outstretched hand he could conveniently reach them. His arrangements were now completed, and the "charm" commenced.

Laying aside the forked sapling ready to his hand, he took the piece of split reed, and drew it backward and forward across the row of upright canes. This produced a sound which was an exact imitation of the "skerr" of the rattlesnake; go like, that a person hearing it, without knowing what caused it, would undoubtedly have mistaken it for the latter; so like, that the black knew the reptile itself would be deceived by it! He did not, however, trust to this alone to allure his victim. Aided by an instrument which he had hastily constructed out of the lanceolate leaves of the cane, he at the same time imitated the scream and chatter of the red cardinal (*Loxia cardinalis*), just as when that bird is engaged in battle, either with a serpent, an opossum, or some other of its habitual enemies.

The sounds produced were exactly similar to those often heard in the depths of the American forest, when the dread *crotalus* plunders the nest of the Virginian nightingale.

The stratagem proved successful. In a few moments the lozenge-shaped head of the reptile appeared outside the cavity. Its forking tongue was protruded at short intervals, and its small dark eyes glittered with rage. Its rattle could be heard, announcing its determination to take part in the fray—which it supposed was going on outside.

It had glided out nearly the full length of its body, and seemed to have discovered the deception, for it was turning round to retreat. But the *crotalus* is one of the most sluggish of snakes; and, before it could get back within the log, the forked sapling descended upon its neck, and pinned it fast to the ground!

Its body now writhed over the grass in helpless contortions—a formidable creature to behold. It was a snake of the largest size for its species, being nearly eight feet in length, and as thick as the wrist of the Bambarra himself. Even he was astonished at its proportions; and assured me it was the largest of its kind he had ever encountered.

I expected to see the black put an end to its struggles at once by killing it; and I essayed to help him with my gun.

"No, mass'," cried he, in a tone of entreaty, "for luv ob de Ormighty! don't fire de gun. Mass' forget dat dis poor nigga am runaway."

I understood his meaning, and lowered the piece.

"B'side," continued he, "I'se got somethin' show mass' yet—he like see curious thing—he like see de big snake trick?"

I replied in the affirmative.

"Well, den, please, mass', hold dis stick. I for something go. Jes now berry curious plant I see—berry curious—berry scace dat plant. I seed it in de cane-brake. Catch 'old, mass', while I go get um."

I took hold of the sapling, and held it as desired, though not without some apprehension of the hideous reptile that curled and writhed at my feet. I had no need to fear, however. The fork was exactly across the small of the creature's neck, and it could not raise its head to strike me. Large as it was, there was no danger from anything but its fangs; for the *crotalus*, unlike serpents of the genus *constrictor*, possesses but a very feeble power of compression.

Gabriel had gone off among the bushes, and in a few minutes I saw him returning. He carried in his hand a plant which, as before, he had pulled up by the roots. Like the former, it was a herbaceous plant, but of a very different appearance. The leaves of this one were heart-shaped and acuminate, its stem sinuous, and its flowers of a dark purple colour.

As the black approached, I saw that he was chewing some parts both of the leaves and root. What did he mean to do?

I was not left long in suspense. As soon as he had arrived upon the ground, he stooped down, and spat a quantity of the juice over the head of the snake. Then, taking the sapling out of my hand, he plucked it up and flung it away.

To my dismay, the snake was now set free; and I lost no time in springing backward, and mounting upon the log.

Not so my companion, who once more stooped down, caught hold of the hideous reptile, fearlessly raised it from the ground, and flung it around his neck as coolly as if it had been a piece of rope!

The snake made no effort to bite him. Neither did it seem desirous of escaping from his grasp. It appeared rather to be stupefied, and without the power of doing injury!

After playing with it for some moments, the Bambarra threw it back to the ground. Even there it made no effort to escape!

The charmer now turned to me, and said, in a tone of triumph, "Now, mass' Edward, you shall hab rebenge. Look at dis!"

As he spoke he pressed his thumb against the fauces of the serpent, until its mouth stood wide open. I could plainly see its terrible fangs and poison glands. Then, holding its head close up to his lips, he injected the dark saliva into its throat, and once more flung it to the ground. Up to this time he had used no violence—nothing that would have killed a creature so retentive of life as a snake; and I still expected to see the reptile make its escape. Not so, however. It made no effort to move from the spot, but lay stretched out in loose irregular folds, without any perceptible motion beyond a slight quivering of the body. In less than two minutes after, this motion ceased and the snake had all the appearance of being dead!

"It am dead, mass'," replied the black to my inquiring glance, "dead as Julium Caesar."

"And what is this plant, Gabriel?"

"Ah, dat is a great yerb, mass'; dat is a scace plant—a berry scace plant. Eat some ob dat—no snake bite you, as you jes seed. Dat is de plant ob de *snake-charmer*."

The botanical knowledge of my sable companion went no farther. In after years, however, I was enabled to classify his "charm," which was no other than the *Aristolochia serpentaria*—a species closely allied to the "bejuco de guaco," that alexipharmic rendered so celebrated by the pens of Mutis and Humboldt.

My companion now desired me to chew some of the roots; for though he had every confidence in the other remedy, he deemed it no harm to make assurance doubly sure. He extolled the virtues of the new-found plant, and told me he should have administered it instead of the seneca root, but he had despaired of finding it—as it was of much more rare occurrence in that part of the country.

I eagerly complied with his request, and swallowed some of the juice. Like the seneca root, it tasted hot and pungent, with something of the flavour of spirits of camphor. But the polygala is quite inodorous, while the guaco gives forth a strong aromatic smell, resembling valerian.

I had already experienced relief—this would have given it to me almost instantaneously. In a very short time time the swelling completely subsided; and had it not been for the binding around my wrist, I should have forgotten that I had been wounded.

Chapter Thirty Seven
Killing a Trail

An hour or more we had spent since entering the glade—now no longer terrible. Once more its flowers looked bright, and their perfume had recovered its sweetness. Once more the singing of the birds and the hum of the insect-world fell soothingly upon my ears; and there, as before, sat the pretty doves, still repeating their soft "co-co-a"—the endearing expression of their loves.

I could have lingered long in the midst of this fair scene—long have enjoyed its sylvan beauty; but the intellectual must over yield to the physical. I felt sensations of hunger, and soon the appetite began to distress me. Where was I to obtain relief from this pain—where obtain food? I could not ask my companion to guide me to the plantations, now that I knew the risk he would run in so doing. I knew that it really was as he had stated—*the loss of an arm, perhaps of life, should he be caught*. There was but little hope of mercy for him—the less so as he had no master with power to protect him, and who might be *interested* in his not being thus crippled!

By approaching the open country on the edge of the clearings, he would not only run the hazard of being seen, but, what he feared still more, being *tracked by hounds*! This mode of searching for "runaways" was not uncommon, and there were even white men base enough to follow it as a calling! So learnt I from my companion. His information was afterwards confirmed *by my own experience*!

I was hungry—what was to be done? I could not find my way alone. I might again get lost, and have to spend the night in the swamp. What had I best do?

I appealed to my companion. He had been silent for some time—busy with his thoughts. They were running on the same subject as my own. The brave fellow had not forgotten me.

"Jes what dis nigga am thinkin' 'bout," replied he. "Well, mass'," he continued, "when sun go down, den I guide you safe—no fear den. Gabr'l take you close to de Lebee road. Mass' must wait till sun go down."

"But—"

"Mass' hungry?" inquired he, interrupting me.

I assented.

"Jes thot so. Dar's nuffin' yeer to eat 'cept dis ole snake. Mass' no care to eat snake: dis nigga eat 'im. Cook 'im at night, when smoke ob de fire not seen ober de woods. Got place to cook 'im, mass' see. Gabr'l truss mass' Edwad. He take him to caboose ob de runaway."

He had already cut off the head of the reptile while he was talking; and having pinned neck and tail together with a sharp stick, he lifted the glittering body, and flinging it over his shoulders, stood ready to depart.

"Come, now, mass'," continued he, "come 'long wi' Ole Gabe; he find you somethin' to eat."

So saying, he turned round and walked off into the bushes.

I took up my gun and followed. I could not do better. To have attempted to find my own way back to the clearings might again have resulted in failure, since I had twice failed. I had nothing to hurry me back. It would be quite as well if I returned to the village after night—the more prudent course, in fact—as then my mud-bedaubed and blood-stained habiliments would be less likely to attract attention; and this I desired to avoid. I was contented, therefore, to follow the runaway to his "lair," and share it with him till after sunset.

For some hundred yards he led on in silence. His eyes wandered around the forest, as though he was seeking for something. They were not directed upon the ground, but upward to the trees; and, therefore, I know it was not the path he was in search of.

A slight exclamation escaped him, and, suddenly turning in his tracks, he struck off in a direction different to that we had been following. I walked after; and now saw that he had halted by a tall tree, and was looking up among its branches.

The tree was the frankincense, or loblolly pine (*Pinus toeda*). That much of botany I knew. I could tell the species by the large spinous cones and light-green needles. Why had he stopped there?

"Mass' Edwad soon see," he said, in answer to my interrogatory. "Please, mass'," he continued, "hold de snake a bit—don't let um touch de groun'—dam dogs dey smell um!"

I relieved him of his burden; and, holding it as he desired, stood watching him in silence.

The loblolly pine grows with a straight, naked shaft and pyramidal head, often without branches, to the height of fifty feet. In this case, however, several fronds stood out from the trunk, at less than twenty feet from the ground. These were loaded with large green cones, full five inches in length; and it appeared to be these that my companion desired to obtain—though for what purpose I had not the remotest idea.

After a while he procured a long pole; and with the end of this knocked down several of the cones, along with pieces of the branchlets to which they adhered.

As soon as he believed he had a sufficient quantity for his purpose, he desisted, and flung the pole away.

What next? I watched with increasing interest.

He now gathered up both the cones and the adhering spray; but to my surprise he flung the former away. It was not the cones, then, he wanted, but the young shoots that grew on the very tops of the branches. These were of a brownish-red colour, and thickly coated with resin—for the *Pinus taeda* is more resinous than any tree of its kind—emitting a strong aromatic odour, which has given to it one of its trivial names.

Having collected the shoots until he had both hands full, my guide now bent down, and rubbed the resin over both the soles and upper surface of his coarse brogans. He then advanced to where I stood, stooped down again, and treated my boots to a similar polishing!

"Now, mass', all right—de dam, blood-dogs no scent Ole Gabe now—dat *hill de trail*. Come, mass' Edwad, come 'long."

Saying this, he again shouldered the snake and started off, leaving me to follow in his tracks.

Chapter Thirty Eight
The Pirogue

We soon after entered the *cyprière*. There the surface was mostly without underwood. The black taxodiums, standing thickly, usurped the ground, their umbellated crowns covered with hoary epiphytes, whose pendulous drapery shut out the sun, that would otherwise have nourished on that rich soil a luxuriant herbaceous vegetation. But we were now within the limits of the annual inundation; and but few plants can thrive there.

After a while I could see we were approaching a stagnant water. There was no perceptible descent, but the dank damp odour of the swamp, the noise of the piping frogs, the occasional scream of some wading bird, or the bellowing of the alligator, admonished me that some constant water—some lake or pond—was near.

We were soon upon its margin. It was a large pond, though only a small portion of it came under the eye; for, as far as I could see, the cypress-trees grew up out of the water, their huge buttresses spreading out so as almost to touch each other! Here and there the black "knees" protruded above the surface, their fantastic shapes suggesting the idea of horrid water-demons, and lending a supernatural character to the scene. Thus canopied over, the water looked black as ink, and the atmosphere felt heavy and oppressive. The picture was one from which Dante might have drawn ideas for his "Inferno."

On arriving near this gloomy pond, my guide came to a stop. A huge tree that had once stood near the edge had fallen, and in such a position that its top extended far out into the water. Its branches were yet undecayed, and the parasites still clung to them in thick tufts, giving the whole the appearance of a mass of hay loosely thrown together. Part of this was under water, but a still larger portion remained above the surface, high and dry. It was at the root of this fallen tree that my guide had halted.

He remained but a moment, waiting only till I came up.

As soon as I had reached the spot, he mounted upon the trunk; and, beckoning me to follow him, walked along the log in the direction of its top. I climbed up, and balancing myself as well as I could, followed him out into the water.

On reaching the head of the tree, we entered among the thick limbs; and, winding around these, kept still farther towards the top branches. I expected that there we should reach our resting-place.

At length my companion came to a stop, and I now saw, to my astonishment, a small "pirogue" resting upon the water, and hidden under the moss! So completely was it concealed, that it was not possible to have seen it from any point except that where we now stood.

"This, then," thought I, "is the object for which we have crawled out upon the tree."

The sight of the pirogue led me to conjecture that we had farther to go. The black now loosed the canoe from its moorings, and beckoned me to get in.

I stepped into the frail craft and sat down. My companion followed, and, laying hold of the branches, impelled the vessel outward till it was clear of the tops of the tree. Then, seizing the paddle, under its repeated strokes we passed silently over the gloomy surface of the water.

For the first two or three hundred yards our progress was but slow. The cypress knees, and huge "buttocks" of the trees, stood thickly in the way, and it was necessary to observe some caution in working the pirogue through among them. But I saw that my companion well understood the *manège* of his craft, and wielded a "paddle" with the skill of a Chippewa. He had the reputation of being a great "'coon-hunter" and "bayou fisherman;" and in these pursuits no doubt he had picked up his canoe-craft.

It was the most singular voyage I had ever made. The pirogue floated in an element that more resembled ink than water. Not a ray of sun glanced across our path. The darkness of twilight was above and around us.

We glided along shadowy aisles, and amidst huge black trunks that rose like columns supporting a canopy of close-woven fronds. From this vegetable root hung the mournful *bromelia*, sometimes drooping down to the very surface of the water, so as to sweep our faces and shoulders as we passed under it.

We were not the only living things. Even this hideous place had its denizens. It was the haunt and secure abode of the great *saurian*, whose horrid form could be distinguished in the gloom, now crawling along some prostrate trunk, now half mounted upon the protruding knees of the cypresses, or swimming with slow and stealthy stroke through the black liquid. Huge water-snakes could be seen, causing a tiny ripple as they passed from tree to tree, or lying coiled upon the projecting buttocks. The swamp-owl hovered on silent wing, and large brown bats pursued their insect prey. Sometimes these came near, fluttering in our very faces, so that we could perceive the mephitic odour of their bodies, while their horny jaws gave forth a noise like the clinking of castanets.

The novelty of the scene interested me; but I could not help being impressed with a slight feeling of awe. Classic memories, too, stirred within me. The fancies of the Roman poet were here realised. I was upon the Styx, and in my rower I recognised the redoubtable Charon.

Suddenly a light broke through the gloom. A few more strokes of the paddle, and the pirogue shot out into the bright sunlight. What a relief!

I now beheld a space of open water,—a sort of circular lake. It was in reality the lake, for what we had been passing over was but the inundation; and at certain seasons this portion covered with forest became almost dry. The open water, on the contrary, was constant, and too deep even for the swamp-loving cypress to grow in it.

The space thus clear of timber was not of very large extent,—a surface of half-a-mile or so. On all sides it was enclosed by the moss-draped forest that rose around it, like a grey wall; and in the very centre grew a clump of the same character, that in the distance appeared to be an island.

This solitary tarn was far from being silent. On the contrary, it was a scene of stirring life. It seemed the rendezvous for the many species of wild winged creatures that people the great *marais* of Louisiana. There were the egrets, the ibises—both white and scarlet—the various species of *Ardeidae*, the cranes, and the red flamingoes. There, too, was the singular and rare darter, swimming with body immersed, and snake-like head just appearing above the water; and there were the white unwieldy forms of the tyrant pelicans standing on the watch for their finny prey. Swimming birds speckled the surface; various species of *Anatidae*—swans, geese, and ducks,—while the air was filled with flights of gulls and curlews, or was cut by the strong whistling wings of the mallards.

Other than waterfowl had chosen this secluded spot for their favourite dwelling-place. The osprey could be seen wheeling about in the air, now shooting down like a star upon the unfortunate fish that had approached too near the surface, and anon yielding up his prey to the tyrant *Haliaetus*. Such were the varied forms of feathered creatures that presented themselves to my eye on entering this lonely lake of the woods.

I looked with interest upon the scene. It was a true scene of nature, and made a vivid impression upon me at the moment. Not so with my companion, to whom it was neither novel nor interesting. It was an old picture to his eyes, and he saw it from a different point of view. He did not stay to look at it, but, lightly dipping his paddle, pressed the pirogue on in the direction of the island.

A few strokes carried us across the open water, and the canoe once more entered under the shadow of trees. But to my surprise, *there was no island*! What I had taken for an island was but a single cypress-tree, that grew upon a spot where the lake was shallow. Its branches extending on every side were loaded with the hoary parasites that drooped down to the very surface of the water, and shadowed a space of half an acre in extent. Its trunk rested upon a base of enormous dimensions. Huge buttresses flanked it on every side, slanting out into the water and rising along its stem to a height of many yards, the whole mass appearing as large as an ordinary cabin. Its sides were indented with deep bays; and, as we approached under the screen, I could perceive a dark cavity which showed that this singular "buttock" was hollow within.

The bow of the pirogue was directed into one of the bays, and soon struck against the tree. I saw several steps cut into the wood, and leading to the cavity above. My companion pointed to these steps. The screaming of the startled birds prevented me from hearing what he said, but I saw that it was a sign for me to mount upward. I hastened to obey his direction; and, climbing out of the canoe, sprawled up the sloping ridge.

At the top was the entrance, just large enough to admit the body of a man; and, pressing through this, I stood inside the hollow tree.

We had reached our destination—I was in the *lair of the runaway*!

Chapter Thirty Nine
The Tree-Cavern

The interior was dark, and it was some time before I could distinguish any object. Presently my eyes became accustomed to the sombre light, and I was enabled to trace the outlines of this singular tree-cavern.

Its dimensions somewhat astonished me. A dozen men could have been accommodated in it, and there was ample room for that number either sitting or standing. In fact, the whole pyramidal mass which supported the tree was nothing more than a thin shell, all the heart having perished by decay. The floor, by the falling of this *débris* of rotten wood, was raised above the level of the water, and felt firm and dry underfoot. Near its centre I could perceive the ashes and half-burnt embers of an extinct fire; and along one side was strewed a thick covering of dry *tillandsia*, that had evidently been used as a bed. An old blanket lying upon the moss gave further testimony that this was its purpose.

There was no furniture. A rude block,—a cypress knee that had been carried there—formed, the only substitute for a chair, and there was nothing to serve for a table. He who had made this singular cave his residence required no luxuries to sustain him. Necessaries, however, he had provided. As my eyes grew more accustomed to the light, I could make out a number of objects I had not at first seen. An earthen cooking-pot, a large water gourd, a tin cup, an old axe, some fishing-tackle, and one or two coarse rags of clothing. What interested me more than all these was the sight of several articles that were *eatable*. There was a good-sized "chunk" of cooked pork, a gigantic "pone" of corn-bread, several boiled ears of maize, and the better half of a roast fowl. All these lay together upon a large wooden dish, rudely carved from the wood of the tulip-tree—of such a fashion as I had often observed about the cabins of the negro quarter. Beside this dish lay several immense egg-shaped bodies of dark-green colour, with other smaller ones of a yellow hue. These were water and musk melons,—not a bad prospect for a dessert.

I had made this reconnoissance while my companion was engaged in fastening his pirogue to the tree. I had finished my survey as he entered.

"Now, mass'," said he, "dis am ole Gabe's nest; de dam man-hunter no found 'im yeer."

"Why, you are quite at home here, Gabriel! How did you ever find such a place?"

"Lor', mass', knowd it long time. He not de fust darkie who hid in dis old cypress,—nor de fust time for Gabr'l neider. He runaway afore,—dat war when he libbed with Mass' Hicks, 'fore ole mass' bought him. He nebber had 'casion to run away from old Mass 'Sançon. He good to de brack folks, and so war Mass Antoine—he good too, but now de poor nigga can't stan no longer; de new oberseer, he flog hard,—he flog till do blood come,—he use de cobbin board, an dat pump, an de red cowhide, an de wagon whip,— ebberything he use,—dam! I nebber go back,—nebber!"

"But how do you intend to live? you can't always exist in this way. Where will you get your provisions?"

"Nebber fear, mass' Edwad, always get nuff to eat; no fear for dat. Da poor runaway hab some friend on de plantations. Beside he steal nuff to keep 'im 'live—hya! hya!"

"Oh!"

"Gabr'l no need steal now, 'ceptin' de roasting yeers and de millyuns. See! what Zip fetch im! Zip come las night to de edge ob de woods an' fetch all dat plunder. But, mass', you 'skoose me. Forgot you am hungry. Hab some pork some chicken. Chloe cook 'em—is good—you eat."

So saying he set the wooden platter with its contents before me; and the conversation was now interrupted, as both myself and my companion attacked the viands with right good-will.

The "millyuns" constituted a delicious dessert, and for a full half-hour we continued to fight against the appetite of hunger. We conquered it at length, but not until the store of the runaway had been greatly reduced in bulk.

After dinner we sat conversing for a long time. We were not without the soothing nicotian weed. My companion had several bunches of dry tobacco-leaf among his stores; and a corn-cob with a piece of cane-joint served for a pipe, through which the smoke was inhaled with all the aromatic fragrance of the costliest Havanna.

Partly from gratitude for the saving of my life, I had grown to feel a strong interest in the runaway, and his future prospects became the subject of our converse. He had formed no plan of escape—though some thoughts of an attempt to reach Canada or Mexico, or to get off in a ship by New Orleans, had passed through his mind.

A plan occurred to me, though I did not communicate it to him, as I might never be able to carry it out. I begged of him, however, not to leave his present abode until I could see him again, promising that I should do what I could to find him a kinder master.

He readily agreed to my proposal; and as it was now sunset, I made preparations for my departure from the lake.

A signal was agreed upon, so that when I should return to visit him, he could bring the pirogue to ferry me across; and this being arranged, we once more entered the canoe, and set out for the plantations.

We soon recrossed the lake; and, leaving the little boat safely moored by the fallen tree, started off through the woods. The path, with Gabriel for my guide, was now easy; and at intervals, as we went along, he directed my attention to certain blazes upon the trees, and other marks by which I should know it again.

In less than an hour after, we parted on the edge of the clearings—he going to some rendezvous already appointed—whilst I kept on to the village, the road to which now ran between parallel fences that rendered it impossible for me to go astray.

Chapter Forty
Hotel Gossip

It was yet early when I entered the village. I glided stealthily through the streets, desirous to avoid observation. Unfortunately I had to pass through the bar of the hotel in order to reach my room. It was just before the hour of supper, and the guests had assembled in the bar saloon and around the porch.

My tattered habiliments, in places stained with blood, and profusely soiled with mud, could not escape notice; nor did they. Men turned and gazed after me. Loiterers looked with eyes that expressed their astonishment. Some in the portico, and others in the bar, hailed me as I passed, asking me where I had been to. One cried out: "Hillow, mister! you've had a tussle with the cats: hain't you?"

I did not make reply. I pushed on up-stairs, and found relief in the privacy of my chamber.

I had been badly torn by the bushes. My wounds needed dressing. I despatched a messenger for Reigart. Fortunately he was at home, and in a few minutes followed my messenger to the hotel. He entered my room, and stood staring at me with a look of surprise.

"My dear R—, where have you been?" he inquired at length.

"To the swamp."

"And those wounds—your clothes torn—blood?"

"Thorn-scratches—that's all."

"But where have you been?"

"In the swamp."

"In the swamp! but how came you to get such a mauling?"

"I have been bitten by a rattlesnake."

"What! bitten by a rattlesnake? Do you speak seriously?"

"Quite true it is—but I have taken the antidote. I am cured."

"Antidote! Cured! And what cure? who gave you an antidote?"

"A friend whom I met in the swamp!"

"A friend in the swamp!" exclaimed Reigart, his astonishment increasing.

I had almost forgotten the necessity of keeping my secret. I saw that I had spoken imprudently. Inquisitive eyes were peeping in at the door. Ears were listening to catch every sound.

Although the inhabitant of the Mississippi is by no means of a curious disposition—*malgré* the statements of gossiping tourists—the unexplained and forlorn appearance I presented on my return was enough to excite a degree of interest even among the most apathetic people; and a number of the guests of the hotel had gathered in the lobby around the door of my chamber, and were eagerly asking each other what had happened to me. I could overhear their conversation, though they did not know it.

"He's been fightin' a painter?" said one, interrogatively.

"A painter or a bar," answered another.

"'Twur some desprit varmint anyhow—it hez left its mark on him,—that it hez."

"It's the same fellow that laid out Bully Bill: ain't it?"

"The same," replied some one.

"English, ain't he?"

"Don't know. He's a Britisher, I believe. English, Irish, or Scotch, he's a hull team an' a cross dog under the wagon. By God! he laid out Bully Bill straight as a fence-rail, wi' nothin' but a bit o' a whup, and then tuk Bill's pistols away from him! Ha! ha! ha!"

"Jehosophat!"

"He's jest a feller to whip his weight in wild-cats. He's killed the catamount, I reckon."

"No doubt he's done that."

I had supposed that my encounter with Bully Bill had made me enemies among his class. It was evident from the tone and tenor of their conversation that such was not the case. Though, perhaps, a little piqued that a stranger—a mere youth as I then was—should have conquered one of their bullies, these backwoodsmen are not intensely clannish, and Bully Bill was no favourite. Had I "whipped" him on any other grounds, I should have gained a positive popularity by the act. But in defence of a slave—and I a foreigner—a Britisher, too—that was a presumption not to be pardoned. That was the drawback on my victory, and henceforth I was likely to be a "marked man" in the neighbourhood.

These observations had served to amuse me while I was awaiting the arrival of Reigart, though, up to a certain point, I took but little interest in them. A remark that now reached my ears, however, suddenly changed the nature of my thoughts. It was this:—

"He's after Miss Besançon, they say."

I was now interested. I stepped to the door, and, placing my ear close to the keyhole, listened.

"I guess he's arter *the plantation*," said another; and the remark was followed by a significant laugh.

"Well, then," rejoined a voice, in a more solemn and emphatic tone, "he's after what he won't get."

"How? how?" demanded several.

"He may get *thee* lady, preehaps," continued the same voice, in the same measured tones; "but not *thee* plantation."

"How? What do you mean, Mr Moxley?" again demanded the chorus of voices.

"I mean what I say, gentlemen," replied the solemn speaker; and then repeated again his former words in a like measured drawl. "He may get the lady, *pree*haps, but not *thee* plantation."

"Oh! the report's true, then?" said another voice, interrogatively. "Insolvent? Eh? Old Gayarre—"

"Owns *thee* plantation."

"And niggers?"

"Every skin o' them; the sheriff will take possession to-morrow."

A murmur of astonishment reached my ears. It was mingled with expressions of disapprobation or sympathy.

"Poor girl! it's a pity o' *her*!"

"Well, it's no wonder. She made the money fly since the old 'un died."

"Some say he didn't leave so much after all. 'Twar most part mortgaged before—"

The entrance of the doctor interrupted this conversation, and relieved me for the moment from the torture which it was inflicting upon me.

"A friend in the swamp, did you say?" again interrogated Reigart.

I had hesitated to reply, thinking of the crowd by the door. I said to the doctor in a low earnest voice—

"My dear friend, I have met with an adventure; am badly scratched, as you see. Dress my wounds, but do not press me for details. I have my reasons for being silent. You will one day learn all, but not now. Therefore—"

"Enough, enough!" said the doctor, interrupting me; "do not be uneasy. Let me look at your scratches."

The good doctor became silent, and proceeded to the dressing of my wounds.

Under other circumstances the manipulation of my wounds, for they now felt painful, might have caused me annoyance. It did not then. What I had just heard had produced a feeling within that neutralised the external pain, and I felt it not.

I was really in mental agony.

I burned with impatience to question Reigart about the affairs of the plantation,—about Eugénie and Aurore. I could not,—we were not alone. The landlord of the hotel and a negro attendant had entered the room, and were assisting the doctor in his operations. I could not trust myself to speak on such a subject in their presence. I was forced to nurse my impatience until all was over, and both landlord and servant had left us.

"Now, doctor, this news of Mademoiselle Besançon?"

"Do *you* not know all?"

"Only what I have heard this moment from those gossips outside the room."

I detailed to Reigart the remarks that had been made.

"Really I thought you must have been acquainted with the whole matter. I had fancied that to be the cause of your long absence to-day; though I did not even conjecture how you might be engaged in the matter."

"I know nothing more than what I have thus accidentally overheard. For heaven's sake tell me all! Is it true?"

"Substantially true, I grieve to say."

"Poor Eugénie!"

"The estate was heavily mortgaged to Gayarre. I have long suspected this, and fear there has been some foul play. Gayarre has foreclosed the mortgage, and, indeed, it is said, is already in possession. Everything is now his."

"Everything?"

"Everything upon the plantation."

"The slaves?"

"Certainly."

"All—all—and—and—Aurore?"

I hesitated as I put the interrogatory, Reigart had no knowledge of my attachment to Aurore.

"The quadroon girl, you mean?—of course, she with the others. She is but a slave like the rest. She will be sold."

"*But a slave! sold with the rest!*"

This reflection was not uttered aloud.

I cannot describe the tumult of my feelings as I listened. The blood was boiling within my veins, and I could scarce restrain myself from some wild expression. I strove to the utmost to hide my thoughts, but scarce succeeded; for I noticed that the usually cold eye of Reigart was kindled in surprise at my manner. If he divined my secret he was generous, for he asked no explanation.

"The slaves are all to be sold then?" I faltered out.

"No doubt,—everything will be sold,—that is the law in such cases. It is likely Gayarre will buy in the whole estate, as the plantation lies contiguous to his own."

"Gayarre! villain! oh! And Mademoiselle Besançon, what will become of her? Has she no friends?"

"I have heard something of an aunt who has some, though not much, property. She lives in the city. It is likely that Mademoiselle will live with her in future. I believe the aunt has no children of her own, and Eugénie will inherit. This, however, I cannot vouch for. I know it only as a rumour."

Reigart spoke these words in a cautious and reserved manner. I noticed something peculiar in the tone in which he uttered them; but I knew his reason for being cautious. He was under a mistaken impression as to the feelings with which I regarded Eugénie! I did not undeceive him.

"Poor Eugénie! a double sorrow,—no wonder at the change I had observed of late,—no wonder she appeared sad!"

All this was but my own silent reflections.

"Doctor!" said I, elevating my voice; "I must go to the plantation."

"Not to-night!"

"To-night,—now!"

"My dear Mr E., you must not."

"Why?"

"It is impossible,—I cannot permit it,—you will have a fever; it may cost you your life!"

"But—"

"I cannot hear you. I assure you, you are now on the verge of a fever. You must remain in your room—at least, until to-morrow. Perhaps then you may go out with safety. Now it is impossible."

I was compelled to acquiesce, though I am not certain but that had I taken my own way it would have been better for my "fever." Within me was a *cause of fever* much stronger than any exposure to the night air. My throbbing heart and wildly-coursing blood soon acted upon my brain.

"Aurore the slave of Gayarre! Ha! ha! ha! His slave! Gayarre! Aurore! ha! ha! ha! Is it his throat I clutch? ha, no! It is the serpent! here—help—help! Water! water! I am choking. No, Gayarre is! I have him now! Again it is the serpent! O God! it coils around my throat—it strangles me! Help! Aurore! lovely Aurore! do not yield to him!"

"I will die rather than yield!"

"I thought so, noble girl! I come to release you! How she struggles in his grasp! Fiend! off—off, fiend! Aurore, you are free—free! Angels of heaven!"

Such was my dream,—the dream of a fevered brain.

Chapter Forty One
The Letter

During all the night my sleep was broken at intervals, and the hours divided between dreaming and half delirium.

I awoke in the morning not much refreshed with my night's rest. I lay for some time passing over in my mind the occurrences of yesterday, and considering what course I should pursue.

After a time I determined upon going direct to the plantation, and learning for myself how matters stood there.

I arose with this intention. As I was dressing, my eye fell upon a letter that lay upon the table. It bore no postmark, but the writing was in a female hand, and I guessed whence it came.

I tore open the seal, and read:—

"*Monsieur!*

"*To-day, by the laws of Louisiana, I am a woman,—and none more unhappy in all the land. The same sun that has risen upon the natal day of my majority looks down upon the ruin of my fortune!*

"*It was my design to have made you happy: to have proved that I am not ungrateful. Alas! it is no longer in my power. I am, no more the proprietor of the plantation Besançon,—no more the mistress of Aurore! All is gone from me, and Eugénie Besançon is now a beggar. Ah, Monsieur! it is a sad tale, and I know not what will be its end.*

"*Alas! there are griefs harder to bear than the loss of fortune. That may in time be repaired, but the anguish of unrequited love,—love strong, and single, and pure, as mine is,—must long endure, perchance for ever!*

"*Know, Monsieur, that in the bitter cup it is my destiny to drink, there is not one drop of jealousy or reproach. I alone have made the misery that is my portion.*

"*Adieu, Monsieur! adieu, and farewell! It is better we should never meet again. O be happy! no plaint of mine shall ever reach your ear, to cloud the sunshine of your happiness. Henceforth the walls of* Sacré Coeur *shall alone witness the sorrows of the unfortunate but grateful.*

"Eugénie."

The letter was dated the day before. I knew that that was the birthday of the writer; in common parlance, the day on which she was "of age."

"Poor Eugénie!" reflected I. "Her happiness has ended with her girlhood. Poor Eugénie!"

The tears ran fast over my cheeks as I finished reading. I swept them hastily away, and ringing the bell I ordered my horse to be saddled. I hurried through with my toilet; the horse was soon brought to the door; and, mounting him, I rode rapidly for the plantation.

Shortly after leaving the village, I passed two men, who were also on horseback—going in the same direction as myself, but riding at a slower pace than I. They were dressed in the customary style of planters, and a casual observer might have taken them for such. There was something about them, however, that led me to think they were not planters, nor merchants, nor men whose calling relates to any of the ordinary industries of life. It was not in their dress I saw this something, but in a certain expression of countenance. This expression I cannot well describe, but I have ever noticed it in the faces and features of men who have anything to do with the execution of the laws. Even in America, where distinctive costume and badge are absent, I have been struck with this peculiarity,—so much so that I believe I could detect a detective in the plainest clothes.

The two men in question had this expression strongly marked. I had no doubt they were in some way connected with the execution of the laws. I had no doubt they were constables or sheriff's officers. With such a slight glance as I gave to them in passing, I might not have troubled myself with this conjecture, had it not been for other circumstances then in my thoughts.

I had not saluted these men; but as I passed, I could perceive that my presence was not without interest to them. On glancing back, I saw that one of them had ridden close up to the other, that they were conversing earnestly; and from their gestures I could tell that I was the subject of their talk.

I had soon ridden far ahead, and ceased to think any more about them.

I had hurried forward without any preconceived plan of action. I had acted altogether on the impulse of the moment, and thought only of reaching the house, and ascertaining the state of affairs, either from Eugénie or Aurore herself.

Thus *impromptu* I had reached the borders of the plantation.

It now occurred to me to ride more slowly, in oder to gain a few moments to manage my thoughts. I even halted awhile. There was a slight bend in the river-bank, and the road crossed this like a chord to its arc. The part cut off was a piece of waste—a common—and as there was no fence I forsook the road, and walked my horse out on the river-bank. There I drew up, but remained seated in my saddle.

I endeavoured to sketch out some plan of action. What should I say to Eugénie? what to Aurore? Would the former see me after what she had written? In her note she had said "farewell," but it was not a time to stand upon punctilious ceremony. And if not, should I find an opportunity to speak with Aurore? I *must* see *her*. Who should prevent me? I had much to say to her; my heart was full. Nothing but an interview with my betrothed could relieve it.

Still without any definite plan, I once more turned my horse's head down the river, used the spur, and galloped onward.

On arriving near the gate I was somewhat surprised to see two saddled horses standing there. I instantly recognised them as the horses I had passed on the road. They had overtaken me again while I was halted by the bend of the river, and had arrived at the gate before me. The saddles were now empty. The riders had gone into the house.

A black man was holding the horses. It was my old friend "Zip."

I rode up, and without dismounting addressed myself to Scipio. Who were they who had gone in?

I was hardly surprised at the answer. My conjecture was right. They were men of the law,—the deputy sheriff of the *parish* and his assistant.

It was scarce necessary to inquire their *business*. I guessed that.

I only asked Scipio the details.

Briefly Scipio gave them; at least so far as I allowed him to proceed without interruption. A sheriff's officer was in charge of the house and all its contents; Larkin still ruled the negro quarter, but the slaves were all to be sold; Gayarre was back and forward; and *"Missa 'Génie am gone away."*

"Gone away! and whither?"

"Don't know, mass'r. B'lieve she gone to de city. She leab last night in de night-time."

"And—"

I hesitated a moment till my heart should still its heavy throbbings.

"Aurore?" I interrogated with an effort.

"'Rore gone too, mass'r;—she gone long wi' Missa 'Génie."

"Aurore gone!"

"Yes, mass'r, she gone; daat's de troof."

I was astounded by the information, as well as puzzled by this mysterious departure. Eugénie gone and in the night! Aurore gone with her! What could it mean? Whither had they gone?

My reiterated appeal to the black threw no light upon the subject. He was ignorant of all their movements,—ignorant of everything but what related to the negro quarter. He had heard that himself, his wife, his daughter,—"the leetle Chloe,"—with all their fellow-slaves, were to be carried down to the city, and to be sold in the slave-market by auction. They were to be taken the following day. They were already advertised. That was all he knew. No, not all,—one other piece of information he had in store for me. It was authentic: he had heard the "white folks" talk of it to one another:—Larkin, Gayarre, and a "negro-trader," who was to be concerned in this sale. It regarded the quadroon. *She was to be sold among the rest*!

The blood boiled in my veins as the black imparted this information. It was authentic. Scipio's statement of what he had heard, minutely detailed, bore the internal evidence of authenticity. I could not doubt the report. I felt the conviction that it was true.

The plantation Besançon had no more attractions. I had no longer any business at Bringiers. New Orleans was now the scene of action for me!

With a kind word to Scipio, I wheeled my horse and galloped away from the gate. The fiery animal caught my excitement, and sprang wildly along the road. It required all his buoyant spirit to keep pace with the quick dancing of my nerves.

In a few minutes I had consigned him to his groom; and, climbing to my chamber, commenced preparing for my departure.

Chapter Forty Two
The Wharf-Boat

I now only waited a boat to convey me to New Orleans. I knew that I should not have long to wait. The annual epidemic was on the decline, and the season of business and pleasure in the "Crescent City" was about commencing. Already the up-river steamers were afloat on all the tributary streams of the mighty Mississippi, laden with the produce of its almost limitless valley, and converging towards the great Southern entrepôt of American commerce. I might expect a "down-boat" every day, or rather indeed every hour.

I resolved to take the first boat that came along.

The hotel in which I dwelt, as well as the whole village, stood at a considerable distance from the boat landing. It had been built so from precaution. The banks of the Mississippi at this place, and for a thousand miles above and below, are elevated but a few feet above the surface level of its water; and, in consequence of the continuous detrition, it is no uncommon occurrence for large slips to give way, and be swept off in the red whirling current. It might be supposed that in time this never-ceasing action of the water would widen the stream to unnatural dimensions. But, no. For every encroachment on one bank there is a corresponding formation against the opposite,—a deposit caused by the eddy which the new curve has produced, so that the river thus preserves its original breadth. This remarkable action may be noted from the *embouchure* of the Ohio to the mouth of the Mississippi itself, though at certain points the extent of the encroachment and the formation that neutralises it is much greater than at others. In some places the "wearing away" of the bank operates so rapidly that in a few days the whole site of a village, or even a plantation, may disappear. Not unfrequently, too, during the high spring-floods this eccentric stream takes a "near cut" across the neck of one of its own "bends," and in a few hours a channel is formed, through which pours the whole current of the river. Perhaps a plantation may have been established in the concavity of this bend,—perhaps three or four of them,—and the planter who has gone to sleep under the full belief that he had built his house upon a *continent*, awakes in the morning to find himself the inhabitant of an island! With dismay he beholds the vast volume of red-brown water rolling past, and cutting off his communication with the mainland. He can no longer ride to his neighbouring village without the aid of an expensive ferry. His wagons will no longer serve him to "haul" to market his huge cotton-bales or hogsheads of sugar and tobacco; and, prompted by a feeling of insecurity—lest the next wild sweep of the current may carry himself, his house, and his several hundred half-naked negroes along with it—he flees from his home, and retires to some other part of the stream, where he may deem the land in less danger of such unwelcome intrusion.

In consequence of these eccentricities a safe site for a town is extremely rare upon the Lower Mississippi. There are but few points in the last five hundred miles of its course where natural elevations offer this advantage. The artificial embankment, known as the "Levee," has in some measure remedied the deficiency, and rendered the towns and plantations *comparatively* secure.

As already stated, my hotel was somewhat out of the way. A boat might touch at the landing and be off again without my being warned of it. A down-river-boat, already laden, and not caring to obtain further freight, would not stop long; and in a "tavern" upon the Mississippi you must not confide in the punctuality of "Boots," as you would in a London hotel. Your chances of being waked by Sambo, ten times sleepier than yourself, are scarcely one in a hundred.

I had ample experience of this; and, fearing that the boat might pass if I remained at the hotel, I came to the resolve to settle my affairs in that quarter and at once transport myself and my *impedimenta* to the landing.

I should not be entirely without shelter. There was no house; but an old steamboat, long since condemned as not "river-worthy," lay at the landing. This hulk, moored by strong cables to the bank, formed an excellent floating wharf; while its spacious deck, cabins, and saloons, served as a storehouse for all sorts of merchandise. It was, in fact, used both as a landing and warehouse, and was known as the "wharf-boat."

It was late,—nearly midnight,—as I stepped aboard the wharf-boat. Stragglers from the town, who may have had business there, had all gone away, and the owner of the store-boat was himself absent. A drowsy negro, his *locum tenens*, was the only human thing that offered itself to my eyes. The lower deck of the boat was tenanted by this individual, who sat behind a counter that enclosed one corner of the apartment. Upon this counter stood a pair of scales, with weights, a large ball of coarse twine, a rude knife, and such other implements as may be seen in a country "store;" and upon shelves at the back were ranged bottles of coloured liquors, glasses, boxes of hard biscuit, "Western reserve" cheeses, kegs of rancid butter, plugs of tobacco, and bundles of inferior cigars,—in short, all the etceteras of a regular "grocery." The remaining portion of the ample room was littered with merchandise, packed in various forms. There were boxes, barrels, bags, and bales; some on their way up-stream, that had come by New Orleans from distant lands, while others were destined downward: the rich product of the soil, to be borne thousands of miles over the wide Atlantic. With these various packages every part of the floor was occupied, and I looked in vain for a spot on which to stretch myself. A better light might have enabled me to discover such a place; but the tallow candle, guttering down the sides of an empty champagne-bottle, but dimly lit up the confusion. It just sufficed to guide me to the only occupant of the place, upon whose sombre face the light faintly flickered.

"Asleep, uncle?" I said, approaching him.

A gruff reply from an American negro is indeed a rarity, and never given to a question politely put. The familiar style of my address touched a sympathetic chord in the bosom of the "darkie," and a smile of satisfaction gleamed upon his features as he made answer. Of course he was *not* asleep. But my idle question was only meant as the prelude to further discourse.

"Ah, Gollys! it be massa Edward. Uncle Sam know'd you, massa Edward. You good to brack folk. Wat can do uncle Sam for massa?"

"I am going down to the city, and have come here to wait for a boat. Is it likely one will pass to-night?"

"Sure, massa—sure be a boat dis night. Bossy 'spect a boat from de Red ribber dis berry night—either de Houma or de Choctuma."

"Good! and now, uncle Sam, if you will find me six feet of level plank, and promise to rouse me when the boat comes in sight, I shall not grudge you this half dollar."

The sudden enlargement of the whites of undo Sam's eyes showed the satisfaction he experienced at the sight of the shining piece of metal. Without more ado he seized the champagne-bottle that hold the candle; and, gliding among the boxes and bales, conducted me to a stairway that led to the second or cabin-deck of the boat. We climbed up, and entered the saloon.

"Dar, massa, plenty of room—uncle Sam he sorry dar's ne'er a bed, but if massa could sleep on these yeer coffee-bags, he berry welcome—berry welcome. I leave dis light wi' massa. I can get anoder for self b'low. Good night, massa Edward—don't fear I wake you—no fear ob dat."

And so saying, the kind-hearted black set the bottle-candlestick upon the floor; and, passing down the stair again, left me to my reflections.

With such poor light as the candle afforded, I took a careless survey of my apartment. There was plenty of room, as uncle Sam had said. It was the cabin of the old steamboat; and as the partition-doors had been broken off and carried away, the ladies' cabin, main saloon, and front, were now all in one. Together they formed a hall of more than a hundred feet in length, and from where I stood, near the centre, both ends were lost to my view in the darkness. The state-rooms on each side were still there, with their green Venetian doors. Some of these were shut, while others stood ajar, or quite open. The gilding and ornaments, dim from age and use, adorned the sides and ceiling of the hall; and over the arched entrance of the main saloon the word "Sultana," in gold letters that still glittered brightly, informed me that I was now inside the "carcase" of one of the most famous boats that ever cleft the waters of the Mississippi.

Strange thoughts came into my mind as I stood regarding this desolate saloon. Silent and solitary it seemed—even more so I thought than would some lonely spot in the midst of a forest. The very absence of those sounds that one is accustomed to hear in such a place—the grinding of the machinery—the hoarse detonations of the 'scape-pipe—the voices of men—the busy hum of conversation, or the ringing laugh—the absence of the sights, too—the brilliant chandeliers—the long tables sparkling with crystal—the absence of these, and yet the presence of the scene associated with such sights and sounds—gave to the place an air of indescribable desolation. I felt as one within the ruins of some old convent, or amidst the tombs of an antique cemetery.

No furniture of any kind relieved the monotony of the place. The only visible objects were the coarse gunny-bags strewed over the floor, and upon which uncle Sam had made me welcome to repose myself.

After surveying my odd chamber, and giving way to some singular reflections, I began to think of disposing of myself for sleep. I was wearied. My health was not yet restored. The clean bast of the coffee-bags looked inviting. I dragged half-a-dozen of them together, placed them side by side, and then, throwing myself upon my back, drew my cloak over me. The coffee-berries yielded to the weight of my body, giving me a comfortable position, and in less than five minutes I fell asleep.

Chapter Forty Three
The Norway Rat

I must have slept an hour or more. I did not think of consulting my watch before going to sleep, and I had little thought about such a thing after I awoke. But that I had slept at least an hour, I could tell by the length of my candle.

A fearful hour that was, as any I can remember to have spent—an hour of horrid dreaming. But I am wrong to call it so. It was no dream, though at the time I thought it one.

Listen!

As I have said, I lay down upon my back, covering myself with my ample cloak from the chin to the ankles. My face and feet were alone free. I had placed one of the bags for a pillow, and thus raised my head in such a position, that I had a full view of the rest of my person. The light, set just a little way beyond my heels, was right before my eyes; and I could see the floor in that direction to the distance of several yards. I have said that in five minutes I was asleep. I thought that I was asleep, and to this hour I think so, and yet my eyes were open, and I plainly saw the candle before them and that portion of the floor illumined by its rays. I thought that I endeavoured to close my eyes, but could not; nor could I change my position, but lay regarding the light and the surface of the floor around it. Presently a strange sight was presented to me. A number of small shining objects began to dance and scintillate in the darkness beyond. At first I took them for "lightning-bugs," but although these were plenty enough without, it was not usual to find them inside an enclosed apartment. Moreover, those I saw were low down upon the floor of the saloon, and not suspended in the air, as they should have been.

Gradually the number of these shining objects increased. There were now some dozens of them, and, what was singular, they seemed to move in pairs. They were *not* fire-flies!

I began to experience a sensation of alarm. I began to feel that there was danger in these fiery spots, that sparkled in such numbers along the floor. What on earth could they be?

I had scarce asked myself the question, when I was enabled to answer it to the satisfaction of my senses, but not to the tranquillising of my fears. The horrid truth now flashed upon me—each pair of sparkling points was a *pair of eyes*!

It was no relief to me to know they were the eyes of rats. You may smile at my fears; but I tell you in all seriousness that I would not have been more frightened had I awaked and found a panther crouching to spring upon me. I had heard such tales of these Norway rats—had, in fact, been witness to their bold and ferocious feats in New Orleans, where at that time they swarmed in countless numbers—that the sight of them filled me with disgust and horror. But what was most horrible of all—I saw that they were approaching me—that they were each moment coming nearer and nearer, and that *I was unable to get out of their way*!

Yes. I could not move. My arms and limbs felt like solid blocks of stone, and my muscular power was quite gone! I *now* thought that I was *dreaming*!

"Yes!" reflected I, for I still possessed the power of reflection. "Yes—I am only dreaming! A horrid dream though—horrid—would I could wake myself—'tis nightmare! I know it—if I could but move something—my toes—my fingers—oh!"

These reflections actually passed through my mind. They have done so at other times when I have been under the influence of nightmare; and I now no longer dread this incubus, since I have learnt how to throw it off. *Then* I could not. I lay like one dead, whose eyelids have been left unclosed; and I thought I was dreaming.

Dreaming or awake, my soul had not yet reached its climax of horror. As I continued to gaze, I perceived that the number of the hideous animals increased every moment. I could now see their brown hairy bodies—for they had approached close to the candle, and were full under its light. They were *thick upon the floor*. It appeared to be alive with them, and in motion like water under a gale. Hideous sight to behold!

Still nearer they came. I could distinguish their sharp teeth—the long grey bristles upon their snouts—the spiteful expression in their small penetrating eyes.

Nearer still! They climb upon the coffee-bags—they crawl along my legs and body—they chase each other over the folds of my cloak—they are gnawing at my boots!—Horror! horror! they will devour me!

They are around me in myriads. I cannot see on either side, but I know that they are all around. I can hear their shrill screaming, the air is loaded with the odour of their filthy bodies. I feel as though it will suffocate me. Horror! horror! oh! merciful God! arouse me from this terrible dream!

Such were my thoughts—such my feelings at that moment. I had a perfect consciousness of all that was passing—so perfect that I believed it a dream.

I made every effort to awake myself—to move hand and limb. It was all in vain. I could not move a muscle. Every nerve of my body was asleep. My blood lay stagnant within my veins!

I lay suffering this monstrous pain for a long, long while. I lay in fear of being eaten up piecemeal!

The fierce animals had only attacked my boots and my cloak, but my terror was complete. I waited to feel them at my throat!

Was it my face and my eyes staring open that kept them off? I am certain my eyes were open all the while. Was it that that deterred them from attacking me? No doubt it was. They scrambled over all parts of my body, even up to my breast, but they seemed to avoid my head and face!

Whether they would have continued under the restraint of this salutary fear, I know not, for a sudden termination was put to the horrid scene.

The candle had burnt to its end, and the remnant fell with a hissing sound through the neck of the bottle, thus extinguishing the light.

Frightened by the sudden transition from light to darkness, the hideous animals uttered their terrible squeaking, and broke off in every direction. I could hear the pattering of their feet upon the planks as they scampered away.

The light seemed to have been the spell that bound me in the iron chain of the nightmare. The moment it went out, I found myself again in possession of muscular strength; and, springing to my feet, I caught up my cloak and swept it wildly around me, shouting at the top of my voice.

The cold perspiration was running from every pore in my skin, and my hair felt as if on end. I still believed I was dreaming; and it was not until the astonished negro appeared with a light, and I had evidence of the presence of my hairy visitors in the condition of my cloak and boots, that I was convinced the terrible episode was a reality.

I remained no longer in the "saloon," but, wrapping my cloak around me, betook myself to the open air.

Chapter Forty Four
The Houma

I had not much longer to remain on the wharf-boat. The hoarse barking of a 'scape-pipe fell upon my ear and shortly after the fires of a steamboat furnace appeared, glittering red upon the stream. Then was heard the crashing plunging sound of the paddle-wheels as they beat the brown water, and then the ringing of the bell, and the shouts of command passing from captain to mate, and from mate to "deck hands," and in five minutes after, the "Houma"—Red River-boat,—lay side by side with the old "Sultana."

I stepped aboard, threw my luggage over the guard, and, climbing upstairs, seated myself under the awning.

Ten minutes of apparent confusion—the quick trampling of feet over the decks and staging—half-a-dozen passengers hastening ashore—others hurrying in the opposite direction—the screeching of the steam—the rattling of huge fire-logs thrust endways up the furnace—at intervals the loud words of command—a peal of laughter at some rude jest, or the murmur of voices in the sadder accents of adieu. Ten minutes of these sights and sounds, and again was heard the ringing of the large bell—the signal that the boat was about to continue her course.

I had flung myself into a chair that stood beside one of the awning-posts, and close to the guards. From my position I commanded a view of the gangway, the staging-plank, and the contiguous wharf-boat, which I had just left.

I was looking listlessly on what was passing below, taking note of nothing in particular. If I had a special thought in my mind the subject of it was not there, and the thought itself caused me to turn my eyes away from the busy groups and bend them downward along the left bank of the river. Perhaps a sigh was the concomitant of these occasional glances; but in the intervals between, my mind dwelt upon nothing in particular, and the forms that hurried to and fro impressed me only as shadows.

This apathy was suddenly interrupted. My eyes, by pure accident, fell upon two figures whose movements at once excited my attention. They stood upon the deck of the wharf-boat—not near the stage-plank, where the torch cast its glare over the hurrying passengers, but in a remote corner under the shadow of the awning. I could see them only in an obscure light,—in fact, could scarce make out their forms, shrouded as they were in dark cloaks—but the attitudes in which they stood, the fact of their keeping thus apart in the most obscure quarter of the boat, the apparent earnestness with which they were conversing—all led me to conjecture that they were lovers. My heart, guided by the sweet instinct of love, at once accepted this explanation, and looked for no other.

"Yes—lovers! how happy! No—perhaps not so happy—it is a *parting*! Some youth who makes a trip down to the city—perhaps some young clerk or merchant, who goes to spend his winter there. What of that? He will return in spring, again to press those delicate fingers, again to fold that fair form in his arms, again to speak those tender words that will sound all the sweeter after the long interval of silence.

"Happy youth! happy girl! Light is the misery of a parting like yours! How easy to endure when compared with that violent separation which I have experienced! Aurore!—Aurore!—Would that you were free! Would that you were some high-born dame! Not that I should love you the more—impossible—but then might I boldly woo, and freely win. Then I might hope—but now, alas! this horrid gulf—this social abyss that yawns between us. Well! it cannot separate souls. Our love shall bridge it—Ha!"

"Hilloa, Mister! What's gwine wrong? Anybody fell overboard!"

I heeded not the rude interrogatory. A deeper pang absorbed my soul, forcing from me the wild exclamation that had given the speaker cause.

The two forms parted—with a mutual pressure of the hand, with a kiss they parted! The young man hastened across the staging. I did not observe his face, as he passed under the light. I had taken no notice of *him*, my eyes by some strange fascination remaining fixed upon *her*. I was curious to observe how *she* would act in this final moment of leave-taking.

The planks were drawn aboard. The signal-bell sounded. I could perceive that we were moving away.

At this moment the shrouded form of the lady glided forward into the light. She was advancing to catch a farewell glance of her lover. A few steps brought her to the edge of the wharf-boat, where the torch was glaring. Her hood-like gun-bonnet was thrown back. The light fell full upon her face, glistened along the undulating masses of black hair that shrouded her temples, and danced in her glorious eyes. Good God! they were the eyes of *Aurore*!

No wonder I uttered the wild ejaculation—

"It is she!"

"What?—a female! overboard, do you say? Where? Where?"

The man was evidently in earnest. My soliloquy had been loud enough to reach his ears.

He believed it to be a reply to his previous question, and my excited manner confirmed him in the belief that a woman had actually fallen into the river!

His questions and exclamations were overheard and repeated in the voices of others who stood near. Like wildfire an alarm ran through the boat. Passengers rushed from the cabins, along the guards, and out to the front awning, and mingled their hurried interrogatories, "Who? What? Where?" A loud voice cried out—

"Some one overboard! A woman! it's a woman!"

Knowing the cause of this ridiculous alarm, I gave no heed to it. My mind was occupied with a far different matter. The first shock of a hideous passion absorbed my whole soul, and I paid no attention to what was going on around me.

I had scarce recognised the face, when the boat rounding up-stream brought the angle of the cabin between it and me. I rushed forward, as far as the gangway. I was too late:—the wheel-house obstructed the view. I did not halt, but ran on, directing myself towards the top of the wheel-house. Passengers in their excitement were rushing along the guards. They hindered my progress, and it was some time before I could climb up the wheel-house, and stand upon its rounded roof. I did so at length, but too late. The boat had forged several hundred yards into the stream. I could see the wharf-boat with its glaring lights. I could even see human forms standing along its deck, but I could no longer distinguish that one that my eyes were in search of.

Disappointed I stepped on to the hurricane-deck, which was almost a continuation of the roof of the wheel-house. There I could be alone, and commune with my now bitter thoughts.

I was not to have that luxury just then. Shouts, the trampling of heavy boots bounding over the planks, and the pattering of lighter feet, sounded in my ears; and next moment a stream of passengers, male and female, came pouring up the sides of the wheel-house.

"That's the gentleman—that's him!" cried a voice.

In another instant the excited throng was around me, several inquiring at once—

"Who's overboard? Who? Where?"

Of course I saw that these interrogatories were meant for me. I saw, too, that an answer was necessary to allay their ludicrous alarm.

"Ladies and gentlemen!" I said, "there is no one overboard that I am aware of. Why do you ask *me*?"

"Hilloa, Mister!" cried the cause of all this confusion, "didn't you tell me—?"

"I told you nothing."

"But didn't I ask you if thar wan't some one overboard?"

"You did."

"And you said in reply—"

"I said nothing in reply."

"Darned if you didn't! you said 'Thar she is!' or, 'It was she!' or something o' that sort."

I turned towards the speaker, who I perceived was rather losing credit with his auditory.

"Mister!" said I, imitating his tone, "it is evident you have never heard of the man who grew immensely rich by minding his own business."

My remark settled the affair. It was received by a yell of laughter, that completely discomfited my meddling antagonist, who, after some little swaggering and loud talk, at length went below to the "bar" to soothe his mortified spirit with a "gin-sling."

The others dropped away one by one, and dispersed themselves through the various cabins and saloons; and I found myself once more the sole occupant of the hurricane-deck.

Chapter Forty Five
Jealousy

Have you ever loved in humble life? some fair young girl, whose lot was among the lowly, but whose brilliant beauty in your eyes annihilated all social inequalities? Love levels all distinctions, is an adage old as the hills. It brings down the proud heart, and teaches condescension to the haughty spirit; but its tendency is to elevate, to ennoble. It does not make a peasant of the prince, but a prince of the peasant.

Behold the object of your adoration engaged in her ordinary duties! She fetches a jar of water from the well. Barefoot she treads the well-known path. Those nude pellucid feet are fairer in their nakedness than the most delicate *chaussure* of silk and satin. The wreaths and pearl circlets, the pins of gold and drupes of coral, the costliest *coiffures* of the dress circle,—all seem plain and poor compared with the glossy *negligé* of those bright tresses. The earthen jar sits upon her head with the grace of a golden coronet—every attitude is the *pose* of a statue, a study for a sculptor; and the coarse garment that drapes that form is in your eyes more becoming than a robe of richest velvet. You care not for that. You are not thinking of the casket, but of the pearl it conceals.

She disappears within the cottage—her humble home. Humble? In your eyes no longer humble; that little kitchen, with its wooden chairs, and scoured dresser, its deal shelf, with mugs, cups, and willow-pattern plates, its lime-washed walls and cheap prints of the red soldier and the blue sailor—that little museum of the *penates* of the poor, is now filled with a light that renders it more brilliant than the gilded saloons of wealth and fashion. That cottage with its low roof, and woodbine trellis, has become a palace. The light of love has transformed it! A paradise you are forbidden to enter. Yes, with all your wealth and power, your fine looks and your titles of distinction, your superfine cloth and bright lacquered boots, mayhap you dare not enter there.

And oh! how you envy those who dare!—how you envy the spruce apprentice, and the lout in the smock who cracks his whip, and whistles with as much *nonchalance* as if he was between the handles of his plough! as though the awe of that fair presence should not freeze his lips to stone!

Gauché that he is, how you envy him his *opportunities*! how you could slaughter him for those sweet smiles that appear to be lavished upon him!

There maybe no meaning in those smiles. They may be the expressions of good-nature of simple friendship, perhaps of a little coquetry. For all that, you cannot behold them without envy—without *suspicion* If there be a meaning—if they be the smiles of love—if the heart of that simple girl has made its lodgement either upon the young apprentice or him of the smock— then are you fated to the bitterest pang that human breast can know. It is not jealousy of the ordinary kind. It is far more painful. Wounded vanity adds a poison to the sting. Oh! it is hard to bear!

A pang of this nature I suffered, as I paced that high platform. Fortunately they had left me alone. The feelings that worked within me could not be concealed. My looks and wild gestures must have betrayed them. I should have been a subject for satire and laughter. But I was alone. The pilot in his glass-box did not notice me. His back was towards me, and his keen eye, bent steadily upon the water, was too busy with logs and sand-bars, and snags and sawyers, to take note of my delirium.

It *was* Aurore! Of that I had no doubt whatever. Her face was not to be mistaken for any other. There was none like it—none so lovely—alas! too fatally fair.

Who could *he* be? Some young spark of the town? Some clerk in one of the stores? a young planter? who? Maybe—and with this thought came that bitter pang—one of her own proscribed race—a young man of "colour"—a mulatto—a quadroon—a slave! Ha! to be rivalled by a slave!—worse than rivalled.—Infamous coquette! Why had I yielded to her fascinations? Why had I mistaken her craft for *naïveté?*—her falsehood for truth?

Who could *he* be? I should search the boat till I found him. Unfortunately I had taken no marks, either of his face or his dress. My eyes had remained fixed upon her after their parting. In the shadow I had seen him only indistinctly; and as he passed under the lights I saw him not. How preposterous then to think of looking for him! I could not recognise him in such a crowd.

I went below, and wandered through the cabins, under the front awning, and along the guard-ways. I scanned every face with an eagerness that to some must have appeared impertinence. Wherever one was young and handsome, he was an object of my scrutiny and jealousy. There were several such among the male passengers; and I endeavoured to distinguish those who had come aboard at Bringiers. There were some young men who appeared as if they had lately shipped, themselves, but I had no clue to guide me, and I failed to find my rival.

In the chagrin of disappointment I returned once more to the roof; but I had hardly reached it, when a new thought came into my mind. I remembered that the slaves of the plantation were to be sent down to the city by the first boat. Were they not travelling by that very one? I had seen a crowd of blacks—men, women, and children—hastily driven aboard. I had paid but little heed to such a common spectacle—one that may be witnessed daily, hourly. I had not thought of it, that those might be the slaves of the plantation Besançon!

If they were, then indeed there might still be hope; Aurore had not gone with them—but what of that? Though, like them, only a slave, it was not probable she would have been forced to herd with them upon the deck. But she had not come aboard! The staging had been already taken in, as I recognised her on the wharf-boat. On the supposition that the slaves of Besançon were aboard, my heart felt relieved. I was filled with a hope that all might yet be well.

Why? you may ask. I answer—simply because the thought occurred to me, that the youth, who so tenderly parted from Aurore, *might be a brother, or some near relative.* I had not heard of such relationship. It might be so, however; and my heart, reacting from its hour of keen anguish, was eager to relieve itself by any hypothesis.

I could not endure doubt longer; and turning on my heel, I hastened below. Down the kleets of the wheel-house, along the guard-way, then down the main stairs to the boiler-deck. Threading my way among bags of maize and hogsheads of sugar, now stooping under the great axle, now climbing over huge cotton-bales, I reached the after-part of the lower deck, usually appropriated to the "deck passengers"—the poor immigrants of Ireland and Germany, who here huddle miscellaneously with the swarthy bondsmen of the South.

As I had hoped, there were they,—those black but friendly faces,—every one of them. Old Zip, and Aunt Chloe, and the little Chloe; Hannibal, the new coachman, and Caesar and Pompey, and all,—all on their way to the dreaded mart.

I had halted a second or two before approaching them. The light was in my favour, and I saw them before discovering my presence. There were no signs of mirth in that sable group. I heard no laughter, no light revelry, as was their wont to indulge in in days gone by, among their little cabins in the quarter. A deep melancholy had taken possession of the features of all. Gloom was in every glance. Even the children, usually reckless of the unknown future, seemed impressed with the same sentiment. They rolled not about, tumbling over each other. They played not at all. They sat without stirring, and silent. Even they, poor infant helots, knew enough to fear for their dark future,—to shudder at the prospect of the slave-market.

All were downcast. No wonder. They had been used to kind treatment. They might pass to a hard taskmaster. Not one of them knew where in another day should be his home—what sort of tyrant should be his lord. But that was not all. Still worse. Friends, they were going to be parted; relatives, they would be torn asunder—perhaps never to meet more. Husband looked upon wife, brother upon sister, father upon child, mother upon infant, with dread in the heart and agony in the eye.

It was painful to gaze upon this sorrowing group, to contemplate the suffering, the mental anguish that spoke plainly in every face; to think of the wrongs which one man can legally put upon another—the deep sinful wrongs, the outrage of every human principle. Oh, it was terribly painful to look on that picture!

It was some relief to me to know that my presence threw at least a momentary light over its shade. Smiles chased away the sombre shadows as I appeared, and joyous exclamations hailed me. Had I been their saviour, I could not have met a more eager welcome.

Amidst their fervid ejaculations I could distinguish earnest appeals that I would buy them—that I would become their master—mingled with zealous protestations of service and devotion. Alas! they knew not how heavily at that moment the price of one of their number lay upon my heart.

I strove to be gay, to cheer them with words of consolation. I rather needed to be myself consoled.

During this while my eyes were busy. I scanned the faces of all. There was light enough glimmering from two oil-lamps to enable me to do so. Several were young mulattoes. Upon these my glance rested, one after the other. How my heart throbbed in this examination! It triumphed at length. Surely there was no face there that *she* could love? Were they all present? Yes, all—so Scipio said; all but Aurore.

"And Aurore?" I asked; "have you heard any more of her?"

"No, mass'; 'blieve 'Rore gone to de city. She go by de road in a carriage—not by de boat, some ob de folks say daat, I b'lieve."

This was strange enough. Taking the black aside—

"Tell me, Scipio," I asked, "has Aurore any relative among you?—any brother, or sister, or cousin?"

"No, mass', ne'er a one. Golly, mass'! 'Rore she near white as missa 'Génie all de rest be black, or leas'wise yeller! 'Rore she quaderoom, yeller folks all mulatto—no kin to 'Rore—no."

I was perplexed and puzzled. My former doubts came crowding back upon me. My jealousy returned.

Scipio could not clear up the mystery. His answer to other questions which I put to him gave me no solution to it; and I returned up-stairs with a heart that suffered under the pressure of disappointment.

The only reflection from which I drew comfort was, that I might have been mistaken. Perhaps, after all, it was *not* Aurore!

Chapter Forty Six
A Scientific Julep

To drown care and sorrow men drink. The spirit of wine freely quaffed will master either bodily pain or mental suffering—for a time. There is no form of the one or phase of the other so difficult to subdue as the pang of jealousy. Wine must be deeply quaffed before that corroding poison can be washed free from the heart.

But there is a partial relief in the wine-cup, and I sought it. I knew it to be only temporary, and that the sorrow would soon return. But even so—even a short respite was to be desired. I could bear my thoughts no longer.

I am not brave in bearing pain. I have more than once intoxicated myself to deaden the pitiful pain of a toothache. By the same means I resolved to relieve the dire aching of my heart.

The spirit of wine was nigh at hand, and might be imbibed in many forms.

In one corner of the "smoking-saloon" was the "bar," with its elegant adornments—its rows of decanters and bottles, with silver stoppers and labels its glasses, and lemons, and sugar-crushers—its bouquet of aromatic mint and fragrant pines—its bunches of straw tubes for "sucking" the "mint-julep," the "sherry-cobbler," or the "claret sangaree."

In the midst of this *entourage* stood the "bar-keeper," and in this individual do not picture to yourself some seedy personage of the waiter class, with bloodless cheeks and clammy skin, such as those monstrosities of an English hotel who give you a very *degoût* for your dinner. On the contrary, behold an *elegant* of latest fashion—that is, the fashion of his country and class, the men of the river. He wears neither coat nor vest while in the exercise of his office, but his shirt will merit an observation. It is of the finest fabric of the Irish loom—too fine to be worn by those who have woven it—and no Bond Street furnishing-house could equal its "make up."

Gold buttons glance at the sleeves, and diamonds sparkle amid the profuse ruffles on the bosom. The collar is turned down over a black silk riband, knotted *à la Byron*; but a tropic sun has more to do with this fashion than any desire to imitate the sailor-poet. Over this shirt stretch silk braces elaborately needle-worked, and still further adorned by buckles of pure gold. A hat of the costly grass from the shores of the South Sea crowns his well-oiled locks, and thus you have the "bar-keeper of the boat." His nether man need not be described. That is the unseen portion of his person, which is below the level of the bar. No cringing, smirking, obsequious counter-jumper he, but a dashing sprig, who, perhaps, *owns* his bar and all its contents, and who holds his head as high as either the clerk or captain.

As I approached this gentleman, he placed a glass upon the counter, and threw into it some broken fragments of ice. All this was done without a word having passed between us.

I had no need to give an order. He saw in my eye the determination to drink.

"Cobbler?"

"No," said I; "a mint-julep."

"Very well, I'll mix you a julep that'll set your teeth for you."

"Thank you. Just what I want."

The gentleman now placed side by side two glasses—tumblers of large size. Into one he put, first, a spoonful of crushed white sugar—then a slice of lemon—ditto of orange—next a few sprigs of green mint—after that a handful of broken ice, a gill of water, and, lastly, a large glass measure of cognac. This done, he lifted the glasses one in each hand, and poured the contents from one to the other so rapidly that ice, brandy, lemons, and all, seemed to be constantly suspended in the air, and oscillating between the glasses. The tumblers themselves at no time approached nearer than two feet from each other! This adroitness, peculiar to his craft, and only obtained after long practice, was evidently a source of professional pride. After some half-score of these revolutions the drink was permitted to rest in one glass, and was then set down upon the counter.

There yet remained to be given the "finishing touch." A thin slice of pine-apple was cut freshly from the fruit. This held between the finger and thumb was doubled over the edge of the glass, and then passed with an adroit sweep round the circumference.

"That's the latest Orleans touch," remarked the bar-keeper with a smile, as he completed the manoeuvre.

There was a double purpose in this little operation. The pine-apple not only cleared the glass of the grains of sugar and broken leaves of mint, but left its fragrant juice to mingle its aroma with the beverage.

"The latest Orleans touch," he repeated; "scientific style."

I nodded my assent.

The julep was now "mixed"—which fact was made known to me by the glass being pushed a little nearer, across the marble surface of the counter.

"Have a straw?" was the laconic inquiry.

"Yes; thank you."

A joint of wheaten straw was plunged into the glass, and taking this between my lips I drew in large draughts of perhaps the most delicious of all intoxicating drinks—the mint-julep.

The aromatic liquid had scarce passed my lips when I began to feel its effects. My pulse ceased its wild throbbing. My blood became cool, and flowed in a more gentle current through my veins, and my heart seemed to be bathing in the waters of Lethe. The relief was almost instantaneous, and I only wondered I had not thought of it before. Though still far from happy, I felt that I held in my hands what would soon make me so. Transitory that happiness might be, yet the reaction was welcome at the moment, and the prospect of it pleasant to my soul. I eagerly swallowed the inspiring beverage—swallowed it in large draughts, till the straw tube, rattling among the fragments of ice at the bottom of the glass, admonished me that the fluid was all gone.

"Another, if you please!"

"You liked it, I guess?"

"Most excellent!"

"Said so. I reckon, stranger, we can get up a mint-julep on board this here boat equal to either Saint Charles or Verandah, if not a leetle superior to either."

"A superb drink!"

"We can mix a sherry-cobbler too, that ain't hard to take."

"I have no doubt of it, but I'm not fond of sherry. I prefer this."

"You're right. So do I. The pine-apple's a new idea, but an improvement, I think."

"I think so too."

"Have a fresh straw?"

"Thank you."

This young fellow was unusually civil. I fancied that his civility proceeded from my having eulogised his mint-juleps. It was not that, as I afterwards ascertained. These Western people are little accessible to cheap flattery. I owed his good opinion of me to a far different cause—*the discomfiture I had put on the meddling passenger*! I believe he had also learnt, that it was I who had chastised the Bully Larkin! Such "feats of arms" soon become known in the region of the Mississippi Valley, where strength and courage are qualities of high esteem. Hence, in the bar-keeper's view, I was one who deserved a civil word; and thus talking together on the best of terms, I swallowed my second julep, and called upon him for a third, Aurore was for the moment forgotten, or when remembered, it was with less of bitterness. Now and then that parting scene came uppermost in my thoughts; but the pang that rose with it was each moment growing feebler, and easier to be endured.

Chapter Forty Seven
A Game of Whist

In the centre of the smoking-saloon, there was a table, and around it some half-dozen men were seated. Other half-dozen stood behind these, looking over their shoulders. The attitudes of all, and their eager glances, suggested the nature of their occupation. The flouting of pasteboard, the chink of dollars, and the oft-recurring words of "ace," "jack," and "trump," put it beyond a doubt that that occupation was gaming. "Euchre" was the game.

Curious to observe this popular American game, I stepped up and stood watching the players. My friend who had raised the false alarm was one of them; but his back was towards me, and I remained for some time unseen by him.

Some two or three of those who played were elegantly-dressed men. Their coats were of the finest cloth, their ruffles of the costliest cambric, and jewels sparkled in their shirt bosoms and glittered upon their fingers. These fingers, however, told a tale. They told plainly as words, that they to whom they belonged had not always been accustomed to such elegant adornment. Toilet soap had failed to soften the corrugated skin, and obliterate the abrasions—the souvenirs of toil.

This was nothing. They might be gentlemen for all that. Birth is of slight consequence in the Far West. The plough-boy may become the President.

Still there was an air about these men—an air I cannot describe, but which led me at the moment to doubt their *gentility*. It was not from any swagger or assumption on their part. On the contrary, they appeared the *most gentlemanly* individuals around the table!

They were certainly the most sedate and quiet. Perhaps it was this very sedateness—this polished reserve—that formed the spring of my suspicion. True gentlemen, bloods from Tennessee or Kentucky, young planters of the Mississippi coast, or French Creoles of Orleans, would have offered different characteristics. The cool complacency with which these individuals spoke and acted—no symptoms of perturbation as the trump was turned, no signs of ruffled temper when luck went against them—told two things; first, that they were men of the world, and, secondly, that they were not now playing their maiden game of "Euchre." Beyond that I could form no judgment about them. They might be doctors, lawyers, or "gentlemen of elegant leisure"—a class by no means uncommon in the work-a-day world of America.

At that time I was still too new to Far West society, to be able to distinguish its features. Besides, in the United States, and particularly in the western portion of the country, those peculiarities of dress and habit, which in the Old-World form, as it were, the landmarks of the professions, do not exist. You may meet the preacher wearing a blue coat and bright buttons; the judge with a green one; the doctor in a white linen jacket; and the baker in glossy black broadcloth from top to toe!

Where every man assumes the right to be a gentleman, the costumes and badges of trade are studiously avoided. Even the tailor is undistinguishable in the mass of his "fellow-citizens." The land of character-dresses lies farther to the south-west—Mexico is that land.

I stood for some time watching the gamesters and the game. Had I not known something of the banking peculiarities of the West, I should have believed that they were gambling for enormous sums. At each man's right elbow lay a huge pile of bank-notes, flanked by a few pieces of silver—dollars, halves, and quarters. Accustomed as my eyes had been to bank-notes of five pounds in value, the table would have presented to me a rich appearance, had I not known that these showy parallelograms of copper-plate and banking-paper, were mere "shin-plasters," representing amounts that varied from the value of one dollar to that of six and a quarter cents! Notwithstanding, the bets were far from being low. Twenty, fifty, and even a hundred dollars, frequently changed hands in a single game.

I perceived that the hero of the false alarm was one of the players. His back was towards me where I stood, and he was too much engrossed with his game to look around.

In dress and general appearance he differed altogether from the rest. He wore a white beaver hat with broad brim, and a coat of great "jeans," wide-sleeved and loose-bodied. He had the look of a well-to-do corn-farmer from Indiana or a pork-merchant from Cincinnati. Yet there was something in his manner that told you river-travelling was not new to him. It was not his first trip "down South." Most probably the second supposition was the correct one—he was a dealer in hog-meat.

One of the fine gentlemen I have described sat opposite to where I was standing. He appeared to be losing considerable sums, which the farmer or pork-merchant was winning. It proved that the luck of the cards was not in favour of the smartest-looking players—an inducement to other plain people to try a hand.

I began to feel sympathy for the elegant gentleman, his losses were so severe. I could not help admiring the composure with which he bore them.

At length he looked up, and scanned the faces of those who stood around. He seemed desirous of giving up the play. His eye met mine. He said, in a careless way—

"Perhaps, stranger, *you* wish to take a hand? You may have my place if you do. I have no luck. I could not win under any circumstances to-night. I shall give up playing."

This appeal caused the rest of the players to turn their faces towards me, and among others the pork-dealer. I expected an ebullition of anger from this individual. I was disappointed. On the contrary, he hailed me in a friendly tone.

"Hilloa, mister!" cried he, "I hope you an't miffed at me?"

"Not in the least," I replied.

"Fact, I meant no offence. Did think thar war a some 'un overboard. Dog-gone me, if I didn't!"

"Oh! I have taken no offence," rejoined I; "to prove it, I ask you now to drink with me."

The juleps and the late reaction from bitter thought had rendered me of a jovial disposition. The free apology at once won my forgiveness.

"Good as wheat!" assented the pork-dealer. "I'm your man; but, stranger, you must allow me to pay. You see, I've won a trifle here. *My* right to pay for the drinks."

"Oh! I have no objection."

"Well, then, let's all licker! *I* stand drinks all round. What say you, fellars?" A murmur of assent answered the interrogatory.

"Good!" continued the speaker. "Hyar, bar-keeper! drinks for the crowd!"

And so saying, he of the white-hat and jeans coat stepped forward to the bar, and placed a couple of dollars upon the counter. All who were near followed him, shouting each out the name of the beverage most to his liking in the various calls of "gin-sling," "cocktail," "cobbler," "julep," "brandy-smash," and such-like interesting mixtures.

In America men do not sit and sip their liquor, but drink standing. *Running*, one might say—for, be it hot or cold, mixed or "neat," it is gone in a gulp, and then the drinkers retire to their chairs to smoke, chew, and wait for the fresh invitation, "Let's all licker!"

In a few seconds we had all liquored, and the players once more took their seats around the table.

The gentleman who had proposed to me to become his successor did not return to his place. He had no luck, he again said, and would not play any more that night.

Who would accept his place and his partner? I was appealed to.

I thanked my new acquaintances, but the thing was impossible, as I had never played Euchre, and therefore knew nothing about the game, beyond the few points I had picked up while watching them.

"That ar awkward," said the pork-dealer. "Ain't we nohow able to get up a set? Come, Mr Chorley—I believe that's your name, sir?" (This was addressed to the gentleman who had risen.) "You ain't a-goin' to desert us that away? We can't make up a game if you do?"

"I should only lose if I played longer," reiterated Chorley. "No," continued he, "I won't risk it."

"Perhaps this gentleman plays 'whist,'" suggested another, alluding to me. "You're an Englishman, sir, I believe. I never knew one of your countrymen who was not a good whist-player."

"True, I can play whist," I replied carelessly.

"Well, then, what say you all to a game of whist?" inquired the last speaker, glancing around the table.

"Don't know much about the game," bluntly answered the pork-dealer. "Mout play it on a pinch rayther than spoil sport; but whoever hez me for a partner 'll have to keep a sharp look-out for himself, I reckon."

"I guess you know the game as well as I do," replied the one who had proposed it.

"I hain't played a rubber o' whist for many a year, but if we can't make up the set at Euchre, let's try one."

"Oh! if you're goin' to play whist," interposed the gentleman who had seceded from the game of Euchre—"if you're going to play whist, I don't mind taking a hand at *that*—it may change my luck—and if this gentleman has no objection, I'd like him for my partner. As you say, sir, Englishmen are good whist-players. It's their national game, I believe."

"Won't be a fair match, Mr Chorley," said the dealer in hog-meat; "but since you propose it, if Mr Hatcher here—your name, sir, I believe?"

"Hatcher is my name," replied the person addressed, the same who suggested whist.

"If Mr Hatcher here," continued white-hat, "has no objection to the arrangement, I'll not back out. Doggoned, if I do!"

"Oh! I don't care," said Hatcher, in a tone of reckless indifference, "anything to get up a game."

Now, I was never fond of gambling, either amateur or otherwise, but circumstances had made me a tolerable whist-player, and I knew there were few who could beat me at it. If my partner knew the game as well, I felt certain we could not be badly damaged; and according to all accounts he understood it well. This was the opinion of one or two of the bystanders, who whispered in my ear that he was a "whole team" at whist.

Partly from the reckless mood I was in—partly that a secret purpose urged me on—a purpose which developed itself more strongly afterwards—and partly that I had been bantered, and, as it were, "cornered" into the thing, I consented to play—Chorley and I *versus* Hatcher and the pork-merchant.

We took our seats—partners *vis-à-vis*—the cards were shuffled, cut, dealt, and the game began.

Chapter Forty Eight
The Game Interrupted

We played the first two or three games for low stakes—a dollar each. This was agreeable to the desire of Hatcher and the pork-merchant—who did not like to risk much as they had nearly forgotten the game. Both, however, made "hedge bets" freely against my partner, Chorley, and against any one who chose to take them up. These bets were on the turn-up, the colour, the "honours," or the "odd trick."

My partner and I won the two first games, and rapidly. I noted several instances of bad play on the part of our opponent. I began to believe that they really were not a match for us. Chorley said so with an air of triumph, as though we were playing merely for the honour of the thing, and the stakes were of no consequence. After a while, as we won another game, he repeated the boast.

The pork-dealer and his partner seemed to get a little nettled.

"It's the cards," said the latter, with an air of pique.

"Of coorse it's the cards," repeated white-hat. "Had nothing but darned rubbish since the game begun. Thar again!"

"Bad cards again?" inquired his partner with a sombre countenance.

"Bad as blazes! couldn't win corn-shucks with 'em."

"Come, gentlemen!" cried my partner, Chorley; "not exactly fair that—no hints."

"Bah!" ejaculated the dealer. "Mout show you my hand, for that matter. Thar ain't a trick in it."

We won again!

Our adversaries, getting still more nettled at our success, now proposed doubling the stakes. This was agreed to, and another game played.

Again Chorley and I were winners, and the pork-man asked his partner if he would double again. The latter consented after a little hesitation, as though he thought the amount too high. Of course we, the winners, could not object, and once more we "swept the shin-plasters," as Chorley euphoniously expressed it.

The stakes were again doubled, and possibly would have increased in the same ratio again and again had I not made a positive objection. I remembered the amount of cash I carried in my pocket, and knew that at such a rate, should fortune go against us, my purse would not hold out. I consented, however, to a stake of ten dollars each, and at this amount we continued the play.

It was well we had not gone higher, for from this time fortune seemed to desert us. We lost almost every time, and at the rate of ten dollars a game. I felt my purse grow sensibly lighter. I was in a fair way of being "cleared out."

My partner, hitherto so cool, seemed to lose patience, at intervals anathematising the cards, and wishing he had never consented to a game of "nasty whist." Whether it was this excitement that caused it I could not tell, but certainly he played badly—much worse than at the beginning. Several times he flung down his cards without thought or caution. It seemed as if his temper, ruffled at our repeated losses, rendered him careless, and even reckless, about the result. I was the more surprised at this, as but an hour before at Euchre I had seen him lose sums of double the amount apparently with the utmost indifference.

We had not bad luck neither. Each hand our cards were good; and several times I felt certain we should have won, had my partner played his hand more skilfully. As it was, we continued to lose, until I felt satisfied that nearly half of my money was in the pockets of Hatcher and the pork-dealer.

No doubt the whole of it would soon have found its way into the same receptacles, had not our game been suddenly, and somewhat mysteriously, interrupted.

Some loud words were heard—apparently from the lower deck—followed by a double report, as of two pistols discharged in rapid succession, and the moment after a voice called out, "Great God! there's a man shot!"

The cards fell from our fingers—each seized his share of the stakes, springing to his feet as he did so; and then players, backers, lookers-on, and all, making for front and side entrances, rushed *pell-mell* out of the saloon.

Some ran down stairs—some sprang up to the hurricane-deck—some took aft, others forward, all crying out "Who is it?" "Where is he?" "Who fired?" "Is he killed?" and a dozen like interrogatories, interrupted at intervals by the screams of the ladies in their cabins. The alarm of the "woman overboard" was nothing to this new scene of excitement and confusion. But what was most mysterious was the fact that no killed or wounded individual could be found, nor any one who had either fired a pistol or had seen one fired! no man had been shot, nor had any man shot him!

What the deuce could it mean? Who had cried out that some one was shot? That no one could tell! Mystery, indeed. Lights were carried round into all the dark corners of the boat, but neither dead nor wounded, nor trace of blood, could be discovered; and at length men broke out in laughter, and stated their belief that the "hul thing was a hoax." So declared the dealer in hog-meat, who seemed rather gratified that he no longer stood alone as a contriver of false alarms.

Chapter Forty Nine
The Sportsmen of the Mississippi

Before things had reached this point, I had gained an explanation of the mysterious alarm. I alone knew it, along with the individual who had caused it.

On hearing the shots, I had run forward under the front awning, and stood looking over the guards. I was looking down upon the boiler-deck—for it appeared to me that the loud words that preceded the reports had issued thence, though I also thought that the shots had been fired at some point nearer.

Most of the people had gone out by the side entrances, and were standing over the gangways, so that I was alone in the darkness, or nearly so.

I had not been many seconds in this situation, when some one glided alongside of me, and touched me on the arm. I turned and inquired who it was, and what was wanted. A voice answered me in French—

"A friend, Monsieur, who wishes to do you a service."

"Ha, that voice! It was you, then, who called out—"

"It was."

"And—"

"I who fired the shots—precisely."

"There is no one killed, then?"

"Not that I know of. My pistol was pointed to the sky—besides it was loaded blank."

"I'm glad of that, Monsieur; but for what purpose, may I ask, have you—"

"Simply to do *you* a service, as I have said."

"But how do you contemplate serving me by firing off pistols, and frightening the passengers of the boat out of their senses?"

"Oh! as to that, there's no harm done. They'll soon got over their little alarm. I wanted to speak with you alone. I could think of no other device to separate you from your new acquaintances. The firing of my pistol was only a *ruse* to effect that purpose. It has succeeded, you perceive."

"Ha! Monsieur, it was you then who whispered the word in my ear as I sat down to play?"

"Yes; have I not prophesied truly?"

"So far you have. It was you who stood opposite me in the corner of the saloon?"

"It was I."

Let me explain these two last interrogatories. As I was about consenting to the game of whist, some one plucked my sleeve, and whispered in French—

"Don't play, Monsieur; you are certain to lose."

I turned in the direction of the speaker, and saw a young man just leaving my side; but was not certain whether it was he who had given this prudent counsel. As is known, I did not heed it.

Again, while engaged in the game, I noticed this same young man standing in front of me, but in a distant and somewhat dark corner of the saloon. Notwithstanding the darkness, I saw that his eyes were bent upon me, as I played. This fact would have drawn my attention of itself, but there was also an expression in the face that at once fixed my interest; and, each time, while the cards were being dealt, I took the opportunity to turn my eyes upon this strange individual.

He was a slender youth, under the medium height, and apparently scarce twenty years of age, but a melancholy tone that pervaded his countenance made him look a little older. His features were small, but finely chiselled—the nose and lips resembling more those of a woman. His cheek was almost colourless, and dark silky hair fell in profuse curls over his neck and shoulders; for such at that time was the Creole fashion. I felt certain the youth was a Creole, partly from his French cast of countenance, partly from the fashion and material of his dress, and partly because he spoke French—for I was under the impression it was he who had spoken to me. His costume was altogether of Creole fashion. He wore a blouse of brown linen—not after the mode of that famous garment as known in France—but as the Creole "hunting-shirt," with plaited body and gracefully-gathered skirt. Its material, moreover,—the fine unbleached linen,—showed that the style was one of choice, not a mere necessary covering. His pantaloons were of the finest sky-blue *cottonade*—the produce of the looms of Opelousas. They were plaited very full below the waist, and open at the bottoms with rows of buttons to close them around the ankles when occasion required. There was no vest. Its place was supplied by ample frills of cambric lace, that puffed out over the breast. The *chaussure* consisted of gaiter-bootees of drab lasting-cloth, tipped with patent leather, and fastened over the front with a silk lace. A broad-brimmed Panama hat completed the dress, and gave the finishing touch to this truly Southern costume.

There was nothing *outré* about either the shirt, the pantaloons, the head-dress, or foot-gear. All were in keeping—all were in a style that at that period was the *mode* upon the lower Mississippi. It was not, therefore, the dress of this youth that had arrested my attention. I had been in the habit of seeing such, every day. It could not be that. No—the dress had nothing to do with the interest which he had excited. Perhaps my regarding him as the author of the brief counsel that had been uttered in my ear had a little to do with it—but not all. Independent of that, there was something in the face itself that forcibly attracted my regard—so forcibly that I began to ponder whether I had ever seen it before. If there had been a better light, I might have resolved the doubt, but he stood in shadow, and I could not get a fair view of him.

It was just about this time that I missed him from his station in the corner of the saloon, and a minute or two later were heard the shouts and shots from without.

"And now, Monsieur, may I inquire why you wish to speak to me, and what you have to say?"

I was beginning to feel annoyed at the interference of this young fellow. A man does not relish being suddenly pulled up from a game of whist; and not a bit the more that he has been losing at it.

"Why I wish to speak to you is, because I feel an interest in you. What I have to say you shall hear."

"An interest in me! And pray, Sir, to what am I indebted for this interest?"

"Is it not enough that you are a stranger likely to be plundered of your purse?—a *green-horn*—"

"How, Monsieur?"

"Nay, do not be angry with me. That is the phrase which I have heard applied to you to-night by more than one of your new acquaintances. If you return to play with them, I think you will merit the title."

"Come, Monsieur, this is too bad: you interfere in a matter that does not concern you."

"True, it does not; but it concerns *you*, and yet—ah!"

I was about to leave this meddling youth, and hurry back to the game, when the strange melancholy tone of his voice caused me to hesitate, and remain by him a little longer.

"Well," I said, "you have not yet told me what you wished to say."

"Indeed, I have said already. I have told you not to play—that you would lose if you did. I repeat that counsel."

"True, I have lost a little, but it does not follow that fortune will be always on one side. It is rather my partner's fault, who seems a bad player."

"Your partner, if I mistake not, is one of the best players on the river. I think I have seen that gentleman before."

"Ha! you know him them?"

"Something of him—not much, but that much I know. Do *you* know him?"

"Never saw him before to-night."

"Nor any of the others?"

"They are all equally strangers to me."

"You are not aware, then, that you are playing with *sportsmen*?"

"No, but I am very glad to hear it. I am something of a sportsman myself—as fond of dogs, horses, and guns, as any of the three, I warrant."

"Ha! Monsieur, you misapprehend. A sportsman in your country, and a sportsman in a Mississippi steamboat, are two very distinct things. Foxes, hares, and partridges, are the game of your sportsman. Greenhorns and their purses are the game of gentry like these."

"The men with whom I am playing, then, are—"

"Professional gamblers—steamboat sharpers."

"Are you sure of this, Monsieur?"

"Quite sure of it. Oh! I often travel up and down to New Orleans. I have seen them all before."

"But one of them has the look of a farmer or a merchant, as I thought—a pork-merchant from Cincinnati—his talk ran that way."

"Farmer—merchant, ha! ha! ha! a farmer without acres—a merchant without trade! Monsieur, that simply-dressed old fellow is said to be the 'smartest'—that is the Yankee word—the smartest sportsman in the Mississippi valley, and such are not scarce, I trow."

"After all, they are strangers to each other, and one of them is my partner—I do not see how they can—"

"Strangers to each other!" interrupted my new friend. "Since when have they become acquainted? I myself have seen the three in company, and at the same business, almost every time I have journeyed on the river. True, they talk to each other as if they had accidentally met. That is part of their arrangement for cheating such as you."

"So you believe they have actually been cheating me?"

"Since the stakes have been raised to ten dollars they have."

"But how?"

"Oh, it is very simple. Sometimes your partner designedly played the wrong card—"

"Ha! I see now; I believe it."

"It did not need that though. Even had you had an honest partner, it would have been all the same in the end. Your opponents have a system of signals by which they can communicate to each other many facts—the sort of cards they hold,—the colour of the cards, their value, and so forth. You did not observe how they placed their fingers upon the edge of the table. *I* did. One finger laid horizontally denoted one trump—two fingers placed in a similar manner, two trumps—three for three, and so on. A slight curving of the fingers told: how many of the trumps were honours; a certain movement of the thumbs bespoke an ace; and in this way each of your adversaries knew almost to a card what his partner had got. It needed not the third to bring about the desired result. As it was, there were seven knaves about the table—four in the cards, and three among the players."

"This is infamous!"

"True, I would have admonished you of it sooner; but, of course, I could not find an opportunity. It would have been no slight danger for me to have told you openly, and exposed the rascals. Hence, the *ruse* I have been compelled to adopt. These are no common swindlers. Any of the three would resent the slightest imputation upon their honour. Two of them are noted duellists. Most likely I should have been called out to-morrow and shot, and you would scarce have thanked me for my 'interference.'"

"My dear sir, I am exceedingly grateful to you. I am convinced that what you say is true. How would you have me act?"

"Simply give up the game—let your losses go—you cannot recover them."

"But I am not disposed to be thus outraged and plundered with impunity. I shall try another game, watch them, and—"

"No, you would be foolish to do so. I tell you, Monsieur, these men are noted duellists as well as black-legs, and possess courage. One of them, your partner, has given proof of it by having travelled over three hundred miles to fight with a gentleman who had slandered him, or rather had spoken the truth about him! He succeeded, moreover, in killing his man. I tell you, Monsieur, you can gain nothing by quarrelling with such men, except a fair chance of having a bullet through you. I know you are a stranger in our country. Be advised, then, and act as I have said. Leave them to their gains. It is late: Retire to your state-room, and think no more on what you have lost."

Whether it was the late excitement consequent upon the false alarm, or whether it was the strange development I had just listened to, aided by the cool river breeze, I know not; but the intoxication passed away, and my brain became clear. I doubted not for a moment that the young Creole had told me the truth. His manner as well as words, connected with the circumstances that had just transpired, produced full conviction.

I felt impressed with a deep sense of gratitude to him for the service he had rendered, and at such risk to himself—for even the *ruse* he had adopted might have had an awkward ending for him, had any one seen him fire off his pistols.

Why had he acted thus? Why this interest in my affairs? Had he assigned the true reason? Was it a feeling of pure chivalry that had prompted him? I had heard of just such instances of noble nature among the Creole-French of Louisiana. Was this another illustration of that character?

I say I was impressed with a deep sense of gratitude, and resolved to follow his advice.

"I shall do as you say," I replied, "on one condition."

"Name it, Monsieur."

"That you will give me your address, so that when we arrive in New Orleans, I may have the opportunity of renewing your acquaintance, and proving to you my gratitude."

"Alas, Monsieur! I have no address."

I felt embarrassed. The melancholy tone in which these words were uttered was not to be mistaken; some grief pressed heavily on that young and generous heart.

It was not for me to inquire into its cause, least of all at that time; but my own secret sorrow enabled me to sympathise the more deeply with others, and I felt I stood beside one whose sky was far from serene. I felt embarrassed by his answer. It left me in a delicate position to make reply. I said at length—

"Perhaps you will do me the favour to call upon me? I live at the Hotel Saint Luis."

"I shall do so with pleasure."

"To-morrow?"

"To-morrow night."

"I shall stay at home for you. *Bon soir*, Monsieur."

We parted, each taking the way to his state-room.

In ten minutes after I lay in my shelf-like bed, asleep; and in ten hours after I was drinking my *café* in the Hotel Saint Luis.

Chapter Fifty
The City

I am strongly in favour of a country life. I am a lover of the chase and the angle.

Perhaps if I were to analyse the feeling, I might find that these predilections have their source in a purer fountain—the love of Nature herself. I follow the deer in his tracks, because they lead me into the wildest solitudes of the forest—I follow the trout in its stream, because I am guided into still retreats, by the margin of shady pools, where human foot rarely treads. Once in the haunts of the fish and the game, my sporting energy dies within me. My rod-spear pierces the turf, my gun lies neglected by my side, and I yield up my soul to a diviner dalliance with the beauties of Nature. Oh, I am a rare lover of the sylvan scene!

And yet, for all this, I freely admit that the first hours spent in a great city have for me a peculiar fascination. A world of new pleasures is suddenly placed within reach—a world of luxury opened up. The soul is charmed with rare joys. Beauty and song, wine and the dance, vary their allurements. Love, or it may be passion, beguiles you into many an incident of romantic adventure; for romance may be found within the walled city. The human heart is its home, and they are but Quixotic dreamers who fancy that steam and civilisation are antagonistic to the purest aspirations of poetry. A sophism, indeed, is the chivalry of the savage. His rags, so picturesque, often cover a shivering form and a hungry stomach. Soldier though I may claim to be, I prefer the cheering roll of the busy mill to the thunder of the cannon—I regard the tall chimney, with its banner of black smoke, a far nobler sight than the fortress turret with its flouting and fickle flag. I hear sweet music in the plashing of the paddle-wheel; and in my ears a nobler sound is the scream of the iron horse than the neigh of the pampered war-steed. A nation of monkeys may manage the business of gunpowder: they must be men to control the more powerful element of steam.

These ideas will not suit the puling sentimentalism of the boudoir and the boarding-school. The Quixotism of the modern time will be angry with the rough writer who thus rudely lays his hand upon the helm of the mailed knight, and would deflower it of its glory and glossy plumes. It is hard to yield up prejudices and preconceptions, however false; and the writer himself in doing so confesses to the cost of a struggle of no ordinary violence. It was hard to give up the Homeric illusion, and believe that Greeks were men, not demigods—hard to recognise in the organ-man and the opera-singer the descendants of those heroes portrayed in the poetic pictures of a Virgil; and yet in the days of my dreamy youth, when I turned my face to the West, I did so under the full conviction that the land of prose was before me and the land of poetry behind my back!

Thanks to Saint Hubert and the golden ring of the word "Mexico," I did turn my face in that direction: and no sooner had I set foot on those glorious shores, trodden by a Columbus and a Cortez, than I recognised the home both of the poetic and the picturesque. In that very land, called prosaic—the land of dollars—I inhaled the very acmé of the poetic spirit; not from the rhythm of books, but expressed in the most beautiful types of the human form, in the noblest impulses of the human soul, in rock and stream, in bird, and leaf and flower. In that very city, which, thanks to perjured and prejudiced travellers, I had been taught to regard as a sort of outcast camp, I found humanity in its fairest forms—progress blended with pleasure—civilisation adorned with the spirit of chivalry as with a wreath. Prosaic indeed! a dollar-loving people! I make bold to assert, that in the concave of that little crescent where lies the city of New Orleans will be found a psychological *mélange* of greater variety and interest than exists in any space of equal extent on the globe's surface. There the passions, favoured by the clime, reach their fullest, highest development, Love and hate, joy and grief, avarice, ambition—all attain to perfect vigour. There, too, the moral virtues are met with in full purity. Cant has there no home, hypocrisy must be deep indeed to avoid exposure and punishment. Genius is almost universal—universal, too, is activity. The stupid and the slothful cannot exist in this moving world of busy life and enjoyment.

An ethnological *mélange* as well this singular city presents. Perhaps no other city exhibits so great a variety of nationalities as in its streets. Founded by the French, held by the Spaniards, "annexed" by the Americans, these three nations form the elements of its population. But you may, nevertheless, there meet with representatives of most other civilised, and of many "savage" people. The Turk in his turban, the Arab in his burnouse, the Chinaman with shaven scalp and queue, the black son of Africa, the red Indian, the swarthy Mestize, yellow Mulatto, the olive Malay, the light graceful Creole, and the not less graceful Quadroon, jostle each other in its streets, and jostle with the red-blooded races of the North, the German and Gael, the Russ and Swede, the Fleming, the Yankee, and the Englishman. An odd human mosaic—a mottled piebald mixture is the population of the Crescent City.

In truth, New Orleans is a great metropolis, more of a city than places of much greater population either in Europe or America. In passing through its streets you feel that you are not in a provincial town. Its shops exhibit the richest goods, of best workmanship. Palace-like hotels appear in every street. Luxurious *cafés* invite you into their elegant saloons. Theatres are there—grand architectural temples—in which you may witness the drama well performed in French, and German, and English, and in its season you may listen to the soul-moving music of the Italian opera. If you are a lover of the Terpsichorean art, you will fold New Orleans, *par excellence*, the town to your taste.

I knew the capacities of New Orleans to afford pleasure. I was acquainted with the sources of enjoyment, yet I sought them not. After a long interval of country life I entered the city without a thought of its gaieties—a rare event in the life even of the most sedate. The masquerades, the quadroon-balls, the drama, the sweet strains of the Opera, had lost their attractions for me. No amusement could amuse me at that moment. One thought alone had possession of my heart—Aurore! There was room for no other.

I pondered as to how I should act.

Place yourself in my position, and you will surely acknowledge it a difficult one. First, I was in love with this beautiful quadroon—in love beyond redemption. Secondly, she, the object of my passion, was for *sale*, and by *public auction*! Thirdly, I was jealous—ay jealous, of that which might be sold and bought like a bale of cotton,—a barrel of sugar! Fourthly, I was still uncertain whether I should have it in my power to become the purchaser. I was still uncertain whether my banker's letter had yet reached New Orleans. Ocean steamers were not known at this period, and the date of a European mail could not be relied upon with any degree of certainty. Should that not come to hand in due time, then indeed should my misery reach its culminating point. Some one else would become possessed of all I held dear on earth—would be her lord and master—with power to do aught—oh God! the idea was fearful. I could not bear to dwell upon it.

Again, even should my letter reach me in time, would the amount I expected be enough? Five hundred pounds sterling—five times five—twenty-five hundred dollars! Would twenty-five hundred be the price of that which was priceless?

I even doubted whether it would. I knew that a thousand dollars was at that time the "average value" of a slave, and it was rare when one yielded twice that amount. It must be a strong-bodied man—a skilful mechanic, a good blacksmith, an expert barber, to be worth such a sum!

But for Aurore. Oh! I had heard strange tales of "fancy prices," for such a "lot"—of brisk competition in the bidding—of men with long purses and lustful thoughts eagerly contending for such a prize.

Such thoughts might harrow the soul even under the most ordinary circumstances! what was their effect upon me? I cannot describe the feelings I experienced.

Should the sum reach me in time—should it prove enough—should I even succeed in becoming the *owner* of Aurore, what then? What if my jealousy were well founded? What if she loved me not? Worse dilemma than ever. I should only have her body—then her heart and soul would be another's. I should live in exquisite torture—the slave of a slave!

Why should I attempt to purchase her at all? Why not make a bold effort, and free myself from this delirious passion? She is not worthy of the sacrifice I would make for her. No—she has deceived me—surely she has deceived me. Why not break my promise, plighted though it be in words of fervid love? Why not flee from the spot, and endeavour to escape the torture that is maddening both my heart and brain? Oh! why not?

In calmer moments, such questions might be thought worthy of an answer. I could not answer them. I did not even entertain them,—though, like shadows, they flitted across my mind. In the then state of my feelings, prudence was unknown. Expediency had no place. I would not have listened to its cold counsels. You who have passionately loved can alone understand me. I was resolved to risk fortune, fame, life—all—to possess the object I so deeply adored.

Chapter Fifty One
Vente Importante des Nègres

"*L'abeille*, Monsieur?"

The *garçon* who helped me to the fragrant cup, at the same time handed me a newspaper fresh from the press.

It was a large sheet, headed upon one side "L'Abeille", on the reverse its synonyme in English, "The Bee." Half of its contents were in French, half in English: each half was a counterpart—a translation of the other.

I mechanically took the journal from the hand of the waiter, but without either the design or inclination to read it. Mechanically my eyes wandered over its broad-sheet—scarce heeding the contents.

All at once, the heading of an advertisement fixed my gaze and my attention. It was on the "French side" of the paper.

"Annoncement."

"*Vente importante des Nègres!*" Yes—it was they. The announcement was no surprise to me. I expected as much.

I turned to the translation on the reverse page, in order to comprehend it more clearly. There it was in all its broad black meaning:—

"*Important Sale of Negroes!*" I read on:—"*Estate in Bankruptcy. Plantation Besançon!*"

"Poor Eugénie!"

Farther:—

"*Forty able-bodied field-hands, of different ages. Several first-rate domestic servants, coachman, cooks, chamber-maids, wagon-drivers. A number of likely mulatto boys and girls, from ten to twenty,*" etcetera, etcetera.

The list followed *in extenso*. I read—

"Lot 1. *Scipio, 48. Able-bodied black, 5 foot 11 inches, understands house-work, and the management of horses. Sound and without blemish.*

"Lot 2. *Hannibal, 40. Dark mulatto, 5 foot 9 inches, good coachman, sound and steady.*

"Lot 3. *César, 43. Black field-hand. Sound,*" etcetera, etcetera.

My eyes could not wait for the disgusting details. They ran down the column in search of that name. They would have lit upon it sooner, but that my hands trembled, and the vibratory motion of the sheet almost prevented me from reading. It was there at length—*last upon the list*! "Why last?" No matter—her "description" was there.

Can I trust myself to read it? Down, burning heart, still your wild throbbings!

"Lot 65. *Aurore. 19. Quadroon. Likely—good housekeeper, and sempstress.*"

Portrait sketched by refined pen—brief and graphic.

"Likely," ha! ha! ha! "Likely," ha! ha! The brute who wrote that paragraph would have described Venus as a likely gal.

'Sdeath! I cannot jest—this desecration of all that is lovely—all that is sacred—all that is dear to my heart, is torture itself. The blood is boiling in my veins—my bosom is wrung with dire emotions!

The journal fell from my hands, and I bent forward over the table, my fingers clutching each other. I could have groaned aloud had I been alone. But I was not. I sat in the great refectory of the hotel. Men were near who would have jeered at my agony had they but known its cause.

Some minutes elapsed before I could reflect on what I had read. I sat in a kind of stupor, brought on by the violence of my emotions.

Reflection came at length, and my first thought was of action. More than ever did I now desire to become the purchaser of the beautiful slave—to redeem her from this hideous bondage. I should buy her. I should set her free. True or false to me, I should accomplish this all the same. I should make no claim for gratitude. She should choose for herself. She should be free, if not in the disposal of her gratitude, at least in that of her love. A love based only on gratitude would not content me. Such could not last. Her heart should freely bestow itself. If I had already won it, well. If not, and it had fixed its affection upon another—mine be the grief. Aurore, at all events, shall be happy.

My love had elevated my soul—had filled it with such noble resolves.

And now to set her free.

When was this hideous exhibition—this "Important Sale," to come off? When was my betrothed to be sold, and I to assist at the spectacle?

I took up the paper again to ascertain the time and place. The place I knew well—the Rotundo of the Saint Louis exchange—adjoining the hotel, and within twenty yards of where I sat. That was the slave-market. But the time—it was of more importance—indeed of all importance. Strange I did not think of this before! Should it be at an early date, and my letter not have arrived! I dared not trust myself with such a supposition. Surely it would be a week—several days, at the least—before a sale of so much importance would take place. Ha! it may have been advertised for some days. The negroes may have been brought down only at the last moment!

My hands trembled, as my eyes sought the paragraph. At length they rested upon it. I read with painful surprise:—

"*To-morrow at twelve!*"

I looked to the date of the journal. All correct. It was the issue of that morning. I looked to the dial on the wall. The clock was on the stroke of *twelve*! Just one day to elapse.

"O God! if my letter should not have arrived!"

I drew forth my purse, and mechanically told over its contents. I knew not why I did so. I knew it contained but a hundred dollars. The "sportsmen" had reduced it in bulk. When I had finished counting it, I could not help smiling at the absurdity of the thing. "A hundred dollars *for the quadroon! Likely—good housekeeper, etcetera! a hundred dollars bid*!" The auctioneer would not be likely to repeat the bid.

All now depended on the English mail. If it had not arrived already, or did not before the morning, I would be helpless. Without the letter on my New Orleans banker, I could not raise fifty pounds—watch, jewels, and all. As to borrowing, I did not think of such a thing. Who was to lend me money? Who to an almost perfect stranger would advance such a sum as I required? No one I felt certain. Reigart could not have helped me to so large an amount, even had there been time to communicate with him. No—there was no one who *would*, that *could* have favoured me. No one I could think of.

"Stop:"—the banker himself! Happy thought, the banker Brown! Good, generous Brown, of the English house, Brown and Co., who, with smiling face, has already cashed my drafts for me. He will do it! The very man! Why did I not think of him sooner? Yes; if the letter have not reached him I shall tell him that I expect it every day, and its amount. He will advance the money.

"Twelve o'clock gone. There is no time to be lost. He's in his counting-house by this. I shall at once apply to him."

I seized my hat, and hastening out of the hotel, took my way through the streets towards the banking-house of Brown and Co.

Chapter Fifty Two
Brown and Co

The banking-house of Brown and Co. was in Canal Street. From the Saint Louis Exchange, Canal Street may be approached by the Rue Conti, or the parallel street of the Rue Royale. The latter is the favourite promenade of the gay Creole-French, as Saint Charles Street is for the fashionable Americans.

You will wonder at this *mélange* of French and English in the nomenclature of streets. The truth is, that New Orleans has a peculiarity somewhat rare. It is composed of two distinct cities—a French and an American one. I might even say *three*, for there is a Spanish quarter with a character distinct from either, and where you may see on the corner the Spanish designation "Calle," as the *Calle de Casacalvo, Calle del Obispo*, etcetera. This peculiarity is explained by referring to the history of Louisiana. It was colonised by the French in the early part of the eighteenth century, New Orleans being founded in 1717. The French held Louisiana till 1762, when it was ceded to Spain, and remained in her possession for a period of nearly fifty years—till 1798, when France once more became its master. Five years after, in 1803, Napoleon sold this valuable country to the American government for 15,000,000 of dollars—the best bargain which Brother Jonathan has ever made, and apparently a slack one on the part of Napoleon. After all, Napoleon was right. The sagacious Corsican, no doubt, foresaw that it could not have long remained the property of France. Sooner or later the American flag would wave over the Crescent City, and Napoleon's easy bargain has no doubt saved America a war, and France a humiliation.

This change of masters will explain the peculiarity of the population of New Orleans. The characteristics of all three nations are visible in its streets, in its houses, in the features, habits, and dress of its citizens. In nothing are the national traces more distinctly marked than in the different styles of architecture. In the American quarter you have tall brick dwellings, several stories in height, their shining fronts half occupied with rows of windows, combining the light and ornamental with the substantial and useful. This is typical of the Anglo-American. Equally typical of the French character are the light wooden one-storey houses, painted in gay colours, with green verandah palings; windows that open as doors, and a profusion of gauzy curtains hanging behind them.

Equally a type of the grand solemn character of the Spaniard, are the massive sombre structures of stone and lime, of the imposing Moorish style, that is still seen in many of the streets of New Orleans. Of these, the Great Cathedral is a fine specimen—that will stand as a monument of Spanish occupancy, long after both the Spanish and French population has been absorbed and melted down in the alembic of the Anglo-American propagandism. The American part of New Orleans is that which is highest on the river—known as the Faubourgs Saint Mary and Annunciation. Canal Street separates it from the French quarter—which last is the old city, chiefly inhabited by Creole-French and Spaniards.

A few years ago, the French and American populations were about equal. Now the Saxon element predominates, and rapidly absorbs all the others. In time the indolent Creole must yield to the more energetic American—in other words, New Orleans will be Americanised. Progress and civilisation will gain by this, at the expense—according to the sentimental school—of the poetic and picturesque.

Two distinct cities, then, are there in New Orleans. Each has its Exchange distinct from the other—a distinct municipal court and public offices—each has its centre of fashionable resort—its favourite promenade for the *flaneurs*, of which the South-western metropolis can boast a large crowd—its own theatres, ballrooms, hotels, and cafés. In fact, a walk of a few paces transports one into quite a different world. The crossing of Canal Street is like being transferred from Broadway to the Boulevards.

In their occupations there is a wide difference between the inhabitants of the two quarters. The Americans deal in the strong staples of human life. The great depôts of provisions, of cotton, of tobacco, of lumber, and the various sorts of raw produce, will be found among them. On the other hand, the finer fabrics, the laces, the jewels, the modes and modistes, the silks and satins, and all articles of *bijouterie* and *virtu*, pass through the lighter fingers of the Creoles—for these inherit both the skill and taste of their Parisian progenitors. Fine old rich wine-merchants, too, will be found in the French part, who have made fortunes by importing the wines of Bordeaux and Champagne—for claret and champagne are the wines that flow most freely on the banks of the Mississippi.

A feeling of jealousy is not wanting between the two races. The strong energetic Kentuckian affects to despise the gay pleasure-loving Frenchman, while the latter—particularly the old Creole noblesse—regard with contempt the *bizarrerie* of the Northern, so that feuds and collisions between them are not infrequent. New Orleans is, *par excellence*, the city of the duello. In all matters of this kind the Kentuckian finds the Creole quite his equal—his full match in spirit, courage, and skill. I know many Creoles who are notorious for the number of their duels. An opera-singer or *danseuse* frequently causes half a score or more—according to her merits, or mayhap her demerits. The masqued and quadroon-balls are also frequent scenes of quarrel among the wine-heated bloods who frequent them. Let no one fancy that life in New Orleans is without incident or adventure. A less prosaic city it would be hard to find.

These subjects did *not* come before my mind as I walked towards the banking-house of Brown and Co. My thoughts were occupied with a far different theme—one that caused me to press on with an agitated heart and hurried steps.

The walk was long enough to give me time for many a hypothetic calculation. Should my letter and the bill of exchange have arrived, I should be put in possession of funds at once,—enough, as I supposed, for my purpose—enough to buy my slave-bride! If not yet arrived, how then? Would Brown advance the money? My heart throbbed audibly as I asked myself this question. Its answer, affirmative or negative, would be to me like the pronouncement of a sentence of life or death.

And yet I felt more than half certain that Brown would do so. I could not fancy his smiling generous John-Bull face clouded with the seriousness of a refusal. Its great importance to me at that moment—the certainty of its being repaid, and in a few days, or hours at the farthest—surely he would not deny me! What to him, a man of millions, could be the inconvenience of advancing five hundred pounds? Oh! he would do it to a certainty. No fear but he would do it!

I crossed the threshold of the man of money, my spirits buoyant with sweet anticipation. When I recrossed it my soul was saddened with bitter disappointment. My letter had not yet arrived—Brown refused the advance!

I was too inexperienced in business to comprehend its sordid calculations—its cold courtesy. What cared the banker for my pressing wants? What to him was my ardent appeal? Even had I told him my motives, my object, it would have been all the same. That game cold denying smile would have been the reply—ay, even had my life depended upon it.

I need not detail the interview. It was brief enough. I was told, with a bland smile, that my letter had not yet come to hand. To my proposal for the advance the answer was blunt enough. The kind generous smile blanked off

Brown's ruddy face. It was not business. It could not be done. There was no sign thrown out—no invitation to talk farther. I might have appealed in a more fervent strain. I might have confessed the purpose for which I wanted the money, but Brown's face gave me no encouragement. Perhaps it was as well I did not. Brown would have chuckled over my delicate secret. The town, over its tea-table, would have relished it as a rich joke.

Enough—my letter had not arrived—Brown refused the advance. With Hope behind me and Despair in front, I hurried back to the hotel.

Chapter Fifty Three
Eugène d'Hauteville

The remainder of the day I was occupied in searching for Aurore. I could learn nothing of her—not even whether she had yet reached the city!

In search of her I went to the quarters where the others had their temporary lodgment. She was not these. She had either not yet arrived, or was kept at some other place. They had not seen her! They knew nothing about her.

Disappointed and wearied with running through the hot and dusty streets, I returned to the hotel.

I waited for night. I waited for the coming of Eugène d'Hauteville, for such was the name of my new acquaintance.

I was strangely interested in this young man. Our short interview had inspired me with a singular confidence in him. He had given proof of a friendly design towards me; and still more had impressed me with a high idea of his knowledge of the world. Young as he was, I could not help fancying him a being possessed of some mysterious power. I could not help thinking that in some way he might aid me. There was nothing remarkable in his being so young and still *au-fait* to all the mysteries of life. Precocity is the privilege of the American, especially the native of New Orleans. A Creole at fifteen is a man.

I felt satisfied that D'Hauteville—about my own age—knew far more of the world than I, who had been half my life cloistered within the walls of an antique university.

I had an instinct that he both *could* and *would* serve me.

How? you may ask. By lending me the money I required?

It could not be thus. I believed that he was himself without funds, or possessed of but little—far too little to be of use to me. My reason for thinking so was the reply he had made when I asked for his address. There was something in the tone of his answer that led me to the thought that he was without fortune—even without a home. Perhaps a clerk out of place, thought I; or a poor artist. His dress was rich enough—but dress is no criterion on a Mississippi steamboat.

With these reflections it was strange I should have been impressed with the idea *he* could serve me! But I was so, and had therefore resolved to make him the confidant of my secret—the secret of my love—the secret of my misery.

Perhaps another impulse acted upon me, and aided in bringing me to this determination. He whose heart has been charged with a deep grief must know the relief which sympathy can afford. The sympathy of friendship is sweet and soothing. There is balm in the counsel of a kind companion.

My sorrow had been long pent up within my own bosom, and yearned to find expression. Stranger among strangers, I had no one to share it with me. Even to the good Reigart I had not confessed myself. With the exception of Aurore herself, Eugénie—poor Eugénie—was alone mistress of my secret. Would that she of all had never known it!

Now to this youth Eugène—strange coincidence of name!—I was resolved to impart it—resolved to unburden my heart. Perhaps, in so doing I might find consolation or relief.

I waited for the night. It was at night he had promised to come. I waited with impatience—with my eyes bent almost continuously on the index finger of time, and chafing at the slow measured strokes of the pendulum.

I was not disappointed. He came at length. His silvery voice rang in my ears, and he stood before me.

As he entered my room, I was once more struck with the melancholy expression of his countenance—the pale cheek—the resemblance to some face I had met before.

The room was close and hot. The summer had not yet quite departed. I proposed a walk. We could converse as freely in the open air, and there was a lovely moon to light us on our way.

As we sallied forth, I offered my visitor a cigar. This he declined, giving his reason. He did not smoke.

Strange, thought I, for one of a race, who almost universally indulge in the habit. Another peculiarity in the character of my new acquaintance!

We passed up the Rue Royale, and turned along Canal Street in the direction of the "Swamp." Presently we crossed the Rue des Rampartes, and soon found ourselves outside the limits of the city.

Some buildings appeared beyond, but they were not houses—at least not dwelling-places for the living. The numerous cupolas crowned with crosses—the broken columns—the monuments of white marble, gleaming under the moon, told us that we looked upon a city of the dead. It was the great cemetery of New Orleans—that cemetery where the poor after death are *drowned*, and the rich fare no better, for they are *baked*!

The gate stood open—the scene within invited me—its solemn character was in unison with my spirit. My companion made no objection, and we entered.

After wending our way among tombs, and statues, and monuments; miniature temples, columns, obelisks, sarcophagi carved in snow-white marble—passing graves that spoke of recent affliction—others of older date, but garnished with fresh flowers—the symbols of lore or affection that still lingered—we seated ourselves upon a moss-grown slab, with the fronds of the Babylonian willow waving above our heads, and drooping mournfully around us.

Chapter Fifty Four
Pity for Love

Along the way we had conversed upon several topics indifferently—of my gambling adventure on the boat—of the "sportsmen" of New Orleans—of the fine moonlight.

Until after entering the cemetery, and taking our seats upon the tomb, I had disclosed nothing of that which altogether engrossed my thoughts. The time had now arrived for unbosoming myself, and half-an-hour after Eugène D'Hauteville knew the story of my love.

I confided to him all that had occurred from the time of my leaving New Orleans, up to the period of our meeting upon the Houma. My interview with the banker Brown, and my fruitless search that day for Aurore, were also detailed.

From first to last he listened without interrupting me; only once, when I described the scene of my confession to Eugénie, and its painful ending. The details of this seemed to interest him exceedingly—in fact, to give him pain. More than once I was interrupted by his sobs, and by the light of the moon I could see that he was in tears!

"Noble youth!" thought I, "thus to be affected by the sufferings of a stranger!"

"Poor Eugénie!" murmured he, "is *she* not to be pitied?"

"Pitied! ah, Monsieur; you know not how much I pity her! That scene will never be effaced from my memory. If pity—friendship—any sacrifice could make amends, how willingly would I bestow it upon her—all but that which is not in my power to give—my love. Deeply, Monsieur D'Hauteville—deeply do I grieve for that noble lady. Oh, that I could pluck the sting from her heart which I have been the innocent cause of placing there. But surely she will recover from this unfortunate passion? Surely in time—"

"Ah! never! never!" interrupted D'Hauteville, with an earnestness of manner that surprised me.

"Why say you so, Monsieur?"

"Why?—because I have some skill in such affairs; young as you think me, *I* have experienced a similar misfortune. Poor Eugénie! *Such a wound is hard to heal*; she will not recover from it. Ah—never!"

"Indeed, I pity her—with my whole soul I pity her."

"You should seek her and say so."

"Why?" I asked, somewhat astonished at the suggestion.

"Perhaps your pity expressed to her might give consolation."

"Impossible. It would have the contrary effect."

"You misjudge, Monsieur. Unrequited love is far less hard to bear when it meets with sympathy. It is only haughty contempt and heartless triumph that wring blood-drops from the heart. Sympathy is balm to the wounds of love. Believe me it is so. *I feel it to be so. Oh! I feel it to be so!*"

The last two phrases he spoke with an earnestness that sounded strangely in my ears.

"Mysterious youth!" thought I. "So gentle, so compassionate, and yet so worldly-wise!"

I felt as though I conversed with some spiritual being—some superior mind, who comprehended all.

His doctrine was new to me, and quite contrary to the general belief. At a later period of my life I became convinced of its truth.

"If I thought my sympathy would have such an effect," replied I, "I should seek Eugénie—I should offer her—"

"There will be a time for that afterward," said D'Hauteville, interrupting me; "your present business is more pressing. You purpose to *buy this quadroon?*"

"I did so this morning. Alas! I have no longer a hope. It will not be in my power."

"How much money have these sharpers left you?"

"Not much over one hundred dollars."

"Ha! that will not do. From your description of her she will bring ten times the amount. A misfortune, indeed! My own purse is still lighter than yours. I have not a hundred dollars. *Pardieu*! it is a sad affair."

D'Hauteville pressed his head between his hands, and remained for some moments silent, apparently in deep meditation. From his manner I could not help believing that he really sympathised with me, and that he was thinking of some plan to assist me.

"After all," he muttered to himself, just loud enough for me to hear what was said, "if she should not succeed—if she should not find the papers—then she, too, must be a sacrifice. Oh! it is a terrible risk. It might be better not—it might be—"

"Monsieur!" I said, interrupting him, "of what are you speaking?"

"Oh!—ah! pardon me: it is an affair I was thinking of—*n'importe*. We had better return, Monsieur. It is cold. The atmosphere of this solemn place chills me."

He said all this with an air of embarrassment, as though he had been speaking his thoughts unintentionally.

Though astonished at what he had uttered, I could not press him for an explanation; but, yielding to his wish, I rose up to depart. I had lost hope. Plainly he had it not in his power to serve me.

At this moment a resource suggested itself to my mind, or rather the forlorn hope of a resource.

I communicated it to my companion.

"I have still these two hundred dollars," said I, "They are of no more service to me for the purchase of Aurore than if they were so many pebbles. Suppose I try to increase the amount at the gaming-table?"

"Oh, I fear it would be an idle attempt. You would lose as before."

"That is not so certain, Monsieur. The chances at least are equal. I need not play with men of skill, like those upon the boat. Here in New Orleans there are gaming-houses, plenty of them, where *games of chance* are carried on. These are of various kinds—as *faro, craps, loto,* and *roulette*. I can choose some one of these, where bets are made on the tossing of a die or the turning of a card. It is just as likely I may win as lose. What say you, Monsieur? Give me your counsel."

"You speak truly," replied he. "There is a chance in the game. It offers a hope of your winning. If you lose, you will be no worse off as regards your intentions for to-morrow. If you win—"

"True, true—if I win—"

"You must not lose time, then. It is growing late. These gaming-houses should be open at this hour: no doubt, they are now in the very tide of their business. Let us find one."

"You will go with me? Thanks, Monsieur D'Hauteville! Thanks—*allons*!"

We hastily traversed the walk that led to the entrance of the cemetery; and, issuing from the gate, took our way back into the town.

We headed for our point of departure—the Rue Saint Louis; for I knew that in that neighbourhood lay the principal gambling hells.

It was not difficult to find them. At that period there was no concealment required in such matters. The gambling passion among the Creoles, inherited from the original possessors of the city, was too rife among all classes to be put down by a police. The municipal authorities in the American quarter had taken some steps toward the suppression of this vice; but their laws had no force on the French side of Canal Street; and Creole police had far different ideas, as well as different instructions. In the French faubourgs gaming was not considered so hideous a crime, and the houses appropriated to it were open and avowed.

As you passed along Rue Conti, or Saint Louis, or the Rue Bourbon, you could not fail to notice several large gilded lamps, upon which you might read "faro" and "craps", "loto" or "roulette,"—odd words to the eyes of the uninitiated, but well enough understood by those whose business it was to traverse the streets of the "First Municipality."

Our hurrying stops soon brought us in front of one of these establishments, whose lamp told us in plain letters that "faro" was played inside.

It was the first that offered; and, without hesitating a moment, I entered, followed by D'Hauteville.

We had to climb a wide stairway, at the top of which we were received by a whiskered and moustached fellow in waiting. I supposed that he was about to demand some fee for admission. I was mistaken in my conjecture. Admission was perfectly free. The purpose of this individual in staying us was to divest us of arms, for which he handed us a ticket, that we might reclaim them in going out. That he had disarmed a goodly number before our turn came, was evident from the numerous butts of pistols, hafts of bowie-knives, and handles of daggers, that protruded from the pigeon-holes of a shelf-like structure standing in one corner of the passage.

The whole proceeding reminded me of the scenes I had often witnessed—the surrender of canes, umbrellas, and parasols, on entering a picture-gallery or a museum. No doubt it was a necessary precaution—the non-observance of which would have led to many a scene of blood over the gaming-table.

We yielded up our weapons—I a pair of pistols, and my companion a small silver dagger. These were ticketed, duplicates delivered to us, and we were allowed to pass on into the *"saloon."*

Chapter Fifty Five
On Games and Gambling

The passion of gaming is universal amongst men. Every nation indulges in it to a greater or less extent. Every nation, civilised or savage, has its game, from whist and cribbage at Almacks to "chuck-a-luck" and "poke-stick" upon the prairies.

Moral England fancies herself clear of the stain. Her gossiping traveller rarely fails to fling a stone at the foreigner on this head. French, German, Spaniard, and Mexican, are in turn accused of an undue propensity for this vice. Cant—all cant! There is more gambling in moral England than in any country of my knowing. I do not speak of card-playing about the purlieus of Piccadilly. Go to Epsom races on a "Derby day," and there you may form an idea of the scale upon which English gaming is carried on—for gaming it is in the very lowest sense of the word. Talk of "noble sport,"—of an admiration for that fine animal—the horse. Bah! Noble, indeed! Fancy those seedy scamps, who in thousands and tens of thousands flock upon every race-course,—fancy them and their harlotic companions possessed with the idea of anything fine or noble! Of all who crowd there the horse alone is noble—naught could be more ignoble than his *entourage*.

No, moral England! You are no pattern for the nations in this respect. You are not free from the stain, as you imagine yourself. You have a larger population of gamblers,—*horse-gamblers* if you will, than any other people; and, however noble be your game, I make bold to affirm that your gamesters are the seediest, snobbiest, and most revolting of the tribe. There is something indescribably mean in the life and habits of those hungry-looking vultures who hang about the corners of Coventry Street and the Haymarket, out at elbows, out at heels, sneaking from tavern to betting-house, and from betting-house to tavern. There is a meanness, a positive cowardice in the very nature of their game,—their small ventures and timid "hedging" of bets. In comparison, the bold ringer of dice has something *almost* noble in him. Your apathetic Don, who stakes his gold onzas on a single throw of the ivory—your Mexican monte-player, who risks his doubloons on each turn of the cards,—are, to some extent, dignified by the very boldness of their venture. With them gambling is a passion—its excitement their lure;

but Brown, and Smith, and Jones, cannot even plead *the passion*. Even *that* would exalt them.

Of all gamblers by profession the "sportsman" of the Mississippi Valley is perhaps the most picturesque. I have already alluded to their elegant style of attire, but, independent of that, there is a dash of the gentleman—a certain *chivalresqueness* of character which distinguishes them from all others of their calling. During the wilder episodes of my life I have been *honoured* with the acquaintance of more than one of these *gentlemen*, and I cannot help bearing a somewhat high testimony in their favour. Several have I met of excellent moral character,—though, perhaps, not quite up to the standard of Exeter Hall. Some I have known of noble and generous hearts—doers of noble actions—who, though outcasts in society, were not outcasts to their own natures; men who would bravely resent the slightest insult that might be put upon them. Of course there were others, as the Chorleys and Hatchers, who would scarce answer to this description of Western "sportsmen"—but I really believe that such are rather the exception than the rule. A word about the "games of America." The true national game of the United States is the "election." The local or state elections afford so many opportunities of betting, just as the minor horse-races do in England; while the great quadrennial, the Presidential election, is the "Derby day" of America. The enormous sums that change hands upon such occasions, and the enormous number of them, would be incredible. A statistic of these bets, could such be given, and their amount, would surprise even the most "enlightened citizen" of the States themselves. Foreigners cannot understand the intense excitement which is felt during an election time throughout the United States. It would be difficult to explain it, in a country where men generally know that the fate of the particular candidate has, after all, but a slight influence on their material interests. True, party spirit and the great stake of all—the "spoils" of office—will account for some of the interest taken in the result, but not for all. I am of opinion that the "balance" of the excitement may be set down to the credit of the gaming passion. Nearly every second man you meet has a bet, or rather a "book," upon the Presidential election!

Election, therefore, is the true national game, indulged in by high, low, rich, and poor.

To bet upon an election, however, is not considered *infra dig*. It is not *professional* gambling.

The games for that purpose are of various kinds—in most of which cards are relied upon to furnish the chances. Dice and billiards are also in vogue—billiards to a considerable extent. It is a very mean village in the United States—particularly in the South and West—that does not furnish one or more public billiard-tables; and among Americans may be found some of the most expert (crack) players in the world. The "Creoles" of Louisiana are distinguished at this game.

"Ten-pins" is also a very general game, and every town has its "ten-pin alley." But "billiards" and "ten-pins" are not true "gambling games." The first is patronised rather as an elegant amusement, and the latter as an excellent exercise. Cards and dice are the real weapons of the "sportsman," but particularly the former. Besides the English games of whist and cribbage, and the French games of "vingt-un," "rouge-et-noir," etcetera, the American gambler plays "poker," "euchre," "seven-up," and a variety of others. In New Orleans there is a favourite of the Creoles called "craps," a dice game, and "keno," and "loto," and "roulette," played with balls and a revolving wheel. Farther to the South, among the Spano-Mexicans, you meet the game of "monte," — a card game, distinct from all the others. Monte is the national game of Mexico.

To all other modes of getting at your money, the South-Western sportsman prefers "faro." It is a game of Spanish origin, as its name imports; indeed, it differs but little from monte, and was no doubt obtained from the Spaniards of New Orleans. Whether native or exotic to the towns of the Mississippi Valley, in all of them it has become perfectly naturalised; and there is no sportsman of the West who does not understand and practise it.

The game of faro is simple enough. The following are its leading features:—

A green cloth or baize covers the table. Upon this the thirteen cards of a suite are laid out in two rows, with their faces turned up. They are usually attached to the cloth by gum, to prevent them from getting out of place.

A square box, like an overgrown snuff-box, is next produced. It is of the exact size and shape to hold two packs of cards. It is of solid silver. Any other metal would serve as well; but a professed "faro dealer" would scorn to carry a mean implement of his calling. The object of this box is to hold the cards to be dealt, and to assist in dealing them. I cannot explain the internal mechanism of this mysterious box; but I can say that it is without a lid, open at one edge—where the cards are pressed in—and contains an interior spring, which, touched by the finger of the dealer, pushes out the cards one by one as they lie in the pack. This contrivance is not at all essential to the game, which may be played without the box. Its object is to insure a fair deal, as no card can be recognised by any mark on its back, since up to the moment of drawing they are all invisible within the box. A stylish "faro box" is the ambition of every "faro dealer"—the specific title of all "sportsmen" whose game is faro.

Two packs of cards, well shuffled, are first put into the box; and the dealer, resting the left hand upon it, and holding the right in readiness, with the thumb extended, pauses a moment until some bets are made. The "dealer" is in reality your antagonist in the game; he is the "banker" who pays all your gains, and pockets all your losses. As many may bet as can sit or stand around the table; but all are betting against the dealer himself. Of course, in this case, the faro dealer must be something of a proprietor to play the game at all; and the "faro bank" has usually a capital of several thousands of dollars—often hundreds of thousands to back it! Not unfrequently, after an unlucky run, the bank gets "broke;" and the proprietor of it may be years before he can establish another. An assistant or "croupier" usually sits beside the dealer. His business is to exchange the "cheques" for money, to pay the bets lost, and gather in those which the bank has won.

The cheques used in the game are pieces of ivory of circular form, of the diameter of dollars: they are white, red, or blue, with the value engraved upon them, and they are used as being more convenient than the money itself. When any one wishes to leave off playing, he can demand from the bank to the amount specified on the cheques he may then hold.

The simplest method of betting "against faro" is by placing the money on the face of any particular one of the cards that lie on the table. You may choose which you will of the thirteen. Say you have selected the ace, and placed your money upon the face of that card. The dealer then commences, and "draws" the cards out of the box one by one. After drawing each two he makes a pause. Until two aces follow each other, with no other card between, there is no decision. When two aces come together the bet is declared. If both appear in the drawing of the two cards, then the dealer takes your money; if only one is pulled out, and the other follows in the next drawing, you have won. You may then renew your bet upon the ace—double it if you will, or remove it to any other card—and these changes you may make at any period of the deal—provided it is not done after the first of the two cards has been drawn.

Of course the game goes on, whether you play or not. The table is surrounded by betters; some on one card, some on another; some by "paralee," on two or more cards at a time; so that there is a constant "falling due" of bets, a constant rattling of cheques and chinking of dollars.

It is all a game of chance. "Skill" has naught to do with the game of faro; and you might suppose, as many do, that the chances are exactly equal for the dealer and his opponents. Such, however, is not the case; a peculiar arrangement of the cards produces a percentage in favour of the former, else there would be no faro bank; and although a rare run of ill-fortune may go against the dealer for a time, if he can only hold out long enough, he is "bound to beat you" in the end.

A similar percentage will be against you in all games of chance—"faro," "monte," or "craps," wherever you bet against a "banker." Of course the banker will not deny this, but answers you, that that *small* percentage is to "pay for the game." It usually does, and well.

Such is faro—the game at which I had resolved to empty my purse, or win the price of my betrothed.

Chapter Fifty Six
The Faro Bank

We entered the saloon. The game *voilà*!

At one end was the table—the bank. We could see neither bank nor dealer; both were hidden by the double ring of bettors, who encircled the table—one line seated, the other standing behind. There were women, too, mingled in the crowd—seated and standing in every attitude—gay and beautiful women, decked out in the finery of fashion, but with a certain *braverie* of manner that betokened their unfortunate character.

D'Hauteville had guessed aright—the game was at its height. The look and attitudes of the betters—their arms constantly in motion, placing their stakes—the incessant rattling of the ivory cheques, and the clinking together of dollars—all told that the game was progressing briskly.

A grand chandelier, suspended above the table, cast its brilliant light over the play and the players.

Near the middle of the saloon stood a large table, amply furnished with "refreshments." Cold fowls, ham and tongue, chicken salad, and lobsters, cut-glass decanters tilled with wine, brandy, and other liquors, garnished this table. Some of the plates and glasses bore the traces of having been already used, while others were clean and ready for anyone who chose to play knife and fork a while. It was, in fact, a "free lunch," or rather supper—free to any guest who chose to partake of it. Such is the custom of an American gambling-house.

The rich viands did not tempt either my companion or myself. We passed the table without halting, and walked directly up to the "bank."

We reached the outer circle, and looked over the shoulders of the players. "*Shade of Fortuna! Chorley and Hatcher!*"

Yes—there sat the two sharpers, side by side, behind the faro-table—not as mere bettors, but acting respectively as banker and croupier of the game! Chorley held the dealing-box in his fingers, while Hatcher sat upon his right, with cheques, dollars, and bank-notes piled upon the table in front of him! A glance around the ring of faces showed us the pork-merchant as well. There sat he in his loose jeans coat and broad white-hat, talking farmer-like, betting bravely, and altogether a stranger to both banker and croupier!

My companion and I regarded each other with a look of surprise.

After all, there was nothing to surprise us. A faro bank needs no charter, no further preliminaries to its establishment than to light up a table, spread a green baize over it, and commence operations. The sportsmen were no doubt quite at home here. Their up-river excursion was only by way of a little variety—an interlude incidental to the summer. The "season" of New Orleans was now commencing, and they had just returned in time for it. Therefore there was nothing to be surprised at, in our finding them where we did.

At first seeing them, however, I felt astonishment, and my companion seemed to share it. I turned towards him, and was about proposing that we should leave the room again, when the wandering eye of the pseudo pork-merchant fell upon me.

"Hilloa, stranger!" he cried out, with an air of astonishment, "you hyar?"

"I believe so," I replied unconcernedly.

"Wal! wal! I tho't you war lost. Whar did you go, anyhow?" he inquired in a tone of vulgar familiarity, and loud enough to turn the attention of all present upon myself and my companion.

"Ay—*whar* did I go?" I responded, keeping my temper, and concealing the annoyance I really felt at the fellow's impudence.

"Yes—that's jest what I wanted to know."

"Are you very anxious?" I asked.

"Oh, no—not particklerly so."

"I am glad of that," I responded, "as I don't intend telling you."

With all his swagger I could see that his crest fell a little at the general burst of laughter that my somewhat *bizarre* remark had called forth.

"Come, stranger," he said, in a half-deprecatory, half-spiteful tone, "you needn't a be so short-horned about it, I guess; I didn't mean no offence—but you know you left us so suddintly—never mind—'taint no business o' mine. You're going to take a hand at faro, ain't you?"

"Perhaps."

"Wal, then, it appears a nice game. I'm jest trying it for the first time myself. It's all chance, I believe—jest like odds and evens. I'm a winnin' anyhow."

He turned his face to the bank, and appeared to busy himself in arranging his bets.

A fresh deal had commenced, and the players, drawn off for a moment by our conversation, became once more engaged in what was of greater interest to them—the little money-heaps upon the cards.

Of course, both Chorley and Hatcher recognised me; but they had restricted their recognitions to a friendly nod, and a glance that plainly said—

"He's here! all right! he'll not go till he has tried to get back his hundred dollars—he'll have a shy at the bank—no fear but he will."

If such were their thoughts they were, not far astray. My own reflections were as follows:—

"I may as well risk my money here as elsewhere. A faro bank is a faro bank all the same. There is no opportunity for cheating, where cards are thus dealt. The arrangement of the bets precludes every possibility of such a thing. Where one player loses to the bank, another may win from it by the very same turn, and this of course checks the dealer from drawing the cards falsely, even if it were possible for him to do so. So I may as well play against Messrs Chorley and Hatcher's bank as any other—better, indeed; for if I am to win I shall have the satisfaction of the *revanche*, which those gentlemen owe me. I shall play here then. Do you advise me, Monsieur?"

Part of the above reflections, and the interrogatory that wound them up, were addressed in a whisper to the young Creole.

He acknowledged their justice. He advised me to remain. He was of the opinion I might as well tempt fortune there as go farther.

Enough—I took out a five-dollar gold-piece, and placed it upon the ace.

No notice was taken of this—neither banker nor croupier even turning their eyes in the direction, of the bet. Such a sum as five dollars would not decompose the well-practised nerves of these gentlemen—where sums of ten, twenty, or even fifty times the amount, were constantly passing to and from their cash-box.

The deal proceeded, Chorley drawing the cards with that air of imperturbable *sang-froid* so characteristic of his class.

"Ace wins," cried a voice, as two aces came forth together.

"Pay you in cheques, sir?" asked the croupier.

I assented, and a flat round piece of ivory, of a red colour, with the figure 5 in its centre, was placed upon my half-eagle. I permitted both to remain upon the ace. The deal went on, and after a while two aces came out together, and two more of the red cheques were mine.

I suffered all four pieces, now worth twenty dollars, to lie. I had not come there to amuse myself. My purpose was very different; and, impelled by that purpose, I was resolved not to waste time. If Fortune was to prove favourable to me, her favours were as likely to be mine soon as late; and when I thought of the real stake for which I was playing, I could not endure the suspense. No more was I satisfied at contact with the coarse and bawd company that surrounded the table.

The deal went on—and after some time aces again came out. This time I lost.

Without a word passing from his lips, the croupier drew in the cheques and gold-piece, depositing them in his japanned cash-box, I took out my purse, and tried ten dollars upon the queen, I won. I doubled the bet, and lost again.

Another ten dollars won—another lost—another and another, and so on, now winning, now losing, now betting with cheques, now with gold-pieces—until at length I felt to the bottom of my purse without encountering a coin!

Chapter Fifty Seven
The Watch and Ring

I rose from my seat, and turned towards D'Hauteville with a glance of despair. I needed not to tell him the result. My look would have announced it, but he had been gazing over my shoulder and knew all.

"Shall we go, Monsieur?" I asked.

"Not yet—stay a moment," replied he, placing his hand upon my arm.

"And why?" I asked; "I have not a dollar. I have lost all. I might have known it would be so. Why stay here, sir?"

I spoke somewhat brusquely. I confess I was at the moment in anything but an amiable mood. In addition to my prospects for the morrow, a suspicion had flashed across my mind that my new friend was not loyal. His knowledge of these men—his having counselled me to play there—the accident, to say the least, a strange one, of our again meeting with the "sportsmen" of the boat, and under such a new phase—the great celerity with which my purse had been "cleared out"—all these circumstances passing rapidly through my mind, led me naturally enough to suspect D'Hauteville of treason. I ran rapidly over our late conversation. I tried to remember whether he had said or done anything to guide me into this particular hell. Certainly he had not proposed my playing, but rather opposed it; and I could not remember that by word or act he had endeavoured to introduce me to the game. Moreover, he seemed as much astonished as myself at seeing these gentlemen behind the table.

What of all that? The surprise might have been well feigned. Possibly enough; and after my late experience of the pork-merchant, probably enough, Monsieur D'Hauteville was also a partner in the firm of Chorley, Hatcher, and Co. I wheeled round with an angry expression on my lips, when the current of my thoughts was suddenly checked, and turned into a new channel. The young Creole stood looking up in my face—he was not so tall as I—gazing upon me out of his beautiful eyes, and waiting until my moment of abstraction should pass. Something glittered in his outstretched hand. It was a purse. I could see the yellow coins shining through the silken network. It was a purse of gold!

"Take it!" he said, in his soft silvery voice.

My heart fell abashed within me. I could scarce stammer forth a reply. Had he but known my latest thoughts, he might have been able to read the flush of shame that so suddenly mantled my cheeks.

"No, Monsieur," I replied; "this is too generous of you. I cannot accept it."

"Come—come! Why not? Take it, I pray—try Fortune again. She has frowned on you of late, but remember she is a fickle goddess, and may yet smile on you. Take the purse, man!"

"Indeed, Monsieur, I cannot after what I—pardon me—if you knew—"

"Then must *I* play for you—remember the purpose that brought us here! Remember Aurore!"

"Oh!"

This ejaculation, wrung from my heart, was the only answer I could make, before the young Creole had turned to the faro-table, and was placing his gold upon the cards.

I stood watching him with feelings of astonishment and admiration, mingled with anxiety for the result.

What small white hands! What a brilliant jewel, sparkling on his finger—a diamond! It has caught the eyes of the players, who gloat upon it as it passes back and forward to the cards. Chorley and Hatcher have both noticed it. I saw them exchange their peculiar glance as they did so. Both are polite to him. By the large bets he is laying he has won their esteem. Their attention in calling out the card when he wins, and in handing him his cheques, is marked and assiduous. He is the favoured better of the ring; and oh! how the eyes of those fair lemans gleam upon him with their wild and wicked meaning! Not one of them that would not love him for that sparkling gem!

I stood on one side watching with great anxiety—greater than if the stake had been my own. But it *was* my own. It was *for me*. The generous youth was playing away his gold for *me*.

My suspense was not likely to be of long duration. He was losing rapidly—recklessly losing. He had taken my place at the table, and along with it my ill-luck. Almost every bet he made was "raked" into the bank, until his last coin lay upon the cards. Another turn, and that, too, chinked as it fell into the cash-box of the croupier!

"Come now, D'Hauteville! Come away!" I whispered, leaning over, and laying hold of his arm.

"How much against this?" he asked the banker, without heeding me—"how much, sir?"

As he put the question, he raised the gold guard over his head, at the same time drawing forth his watch.

I suspected this was his intention when I first spoke. I repeated my request in a tone of entreaty—all in vain. He pressed Chorley for a reply.

The latter was not the man to waste words at such a crisis.

"A hundred dollars," said he, "for the watch—fifty more upon the chain."

"Beautiful!" exclaimed one of the players.

"They're worth more," muttered another.

Even in the *blazé* hearts around that table there were human feelings. There is always a touch of sympathy for him who loses boldly; and an expression of this in favour of the Creole youth could be heard, from time to time, as his money parted from him.

"Yes, that watch and chain are worth more," said a tall dark-whiskered man, who sat near the end of the table. This remark was made in a firm confident tone of voice, that seemed to command Chorley's attention.

"I'll look at it again, if you please?" said he, stretching across the table to D'Hauteville, who still held the watch in his hand.

The latter surrendered it once more to the gambler, who opened the case, and commenced inspecting the interior. It was an elegant watch, and chain also—of the fashion usually worn by ladies. They were worth more than Chorley had offered, though that did not appear to be the opinion of the pork-merchant.

"It's a good pile o' money, is a hundred an' fifty dollars," drawled he; "a good biggish pile, I reckon. I don't know much about such fixins meself, but it's full valley for that ar watch an' chain, I shed say."

"Nonsense!" cried several: "two hundred dollars—it's worth it all. See the jewels!"

Chorley cut short the discussion.

"Well," said he, "I don't think it worth more than what I've bid, sir. But since you wish to get back what you've already lost, I don't mind staking two hundred against watch and chain together. Does that satisfy you?"

"Play on!" was the only answer made by the impatient Creole, as he took back his watch, and laid it down upon one of the cards.

It was a cheap watch to Chorley. It cost him but the drawing out of half-a-dozen cards, and it became his!

"How much against this?"

D'Hauteville drew off his ring, and held it before the dazzled eyes of the dealer.

At this crisis I once more interfered, but my remonstrance was unheeded. It was of no use trying to stay the fiery spirit of the Creole.

The ring was a diamond, or rather a collection of diamonds in a gold setting. It, like the watch, was also of the fashion worn by ladies; and I could hear some characteristic remarks muttered around the table, such as, "That young blood's got a rich girl somewhere," "There's more where they come from," and the like!

The ring was evidently one of much value, as Chorley, after an examination of it, proposed to stake four hundred dollars. The tall man in dark whiskers again interfered, and put it at five hundred. The circle backed him, and the dealer at length agreed to give that sum.

"Will you take cheques, sir?" he inquired, addressing D'Hauteville, "or do you mean to stake it at one bet?"

"At one bet," was the answer.

"No, no!" cried several voices, inclined to favour D'Hauteville.

"At one bet," repeated he, in a determined tone. "Place it upon the ace!"

"As you wish, sir," responded Chorley, with perfect *sang-froid*, at the same time handing back the ring to its owner.

D'Hauteville took the jewel in his slender white fingers, and laid it on the centre of the card. It was the only bet made. The other players had become so interested in the result, that they withheld their stakes in order to watch it.

Chorley commenced drawing the cards. Each one as it came forth caused a momentary thrill of expectancy; and when aces, deuces, or trés with their broad white margins appeared outside the edge of that mysterious box, the excitement became intense.

It was a long time before two aces came together. It seemed as if the very importance of the stakes called for more than the usual time to decide the bet.

It was decided at length. The ring followed the watch.

I caught D'Hauteville by the arm, and drew him away from the table. This time he followed me unresistingly—as he had nothing more to lay.

"What matters it?" said he, with a gay air as we passed together out of the saloon. "Ah! yes," he continued, changing his tone, "ah, yes, it does matter! It matters to *you*, and *Aurore*!"

Chapter Fifty Eight
My Forlorn Hope

It was pleasant escaping from that hot hell into the cool night air—into the soft light of a Southern moon. It would have been pleasant under other circumstances; but then the sweetest clime and loveliest scene would have made no impression upon me.

My companion seemed to share my bitterness of soul. His words of consolation were not without their influence; I knew they were the expressions of a real sympathy. His acts had already proved it.

It was, indeed, a lovely night. The white moon rode buoyantly through fleecy clouds, that thinly dappled the azure sky of Louisiana, and a soft breeze played through the now silent streets. A lovely night—too sweet and balmy. My spirit would have preferred a storm. Oh! for black clouds, red lightning, and thunder rolling and crashing through the sky. Oh! for the whistling wind, and the quick pattering of the rain-drops. Oh! for a hurricane without, consonant to the storm that was raging within me!

It was but a few steps to the hotel; but we did not stop there. We could think better in the open air, and converse as well. Sleep had no charms for me, and my companion seemed to share my impulses; so passing once more from among the houses, we went on towards the Swamp, caring not whither we went.

We walked side by side for some time without exchanging speech. Our thoughts were running upon the same theme,—the business of to-morrow. To-morrow no longer, for the tolling of the great cathedral clock had just announced the hour of midnight. In twelve hours more the *vente de l'ençan* would commence—in twelve hours more they would be bidding, for my betrothed!

Our steps were towards the "Shell Road," and soon our feet crunched upon the fragments of unios and bivalves that strewed the path. Here was a scene more in unison with our thoughts. Above and around waved the dark solemn cypress-trees, fit emblems of grief—rendered doubly lugubrious in their expression by the hoary *tillandsia*, that draped them like a couch of the dead. The sounds, too, that here saluted our ears had a soothing effect; the melancholy "coowhoo-a" of the swamp-owl—the creaking chirp of the tree-crickets and cicadas—the solemn "tong-tong" of the bell-frog—the hoarse trumpet-note of the greater batrachian—and high overhead the wild treble of the bull-bat, all mingled together in a concert, that, however disagreeable under other circumstances, now fell upon my ears like music, and even imparted a kind of sad pleasure to my soul.

And yet it was not my darkest hour. A darker was yet in store for me. Despite the very hopelessness of the prospect, I still clung to hope. A vague feeling it was; but it sustained me against despair. The trunk of a taxodium lay prostrate by the side of our path. Upon this we sat down.

We had exchanged scarce a dozen words since emerging from the hell. I was busy with thoughts of the morrow: my young companion, whom I now regarded in the light of an old and tried friend, was thinking of the same.

What generosity towards a stranger! what self-sacrifice! *Ah! little did I then know of the vast extent—the noble grandeur of that sacrifice*!

"There now remains but one chance," I said; "the chance that to-morrow's mail, or rather to-day's, may bring my letter. It might still arrive in time; the mail is due by ten o'clock in the morning."

"True," replied my companion, seemingly too busy with his own thoughts to give much heed to what I had said.

"If not," I continued, "then there is only the hope that he who shall become the purchaser, may afterwards sell her to *me*. I care not at what price, if I—"

"Ah!" interrupted D'Hauteville, suddenly waking from his reverie; "it is just that which troubles me—that is exactly what I have been thinking upon. I fear, Monsieur, I fear—"

"Speak on!"

"I fear there is no hope that he who buys her will be willing to sell her again."

"And why? Will not a large sum—?"

"No—no—I fear that he who buys will not give her up again, *at any price*."

"Ha! Why do you think so, Monsieur D'Hauteville."

"I have my suspicion that a certain individual designs—"

"Who?"

"Monsieur Dominique Gayarre."

"Oh! heavens! Gayarre! Gayarre!"

"Yes; from what you have told me—from what I know myself—for I, too, have some knowledge of Dominique Gayarre."

"Gayarre! Gayarre! Oh, God!"

I could only ejaculate. The announcement had almost deprived me of the power of speech. A sensation of numbness seemed to creep over me—a prostration of spirit, as if some horrid danger was impending and nigh, and I without the power to avert it.

Strange this thought had not occurred to me before. I had supposed that the quadroon would be sold to some buyer in the ordinary course; some one who would be disposed to *resell* at a profit—perhaps an enormous one; but in time I should be prepared for that. Strange I had never thought of Gayarre becoming the purchaser. But, indeed, since the hour when I first heard of the bankruptcy, my thoughts had been running too wildly to permit me to reflect calmly upon anything.

Now it was clear. It was no longer a conjecture; most certainly, Gayarre would become the master of Aurore. Ere another night her body would be his property. Her soul—Oh, God! Am I awake?—do I dream?

"I had a suspicion of this before," continued D'Hauteville; "for I may tell you I know something of this family history—of Eugénie Besançon—of Aurore—of Gayarre the avocat. I had a suspicion before that Gayarre might desire to be the owner of Aurore. But now that you have told me of the scene in the dining-room, I no longer doubt this villain's design. Oh! it is infamous."

"Still further proof of it," continued D'Hauteville. "There was a man on the boat—you did not notice him, perhaps—an agent for Gayarre in such matters. A negro-trader—a fit tool for such a purpose. No doubt his object in coming down to the city is to be present at the sale—to bid for the poor girl."

"But why," I asked, catching at a straw of hope,—"why, since he wishes to possess Aurore, could he not have effected it by private contract?—why send her to the slave-market to public auction?"

"The law requires it. The slaves of an estate in bankruptcy must be sold publicly to the highest bidder. Besides, Monsieur, bad as may be this man, he dare not for the sake of his character act as you have suggested. He is a thorough hypocrite, and, with all his wickedness, wishes to stand well before the world. There are many who believe Gayarre a good man! He dare not act openly in this villainous design, and will not appear in it. To save scandal, the negro-trader will be supposed to purchase for himself. It is infamous!"

"Beyond conception! Oh! what is to be done to save her from this fearful man? to save me—"

"It is of that I am thinking, and have been for the last hour. Be of good cheer, Monsieur! all hope is not lost. There is still one chance of saving Aurore. There is one hope left. Alas! I have known the time,—I, too, have been unfortunate—sadly—sadly—unfortunate. No matter now. We shall not talk of my sorrows till yours have been relieved. Perhaps, at some future time you may know me, and my griefs—no more of that now. There is still one chance for Aurore, and she and you—both—may yet be happy. It must be so; I am resolved upon it. 'Twill be a wild act; but it is a wild story. Enough—I have no time to spare—I must be gone. Now to your hotel!—go and rest. To-morrow at twelve I shall be with you—at twelve in the Rotundo. Good night! Adieu."

Without allowing me time to ask for an explanation, or make any reply, the Creole parted from me; and, plunging into a narrow street, soon passed out of sight!

Pondering over his incoherent words—over his unintelligible promise—upon his strange looks and manner,—I walked slowly to my hotel.

Without undressing I flung myself on my bed, without a thought of going to sleep.

Chapter Fifty Nine
The Rotundo

The thousand and one reflections of a sleepless night—the thousand and one alternations of hope, and doubt, and fear—the theoretic tentation of a hundred projects—all passed before my waking spirit. Yet when morning came, and the yellow sunlight fell painfully on my eyes, I had advanced no farther in any plan of proceeding. All my hopes centred upon D'Hauteville— for I no longer dwelt upon the chances of the mail.

To be assured upon this head, however, as soon as it had arrived, I once more sought the banking-house of Brown and Co. The negative answer to my inquiry was no longer a disappointment. I had anticipated it. When did money ever arrive in time for a crisis? Slowly roll the golden circles—slowly are they passed from hand to hand, and reluctantly parted with. This supply was due by the ordinary course of the mail; yet those friends at home, into whose executive hands I had intrusted my affairs, had made some cause of delay.

Never trust your business affairs to a *friend*. Never trust to a day for receiving a letter of credit, if to a friend belongs the duty of sending it. So swore I, as I parted from the banking-house of Brown and Co.

It was twelve o'clock when I returned to the Rue Saint Louis. I did not re-enter the hotel—I walked direct to the *Rotundo*.

My pen fails to paint the dark emotions of my soul, as I stepped under the shadow of that spacious dome. I remember no fooling akin to what I experienced at that moment.

I have stood under the vaulted roof of the grand cathedral, and felt the solemnity of religious awe—I have passed through the gilded saloons of a regal palace, that inspired me with pity and contempt—pity for the slaves who had sweated for that gilding, and contempt for the sycophants who surrounded me—I have inspected the sombre cells of a prison with feelings of pain—but remembered no scene that had so painfully impressed me as that which now presented itself before my eyes.

Not sacred was that spot. On the contrary, I stood upon *desecrated* ground—desecrated by acts of the deepest infamy. This was the famed *slave-market of New Orleans*—the place where human bodies—I might almost say *human souls*—were bought and sold!

Many a forced and painful parting had these walls witnessed. Oft had the husband been here severed from his wife—the mother from her child. Oft had the bitter tear-bedewed that marble pavement—oft had that vaulted dome echoed back the sigh—nay more—the cry of the anguished heart!

I repeat it—my soul was filled with dark emotions as I entered within the precincts of that spacious hall. And no wonder—with such thoughts in my heart, and such a scene before my eyes, as I then looked upon.

You will expect a description of that scene. I must disappoint you. I cannot give one. Had I been there as an ordinary spectator—a reporter cool and unmoved by what was passing—I might have noted the details, and set them before you. But the case was far otherwise. One thought alone was in my mind—my eyes sought for one sole object—and that prevented me from observing the varied features of the spectacle.

A few things I do remember. I remember that the Rotundo, as its name imports, was a circular hall, of large extent, with a flagged floor, an arched coiling, and white walls. These were without windows, for the hall was lighted from above. On one side, near the wall, stood a desk or rostrum upon an elevated daïs, and by the side of this a large block of cut stone of the form of a parallelopipedon. The use of these two objects I divined.

A stone "kerb," or banquette, ran around one portion of the wall. The purpose of this was equally apparent.

The hall when I entered was half filled with people. They appeared to be of all ages and sorts. They stood conversing in groups, just as men do when assembled for any business, ceremony, or amusement, and waiting for the affair to begin. It was plain, however, from the demeanour of these people, that what they waited for did not impress them with any feelings of solemnity. On the contrary a merry-meeting might have been anticipated, judging from the rough jests and coarse peals of laughter that from time to time rang through the hall.

There was one group, however, which gave out no such signs or sounds. Seated along the stone banquette, and standing beside it, squatted down upon the floor, or leaning against the wall in any and every attitude, were the individuals of this group. Their black and brown skins, the woolly covering of their skulls, their rough red "brogans," their coarse garments of cheap cottonade, of jeans, of "nigger cloth" died cinnamon colour by the juice of the catalpa-tree,—these characteristics marked them as distinct from all the other groups in the hall—a distinct race of beings.

But even without the distinctions of dress or complexion—even without the thick lips or high cheekbones and woolly hair, it was easy to tell that those who sat upon the banquette were under different circumstances from these who strutted over the floor. While these talked loudly and laughed gaily, those were silent and sad. These moved about with the air of the conqueror—those were motionless with the passive look and downcast mien of the captive. These were *masters*—those were *slaves*! They were the slaves of the plantation Besançon.

All were silent, or spoke only in whispers. Most of them seemed ill at ease. Mothers sat holding their "piccaninnies" in their sable embrace, murmuring expressions of endearment, or endeavouring to hush them to rest. Here and there big tears rolled over their swarthy cheeks, as the maternal heart rose and fell with swelling emotions. Fathers looked on with drier eyes, but with the stern helpless gaze of despair, which bespoke the consciousness, that they had no power to avert their fate—no power to undo whatever might be decreed by the pitiless wretches around them.

Not all of them wore this expression. Several of the younger slaves, both boys and girls, were gaily-dressed in stuffs of brilliant colours, with flounces, frills, and ribbons. Most of these appeared indifferent to their future. Some even seemed happy—laughing and chatting gaily to each other, or occasionally exchanging a light word with one of the "white folks." A change of masters could not be such a terrible idea, after the usage they had lately had. Some of them rather anticipated such an event with hopeful pleasure. These were the dandy young men, and the yellow belles of the plantation. They would, perhaps, be allowed to remain in that great city, of which they had so often heard—perhaps a brighter future was before them. Dark must it be to be darker than their proximate past.

I glanced over the different groups, but my eyes rested not long upon them. A glance was enough to satisfy me that *she* was not there. There was no danger of mistaking any one of those forms or faces for that of Aurore. She was not there, Thank Heaven! I was spared the humiliation of seeing her in such a crowd! She was, no doubt, near at hand and would be brought in when her turn came.

I could ill brook the thought of seeing her exposed to the rude and insulting glances—perhaps insulting speeches—of which she might be the object. And yet that ordeal was in store for me.

I did not discover myself to the slaves. I knew their impulsive natures, and that a scene would be the result. I should be the recipient of their salutations and entreaties, uttered loud enough to draw the attention of all upon me.

To avoid this, I took my station behind one of the groups of white men that screened me from their notice, and kept my eyes fixed upon the entrance, watching for D'Hauteville. In him now lay my last and only hope.

I could not help noting the individuals who passed out and in. Of course they were all of my own sex, but of every variety. There was the regular "negro-trader," a tall lathy fellow, with harsh horse-dealer features, careless dress, loose coat, slouching broad-brimmed hat, coarse boots, and painted quirt of raw hide, — the "cowskin," — fit emblem of his calling.

In strong contrast to him was the elegantly-attired Creole, in coat of claret or blue, full-dress, with gold buttons, plated pantaloons, gaiter "bootees," laced shirt, and diamond studs.

An older variety of the same might be seen in trousers of buff, nankeen jacket of the same material, and hat of Manilla or Panama set over his short-cropped snow-white hair.

The American merchant from Poydras or Tehoupitoulas Street, from Camp, New Levee, or Saint Charles, in dress-coat of black cloth, vest of black satin, shining like glaze—trousers of like material with the coat—boots of calf-skin, and gloveless hands.

The dandy clerk of steamboat or store, in white grass frock, snowy ducks, and beaver hat, long furred and of light yellowish hue. There, too, the snug smooth banker—the consequential attorney, here no longer sombre and professional, but gaily caparisoned—the captain of the river-boat, with no naval look—the rich planter of the coast—the proprietor of the cotton press or "pickery"—with a sprinkling of nondescripts made up the crowd that had now assembled in the Rotundo.

As I stood noting these various forms and costumes, a large heavy-built man, with florid face, and dressed in a green "shad-bellied" coat, passed through the entrance. In one hand he carried a bundle of papers, and in the other a small mallet with ivory head—that at once proclaimed his calling.

His entrance produced a buzz, and set the various groups in motion. I could hear the phrases, "Here he comes!" "Yon's him!" "Here comes the major!"

This was not needed to proclaim to all present, who was the individual in the green "shad-belly." The beautiful dome of Saint Charles itself was not better known to the citizens of New Orleans than was Major B—, the celebrated auctioneer.

In another minute, the bright bland face of the major appeared above the rostrum. A few smart raps of his hammer commanded silence, and the sale began.

Scipio was ordered first upon the block. The crowd of intended bidders pressed around him, poked their fingers between his ribs, felt his limbs as if he had been a fat ox, opened his mouth and examined his teeth as if he had been a horse, and then bid for him just like he had been one or the other.

Under other circumstances I could have felt compassion for the poor fellow; but my heart was too full—there was no room in it for Scipio; and I averted my face from the disgusting spectacle.

Chapter Sixty
The Slave-Mart

I once more fixed my eyes upon the entrance, scrutinising every form that passed in. As yet no appearance of D'Hauteville! Surely he would soon arrive. He said at twelve o'clock. It was now one, and still he had not come.

No doubt he would come, and in proper time. After all, I need not be so anxious as to the time. Her name was last upon the list. It would be a long time.

I had full reliance upon my new friend—almost unknown, but not untried. His conduct on the previous night had inspired me with perfect confidence. He would not disappoint me. His being thus late did not shake my faith in him. There was some difficulty about his obtaining the money, for it was *money* I expected him to bring. He had hinted as much. No doubt it was that that was detaining him; but he would be in time. He knew that her name was at the bottom of the list—the last lot—Lot 65!

Notwithstanding my confidence in D'Hauteville I was ill-at-ease. It was very natural I should be so, and requires no explanation. I kept my gaze upon the door, hoping *every* moment to see him enter.

Behind me I heard the voice of the auctioneer, in constant and monotonous repetition, interrupted at intervals by the smart rap of his ivory mallet. I knew that the sale was going on; and, by the frequent strokes of the hammer, I could tell that it was rapidly progressing. Although but some half-dozen of the slaves had yet been disposed of, I could not help fancying that they were galloping down the list, and that *her* turn would soon come—too soon. With the fancy my heart beat quicker and wilder. Surely D'Hauteville will not disappoint me!

A group stood near me, talking gaily. They were all young men, and fashionably dressed,—the scions I could tell of the Creole noblesse. They conversed in a tone sufficiently loud for me to overhear them. Perhaps I should not have listened to what they were saying, had not one of them mentioned a particular name that fell harshly upon my ear. The name was *Marigny*. I had an unpleasant recollection associated with this name. It was a Marigny of whom Scipio had spoken to me—a Marigny who had proposed to *purchase Aurore*. Of course I remembered the name.

"Marigny!" I listened.

"So, Marigny, you really intend to bid for her?" asked one.

"*Qui,*" replied a young sprig, stylishly and somewhat foppishly dressed. "*Oui—oui—oui,*" he continued with a languid drawl, as he drew tighter his lavender gloves, and twirled his tiny cane. "I do intend—*ma foi!*—yes."

"How high will you go?"

"Oh—ah! *une petite somme, mon cher ami.*"

"A *little sum* will not do, Marigny," said the first speaker. "I know half-a-dozen myself who intend bidding for her—rich dogs all of them."

"Who?" inquired Marigny, suddenly awaking from his languid indifference, "Who, may I inquire?"

"Who? Well there's Gardette the dentist, who's half crazed about her; there's the old Marquis; there's planter Tillareau and Lebon, of Lafourche; and young Moreau, the wine-merchant of the Rue Dauphin; and who knows but half-a-dozen of those rich Yankee cotton-growers may want her for a *housekeeper!* Ha! ha! ha!"

"I can name another," suggested a third speaker.

"Name!" demanded several; "yourself, perhaps, Le Ber; you want a sempstress for your shirt-buttons."

"No, not myself," replied the speaker; "I don't buy *coturiers* at that price—*deux mille dollares,* at the least, my friends. *Pardieu!* no. I find my sempstresses at a cheaper rate in the Faubourg Tremé."

"Who, then? Name him!"

"Without hesitation I do,—the old wizen-face Gayarre."

"Gayarre the avocat?"

"Monsieur Dominique Gayarre!"

"Improbable," rejoined one. "Monsieur Gayarre is a man of steady habits—a moralist—a miser."

"Ha! ha!" laughed Le Ber; "it's plain, Messieurs, you don't understand the character of Monsieur Gayarre. Perhaps I know him better. Miser though he be, in a general sense, there's one class with whom he's generous enough. *Il a une douzaine des maîtresses!* Besides, you must remember that Monsieur Dominique is a bachelor. He wants a good housekeeper—a *femme-de-chambre.* Come, friends, I have heard something—*un petit chose.* I'll lay a wager the miser outbids *every* one of you,—even rich generous Marigny here!"

Marigny stood biting his lips. His was but a feeling of annoyance or chagrin—mine was utter agony. I had no longer a doubt as to who was the subject of the conversation.

"It was at the suit of Gayarre the bankruptcy was declared, was it not?" asked one.

"'Tis so said."

"Why, he was considered the great friend of the family—the associate of old Besançon?"

"Yes, the *lawyer-friend* of the family—Ha! ha!" significantly rejoined another.

"Poor Eugénie! she'll be no longer the belle. She'll now be less difficult to please in her choice of a husband."

"That's some consolation for you, Le Ber. Ha! ha!"

"Oh!" interposed another, "Le Ber had no chance lately. There's a young Englishman the favourite now—the same who swam ashore with her at the blowing-up of the Belle steamer. So I have heard, at least. Is it so, Le Ber?"

"You had better inquire of Mademoiselle Besançon," replied the latter, in a peevish tone, at which the others laughed, "I would," replied the questioner, "but I know not where to find her. Where is she? She's not at her plantation. I was up there, and she had left two days before. She's not with the aunt here. Where is she, Monsieur?"

I listened for the answer to this question with a degree of interest. I, too, was ignorant of the whereabouts of Eugénie, and had sought for her that day, but in vain. It was said she had come to the city, but no one could tell me anything of her. And I now remembered what she had said in her letter of *"Sacré Coeur."* Perhaps, thought I, she has really gone to the convent. Poor Eugénie!

"Ay, where is she, Monsieur?" asked another of the party.

"Very strange!" said several at once. "Where can she be? Le Ber, you must know."

"I know nothing of the movements of Mademoiselle Besançon," answered the young man, with an air of chagrin and surprise, too, as if he was really ignorant upon the subject, as well as vexed by the remarks which his companions were making.

"There's something mysterious in all this," continued one of the number. "I should be astonished at it, if it were any one else than Eugénie Besançon."

It is needless to say that this conversation interested me. Every word of it fell like a spark of fire upon my heart; and I could have strangled these fellows, one and all of them, as they stood. Little knew they that the "young Englishman" was near, listening to them, and as little the dire effect their words were producing.

It was not what they said of Eugénie that gave me pain. It was their free speech about Aurore. I have not repeated their ribald talk in relation to her—their jesting innuendoes, their base hypotheses, and coldly brutal sneers whenever her chastity was named.

One in particular, a certain Monsieur Sévigné, was more *bizarre* than any of his companions; and once or twice I was upon the point of turning upon him. It cost me an effort to restrain myself, but that effort was successful, and I stood unmoved. Perhaps I should not have been able to endure it much longer, but for the interposition of an event, which at once drove these gossips and their idle talk out of my mind. That event was *the entrance of Aurore*!

They had again commenced speaking of her—of her chastity—of her rare charms. They were dismissing the probabilities as to who would become possessed of her, and the *certainty* that she would be the *maîtresse* of whoever did; they were waxing warmer in their eulogium of her beauty, and beginning to lay wagers on the result of the sale, when all at once the clack of their conversation ceased, and two or three cried out—

"*Voilà! voilà! elle vient!*"

I turned mechanically at the words. Aurore was in the entrance.

Chapter Sixty One
Bidding for my Betrothed

Yes, Aurore appeared in the doorway of that infernal hall, and stood timidly pausing upon its threshold.

She was not alone. A mulatto girl was by her side—like herself a slave—like herself brought there *to be sold*!

A third individual was of the party, or rather with it; for he did not walk by the side of the girls, but in front, evidently conducting them to the place of sale. This individual was no other than Larkin, the brutal overseer.

"Come along!" said he, roughly, at the same time beckoning to Aurore and her companion: "this way, gals—foller me!"

They obeyed his rude signal, and, passing in, followed him across the hall towards the rostrum.

I stood with slouched hat and averted face. Aurore saw me not.

As soon as they were fairly past, and their backs towards me, my eyes followed them. Oh, beautiful Aurore!—beautiful as ever!

I was not single in my admiration. The appearance of the Quadroon created a sensation. The din ceased as if by a signal; every voice became hushed, and every eye was bent upon her as she moved across the floor. Men hurried forward from distant parts of the hall to get a nearer glance; others made way for her, stepping politely back as if she had been a queen. Men did this who would have scorned to offer politeness to another of her race—to the "yellow girl" for instance, who walked by her side! Oh, the power of beauty! Never was it more markedly shown than in the *entrée* of that poor slave.

I heard the whispers, I observed the glances of admiration, of passion. I marked the longing eyes that followed her, noting her splendid form and its undulating outlines as she moved forward.

All this gave me pain. It was a feeling worse than mere jealousy I experienced. It was jealousy embittered by the very brutality of my rivals.

Aurore was simply attired. There was no affectation of the fine lady—none of the ribbons and flounces that bedecked the dresses of her darker-skinned companion. Such would have ill assorted with the noble melancholy that appeared upon her beautiful countenance. None of all this.

A robe of light-coloured muslin, tastefully made, with long skirt and tight sleeves—as was the fashion of the time—a fashion that displayed the pleasing rotundity of her figure. Her head-dress was that worn by all quadroons—the "toque" of the Madras kerchief, which sat upon her brow like a coronet, its green, crimson, and yellow checks contrasting finely with the raven blackness of her hair. She wore no ornaments excepting the broad gold rings that glittered against the rich glow of her cheeks; and upon her finger one other circlet of gold—the token of her betrothal. I knew it well.

I buried myself in the crowd, slouching my hat on that side towards the rostrum. I desired she should not see me, while I could not help gazing upon her. I had taken my stand in such a situation, that I could still command a view of the entrance. More than ever was I anxious about the coming of D'Hauteville.

Aurore had been placed near the foot of the rostrum. I could just see the edge of her turban over the shoulders of the crowd. By elevating myself on my toes, I could observe her face, which by chance was turned towards me. Oh! how my heart heaved as I struggled to read its expression—as I endeavoured to divine the subject of her thoughts!

She looked sad and anxious. That was natural enough. But I looked for another expression—that unquiet anxiety produced by the alternation of hope and fear.

Her eye wandered over the crowd. She scanned the sea of faces that surrounded her. *She was searching for some one. Was it for me?*

I held down my face as her glance passed over the spot. I dared not meet her gaze. I feared that I could not restrain myself from addressing her. Sweet Aurore!

I again looked up. Her eye was still wandering in fruitless search—oh! surely it is for me!

Again I cowered behind the crowd, and her glance was carried onward.

I raised myself once more. I saw the shadow darkening upon her face. Her eye filled with a deeper expression—it was the look of despair.

"Courage! courage!" I whispered to myself. "Look again, lovely Aurore! This time I shall meet you. I shall speak to you from mine eyes—I shall give back glance for glance—"

"She sees—she recognises me! That start—the flash of joy in her eyes—the smile curling upon her lips! Her glance wanders no more—her gaze is fixed—proud heart! It *was* for me!"

Yes, our eyes met at length—met, melting and swimming with love. Mine had escaped from my control. For some moments I could not turn them aside, but surrendered them to the impulse of my passion. It was mutual. I doubted it not. I felt as though the ray of love-light was passing between us. I had almost forgotten where I stood!

A murmur from the crowd, and a movement, restored me to my senses. Her stedfast gaze had been noticed, and by many—skilled to interpret such glances—had been understood. These, in turning round to see who was the object of that glance, had caused the movement. I had observed it in time, and turned my face in another direction.

I watched the entrance for D'Hauteville. Why had he not arrived? My anxiety increased with the minutes.

True, it would still be an hour—perhaps two—before her time should come.—Ha!—what?

There was silence for a moment—something of interest was going on. I looked towards the rostrum for an explanation. A dark man had climbed upon one of the steps, and was whispering to the auctioneer.

He remained but a moment. He appeared to have asked some favour, which was at once conceded him, and he stepped back to his place among the crowd.

A minute or two intervened, and then, to my horror and astonishment, I saw the overseer take Aurore by the arm, and raise her upon the block! The intention was plain. *She was to be sold next*!

In the moments that followed, I cannot remember exactly how I acted. I ran wildly for the entrance. I looked out into the street. Up and down I glanced with anxious eyes. No D'Hauteville!

I rushed back into the hall—again through the outer circles of the crowd, in the direction of the rostrum.

The bidding had begun. I had not heard the preliminaries, but as I re-entered there fell upon my ears the terrible words—

"*A thousand dollars for the Quadroon.—A thousand dollars bid!*"

"O Heaven! D'Hauteville has deceived me. She is lost!—lost!"

In my desperation I was about to interrupt the sale. I was about to proclaim aloud its unfairness, in the fact that the Quadroon had been *taken out of the order advertised*! Even on this poor plea I rested a hope.

It was the straw to the drowning man, but I was determined to grasp it.

I had opened my lips to call out, when some one pulling me by the sleeve caused me to turn round. It was D'Hauteville! Thank Heaven, it was D'Hauteville!

I could scarce restrain myself from shouting with joy. His look told me that he was the bearer of bright gold.

"In time, and none to spare," whispered he, thrusting a pocket-book between my fingers; "there is three thousand dollars—that will surely be enough; 'tis all I have been able to procure. I cannot stay here—there are those I do not wish to see. I shall meet you after the sale is over. Adieu!"

I scarce thanked him. I saw not his parting. My eyes were elsewhere.

"Fifteen hundred dollars bid for the Quadroon!—good housekeeper—sempstress—fifteen hundred dollars!"

"*Two thousand!*" I called out, my voice husky with emotion. The sudden leap over such a large sum drew the attention of the crowd upon me. Looks, smiles, and innuendoes were freely exchanged at my expense.

I saw, or rather heeded them not. I saw Aurore, only Aurore, standing upon the daïs like a statue upon its pedestal—the type of sadness and beauty. The sooner I could take her thence, the happier for me; and with that object in view I had made my "bid."

"Two thousand dollars bid—two thousand—twenty-one hundred dollars—two thousand, one, two—twenty-two hundred dollars bid—twenty-two—"

"Twenty-five hundred dollars!" I again cried out, in as firm a voice as I could command.

"Twenty-five hundred dollars," repeated the auctioneer, in his monotonous drawl; "twenty-five—six—you, sir? thank you! twenty-six hundred dollars for the Quadroon—twenty-six hundred!"

"Oh God! they will go above three thousand; if they do—"

"Twenty-seven hundred dollars!" bid the fop Marigny.

"Twenty-eight hundred!" from the old Marquis.

"Twenty-eight hundred and fifty!" assented the young merchant, Moreau.

"Nine!" nodded the tall dark man who had whispered to the auctioneer.

Twenty-nine hundred dollars bid—two thousand nine hundred.

"Three thousand!" I gasped out in despair.

It was my last bid. I could go no farther.

I waited for the result, as the condemned waits for the falling of the trap or the descent of the axe. My heart could not have endured very long that terrible suspense. But I had not long to endure it.

"*Three thousand one hundred dollars!*—three thousand one hundred bid—thirty-one hundred dollars—"

I cast one look upon Aurore. It was a look of hopeless despair; and turning away, I staggered mechanically across the hall.

Before I had reached the entrance I could hear the voice of the auctioneer, in the same prolonged drawl, calling out, "Three thousand five hundred bid for the Quadroon girl?"

I halted and listened. The sale was coming to its close.

"Three thousand five hundred—going at three thousand five hundred—going—going—"

The sharp stroke of the hammer fell upon my ear. It drowned the final word "gone!" but my heart pronounced that word in the emphasis of its agony.

There was a noisy scene of confusion, loud words and high excitement among the crowd of disappointed bidders. Who was the fortunate one?

I leant over to ascertain. The tall dark man was in conversation with the auctioneer. Aurore stood beside him. I now remembered having seen the man on the boat. He was the agent of whom D'Hauteville had spoken. The Creole had guessed aright, and so, too, had Le Ber.

Gayarre had outbid them all!

Chapter Sixty Two
The Hackney-Carriage

For a while I lingered in the hall, irresolute and almost without purpose. She whom I loved, and who loved me in return, was wrested from me by an infamous law, ruthlessly torn from me. She would be borne away before my eyes, and I might, perhaps, never behold her again. Probable enough was this thought—I might never behold her again! Lost to me, more hopelessly lost, than if she had become the *bride* of another. Far more hopelessly lost. Then, at least, she would have been free to think, to act, to go abroad, to —. Then I might have hoped to meet her again, to see her, to gaze upon her, even if only at a distance, to worship her in the secret silence of my heart, to console myself with the belief that she still loved me. Yes; the bride, the wife of another! Even that I could have borne with calmness. But now, not the bride of another, but the *slave*, the forced, unwilling *leman*, and that other—. Oh! how my heart writhed under its horrible imaginings!

What next? How was I to act? Resign myself to the situation? Make no further effort to recover, to save her?

No! It had not come to that. Discouraging as the prospect was, a ray of hope was visible; one ray yet illumed the dark future, sustaining and bracing my mind for further action.

The plan was still undefined; but the purpose had been formed, and that purpose was to free Aurore, to make her mine *at every hazard*! I thought no longer of buying her. I knew that Gayarre had become her owner. I felt satisfied that to purchase her was no longer possible. He who had paid such an enormous sum would not be likely to part with her at any price. My whole fortune would not suffice. I gave not a thought to it. I felt certain it would be impossible.

Far different was the resolve that was already forming itself in my mind, and cheering me with new hopes. Forming itself, do I say? It had already taken a definite shape, even before the echoes of the salesman's voice had died upon my ears! With the clink of his hammer my mind was made up. The purpose was formed; it was only the *plan* that remained indefinite.

I had resolved to outrage the laws—to become thief or robber, whichever it might please circumstances to make me. I had resolved to *steal my betrothed*!

Disgrace there might be—danger I knew there was, not only to my liberty, but my life. I cared but little about the disgrace; I recked not of the danger. My purpose was fixed—my determination taken.

Brief had been the mental process that conducted me to this determination—the more brief that the thought had passed through my mind before—the more brief that I believed there was positively no other means I could adopt. It was the only course of action left me—either that, or yield up all that I loved without a struggle—and, passion-led as I was, I was not going to yield. Certain disgrace,—even death itself, appeared more welcome than this alternative.

I had formed not yet the shadow of a plan. That, must be thought of afterwards; but even at that moment was action required. My poor heart was on the rack; I could not bear the thought that a single night should pass and she under the same roof with that hideous man!

Wherever she should pass the night, I was determined that I should not be far-distant from her. Walls might separate us, but she should know I was near. Just that much of a plan *had* I thought of.

Stepping to a retired spot, I took out my note-book, and wrote upon one of its leaves:

"*Ce soir viendrai*!—Edouard."

I had no time to be more particular, for I feared every moment she would be hurried out of my sight. I tore out the leaf; and, hastily folding it, returned to the entrance of the Rotundo.

Just as I got back to the door a hackney-carriage drove up, and halted in front. I conjectured its use, and lost no time in providing another from a stand close by. This done, I returned within the hall. I was yet in time. As I entered, I saw Aurore being led away from the rostrum.

I pressed into the crowd, and stood in such a position that she would have to pass near me. And she did so, our hands met, and the note parted from my fingers. There was no time for a further recognition—not even a love-pressure—for the moment after she was hurried on through the crowd, and the carriage-door closed after her.

The mulatto girl accompanied her, and another of the female slaves. All were put into the carriage. The negro-dealer climbed to the box alongside the coachman, and the vehicle rattled off over the stony pavement.

A word to my driver was enough, who, giving the whip to his horses, followed at like speed.

Chapter Sixty Three
To Bringiers

Coachmen of New Orleans possess their full share of *intelligence*; and the ring of a piece of silver, extra of their fare, is a music well understood by them. They are the witnesses of many a romantic adventure—the necessary confidants of many a love-secret. A hundred yards in front rolled the carriage that had taken Aurore; now turning round corners, now passing among drays laden with huge cotton-bales or hogsheads of sugar—but my driver had fixed his knowing eye upon it, and I had no need to be uneasy.

It passed up the Rue Chartres but a short distance, and then turned into one of the short streets that ran from this at right angles towards the Levee. I fancied for a moment, it was making for the steamboat wharves; but on reaching the corner, I saw that it had stopped about half way down the street. My driver, according to the instructions I had given him, pulled up at the corner, and awaited my further orders. The carriage I had followed was now standing in front of a house; and just as I rounded the corner, I caught a glimpse of several figures crossing the banquette and entering the door. No doubt, all that had ridden in the carriage—Aurore with the rest—had gone inside the house.

Presently a man came out, and handing his fare to the hackney-coachman, turned and went back into the house. The latter, gathering up his reins, gave the whip to his horses, and, wheeling round, came back by the Rue Chartres. As he passed me, I glanced through the open windows of his vehicle. It was empty. She had gone into the house, then.

I had no longer any doubt as to where she had been taken. I read on the corner, "Rue Bienville." The house where the carriage had stopped was the town residence of Monsieur Dominique Gayarre.

I remained for some minutes in the cab, considering what I had best do. Was this to be her future home? or was she only brought here temporarily, to be afterwards taken up to the plantation?

Some thought, or instinct perhaps, whispered me that she was not to remain in the Rue Bienville; but would be carried to the gloomy old mansion at Bringiers. I cannot tell why I thought so. Perhaps it was because I wished it so.

I saw the necessity of watching the house—so that she might not be taken away without my knowing it. Wherever she went I was determined to follow.

Fortunately I was prepared for any journey. The three thousand dollars lent me by D'Hauteville remained intact. With that I could travel to the ends of the earth.

I wished that the young Creole had been with me. I wanted his counsel—his company. How should I find him? he had not said where we should meet—only that he would join me when the sale should be over. I saw nothing of him on leaving the Rotundo. Perhaps he meant to meet me there or at my hotel; but how was I to get back to either of these places without leaving my post?

I was perplexed as to how I should communicate with D'Hauteville. It occurred to me that the hackney-coachman—I had not yet dismissed him— might remain and watch the house, while I went in search of the Creole. I had only to pay the Jehu; he would obey me, of course, and right willingly.

I was about arranging with the man, and had already given him some instructions, when I heard wheels rumbling along the street; and a somewhat old-fashioned coach, drawn by a pair of mules, turned into the Rue Bienville. A negro driver was upon the box.

There was nothing odd in all this. Such a carriage and such a coachman were to be seen every hour in New Orleans, and drawn by mules as often as horses. But this pair of mules, and the negro who drove them, I recognised.

Yes! I recognised the equipage. I had often met it upon the Levee Road near Bringiers. It was the carriage of Monsieur Dominique!

I was further assured upon this point by seeing the vehicle draw up in front of the avocat's house.

I at once gave up my design of going back for D'Hauteville. Climbing back into the hack, I ensconced myself in such a position, that I could command a view of what passed in the Rue Bienville.

Some one was evidently about to become the occupant of the carriage. The door of the house stood open, and a servant was speaking to the coachman. I could tell by the actions of the latter, that he expected soon to drive off.

The servant now appeared outside with several parcels, which he placed upon the coach; then a man came out—the negro-trader—who mounted the box. Another man shot across the banquette, but in such a hurried gait that I could not recognise him. I guessed, however, who *he* was. Two others now came from the house—a mulatto woman and a young girl. In spite of the cloak in which she was enveloped I recognised Aurore. The mulatto woman conducted the girl to the carriage, and then stepped in after. At this moment a man on horseback appeared in the street, and riding up, halted by the carriage. After speaking to some one inside, he again put his horse in motion and rode off. This horseman was Larkin the overseer.

The clash of the closing door was immediately followed by the crack of the coachman's whip; and the mules, trotting off down the street, turned to the right, and headed up the Levee.

My driver, who had already been instructed, gave the whip to his hack, and followed, keeping a short distance in the rear.

It was not till we had traversed the long street of Tehoupitoulas, through the Faubourg Marigny, and were some distance upon the road to the suburban village of Lafayette, that I thought of where I was going. My sole idea had been to keep in sight the carriage of Gayarre.

I now bethought me for what purpose I was driving after him. Did I intend to follow him to his house, some thirty miles distant, in a hackney-coach?

Even had I been so determined, it was questionable whether the driver of the vehicle could have been tempted to humour my caprice, or whether his wretched hack could have accomplished such a feat.

For what purpose, then, was I galloping after? To overtake these men upon the road, and deliver Aurore from their keeping? No, there were three of them—well armed, no doubt—and I alone.

But it was not until I had gone several miles that I began to reflect on the absurdity of my conduct. I then ordered my coachman to pull up.

I remained seated; and from the window of the hack gazed after the carriage, until it was hidden by a turn in the road.

"After all," I muttered to myself, "I have done right in following. I am now sure of their destination. Back to the Hotel Saint Luis!"

The last phrase was a command to my coachman, who turning his horse drove back.

As I had promised to pay for speed, it was not long before the wheels of my hackney rattled over the pavé of the Rue Saint Luis.

Having dismissed the carriage, I entered the hotel. To my joy I found D'Hauteville awaiting my return, and in a few minutes I had communicated to him my determination to carry off Aurore.

Bare friendship his! he approved of my resolve. Rare devotion! he proposed to take part in my enterprise, I warned him of its perils—to no purpose. With an enthusiasm I could not account for, and that greatly astonished me at the time, he still insisted upon sharing them.

Perhaps I might more earnestly have admonished him against such a purpose, but I felt how much I stood in need of him.

I could not explain the strange feeling of confidence, with which the presence of this gentle but heroic youth had inspired me. The reluctance with which I accepted his offer was only apparent—it was not felt. My heart was struggling against my will. I was but too glad when he stated his determination to accompany me.

There was no boat going up that night; but we were not without the means to travel. A pair of horses were hired—the best that money could procure—and before sun-down we had cleared the suburbs of the city, and were riding along the road that conducts to the village of Bringiers.

Chapter Sixty Four
Two Villains

We travelled rapidly. There were no hills to impede our progress. Our route lay along the Levee Road, which leads from New Orleans by the bank of the river, passing plantations and settlements at every few hundred yards' distance. The path was as level as a race-course, and the hoof fell gently upon the soft dusty surface, enabling us to ride with ease. The horses we bestrode were *mustangs* from the prairies of Texas, trained to that gait, the "pace" peculiar to the saddle-bags of the South-western States. Excellent "pacers" both were; and, before the night came down, we had made more than half of our journey.

Up to this time we had exchanged only a few words. I was busy with my thoughts—busy planning my enterprise. My young companion appeared equally occupied with his.

The darkening down of the night brought us closer together; and I now unfolded to D'Hauteville the plan which I had proposed to myself.

There was not much of plan about it. My intention was simply this: To proceed at once to the plantation of Gayarre—stealthily to approach the house—to communicate with Aurore through some of the slaves of the plantation; failing in this, to find out, if possible, in what part of the house she would pass the night—to enter her room after all had gone to sleep— propose to her to fly with me—and then make our escape the best way we could.

Once clear of the house, I had scarce thought of a plan of action. That seemed easy enough. Our horses would carry us back to the city. There we might remain concealed, until some friendly ship should bear us from the country.

This was all the plan I had conceived, and, having communicated it to D'Hauteville, I awaited his response.

After some moments' silence, he replied, signifying his approval of it. Like me, he could think of no other course to be followed. Aurore must be carried away at all hazards.

We now conversed about the details. We debated every chance of failure and success.

Our main difficulty, both agreed, would be in communicating with Aurore. Could we do so? Surely she would not be locked in? Surely Gayarre would not be suspicious enough to have her guarded and watched? He was now the full owner of this coveted treasure—no one could legally deprive him of his slave—no one could carry her away without the risk of a fearful punishment; and although he no doubt suspected that some understanding existed between the quadroon and myself, I would never dream of such a love as that which I felt—a love that would lead me to risk even life itself, as I now intended.

No. Gayarre, judging from his own vile passion, might believe that I, like himself, had been "struck" with the girl's beauty, and that I was willing to pay a certain sum—three thousand dollars—to possess her. But the fact that I had bid no more—no doubt exactly reported to him by his agent—was proof that my love had its limits, and there was an end of it. As a rival he would hear of me no more. No. Monsieur Dominique Gayarre would never suspect a passion like mine—would never dream of such a purpose as the one to which that passion now impelled me. An enterprise so romantic was not within the bounds of probability. Therefore—so reasoned D'Hauteville and I—it was not likely Aurore would be either guarded or watched.

But even though she might not be, how were we to communicate with her? That would be extremely difficult.

I built my hopes on the little slip of paper—on the words *"Ce soir viendrai."* Surely upon this night Aurore would *not sleep*. My heart told me she would not, and the thought rendered me proud and sanguine. That very night should I make the attempt to carry her off. I could not bear the thought that she should pass even a single night under the roof of her tyrant.

And the night promised to befriend us. The sun had scarcely gone down, when the sky became sullen, turning to the hue of lead. As soon as the short twilight passed, the whole canopy had grown so dark, that we could scarce distinguish the outline of the forest from the sky itself. Not a star could be seen. A thick pall of smoke-coloured clouds hid them from the view. Even the yellow surface of the river was scarce perceptible from its bank, and the white dust of the road alone guided us.

In the woods, or upon the darker ground of the plantation fields, to find a path would have been impossible—so intense was the darkness that enveloped us.

We might have augured trouble from this—we might have feared losing our way. But I was not afraid of any such result. I felt assured that the star of love itself would guide me.

The darkness would be in our favour. Under its friendly shadow we could approach the house, and act with safety; whereas had it been a moonlight night, we should have been in great danger of being discovered.

I read in the sudden change of sky no ill augury, but an omen of success.

There were signs of an approaching storm. What to me would have been kindly weather? Anything—a rain-storm—a tempest—a hurricane—anything but a fine night was what I desired.

It was still early when we reached the plantation Besançon—not quite midnight. We had lost no time on the road. Our object in hurrying forward was to arrive at the place before the household of Gayarre should go to rest. Our hopes were that we might find some means of communicating with Aurore—through the slaves.

One of those I know. I had done him a slight favour during my residence at Bringiers. I had gained his confidence—enough to render him accessible to a bribe. He might be found, and might render us the desired assistance.

All was silent upon the plantation Besançon. The dwelling-house appeared deserted. There were no lights to be seen. One glimmered in the rear, in a window of the overseer's house. The negro quarter was dark and silent. The buzz usual at that hour was not heard. They whose voices used to echo through its little street were now far away. The cabins were empty. The song, the jest, and the cheerful laugh, were hushed; and the 'coon-dog howling for his absent master, was the only sound that broke the stillness of the place.

We passed the gate, riding in silence, and watching the road in front of us. We were observing the greatest caution as we advanced. We might meet those whom above all others we desired not to encounter—the overseer, the agent, Gayarre himself. Even to have been seen by one of Gayarre's negroes might have resulted in the defeat of our plans. So fearful was I of this, that but for the darkness of the night, I should have left the road sooner, and tried a path through the woods which I knew of. It was too dark to traverse this path without difficulty and loss of time. We therefore clung to the road, intending to leave it when we should arrive opposite the plantation of Gayarre.

Between the two plantations a wagon-road for wood-hauling led to the forest. It was this road I intended to take. We should not be likely to meet any one upon it; and it was our design to conceal our horses among the trees in the rear of the cane-fields. On such a night not even the negro 'coon-hunter would have any business in the woods.

Creeping along with caution, we had arrived near the point where this wood-road *debouched*, when voices reached our ears. Some persons were coming down the road.

We reined, up and listened. There were men in conversation; and from their voices each moment growing more distinct, we could tell that they were approaching us.

They were coming down the main road from the direction of the village. The hoof-stroke told us they were on horseback, and, consequently, that they were white men.

A large cotton-wood tree stood on the waste ground on one side of the road. The long flakes of Spanish moss hanging from its branches nearly touched the ground. It offered the readiest place of concealment, and we had just time to spur our horses behind its giant trunk, when the horsemen came abreast of the tree.

Dark as it was, we could see them in passing. Their forms—two of them there were—were faintly outlined against the yellow surface of the water. Had they been silent, we might have remained in ignorance as to who they were, but their voices betrayed them. They were Larkin and the trader.

"Good!" whispered D'Hauteville, as we recognised them; "they have left Gayarre's—they are on their way home to the plantation Besançon."

The very same thought had occurred to myself. No doubt they were returning to their homes—the overseer to the plantation Besançon, and the trader to his own house—which I know to be farther down the coast. I now remembered having often seen this man in company with Gayarre.

The thought had occurred to myself as D'Hauteville spoke, but how knew *he*? He must be well acquainted with the country, thought I.

I had no time to reflect or ask him any question. The conversation of these two ruffians—for ruffians both were—occupied all my attention. They were evidently in high glee, laughing as they went, and jesting as they talked. No doubt their vile work had been remunerative.

"Wal, Bill," said the trader, "it air the biggest price I ever giv for a nigger."

"Darn the old French fool! He's paid well for his whistle this time—he ain't allers so open-fisted. Dog darned if he is!"

"Wal—she air dear; an she ain't when a man has the dollars to spare. She's as putty a piece o' goods as there air in all Louisiana. I wouldn't mind myself—"

"Ha! ha! ha!" boisterously laughed the overseer. "I guess you can get a chance if you've a mind to," he added, in a significant tone.

"Say, Bill!—tell me—be candid, old feller—have you ever—?"

"Wal, to tell the truth, I hain't; but I reckon I mout if I had pushed the thing. I wan't long enough on the plantation. Beside, she's so stuck up with cussed pride an larnin', that she thinks herself as good as white. I calclate old Foxey 'll bring down her notions a bit. She won't be long wi' him till she'll be glad to take a ramble in the woods wi' anybody that asks her. There'll be chance enough yet, I reckon."

The trader muttered some reply to this prophetic speech; but both were now so distant that their conversation was no longer audible. What I had heard, absurd as it was, caused me a feeling of pain, and, if possible, heightened my desire to save Aurore from the terrible fate that awaited her.

Giving the word to my companion, we rode out from behind the tree, and a few minutes after turned into the by-path that led to the woods.

Chapter Sixty Five
The Pawpaw Thicket

Our progress along this by-road was slow. There was no white dust upon the path to guide us. We had to grope our way as well as we could between the zigzag fences. Now and then our horses stumbled in the deep ruts made by the wood-wagons, and it was with difficulty we could force them forward.

My companion seemed to manage better than I, and whipped his horse onward as if he were more familiar with the path, or else more reckless! I wondered at this without making any remark.

After half-an-hour's struggling we reached the angle of the rail-fence, where the enclosure ended and the woods began. Another hundred yards brought us under the shadow of the tall timber; where we reined up to take breath, and concert what was next to be done.

I remembered that there was a pawpaw thicket near this place.

"If we could find it," I said to my companion, "and leave our horses there?"

"We may easily do that," was the reply; "though 'tis scarce worth while searching for a thicket—the darkness will sufficiently conceal them.—Ha! not so—*Voilà l'éclair*!"

As D'Hauteville spoke, a blue flash lit up the whole canopy of heaven. Even the gloomy aisles of the forest were illuminated, so that we could distinguish the trunks and branches of the trees to a long distance around us. The light wavered for some seconds, like a lamp about being extinguished; and then went suddenly out, leaving the darkness more opaque than before.

There was no noise accompanying this phenomenon—at least none produced by the lightning itself. It caused some noise, however, among the wild creatures of the woods. It woke the white-headed haliaetus, perched upon the head of the tall taxodium, and his maniac laugh sounded harsh and shrill. It woke the grallatores of the swamp—the qua-bird, the curlews, and the tall blue herons—who screamed in concert. The owl, already awake, hooted louder its solemn note; and from the deep profound of the forest came the howl of the wolf, and the more thrilling cry of the cougar.

All nature seemed startled by this sudden blaze of light that filled the firmament. But the moment after all was darkness and silence as before. "The storm will soon be on?" I suggested. "No," said my companion, "there will be no storm—you hear no thunder—when it is thus we shall have no rain—a very black night, with lightning at intervals—nothing more. Again!"

The exclamation was drawn forth by a second blaze of lightning, that like the first lit up the woods on all sides around us, and, as before, unaccompanied by thunder. Neither the slightest rumble nor clap was heard, but the wild creatures once more uttered their varied cries.

"We must conceal the horses, then," said my companion; "some straggler might be abroad, and with this light they could be seen far off. The pawpaw thicket is the very place. Let us seek it! It lies in this direction."

D'Hauteville rode forward among the tree-trunks. I followed mechanically. I felt satisfied he know the ground better than I! He must have been here before, was my reflection.

We had not gone many steps before the blue light blazed a third time; and we could see, directly in front of us, the smooth shining branches and broad green leaves of the *Asiminas*, forming the underwood of the forest.

When the lightning flashed again, we had entered the thicket.

Dismounting in its midst, we hastily tied our bridles to the branches; and then, leaving our horses to themselves, we returned towards the open ground.

Ten minutes' walking enabled us to regain the zigzag railing that shut in the plantation of Gayarre.

Directing ourselves along this, in ten minutes after we arrived opposite the house—which by the electric blaze we could distinguish shining among the tall cotton-wood trees that grew around it. At this point we again made a stop to reconnoitre the ground, and consider how we should proceed.

A wide field stretched from the fence almost to the walls. A garden enclosed by palings lay between the field and the house; and on one side we could perceive the roofs of numerous cabins denoting the negro quarter. At some distance in the same direction, stood the sugar-mill and other outbuildings, and near these the house of Gayarre's overseer.

This point was to be avoided. Even the negro quarter must be shunned, lest we might give alarm. The dogs would be our worst enemies. I knew that Gayarre kept several. I had often seen them along the roads. Large fierce animals they were. How were they to be shunned? They would most likely be rambling about the outbuildings or the negro cabins; therefore, our safest way would be to approach from the opposite side.

If we should fail to discover the apartment of Aurore, then it would be time to make reconnaissance in the direction of the "quarter," and endeavour to find the boy Caton.

We saw lights in the house. Several windows—all upon the ground-floor—were shining through the darkness. More than one apartment therefore was occupied.

This gave us hope. One of them might be occupied by Aurore.

"And now, Monsieur!" said D'Hauteville, after we had discussed the various details, "suppose we fail? suppose some alarm be given, and we be detected before—?"

I turned, and looking my young companion full in the face, interrupted him in what he was about to say. "D'Hauteville!" said I, "perhaps, I may never be able to repay your generous friendship. It has already exceeded all bounds—but *life* you must not risk for me. That I cannot permit."

"And how risk life, Monsieur?"

"If I fail—if alarm be given—if I am opposed, *voilà*—!"

I opened the breast of my coat, exposing to his view my pistols.

"Yes!" I continued; "I am reckless enough. I shall use them if necessary. I shall take life if it stand in the way. I am resolved; but you must not risk an encounter. You must remain here—I shall go to the house alone."

"No—no!" he answered promptly; "I go with you."

"I cannot permit it, Monsieur. It is better for you to remain here. You can stay by the fence until I return to you—until *we* return, I should say, for I come not back without *her*."

"Do not act rashly, Monsieur!"

"No, but I am determined. I am desperate. We must not go farther."

"And why not? *I, too, have an interest in this affair.*"

"You?" I asked, surprised at the words as well as the tone in which they were spoken. "You an interest?"

"Of course," coolly replied my companion. "I love adventure. That gives me an interest. You must permit me to accompany you—I must go along with you!"

"As you will then, Monsieur D'Hauteville. Fear not. I shall act with prudence. Come on!"

I sprang over the fence, followed by my companion; and, without another word having passed between us, we struck across the field in the direction of the house.

Chapter Sixty Six
The Elopement

It was a field of sugar-cane. The canes were of that species known as "ratoons"—suckers from old roots—and the thick bunches at their bases, as well as the tall columns, enabled us to pass among them unobserved. Even had it been day, we might have approached the house unseen.

We soon reached the garden-paling. Here we stopped to reconnoitre the ground. A short survey was sufficient. We saw the very place where we could approach and conceal ourselves.

The house had an antique weather-beaten look—not without some pretensions to grandeur. It was a wooden building, two stories in height, with gable roofs, and large windows—all of which had Venetian shutters that opened to the outside. Both walls and window-shutters had once been painted, but the paint was old and rusty; and the colour of the Venetians, once green, could hardly be distinguished from the grey wood-work of the walls. All round the house ran an open gallery or verandah, raised some three or four feet from the ground. Upon this gallery the windows and doors opened, and a paling or guard-rail encompassed the whole. Opposite the doors, a stairway of half-a-dozen steps led up; but at all other parts the space underneath was open in front, so that, by stooping a little, one might get under the floor of the gallery.

By crawling close up in front of the verandah, and looking through the rails, we should be able to command a full view of all the windows in the house;—and in case of alarm, we could conceal ourselves in the dark cavity underneath. We should be safe there, unless scented by the dogs.

Our plan was matured in whispers. It was not much of a plan. We were to advance to the edge of the verandah, peep through the windows until we could discover the apartment of Aurore; then do our best to communicate with her, and get her out. Our success depended greatly upon accident or good fortune.

Before we could make a move forward, fortune seemed as though she was going to favour us. In one of the windows, directly before our face, a figure appeared. A glance told us it was the Quadroon!

The window, as before stated, reached down to the floor of the verandah; and as the figure appeared behind the glass, we could see it from head to foot. The Madras kerchief on the head, the gracefully undulating figure, outlined upon the background of the lighted room, left no doubt upon our minds as to who it was.

"'Tis Aurore!" whispered my companion.

How could *he* tell? Did he know her? Ah! I remembered—he had seen her that morning in the Rotundo.

"It is she!" I replied, my beating heart scarce allowing me to make utterance.

The window was curtained, but she had raised the curtain in one hand, and was looking out. There was that in her attitude that betokened earnestness. She appeared as if trying to penetrate the gloom. Even in the distance I could perceive this, and my heart bounded with joy. She had understood my note. She was looking for me!

D'Hauteville thought so as well. Our prospects were brightening. If she guessed our design, our task would be easier.

She remained but a few moments by the window. She turned away and the curtain dropped into its place; but before it had screened the view, the dark shadow of a man fell against the back wall of the room. Gayarre, no doubt!

I could hold back no longer; but climbing over the garden-fence, I crept forward, followed by D'Hauteville.

In a few seconds both of us had gained the desired position—directly in front of the window, from which we were now separated only by the wood-work of the verandah. Standing half-bent our eyes were on a level with the floor of the room. The curtain had not fallen properly into its place. A single pane of the glass remained unscreened, and through this we could see nearly the whole interior of the apartment. Our ears, too, were at the proper elevation to catch every sound; and persons conversing within the room we could hear distinctly.

We were right in our conjecture. It was Aurore we had seen. Gayarre was the other occupant of the room.

I shall not paint that scene. I shall not repeat the words to which we listened. I shall not detail the speeches of that mean villain—at first fulsome and flattering—then coarse, bold, and brutal; until at length, failing to effect his purpose by entreaties, he had recourse to threats.

D'Hauteville held me back, begging me in earnest whispers to be patient. Once or twice I had almost determined to spring forward, dash aside the sash, and strike the ruffian to the floor. Thanks to the prudent interference of my companion, I restrained myself.

The scene ended by Gayarre going out of the room indignant, but somewhat crest-fallen. The bold, upright bearing of the Quadroon—whose strength, at least, equalled that of her puny assailant—had evidently intimidated him for the moment, else he might have resorted to personal violence.

His threats, however, as he took his departure; left no doubt of his intention soon to renew his brutal assault. He felt certain of his victim—she was his slave, and must yield. He had ample time and opportunity. He need not at once proceed to extremes. He could wait until his valour, somewhat cowed, should return again, and imbue him with a fresh impulse.

The disappearance of Gayarre gave us an opportunity to make our presence known to Aurore. I was about to climb up to the verandah and tap on the glass; but my companion prevented me from doing so.

"It is not necessary," he whispered; "she certainly knows you will be here. Leave it to *her*. She will return to the window presently. Patience, Monsieur! a false step will ruin all. Remember the dogs!"

There was prudence in these counsels, and I gave way to them. A few minutes would decide; and we both crouched close, and watched the movements of the Quadroon.

The apartment in which she was attracted our notice. It was not the drawing-room of the house, nor yet a bedroom. It was a sort of library or studio—as shelves filled with books, and a table, covered with papers and writing-materials, testified. It was, no doubt, the office of the avocat, in which he was accustomed to do his writing.

Why was Aurore in that room? Such a question occurred to us; but we had little time to dwell upon it. My companion suggested that as they had just arrived, she may have been placed there while an apartment was being prepared for her. The voices of servants overhead, and the noise of furniture being moved over the floor, was what led him to make this suggestion; it was just as if a room was being set in order.

This led me into a new train of reflection. She might be suddenly removed from the library, and taken up-stairs. It would then be more difficult to communicate with her. It would be better to make the attempt at once.

Contrary to the wish of D'Hauteville, I was about to advance forward to the window, when the movements of Aurore herself caused me to hesitate.

The door through which Gayarre had just made his exit was visible from where we stood. I saw the Quadroon approach this with silent tread, as if meditating some design. Placing her hand upon the key, she turned it in the lock, so that the door was thus bolted inside. With what design had she doing this?

It occurred to us that she was about to make her escape out by the window, and that she had fastened the door for the purpose of delaying pursuit. If so, it would be better for us to remain quiet, and leave her to complete the design. It would be time enough to warn her of our presence when she should reach the window. This was D'Hauteville's advice.

In one corner of the room stood a large mahogany desk, and over its head was ranged a screen of box-shelves—of the kind known as "pigeon-holes." These were filled with papers and parchments—no doubt, wills, deeds, and other documents relating to the business of the lawyer.

To my astonishment I saw the Quadroon, as soon as she had secured the door, hastily approach this desk, and stand directly in front of it—her eyes eagerly bent upon the shelves, as though she was in search of some document!

Such was in reality the case, for she now stretched forth her hand, drew a bundle of folded papers from the box, and after resting her eyes upon them for a moment, suddenly concealed them in the bosom of her dress!

"Heavens!" I mentally ejaculated, "what can it mean?"

I had no time to give way to conjectures—for in a second's time Aurore had glided across the floor, and was standing in the window.

As she raised the curtain, the light streamed full on the faces of myself and my companion, and at the first glance she saw us. A slight exclamation escaped her, but it was of joy, not surprise; and she suddenly checked herself.

The ejaculation was not loud enough to be heard across the room. The sash opened noiselessly—with silent tread the verandah was crossed—and in another moment my betrothed was in my arms! I lifted her over the balustrade, and we passed hastily along the walks of the garden.

The outer field was reached without any alarm having been given; and, directing ourselves between the rows of the canes, we speeded on towards the woods, that loomed up like a dark wall in the distance.

Chapter Sixty Seven
The Lost Mustangs

The lightning continued to play at intervals, and we had no difficulty in finding our way. We recrossed near the same place where we had entered the field; and, guiding ourselves along the fence, hurried on towards the thicket of pawpaws, where we had left our horses.

My design was to take to the road at once, and endeavour to reach the city before daybreak. Once there, I hoped to be able to keep concealed—both myself and my betrothed—until some opportunity offered of getting out to sea, or up the river to one of the free states. I never thought of taking to the woods. Chance had made me acquainted with a rare hiding-place, and no doubt we might have found concealment there for a time. The advantage of this had crossed my mind, but I did not entertain the idea for a moment. Such a refuge could be but temporary. We should have to flee from it in the end, and the difficulty of escaping from the country would be as great as ever. Either for victim or criminal there is no place of concealment so safe as the crowded haunts of the populous city; and in New Orleans—half of which consists of a "floating" population—incognito is especially easily to be preserved.

My design, therefore—and D'Hauteville approved it—was to mount our horses, and make direct for the city.

Hard work I had cut out for our poor animals, especially the one that should have to "carry double." Tough hacks they were, and had done the journey up cleverly enough, but it would stretch all their muscle to take us back before daylight.

Aided by the flashes, we wound our way, amid the trunks of the trees, until at length we came within sight of the pawpaw thicket—easily distinguished by the large oblong leaves of the *asiminiers*, which had a whitish sheen under the electric light. We hurried forward with joyful anticipation. Once mounted, we should soon get beyond the reach of pursuit.

"Strange the horses do not neigh, or give some sign of their presence! One would have thought our approach would have startled them. But no, there is no whimper, no hoof-stroke; yet we must be close to them now. I never knew of horses remaining so still? What can they be doing? Where are they?"

"Ay, where are they?" echoed D'Hauteville; "surely this is the spot where we left them?"

"Here it certainly was! Yes—here—this is the very sapling to which I fastened my bridle. See! here are their hoof-prints. By Heaven! the *horses are gone!*"

I uttered this with a full conviction of its truth. There was no room left for doubt. There was the trampled earth where they had stood—there the very tree to which we had tied them. I easily recognised it—for it was the largest in the grove.

Who had taken them away? This was the question that first occurred to us. Some one had been dogging us? Or had it been some one who had come across the animals by accident? The latter supposition was the less probable. Who would have been wandering in the woods on such a night? or even if any one had, what would have taken them into the pawpaw thicket? Ha! a new thought came into my head—perhaps the horses had got loose of themselves?

That was likely enough. Well, we should be able to tell as soon as the lightning flashed again, whether they had set themselves free; or whether some human hand had undone the knotted bridles. We stood by the tree waiting for the light. It did not tarry long; and when it came it enabled us to solve the doubt. My conjecture was correct; the horses had freed themselves. The broken branches told the tale. Something—the lightning—or more likely a prowling wild beast, had *stampeded* them; and they had broken off into the woods.

We now reproached ourselves for having so negligently fastened them—for having tied them to a branch of the *asiminier*, whose soft succulent wood possesses scarcely the toughness of an ordinary herbaceous plant. I was rather pleased at the discovery that the animals had freed themselves. There was a hope they had not strayed far. We might yet find them near at hand, with trailing bridles, cropping the grass.

Without loss of time we went in search of them—D'Hauteville took one direction, I another, while Aurore remained in the thicket of the pawpaws.

I ranged around the neighbourhood, went back to the fence, followed it to the road, and even went some distance along the road. I searched every nook among the trees, pushed through thickets and cane-brakes, and, whenever it flashed, examined the ground for tracks. At intervals I returned to the point of starting, to find that D'Hauteville had been equally unsuccessful.

After nearly an hour spent in this fruitless search, I resolved to give it up. I had no longer a hope of finding the horses; and, with despairing step, I turned once more in the direction of the thicket. D'Hauteville had arrived before me.

As I approached, the quivering gleam enabled me to distinguish his figure. He was standing beside Aurore. He was conversing familiarly with her. I fancied he was *polite* to her, and that she seemed pleased. There was something in this slight scene that made a painful impression upon me.

Neither had he found any traces of the missing steeds. It was no use looking any longer for them; and we agreed to discontinue the search, and pass the night in the woods.

It was with a heavy heart that I consented to this; but we had no alternative. Afoot we could not possibly reach New Orleans before morning; and to have been found on the road after daybreak would have insured our capture. Such as we could not pass without observation; and I had no doubt that, at the earliest hour, a pursuing party would take the road to the city.

Our most prudent plan was to remain all night where we were, and renew our search for the horses as soon as it became day. If we should succeed in finding them, we might conceal them in the swamp till the following night, and then make for the city. If we should not recover them, then, by starting at an earlier hour, we might attempt the journey on foot.

The loss of the horses had placed us in an unexpected dilemma. It had seriously diminished our chances of escape, and increased the peril of our position.

Peril I have said, and in such we stood—peril of no trifling kind. You will with difficulty comprehend the nature of our situation. You will imagine yourself reading the account of some ordinary lover's escapade—a mere runaway match, *à la Gretna Green*.

Rid yourself of this fancy. Know that all three of us had committed an act for which we were amenable. Know that my *crime* rendered me liable to certain and severe punishment by the *laws of the land*; that a still more terrible sentence might be feared *outside the laws of the land*. I knew all this—I knew that life itself was imperilled by the act I had committed!

Think of our danger, and it may enable you to form some idea of what were our feelings after returning from our bootless hunt after the horses.

We had no choice but stay where we were till morning.

We spent half-an-hour in dragging the *tillandsia* from the trees, and collecting the soft leaves of the pawpaws. With these I strewed the ground; and, placing Aurore upon it, I covered her with my cloak.

For myself I needed no couch. I sat down near my beloved, with my back against the trunk of a tree. I would fain have pillowed her head upon my breast, but the presence of D'Hauteville restrained me. Even that might not have hindered me, but the slight proposal which I made had been declined by Aurore. Even the hand that I had taken in mine was respectfully withdrawn!

I will confess that this coyness surprised and piqued me.

Chapter Sixty Eight
A Night in the Woods

Lightly clad as I was, the cold dews of the night would have prevented me from sleeping; but I needed not that to keep me awake. I could not have slept upon a couch of eider.

D'Hauteville had generously offered me his cloak, which I declined. He, too, was clad in cottonade and linen—though that was not the reason for my declining his offer. Even had I been suffering, I could not have accepted it. I began to fear him!

Aurore was soon asleep. The lightning showed me that her eyes were closed, and I could tell by her soft regular breathing that she slept. This, too, annoyed me!

I watched for each new gleam that I might look upon her. Each time as the quivering light illumined her lovely features, I gazed upon them with mingled feelings of passion and pain. Oh! could there be falsehood under that fair face? Could sin exist in that noble soul? After all was I *not* beloved?

Even so, there was no withdrawing now—no going back from my purpose. The race in which I had embarked must be run to the end—even at the sacrifice both of heart and life. I thought only of the purpose that had brought us there.

As my mind became calmer, I again reflected on the means of carrying it out. As soon as day should break, I would go in search of the horses— track them, if possible, to where they had strayed—recover them, and then remain concealed in the woods until the return of another night.

Should we not recover the horses, what then?

For a long time, I could not think of what was best to be done in such a contingency.

At length an idea suggested itself—a plan so feasible that I could not help communicating it to D'Hauteville, who like myself was awake. The plan was simple enough, and I only wondered I had not thought of it sooner. It was that he (D'Hauteville) should proceed to Bringiers, procure other horses or a carriage there, and at an early hour of the following night meet us on the Levee Road.

What could be better than this? There would be no difficulty in his obtaining the horses at Bringiers—the carriage more likely. D'Hauteville was not known—at least no one would suspect his having any relations with me. I was satisfied that the disappearance of the quadroon would be at once attributed to me. Gayarre himself would know that; and therefore I alone would be suspected and sought after. D'Hauteville agreed with me that this would be the very plan to proceed upon, in case our horses could not be found; and having settled the details, we awaited with less apprehension for the approach of day.

Day broke at length. The grey light slowly struggled through the shadowy tree-tops, until it became clear enough to enable us to renew the search.

Aurore remained upon the ground; while D'Hauteville and I, taking different directions set out after the horses.

D'Hauteville went farther into the woods, while I took the opposite route.

I soon arrived at the zigzag fence bounding the fields of Gayarre; for we were still upon the very borders of his plantation. On reaching this, I turned along its edge, and kept on for the point where the bye-road entered the woods. It was by this we had come in on the previous night, and I thought it probable the horses might have taken it into their heads to stray back the same way.

I was right in my conjecture. As soon as I entered the embouchure of the road, I espied the hoof-tracks of both animals going out towards the river. I saw also those we had made on the previous night coming in. I compared them. The tracks leading both ways were made by the same horses. One had a broken shoe, which enabled me at a glance to tell they were the same. I noted another "sign" upon the trail. I noted that our horses in passing out dragged their bridles, with branches adhering to them. This confirmed the original supposition, that they had broken loose.

It was now a question of how far they had gone. Should I follow and endeavour to overtake them? It was now bright daylight, and the risk would be great. Long before this, Gayarre and his friends would be up and on the alert. No doubt parties were already traversing the Levee Road as well as the bye-paths among the plantations. At every step I might expect to meet either a scout or a pursuer.

The tracks of the horses showed they had been travelling rapidly and straight onward. They had not stopped to browse. Likely they had gone direct to the Levee Road, and turned back to the city. They were livery horses, and no doubt knew the road well. Besides, they were of the Mexican breed—"mustangs." With these lively animals the trick of returning over a day's journey without their riders is not uncommon.

To attempt to overtake them seemed hopeless as well as perilous, and I at once gave up the idea and turned back into the woods. As I approached the pawpaw thicket, I walked with lighter tread. I am ashamed to tell the reason. Foul thoughts were in my heart.

The murmur of voices fell upon my ear.

"By Heaven! D'Hauteville has again got back before me!"

I struggled for some moments with my honour. It gave way; and I made my further approach among the pawpaws with the silence of a thief.

"D'Hauteville and she in close and friendly converse! They stand fronting each other. Their faces almost meet—their attitudes betoken a mutual interest. They talk in an earnest tone—in the low murmuring of lovers! O God!"

At this moment the scene on the wharf-boat flashed on my recollection. I remembered the youth wore a cloak, and that he was of low stature. It was he who was standing before me! That puzzle was explained. I was but a waif—a foil—a thing for a coquette to play with!

There stood the *true* lover of Aurore!

I stopped like one stricken. The sharp aching of my heart, oh! I may never describe. It felt as if a poisoned arrow had pierced to its very core, and there remained fixed and rankling. I felt faint and sick. I could have fallen to the ground.

She has taken something from her bosom. She is handing it to him! A love-token—a *gage d'amour*!

No. I am in error. It is the parchment—the paper taken from the desk of the avocat. What does it mean? What mystery is this? Oh! I shall demand a full explanation from both of you. I shall—patience, heart!—patience!

D'Hauteville has taken the papers, and hidden them under his cloak. He turns away. His face is now towards me. His eyes are upon me. I am seen!

"Ho! Monsieur?" he inquired, advancing to meet me. "What success? You have seen nothing of the horses!"

I made an effort to speak calmly.

"Their tracks," I replied.

Even in this short phrase my voice was quivering with emotion. He might easily have noticed my agitation, and yet he did not seem to do so.

"Only their tracks, Monsieur! Whither did they lead?"

"To the Levee Road. No doubt they have returned towards the city. We need have no farther dependence on them."

"Then I shall go to Bringiers at once?"

This was put hypothetically.

The proposal gave me pleasure. I wished him away.

I wished to be alone with Aurore.

"It would be as well," I assented, "if you do not deem it too early?"

"Oh, no! besides, I have business in Bringiers that will occupy me all the day."

"Ah!"

"Doubt not my return to meet you. I am certain to procure either horses or a carriage. Half-an-hour after twilight you will find me at the end of the bye-road. Fear not, Monsieur! I have a strong presentiment that for you all will yet be well. For *me*—ah!"

A deep sigh escaped him as he uttered the last phrase.

What did it mean? Was he mocking me? Had this strange youth a secret beyond *my* secret? Did he *know* that Aurore loved *him*? Was he so confident—so sure of her heart, that he recked not thus leaving her alone with me? Was he playing with me as the tiger with its victim? Were *both* playing with me?

These horrid thoughts crowding up, prevented me from making a definite rejoinder to his remarks. I muttered something about hope, but he seemed hardly to heed my remark. For some reason he was evidently desirous of being gone; and bidding Aurore and myself adieu, he turned abruptly off, and with quick, light steps, threaded his way through the woods.

With my eyes I followed his retreating form, until it was hidden by the intervening branches. I felt relief that he was gone. I could have wished that he was gone for ever. Despite the need we had of his assistance—despite the absolute necessity for his return—at that moment I could have wished that we should never see him again!

Chapter Sixty Nine
Love's Vengeance

Now for an explanation with Aurore! Now to give vent to the dire passion of jealousy—to relieve my heart with recriminations—with the bitter-sweet vengeance of reproach!

I could stifle the foul emotion no longer—no longer conceal it. It must have expression in words.

I had purposely remained standing with my face averted from her, till D'Hauteville was gone out of sight. Longer, too. I was endeavouring to still the wild throbbings of my breast—to affect the calmness of indifference. Vain hypocrisy! To her eyes my spite must have been patent, for in this the keen instincts of woman are not to be baffled.

It was even so. She comprehended all. Hence the wild act—the *abandon* to which at that moment she gave way.

I was turning to carry out my design, when I felt the soft pressure of her body against mine—her arms encircled my neck—her head, with face upturned, rested upon my bosom, and her large lustrous eyes sought mine with a look of melting inquiry.

That look should have satisfied me. Surely no eyes but the eyes of love could have borne such expression?

And yet I was not content. I faltered out—

"Aurore, you do not love me!"

"*Ah, Monsieur! pourquoi cette cruauté? Je t'aime—mon Dieu! avec tout mon coeur je t'aime!*"

Even this did not still my suspicious thoughts. The circumstances had been too strong—jealousy had taken too firm a hold to be plucked out by mere assurances. Explanation alone could satisfy me. That or confession.

Having made a commencement, I went on. I detailed what I had seen at the landing—the after conduct of D'Hauteville—what I had observed the preceding night—what I had just that moment witnessed. I detailed all.

I added no reproaches. There was time enough for them when I should receive her answer.

It came in the midst of tears. She had known D'Hauteville before—that was acknowledged. There *was* a mystery in the relations that existed between them. I was solicited not to require an explanation. My patience was appealed to. It was not her secret. I should soon know all. In due time all would be revealed.

How readily my heart yielded to these delicious words! I no longer doubted. How could I, with those large eyes, full of love-light, shining through the tear-bedewed lashes?

My heart yielded. Once more my arms closed affectionately around the form of my betrothed, and a fervent kiss renewed the vow of our betrothal.

We could have remained long upon this love-hallowed spot, but prudence prompted us to leave it. We were too near to the point of danger. At the distance of two hundred yards was the fence that separated Gayarre's plantation from the wild woods; and from that could even be seen the house itself, far off over the fields. The thicket concealed this, it was true; but should pursuit lead that way, the thicket would be the first place that would be searched. It would be necessary to seek a hiding-place farther off in the woods.

I bethought me of the flowery glade—the scene of my adventure with the *crotalus*. Around it the underwood was thick and shady, and there were spots where we could remain screened from the observation of the keenest eyes. At that moment I thought only of such concealment. It never entered my head that there were means of discovering us, even in the heart of the tangled thicket, or the pathless maze of the cane-brake. I resolved, therefore, to make at once for the glade.

The pawpaw thicket, where we had passed the night, lay near the south-eastern angle of Gayarre's plantation. To reach the glade it would be necessary for us to pass a mile or more to the northward. By taking a diagonal line through the woods, the chances were ten to one we should lose our way, and perhaps not find a proper place of concealment. The chances were, too, that we might not find a path, through the network of swamps and bayous that traversed the forest in every direction.

I resolved, therefore, to skirt the plantation, until I had reached the path that I had before followed to the glade, and which I now remembered.

There would be some risk until we had got to the northward of Gayarre's plantation; but we should keep at a distance from the fence, and as much as possible in the underwood. Fortunately a belt of "palmetto" land, marking the limits of the annual inundation, extended northward through the woods, and parallel to the line of fence. This singular vegetation, with its broad fan-like fronds, formed an excellent cover; and a person passing through it with caution could not be observed from any great distance. The partial lattice-work of its leaves was rendered more complete by the tall flower-stalks of the *altheas*, and other malvaceous plants that shared the ground with the palmettos.

Directing ourselves within the selvage of this rank vegetation, we advanced with caution; and soon came opposite the place where we had crossed the fence on the preceding night. At this point the woods approached nearest to the house of Gayarre. As already stated, but one field lay between, but it was nearly a mile in length. It was dead level, however, and did not appear half so long. By going forward to the fence, we could have seen the house at the opposite end, and very distinctly.

I had no intention of gratifying my curiosity at that moment by such an act, and was moving on, when a sound fell upon my ear that caused me suddenly to halt, while a thrill of terror ran through my veins.

My companion caught me by the arm, and looked inquiringly in my face.

A caution to her to be silent was all the reply I could make; and, leaning a little lower, so as to bring my ear nearer to the ground, I listened.

The suspense was short. I heard the sound again. My first conjecture was right. It was the "growl" of a hound!

There was no mistaking that prolonged and deep-toned note. I was too fond a disciple of Saint Hubert not to recognise the bay of a long-eared Molossian. Though distant and low, like the hum of a forest bee, I was not deceived in the sound. It fell upon my ears with a terrible import!

And why terrible was the baying of a hound? To me above all others, whose ears, attuned to the "tally ho!" and the "view hilloa!" regarded these sounds as the sweetest of music? Why terrible? Ah! you must think of the circumstances in which I was placed—you must think, too, of the hours I spent with the snake-charmer—of the tales he told me in that dark tree-cave—the stories of runaways, of sleuth-dogs, of man-hunters, and "nigger-hunts," —practices long thought to be confined to Cuba, but which I found as rife upon the soil of Louisiana,—you must think of all these, and then you will understand why I trembled at the distant baying of a hound.

The howl I heard was still very distant. It came from the direction of Gayarre's house. It broke forth at intervals. It was not like the utterance of a hound upon the trail, but that of dogs just cleared from the kennel, and giving tongue to their joy at the prospect of sport.

Fearful apprehensions were stirred within me at the moment. A terrible conjecture rushed across my brain. *They were after us with hounds*!

Chapter Seventy
Hounds on our Trail

O God! after us with hounds!

Either after us, or about to be, was the hypothetic form of my conjecture. I could proceed no farther upon our path till I had become satisfied.

Leaving Aurore among the palmettoes. I ran directly forward to the fence, which was also the boundary of the woods. On reaching this, I grasped the branch of a tree, and swung myself up to such an elevation as would enable me to see over the tops of the cane. This gave me a full view of the house shining under the sun that had now risen in all his splendour.

At a glance I saw that I had guessed aright. Distant as the house was, I could plainly see men around it, many of them on horseback. Their heads were moving above the canes; and now and then the deep bay of hounds told that several dogs were loose about the enclosure. The scene was just as if a party of hunters had assembled before going out upon a deer "drive;" and but for the place, the time, and the circumstances that had already transpired, I might have taken it for such. Far different, however, was the impression it made upon me. I knew well why was that gathering around the house of Gayarre. I knew well the game they were about to pursue. I lingered but a moment upon my perch—long enough to perceive that the *hunters* were all mounted and ready to start.

With quick-beating pulse I retraced my steps; and soon rejoined my companion, who stood awaiting me with trembling apprehension.

I did not need to tell her the result of my reconnoissance: she read it in my looks. She, too, had heard the baying of the dogs. She was a native, and knew the customs of the land: she knew that hounds were used to hunt deer and foxes and wild-cats of the woods; but she knew also that on many plantations there were some kept for a far different purpose—sleuth-dogs, *trained to the hunting of men*!

Had she been of slow comprehension, I might have attempted to conceal from her what I had learnt; but she was far from that, and with quick instinct she divined all.

Our first feeling was that of utter hopelessness. There seemed no chance of our escaping. Go where we would, hounds, trained to the scent of a human track, could not fail to follow and find us. It would be of no use hiding in the swamp or the bush. The tallest sedge or the thickest underwood could not give us shelter from pursuers like these.

Our first feeling, then, was that of hopelessness—quickly followed by a half-formed resolve to go no farther, to stand our ground and be taken. We had not death to fear; though I knew that if taken I might make up my mind to some rough handling. I knew the feeling that was abroad in relation to the Abolitionists—at that time raging like a fever. I had heard of the barbarous treatment which some of these "fanatics"—as they were called—had experienced at the hands of the incensed slave-owners. I should no doubt be reckoned in the same category, or maybe, still worse, be charged as a "nigger-stealer." In any case I had to fear chastisement, and of no light kind either.

But my dread of this was nothing when compared with the reflection that, if taken, *Aurore must go back to Gayarre*!

It was this thought more than any other that made my pulse beat quickly. It was this thought that determined me not to surrender until after every effort to escape should fail us.

I stood for some moments pondering on what course to pursue. All at once a thought came into my mind that saved me from despair. That thought was of Gabriel the runaway.

Do not imagine that I had forgotten him or his hiding-place all this time. Do not fancy I had not thought of him before. Often, since we had entered the woods, had he and his tree-cave arisen in my memory; and I should have gone there for concealment, but that the distance deterred me. As we intended to return to the Levee Road after sunset, I had chosen the glade for our resting-place, on account of its being nearer.

Even then, when I learnt that hounds would be after us, I had again thought of making for the Bambarra's hiding-place; but had dismissed the idea, because it occurred to me that *the hounds could follow us anywhere*, and that, by taking shelter with the runaway, we should only guide his tyrants upon *him*.

So quick and confused had been all these reflections, that it had never occurred to me that the hounds *could not trail us across water*. It was only at that moment when pondering how I could throw them off the track— thinking of the snake-charmer and his pine-cones—that I remembered the water.

Sure enough, in that still lay a hope; and I could now appreciate the remarkable cunning with which the lair of the runaway had been chosen. It was just the place to seek refuge from "de dam blood-dogs."

The moment I thought of it, I resolved to flee thither.

I would be sure to know the way. I had taken especial pains to remember it; for even on the day of my snake-adventure, some half-defined thoughts—something more like a presentiment than a plan—had passed through my mind, vaguely pointing to a contingency like the present. Later events, and particularly my design of escaping to the city at once, had driven these thoughts out of my mind. For all that, I still remembered the way by which the Bambarra had guided me, and could follow it with hurried steps—though there was neither road nor path, save the devious tracks made by cattle or the wild animals of the forest.

But I was certain I knew it well. I should remember the signs and "blazes" to which the guide had called my attention. I should remember where it crossed the "big bayou" by the trunk of a fallen tree that served as a foot-bridge. I should remember where it ran through a strip of marsh impassable for horses, through the cane-brake, among the great knees and buttocks of the cypresses, down to the edge of the water. And that huge tree, with its prostrate trunk projecting out into the lake, and its moss-wrapped branches—that cunning harbour for the little pirogue—I should be sure to remember.

Neither had I forgotten the signal, by which I was to warn the runaway whenever I should return. It was a peculiar whistle he had instructed me to give, and also the number of times I was to utter it.

I had not waited for all these reflections. Many of them were after-thoughts, that occurred along the way. The moment I remembered the lake, I resolved upon my course; and, with a word of cheer to my companion, we again moved forward.

Chapter Seventy One
The Signal

The change in our plans made no change in the direction. We continued on in the same course. The way to the lake passed by the glade, where we had purposed going—indeed, through the middle of it lay the nearest path to the lair of the runaway.

Not far from the north-east angle of Gayarre's plantation, was the spot where I had parted with the black on the night of my adventure with him. It was at this point the path entered the woods. The blaze upon a sweet-gum-tree, which I remembered well, showed me the direction. I was but too glad to turn off here, and leave the open woods; the more so that, just as we had reached the turning-point, the cry of the hounds came swelling upon the air, loud and prolonged. From the direction of the sound, I had no doubt but that they were already in the cane-field, and lifting our trail of the preceding night.

For a few hundred yards farther the timber was thin. The axe had been flourished there, as the numerous "stumps" testified. It was there the "firewood" was procured for the use of the plantation, and "cords" of it, already cut and piled, could be seen on both sides of our path. We passed among these with trembling haste. We feared to meet with some of the woodcutters, or the driver of a wood-wagon. Such an encounter would have been a great misfortune; as, whoever might have seen us would have guided our pursuers on the track.

Had I reasoned calmly I would not have felt uneasiness on this head. I might have known, that if the dogs succeeded in tracking us thus far, they would need no direction from either wagoner or wood-chopper. But in the hurry of the moment I did not think of this; and I felt relief when we had passed through the tract of broken woods, and were entering under the more sombre shadow of the virgin forest.

It was now a question of time—a question of whether we should be able to reach the lake, summon the Bambarra with his pirogue, and be paddled out of sight, before the dogs should trail us to the edge of the water. Should we succeed in doing so, we should then have a fair prospect of escape. No doubt the dogs would guide our pursuers to the place of our embarkation—

the fallen tree—but then both dogs and men would be at fault. That gloomy lake of the woods was a rare labyrinth. Though the open water was a surface of small extent, neither it, nor the island-like motte of timber in its centre, was visible from the place of embarkation; and, besides the lake itself, the inundation covered a large tract of the forest. Even should our pursuers be certain that we had escaped by the water, they might despair of finding us in the midst of such a maze—where the atmosphere at that season of fall foliage had the hue of a dark twilight.

But they would hardly be convinced of our escape in that way. There was no trace left where the pirogue was moored—no mark upon the tree. They would scarce suspect the existence of a canoe in such an out-of-the-way spot, where the water—a mere stagnant pond—had no communication either with the river or the adjacent bayous. We were leaving no tracks—I took care of that—that could be perceived under the forest gloom; and our pursuers might possibly conclude that the dogs had been running upon the trail of a bear, a cougar, or the swamp wild-cat (*Lynx rufus*)—all of which animals freely take the water when pursued. With such probabilities I was cheering myself and my companion, as we kept rapidly along our course!

My greatest source of apprehension was the delay we should have to make, after giving the signal to the runaway. Would he hear it at once? Would he attend to it in due haste? Would he arrive in time? These were the points about which I felt chiefly anxious. Time was the important consideration; in that lay the conditions of our danger. Oh! that I had thought of this purpose before!—oh! that we had started earlier!

How long would it take our pursuers to come up? I could scarce trust myself to think of a reply to this question. Mounted as they were, they would travel faster than we: the dogs would guide them at a run!

One thought alone gave me hope. They would soon find our resting-place of the night; they would see where we had slept by the pawpaw-leaves and the moss; they could not fail to be certain of all that; but would they so easily trail us thence? In our search after the horses, we had tracked the woods in all directions. I had gone back to the bye-road, and some distance along it. All this would surely baffle the dogs for a while; besides, D'Hauteville, at starting, had left the pawpaw thicket by a different route from that we had taken. They might go off on *his* trail. Would that they might follow D'Hauteville.

All these conjectures passed rapidly through my mind as we hurried along. I even thought of making an attempt to throw the hounds off the scent. I thought of the *ruse* practised by the Bambarra with the spray of the loblolly pine; but, unfortunately, I could not see any of these trees on our way, and feared to lose time by going in search of one. I had doubts, too, of the efficacy of such a proceeding, though the black had solemnly assured me of it. The common red onion, he had afterwards told me would be equally effective for the like purpose! But the red onion grew not in the woods, and the *pin de l'encens* I could not find.

For all that I did not proceed without precautions. Youth though I was, I was an old hunter, and had some knowledge of "woodcraft," gathered in deerstalking, and in the pursuit of other game, among my native hills. Moreover, my nine months of New-world life had not all been passed within city walls; and I had already become initiated into many of the mysteries of the great American forest.

I did not proceed, then, in mere reckless haste. Where precautions could be observed, I adopted them.

A strip of marsh had to be crossed. It was stagnant water, out of which grew flags, and the shrub called "swamp-wood" (*Bois de marais*). It was knee-deep, and could he waded. I knew this, for I had crossed it before. Hand in hand we waded through, and got safe to the opposite side; but on entering I took pains to choose a place, where we stepped at once from the dry ground into the water. On going out, I observed a like precaution—so that our tracks might not appear in the mud.

Perhaps I should not have taken all this trouble, had I known that, there were "hunters" among those who pursued us. I fancied the crowd I had seen were but planters, or people of the town—hurriedly brought together by Gayarre and his friends. I fancied they might not have much skill in tracking, and that my simple trick might be sufficient to mislead them.

Had I known that at their head was a man, of whom Gabriel had told me much—a man *who made negro-hunting his profession,* and who was the most noted "tracker" in all the country—I might have saved myself both the time and the trouble I was taking. But I knew not that this ruffian and his trained dogs were after us, and I did my utmost to throw my pursuers off.

Shortly after passing the marsh, we crossed the "big bayou" by means of its tree-bridge. Oh! that I could have destroyed that log, or hurled it from its position. I consoled myself with the idea, that though the dogs might follow us over it, it would delay the pursuers awhile, who, no doubt, were all on horseback.

We now passed through the glade, but I halted not there. We stopped not to look upon its bright flowers—we perceived not their fragrance. Once I had wished to share this lovely scene in the company of Aurore. We were now in its midst, but under what circumstances! What wild thoughts were passing through my brain, as we hurried across this flowery tract under bright sunshine, and then plunged once more into the sombre atmosphere of the woods!

The path I remembered well, and was able to pursue it without hesitancy. Now and then only did I pause—partly to listen, and partly to rest my companion, whose bosom heaved quick and high with the rude exertion. But her glance testified that her courage was firm, and her smile cheered *me* on.

At length we entered among the cypress-trees that bordered the lake; and, gliding around their massive trunks, soon reached the edge of the water.

We approached the fallen tree; and, climbing up, advanced along its trunk until we stood among its moss-covered branches.

I had provided myself with an instrument—a simple joint of the cane which grew plenteously around, and which with my knife I had shaped after a fashion I had been already taught by the Bambarra. With this I could produce a sound, that would be heard at a great distance off, and plainly to the remotest part of the lake.

Taking hold of the branches, I now bent down, until my face almost touched the surface of the water, and placing the reed to my lips, I gave utterance to the signal.

Chapter Seventy Two
The Sleuth-Hounds

The shrill whistle, pealing along the water, pierced the dark aisles of the forest. It aroused the wild denizens of the lake, who, startled by such an unusual sound, answered it with their various cries in a screaming concert. The screech of the crane and the Louisiana heron, the hoarse hooting of owls, and the hoarser croak of the pelican, mingled together; and, louder than all, the scream of the osprey and the voice of the bald eagle—the last falling upon the ear with sharp metallic repetitions that exactly resembled the filing of saws.

For some moments this commotion was kept up; and it occurred to me that if I had to repeat the signal then it would not have been heard. Shrill as it was, it could scarce have been distinguished in such a din!

Crouching among the branches, we remained to await the result. We made no attempts at idle converse. The moments were too perilous for aught but feelings of extreme anxiety. Now and then a word of cheer—a muttered hope—were all the communications that passed between us.

With earnest looks we watched the water—with glances of fear we regarded the land. On one side we listened for the plashing of a paddle; on the other we dreaded to hear the "howl" of a hound. Never can I forget those moments—those deeply-anxious moments. Till death I may not forget them.

Every thought at the time—every incident, however minute—now rushes into my remembrance, as if it were a thing of yesterday.

I remember that once or twice, away under the trees, we perceived a ripple along the surface of the water. Our hearts were full of hope—we thought it was the canoe.

It was a fleeting joy. The waves were made by the great saurian, whose hideous body—large almost as the pirogue itself—next moment passed before our eyes, cleaving the water with fish-like velocity.

I remember entertaining the supposition that the runaway *might not be in his lair*! He might be off in the forest—in search of food—or on any other errand. Then the reflection followed—if such were the case, I should have found the pirogue by the tree? Still he might have other landing-places around the lake—on the other side perhaps. He had not told me whether or no, and it was probable enough. These hypothetic conjectures increased my anxiety.

But there arose another, far more dreadful, because far more probable—

The black might be asleep!

Far more probable, because night was his day, and day his night. At night he was abroad, roaming and busy—by day he was at home and slept.

Oh, Heavens! if he should be asleep, and not have heard the signal!

Such was the terrible fancy that rushed across my brain.

I felt suddenly impelled to repeat the signal—though I thought at the time, if my conjecture were correct, there was but little hope he would hear me. A negro sleeps like a torpid bear. The report of a gun or a railway-whistle alone could awake one. There was no chance for a puny pipe like mine—the more especially as the screaming concert still continued.

"Even if he should hear it, he would hardly be able to distinguish the whistle from—Merciful heavens!"

I was speaking to my companion when this exclamation interrupted me. It came from my own lips, but with involuntary utterance. It was called forth by a sound of dread import—a sound that I could hear above the shrill screaming of the birds, and hearing could interpret. It was the trumpet-like baying of a hound!

I stood bent, and listening; I heard it again. There was no mistaking that note. I had the ears of a hunter. I knew the music well.

Oh, how unlike to music then! It fell upon my ears like a cry of vengeance—like a knell of death!

I thought no longer of repeating the signal; even if heard, it would be too late. I flung the reed away, as a useless toy. I drew Aurore along the tree, passing her behind me; and raising myself erect, stood fronting the land.

Again the "gowl" broke out—its loud echoes rolling through the woods—this time so near, that every moment I expected to see the animal that had uttered it.

I had not long to wait. A hundred yards off was a cane-brake. I could perceive a motion among the tall reeds. Their tops swayed to and fro, and their hollow culms rattled against each other, as they were jerked about, and borne downward. Some living thing was pressing through their midst.

The motion reached their verge—the last canes gave way, and I now saw what I had looked for—the spotted body of a hound! With a spring the animal came forth, paused for a moment in the open ground, and then, uttering a prolonged howl, took up the scent, and galloped forward.

Close upon his heels came a second; the waving cane closed behind them, and both ran forward in the direction of the log.

As there was no longer any underwood, I had a full view of their bodies. Gloomy as the place was, I could see them with sufficient distinctness to note their kind—huge, gaunt deer-hounds, black and tan. From the manner of their approach, they had evidently been trained to their work, and that was *not* the hunting of deer. No ordinary hound would have run upon a human track, as they were running upon ours.

The moment I saw these dogs I made ready for a conflict. Their huge size, their broad heavy jaws, and ferocious looks, told what savage brutes they were; and I felt satisfied they would attack me as soon as they came up.

With this belief I drew forth a pistol; and, laying hold of a branch to steady me, I stood waiting their approach.

I had not miscalculated. On reaching the prostrate trunk, he scarcely made a pause; but, leaping upward, came running along the log. He had dropped the scent, and now advanced with eyes glaring, evidently meditating to spring upon me.

My position could not have been better, had I spent an hour in choosing it. From the nature of the ground, my assailant could neither dodge to the right nor the left; but was compelled to approach me in a line as straight as an arrow. I had nought to do but hold my weapon firm and properly directed. A novice with fire-arms could hardly have missed such an object.

My nerves were strung with anger—a feeling of intense indignation was burning in my breast, that rendered me as firm as steel. I was cool from very passion—at the thought of being thus hunted like a wolf!

I waited until the muzzle of the hound almost met that of the pistol, and then I fired. The dog tumbled from the log.

I saw the other close upon his heels. I aimed through the smoke, and again pulled trigger.

The good weapon did not fail me. Again the report was followed by a plunge.

The hounds were no longer upon the log. They had fallen right and left into the black water below!

Chapter Seventy Three
The Man-Hunter

The hounds had fallen into the water—one dead, the other badly wounded. The latter could not have escaped, as one of his legs had been struck by the bullet, and his efforts to swim were but the throes of desperation. In a few minutes he must have gone to the bottom; but it was not his fate to die by drowning. It was predestined that his howling should be brought to a termination in a far different manner.

The voice of the dog is music to the ear of the alligator. Of all other animals, this is the favourite prey of the great saurian; and the howl of hound or cur will attract him from any distance where it may be heard.

Naturalists have endeavoured to explain this in a different way. They say—and such is the fact—that the howling of a dog bears a resemblance to the voice of the young alligator, and that the old ones are attracted towards the spot where it is heard—the mother to protect it, and the male parent to devour it!

This is a disputed point in natural history; but there can be no dispute that the alligator eagerly preys upon the dog whenever an opportunity offers—seizing the canine victim in his terrible jaws, and carrying it off to his aqueous retreat. This he does with an air of such earnest avidity, as to leave no doubt but that he esteems the dog a favourite morsel.

I was not surprised, then, to see half-a-dozen of these gigantic reptiles emerging from amid the dark tree-trunks, and hastily swimming towards the wounded hound.

The continued howling of the latter guided them; and in a few seconds they had surrounded the spot where he struggled, and were dashing forward upon their victim.

A shoal of sharks could not have finished him more expeditiously. A blow from the tail of one silenced his howling—three or four pair of gaunt jaws closed upon him at the same time—a short scuffle ensued—then the long bony heads separated, and the huge reptiles were seen swimming off again—each with a morsel in his teeth. A few bubbles and blotches of red froth mottling the inky surface of the water, were all that remained where the hound had lately been plunging.

Almost a similar scene occurred on the opposite side of the log—for the water was but a few feet in depth, and the dead hound was visible as he lay at the bottom. Several of the reptiles approaching on that side, had seen this one at the same time, and, rushing forward, they served him precisely as his companion had been served by the others. A crumb of bread could not have disappeared sooner among a shoal of hungry minnows, than did the brace of deer-hounds down the throats of these ravenous reptiles.

Singular as was the incident, it had scarce drawn my notice. I had far other things to think of.

After firing the pistol, I remained standing upon the tree, with my eyes fixed in the direction whence came the hounds.

I gazed intently among the tree-trunks, away up the dark vistas of the forest, I watched the cane-brake, to note the slightest motion in the reeds. I listened to every sound, while I stood silent myself, and enjoined silence upon my trembling companion.

I had but little hope then. There would be more dogs, no doubt—slower hounds following in the distance—and with them the mounted man-hunters. They could not be far behind—they could not fail to come up soon—the sooner that the report of my pistol would guide them to the spot. It would be of no use making opposition to a crowd of angry men. I could do nothing else than surrender to them.

My companion entreated me to this course; abjured me not to use my weapons—for I now held the second pistol in my hand. But I had no intention of using them should the crowd of men come up; I had only taken out the pistol as a precaution against the attack of the dogs—should any more appear.

For a good while I heard no sounds from the forest, and saw no signs of our pursuers. What could be detaining them? Perhaps the crossing of the bayou; or the tract of marsh. I knew the horsemen must there leave the trail; but were they all mounted?

I began to hope that Gabriel might yet be in time. If he had not heard the signal-whistle, he must have heard the reports of my pistol? But, on second thoughts, that might only keep him back. He would not understand the firing, and might fear to come with the pirogue!

Perhaps he had heard the first signal, and was now on his way. It was not too late to entertain such a supposition. Notwithstanding what had passed, we had been yet but a short while upon the spot. If on the way, he might think the shots were fired from my double-barrelled gun—fired at some game. He might not be deterred. There was still a hope he might come in time. If so, we would be able to reach his tree-cave in safety.

There was no trace of the dogs, save a blotch or two of blood upon the rough bark of the log, and that was not visible from the shore. Unless there were other dogs to guide them to the spot, the men might not in the darkness so easily discover these marks. We might yet baffle them!

With fresh hope I turned once more towards the water, and gazed in the direction in which I expected the pirogue to come. Alas! there was no sign of it. No sound came from the lake save the wild calling of the affrighted birds.

I turned once more to the land.

I saw the cane-brake in motion. The tall culms vibrated and crackled under the heavy tread of a man, who the next moment emerging into the open ground, advanced at a slinging trot towards the water!

He was alone and afoot—there were no dogs with him—but the long rifle poised upon his shoulder, and the hunting accoutrements around his body, told me at a glance he was the owner of the deer-hounds.

His black bushy beard, his leggings, and buckskin shirt, his red neckcloth and raccoon cap—but above all, the brutal ferocity of his visage, left me in no doubt as to who this character was. The description of the runaway answered him in every particular. He could be no other than *Ruffin the man-hunter*!

Chapter Seventy Four
Shot for Shot

Yes, the individual who now advanced was Ruffin the man-hunter; and the dogs I had killed, were his—a brace of sleuth-hounds, well-known in the settlement as being specially trained to tracking the unfortunate blacks, that, driven by cruel treatment, had taken to the woods.

Well-known, too, was their master—a dissipated brutal fellow, half hunter, half hog-thief, who dwelt in the woods like an Indian savage, and hired himself out to such of the planters as needed the aid of him and his horrid hounds!

As I have said, I had never seen this individual, though I had heard of him often—from Scipio, from the boy Caton, and, lastly, from Gabriel. The Bambarra had described him minutely—had told me wild stories of the man's wickedness and ferocious cruelty—how he had taken the lives of several runaways while in pursuit of them, and caused others to be torn and mangled by his savage dogs!

He was the terror and aversion of every negro quarter along the coast; and his name—appropriate to his character—oft served the sable mother as a "bogey" to frighten her squalling piccaninny into silence!

Such was Ruffin the *man-hunter*, as he was known among the black helots of the plantations. The "cobbing-board" and the red cowhide were not half so terrible as he. In comparison with him, such characters as "Bully Bill," the flogging overseer, might be esteemed mild and humane.

The sight of this man at once deprived me of all farther thought of escape. I permitted my pistol arm to drop loosely by my side, and stood awaiting his advance, with the intention of surrendering ourselves up. Resistance would be vain, and could only lead to the idle spilling of blood. With this intention I remained silent, having cautioned my companion to do the same.

On first emerging from the cane-brake, the hunter did not see us. I was partially screened by the moss where I stood—Aurore entirely so. Besides, the man's eyes were not turned in our direction. They were bent upon the ground. No doubt he had heard the reports of my pistol; but he trusted more to his tracking instincts; and, from his bent attitude. I could tell that he was trailing his own dogs—almost as one of themselves would have done!

As he neared the edge of the pond, the *smell* of the water reached him; and, suddenly halting, he raised his eyes and looked forward. The sight of the pond seemed to puzzle him, and his astonishment was expressed in the short sharp expression—

"Hell!"

The next moment his eyes fell upon the prostrate tree, then quickly swept along its trunk, and rested full upon me.

"Hell and scissors!" he exclaimed, "thar are ye! Whar's my dogs?"

I stood eyeing him back, but made no reply.

"You hear, damn yer! Whar's my dogs?"

I still remained silent.

His eyes fell upon the log. He saw the blood-spots upon the hark. He remembered the shots.

"Hell and damn!" cried he, with horrid emphasis, "you've kilt my dogs!" and then followed a volley of mingled oaths and threats, while the ruffian gesticulated as, if he had suddenly gone mad!

After a while he ceased from these idle demonstrations; and, planting himself firmly, he raised his rifle muzzle towards me, and cried out:—

"Come off that log, and fetch your blue-skin with you! Quick, damn yer! Come off that log! Another minnit, an' I'll plug ye!"

I have said that at first sight of the man I had given up all idea of resistance, and intended to surrender at once; but there was something so arrogant in the demand—so insulting in the tone with which the ruffian made it—that it fired my very flesh with indignation, and determined me to stand at bay.

Anger, at being thus hunted, new-nerved both my heart and my arm. The brute had bayed me, and I resolved to risk resistance.

Another reason for changing my determination—I now saw that he was *alone*. He had followed the dogs afoot, while the others on horseback had no doubt been stopped or delayed by the bayou and morass. Had the crowd come up, I must have yielded *nolens volens*; but the man-hunter himself—formidable antagonist though he appeared—was still but *one*, and to surrender tamely to a single individual, was more than my spirit—inherited from border ancestry—could brook. There was too much of the moss-trooper blood in my veins for that, and I resolved, *coute que coute*, to risk the encounter.

My pistol was once more firmly grasped; and looking the ruffian full into his bloodshot eyes, I shouted back—

"Fire at your peril! Miss and you are mine!"

The sight of my uplifted pistol caused him to quail; and I have no doubt that had opportunity offered, he would have withdrawn from the contest. He had expected no such a reception.

But he had gone too far to recede. His rifle was already at his shoulder, and the next moment I saw the flash, and heard the sharp crack. The "thud" of his bullet, too, fell upon my ear, as it struck into the branch against which I was leaning. Good marksman as he was reputed, the sheen of my pistols had spoiled his aim, and he had missed me!

I did not miss *him*. He fell to the shot with a demoniac howl; and as the smoke thinned off, I could see him writhing and scrambling in the black mud!

I hesitated whether to give him the second barrel—for I was angry and desired his life—but at this moment noises reached me from behind. I heard the plunging paddle, with the sounds of a manly voice; and turning, I beheld the Bambarra.

The latter had shot the pirogue among the tree-tops close to where we stood, and with voice and gesture now urged us to get aboard.

"Quick, mass'. Quick, 'Rore gal! jump into de dugout! Jump in! Truss Ole Gabe!—he stand by young mass' to de deff!"

Almost mechanically I yielded to the solicitations of the runaway—though I now saw but little chance of our ultimate escape—and, having assisted Aurore into the pirogue, I followed and took my seat beside her.

The strong arm of the negro soon impelled us far out from the shore; and in five minutes after we were crossing the open lake toward the cypress clump in its midst.

Chapter Seventy Five
Love in the Hour of Peril

We glided into the shadow of the tree, and passed under its trailing parasites. The pirogue touched its trunk. Mechanically I climbed along the sloping buttress—mechanically assisted Aurore.

We stood within the hollow chamber—the lurking-place of the runaway—and for the present were safe from pursuit. But there was no joy in our hearts. We knew it was but a respite, without any hope of ultimate concealment.

The encounter with Ruffin had ruined all our prospects. Whether the hunter were yet dead or alive, his presence would guide the pursuit. The way we had got off would easily be conjectured, and our hiding-place could not long remain undiscovered.

What had passed would be likely to aggravate our pursuers, and strengthen their determination to capture us. Before Ruffin came up, there was yet a chance of safety. Most of those engaged in the pursuit would regard it as the mere ordinary affair of a chase after a runaway negro—a sport of which they might get tired whenever they should lose the track. Considering for whom the hunt was got up—a man so unpopular as Gayarre,—none would have any great interest in the result, excepting himself and his ruffian aids. Had we left no traces where we embarked in the pirogue, the gloomy labyrinth of forest-covered water might have discouraged our pursuers—most of whom would have given up at the doubtful prospect, and returned to their homes. We might have been left undisturbed until nightfall, and it was my design to have then recrossed the lake, landed at some new point, and, under the guidance of the Bambarra, get back to the Levee Road, where we were to meet D'Hauteville with the horses. Thence, as originally agreed upon, to the city.

All this programme, I had hastily conceived; and previous to the appearance of Ruffin, there was every probability I should succeed in carrying it out.

Even after I had shot the dogs, I did not wholly despair. There were still many chances of success that occurred to me. The pursuers, thought I, detained by the bayou, might have lost the dogs, and would not follow their track so easily. Some time would be wasted at all events. Even should they form a correct guess as to the fate of the hounds, neither men afoot nor on horseback could penetrate to our hiding-place. They would need boats or canoes. More time would be consumed in bringing these from the river, and perhaps night would be down before this could be effected. On night and D'Hauteville I still had confidence.

That was previous to the conflict with the man-hunter.

After that affair, circumstances had undergone a change. Alive or dead, Ruffin would guide the pursuit to where we were. If still living—and now that my angry feeling had passed away I hoped he was—he would at once direct the pursuers upon us.

I believed he was not dead—only wounded. His behaviour, after receiving the shot, had not been like that of a man mortally wounded. I believed, and hoped, that he still lived:—not that I felt at all remorseful at what had happened, but from mere prudential considerations. If dead, his body by the prostrate tree would soon be discovered, and would tell the tale to those who came up. We should be captured all the same, and might expect the more terrible consequences.

The rencontre with this ruffian had been altogether unfortunate. It had changed the face of affairs. Blood had been spilt *in defence of a runaway*. The news would return rapidly to the town. It would spread through the plantations with lightning-speed. The whole community would be fired and roused—the number of our pursuers quadrupled. I should be hunted as a *double* outlaw, and with the hostile energy of vengeance!

I knew all this, and no longer speculated upon the probabilities of deliverance. There was not the remotest prospect of our being able to get away.

I drew my betrothed near me. I folded her in my arms, and pressed her to my heart. Till death she would be mine! She swore it in that shadowy spot—in that dread and darksome hour. Till death she would be mine!

Her love inspired me with courage; and with courage I awaited the result.

Another hour passed.

Despite our fearful anticipations, that hour was pleasantly spent. Strange it is to say so, but it was in reality one of the happiest hours I can remember. It was the first time I had been enabled to hold free converse with Aurore since the day of our betrothal. We were now alone—for the faithful black stood sentinel below by the hawser of his pirogue.

The reaction, consequent upon my late jealousy, had kindled my love to a renewed and fiercer life—for such is the law of nature. In the very ardour of my affection, I almost forgot our desperate situation.

Over and over again we vowed eternal troth—over and over plighted our mutual faith, in fond, burning words—the eloquence of our heartfelt passion. Oh! it was a happy hour!

Alas! it came to an end. It ended with a painful regret, but not with surprise. I was not surprised to hear horns sounding through the woods, and signal shouts answering each other in different directions. I was not surprised when voices came pealing across the water—loud oaths and ejaculations—mingled with the plashing of paddles and the plunging of oars; and, when the negro announced that several boats filled with armed men were in the open water and approaching the tree, it did not take me by surprise. I had foreseen all this.

I descended to the base of the cypress, and, stooping down, looked out under the hanging moss. I could see the surface of the lake. I could see the men in their canoes and skiffs, rowing and gesticulating.

When near the middle of the open water, they lay upon their oars, and held a short consultation. After a moment they separated, and rowed in circles around, evidently with the design of encompassing the tree.

In a few minutes they had executed this manoeuvre, and now closed in, until their vessels floated among the drooping branches of the cypress. A shout of triumph told that they had discovered our retreat; and I now saw their faces peering through the curtain of straggling *tillandsia*.

They could see the pirogue, and both the negro and myself standing by the bow.

"Surrender!" shouted a voice in a loud, firm tone. "If you resist, your lives be on your own heads!"

Notwithstanding this summons, the boats did not advance any nearer. They knew that I carried pistols, and that I knew how to handle them—the proofs, were fresh. They approached, therefore, with caution—thinking I might still use my weapons.

They had no need to be apprehensive. I had not the slightest intention of doing so. Resistance against twenty men—for there were that number in the boats, twenty men well armed—would have been a piece of desperate folly. I never thought of such a thing; though, if I had, I believe the Bambarra would have stood by me to the death. The brave fellow, steeled to a supernatural courage by the prospect of his punishment, had even proposed fight! But his courage was madness; and I entreated him not to resist—as they would certainly have slain him on the spot.

I meant no resistance, but I hesitated a moment in making answer.

"We're all armed," continued the speaker, who seemed to have some authority over the others. "It is useless for you to resist—you had better give up!"

"Damn them!" cried another and a rougher voice; "don't waste talk on them. Let's fire the tree, and smoke 'em out; that moss 'll burn, I reckon!"

I recognised the voice that uttered this inhuman suggestion. It came from Bully Bill.

"I have no intention of making resistance," I called out in reply to the first speaker. "I am ready to go with you. I have committed no crime. For what I have done I am ready to answer to the laws."

"You shall answer to *us*," replied one who had not before spoken; "*we* are the laws here."

There was an ambiguity in this speech that I liked not; but there was no further parley. The skiffs and canoes had suddenly closed in around the tree. A dozen muzzles of pistols and rifles were pointed at me, and a dozen voices commanded the negro and myself to get into one of the boats.

From the fierce, determined glances of these rough men, I saw it was death or obedience.

I turned to bid adieu to Aurore, who had rushed out of the tree-cave, and stood near me weeping.

As I faced round, several men sprang upon the buttress; and, seizing me from behind, held me in their united grasp. Then drawing my arms across my back, tied them fast with a rope.

I could just speak one parting word with Aurore, who, no longer in tears, stood regarding my captors with a look of scornful indignation. As they led me unresistingly into the boat, her high spirit gave way to words, and she cried out in a voice of scorn—

"Cowards! cowards! Not one of you dare meet him in a fair field—no, not one of you!"

The lofty spirit of my betrothed echoed mine, and gave me proof of her love. I was pleased with it, and could have applauded; but my mortified captors gave me no time to reply; for the next moment the pirogue in which I had been placed shot out through the branches, and floated on the open water of the lake.

Chapter Seventy Six
A Terrible Fate

I saw no more of Aurore. Neither was the black brought along. I could gather from the conversation of my captors, that they were to be taken in one of the skiffs that had stayed behind—that they were to be landed at a different point from that to which we were steering. I could gather, too, that the poor Bambarra was doomed to a terrible punishment—the same he already dreaded—the losing of an arm!

I was pained at such a thought, but still more by the rude jests I had now to listen to. My betrothed and myself were reviled with a disgusting coarseness, which I cannot repeat.

I made no attempt to defend either her or myself. I did not even reply. I sat with my eyes bent gloomily upon the water; and it was a sort of relict to me when the pirogue again passed in among the trunks of the cypress-trees, and their dark shadow half concealed my face from the view of my captors. I was brought back to the landing by the old tree-trunk.

On nearing this I saw that a crowd of men awaited us on the shore; and among them I recognised the ferocious Ruffin, with his arm slung in his red kerchief, bandaged and bloody. He was standing up with the rest.

"Thank Heaven! I have not killed him!" was my mental ejaculation. "So much the less have I to answer for."

The canoes and skiffs—with the exception of that which carried Aurore and the black—had all arrived at this point, and my captors were landing. In all there were some thirty or forty men, with a proportion of half-grown boys. Most of them were armed with either pistols or rifles. Under the grey gloom of the trees, they presented a picturesque tableau; but at that moment my feelings were not attuned to enjoy it.

I was landed among the rest; and with two armed men, one before and another immediately at my back, I was marched off through the woods. The crowd accompanied us, some in the advance, some behind, while others walked alongside. These were the boys and the more brutal of the men who occasionally taunted me with rude speech.

I might have lost patience and grown angry, had that served me; but I knew it would only give pleasure to my tormentors, without bettering my condition. I therefore observed silence, and kept my eyes averted or turned upon the ground.

We passed on rapidly—as fast as the crowd could make way through the bushes—and I was glad of this. I presumed I was about to be conducted before a magistrate, or "justice of the peace," as there called. Well, thought I. Under legal authority, and in the keeping of the officers, I should be protected from the gibes and insults that were being showered upon me. Everything short of personal violence was offered; and there were some that seemed sufficiently disposed even for this.

I saw the forest opening in front. I supposed we had gone by some shorter way to the clearings. It was not so, for the next moment we emerged into the glade. Again the glade!

Here my captors came to a halt; and now in the open light I had an opportunity to know who they were. At a glance I saw that I was in the hands of a desperate crowd.

Gayarre himself was in their midst, and beside him his own overseer, and the negro-trader, and the brutal Larkin. With these were some half-dozen Creole-Frenchmen of the poorer class of *proprietaires*, weavers of cottonade, or small planters. The rest of the mob was composed of the very scum of the settlement—the drunken boatmen whom I had used to see gossiping in front of the "groceries," and other dissipated rowdies of the place. Not one respectable planter appeared upon the ground—not one respectable man!

For what had they stopped in the glade? I was impatient to be taken before the justice, and chafed at the delay.

"Why am I detained here?" I asked in a tone of anger.

"Ho, mister!" replied one; "don't be in such a hell of a hurry! You'll find out soon enough, I reckon."

"I protest against this," I continued. "I insist upon being taken before the justice."

"An' so ye will, damn you! You ain't got far to go. *The justice is hyar.*"

"Who? where?" I inquired, under the impression that a magistrate was upon the ground. I had heard of wood-choppers acting as justices of the peace—in fact, had met with one or two of them—and among the rude forms that surrounded me there might be one of these. "Where is the justice?" I demanded. "Oh, he's about—never you fear!" replied one. "Whar's the justice?" shouted another. "Ay, whar's the justice?—whar are ye, judge?" cried a third, as if appealing to some one in the crowd. "Come on hyar, judge!" he added. "Come along!—hyar's a fellar wants to see you!"

I really thought the man was in earnest. I really believed there was such an individual in the mob. The only impression made upon me was astonishment at this rudeness towards the magisterial representative of the law.

My misconception was short-lived, for at this moment Ruffin—the bandaged and bloody Ruffin—came close up to me; and, after scowling upon me with his fierce, bloodshot eyes, bent forward until his lips almost touched my face, and then hissed out—

"Perhaps, Mister nigger-stealer, you've niver heerd ov *Justice Lynch*?"

A thrill of horror run through my veins. The fearful conviction flashed before my mind that *they* were *going to Lynch me*!

Chapter Seventy Seven
The Sentence of Judge Lynch

An undefined suspicion of something of this sort had already crossed my thoughts. I remembered the reply made from the boats, "You shall answer to *us*. *We* are the law." I had heard some mysterious innuendoes as we passed through the woods—I had noticed too, that on our arrival in the glade, we found those who had gone in the advance halted there, as if waiting for the others to come up; and I could not comprehend why we had stopped there at all.

I now saw that the men of the party were drawing to one side, and forming a sort of irregular ring, with that peculiar air of solemnity that bespeaks some serious business. It was only the boys, and some negroes—for these, too, had taken part in our capture—who remained near me. Ruffin had simply approached to gratify his revengeful feelings by tantalising me.

All these appearances had aroused wild suspicions within me, but up to that moment they had assumed no definite form. I had even endeavoured to keep back such a suspicion, under the vague belief, that by the very imagination of it, I might in some way aid in bringing it about!

It was no longer suspicion. It was now conviction. They were going to Lynch me!

The significant interrogatory, on account of the manner in which it was put, was hailed by the boys with a shout of laughter. Ruffin continued—

"No; I guess you han't heerd ov that ar justice, since yur a stranger in these parts, an' a Britisher. You han't got sich a one among yur bigwigs, I reckin. He's the fellar that ain't a-goin' to keep you long in Chancery. No, by God! he'll do yur business in double-quick time. Hell and scissors! yu'll see if he don't."

Throughout all this speech the brutal fellow taunted me with gestures as well as words—drawing from his auditory repeated bursts of laughter.

So provoked was I that, had I not been fast bound, I should have sprung upon him; but, bound as I was, and vulgar brute as was this adversary, I could not hold my tongue.

"Were I free, you ruffian, you would not dare taunt me thus. At all events *you* have come off but second best. I've crippled *you* for life; though it don't matter much, seeing what a clumsy use you make of a rifle."

This speech produced a terrible effect upon the brute—the more so that the boys now laughed at *him*. These boys were not all bad. They were incensed against me as an Abolitionist—or "nigger-stealer," as they phrased it—and, under the countenance and guidance of their elders, their worst passions were now at play; but for all that, they were not essentially wicked. They were rough backwoods' boys, and the spirit of my retort pleased them. After that they held back from jeering me.

Not so with Ruffin, who now broke forth into a string of vindictive oaths and menaces, and appeared as if about to grapple me with his one remaining hand. At this moment he was called off by the men, who needed him in the "caucus;" and, after shaking his fist in my face, and uttering a parting imprecation, he left me.

I was for some minutes kept in suspense. I could not tell what this dread council were debating, or what they meant to do with me—though I now felt quite certain that they did not intend taking me before any magistrate. From frequent phrases that reached my ears, such as, "flog the scoundrel," "tar and feathers," I began to conjecture that some such punishment awaited me. To my astonishment, however, I found, upon listening a while, that a number of my judges were actually opposed to these punishments as being too mild! Some declared openly, that *nothing but my life could satisfy the outraged laws*!

The *majority* took this view of the case; and it was to add to their strength that Ruffin had been summoned!

A feeling of terrible fear crept over me—say rather a feeling of horror—but it was only complete when the ring of men suddenly broke up, and I saw two of their number lay hold of a rope, and commence reeving it over the limb of a gum-tree that stood by the edge of the glade.

There had been a trial and a sentence too. Even Judge Lynch has his formality.

When the rope was adjusted, one of the men—the negro-trader it was—approached me; and in a sort of rude paraphrase of a judge, summed up and pronounced the sentence!

I had outraged the laws; I had committed two capital crimes. I had stolen slaves, and endeavoured to take away the life of a fellow-creature. A jury of twelve men had tried—and found me guilty; and sentenced me to death by hanging. Even this was not permitted to go forth in an informal manner. The very phraseology was adopted. I was to be hung by the neck until I should be dead—dead!

You will deem this relation exaggerated and improbable. You will think that I am sporting with you. You will not believe that such lawlessness can exist in a Christian—a civilised land. You will fancy that these men were sporting with *me*, and that in the end they did not seriously intend to *hang me*.

I cannot help it if you think so; but I solemnly declare that such was their design: and I felt as certain at that moment that they intended to have hanged me, as I now feel that I was not hanged!

Believe it or not, you must remember that I would not have been the first victim by many, and that thought was vividly before my mind at the time.

Along with it, there was the rope—there the tree—there stood my judges before me. Their looks alone might have produced conviction. There was not a ray of mercy to be seen.

At that awful moment I knew not what I said or how I acted.

I remember only that my fears were somewhat modified by my indignation. That I protested, menaced, swore—that my ruthless judges answered me with mockery.

They were actually proceeding to put the sentence into execution—and had already carried me across to the foot of the tree—when the sound of trampling hoofs fell upon our ears, and the next moment a party of horsemen galloped into the glade.

Chapter Seventy Eight
In the Hands of the Sheriff

At sight of these horsemen my heart leaped with joy, for among the foremost I beheld the calm, resolute face of Edward Reigart. Behind him rode the sheriff of the parish, followed by a "posse" of about a dozen men—among whom I recognised several of the most respectable planters of the neighbourhood. Every one of the party was armed either with a rifle or pistols; and the manner in which they rode forward upon the ground, showed that they had come in great haste, and with a determined purpose.

I say my heart leaped with joy. An actual criminal standing upon the platform of the gallows could not have been more joyed at sight of the messenger that brought him reprieve or pardon. In the new-comers I recognised friends: in their countenances I read rescue. I was not displeased, therefore, when the sheriff, dismounting, advanced to my side, and placing his hand upon my shoulder, told me I was his prisoner "in the name of the law." Though brusquely done, and apparently with a degree of rudeness, I was not displeased either by the act or the manner. The latter was plainly assumed for a purpose; and in the act itself I hailed the salvation of my life. I felt like a rescued man.

The proceeding did not equally content my former judges, who loudly murmured their dissatisfaction. They alleged that I had already been tried by a jury of *twelve free citizens*—that I had been found guilty of nigger-stealing—that I had stolen *two niggers*—that I had resisted when pursued, and had "wownded" one of my pursuers; and that, as all this had been "clarly made out," they couldn't see what more was wanted to establish my guilt, and that I ought to be *hung* on the spot, without further loss of time.

The sheriff replied that such a course would be illegal; that the majesty of the law must be respected; that if I was guilty of the crimes alleged against me, the law would most certainly measure out full punishment to me; but that I must first be brought before a justice, and the charge legally and formally made out; and, finally, expressed his intention to take me before Justice Claiborne, the magistrate of the district.

An angry altercation ensued between the mob and the sheriffs party—in which but slight show of respect was paid to the high executive—and for some time I was actually in dread that the ruffians would carry their point. But an American sheriff is entirely a different sort of character from the idle gentleman who fills that office in an English county. The former is, in nine cases out of ten, a man of proved courage and action; and Sheriff Hickman, with whom my *quasi* judges had to deal, was no exception to this rule. His "posse," moreover, hurriedly collected by my friend Reigart, chanced to have among their number several men of a similar stamp. Reigart himself, though a man of peace, was well-known to possess a cool and determined spirit; and there was the landlord of my hotel, and several of the planters who accompanied several of the young planters, behaved in a handsome manner; and the law prevailed.

Yes! thank Heaven and half-a-dozen noble men, the law prevailed—else I should never have gone out of that glade alive!

Justice Lynch had to give way to Justice Claiborne, and a respite was obtained from the cruel verdict of the former. The victorious sheriff and his party bore me off in their midst.

But though my ferocious judges had yielded for the present, it was not certain that they would not still attempt to rescue me from the hands of the law. To prevent this, the sheriff mounted me upon a horse—he himself riding upon one side, while an assistant of tried courage took the opposite. Reigart and the planters kept close to me before and behind; while the shouting, blaspheming mob followed both on horseback and afoot. In this way we passed through the woods, across the fields, along the road leading into Bringiers, and then to the residence of "Squire" Claiborne—Justice of the Peace for that district.

Attached to his dwelling was a large room or office where the Squire was used to administer the magisterial law of the land. It was entered by a separate door from the house itself, and had no particular marks about it to denote that it was a hall of justice, beyond the fact that it was furnished with a bench or two to serve as seats, and a small desk or rostrum in one corner.

At this desk the Squire was in the habit of settling petty disputes, administering affidavits at a quarter of a dollar each, and arranging other small civic matters. But oftener was his magisterial function employed in sentencing the mutinous "darkie" to his due the sheriff—sterling men, who were lovers of the law and lovers of fair play as well—and those, armed to the teeth, would have laid down their lives on the spot in defence of the sheriff and his demand. True, they were in the minority in point of numbers; but they had the law upon their side, and that gave them strength.

There was one point in my favour above all others, and that was, my accusers chanced to be unpopular men. Gayarre, as already stated, although professing a high standard of morality, was not esteemed by the neighbouring planters—particularly by those of American origin. The others most forward against me were known to be secretly instigated by the lawyer. As to Ruffin, whom I had "wounded," those upon the ground had heard the crack of his rifle, and knew that *he had fired first*. In their calmer moments my resistance would have been deemed perfectly justifiable—so far as that individual was concerned.

Had the circumstances been different—had the "two niggers" I had *stolen* belonged to a popular planter, and not to Monsieur Dominique Gayarre—had Ruffin been a respectable citizen, instead of the dissipated half outlaw that he was—had there not been a suspicion in the minds of many present that it was *not* a case of ordinary *nigger-stealing*, then indeed might it have gone ill with me, in spite of the sheriff and his party.

Even as it was, a long and angry altercation ensued—loud words, oaths, and gestures of menace, were freely exchanged—and both rifles and pistols were cocked and firmly grasped before the discussion ended.

But the brave sheriff remained resolute; Reigart acted a most courageous part; my *ci-devant* host, and proportion of stripes on the complaint of a conscientious master—for, after all, such theoretical protection does the poor slave enjoy.

Into this room, then, was I hurried by the sheriff and his assistants—the mob rushing in after, until every available space was occupied.

Chapter Seventy Nine
The Crisis

No doubt a messenger had preceded us, for we found Squire Claiborne in his chair of office, ready to hear the case. In the tall, thin old man, with white hair and dignified aspect, I recognised a fit representative of justice — one of those venerable magistrates, who command respect not only by virtue of age and office, but from the dignity of their personal character. In spite of the noisy rabble that surrounded me, I read in the serene, firm look of the magistrate the determination to show fair play.

I was no longer uneasy. On the way, Reigart had told me to be of good cheer. He had whispered something about "strange developments to be made;" but I had not fully heard him, and was at a loss to comprehend what he meant. In the hurry and crush I had found no opportunity for an explanation.

"Keep up your spirits!" said he, as he pushed his horse alongside me. "Don't have any fear about the result. It's rather an odd affair, and will have an odd ending — rather unexpected for somebody, I should say — ha! ha! ha!"

Reigart actually laughed aloud, and appeared to be in high glee! What could such conduct mean?

I was not permitted to know, for at that moment the sheriff, in a high tone of authority, commanded that no one should "hold communication with the prisoner;" and my friend and I were abruptly separated. Strange, I did not dislike the sheriff for this! I had a secret belief that his manner — apparently somewhat hostile to me — was assumed for a purpose. The mob required conciliation; and all this *brusquerie* was a bit of management on the part of Sheriff Hickman.

On arriving before Justice Claiborne, it required all the authority of both sheriff and justice to obtain silence. A partial lull, however, enabled the latter to proceed with the case.

"Now, gentlemen!" said he, speaking in a firm, magisterial tone, "I am ready to hear the charge against this young man. Of what is he accused, Colonel Hickman?" inquired the justice, turning to the sheriff.

"Of negro-stealing, I believe," replied the latter.

"Who prefers the charge?"

"Dominique Gayarre," replied a voice from the crowd, which I recognised as that of Gayarre himself.

"Is Monsieur Gayarre present?" inquired the justice.

The voice again replied in the affirmative, and the fox-like face of the avocat now presented itself in front of the rostrum.

"Monsieur Dominique Gayarre," said the magistrate, recognising him, "what is the charge you bring against the prisoner? State it in full and upon oath."

Gayarre having gone through the formula of the oath, proceeded with his plaint in true lawyer style.

I need not follow the circumlocution of legal phraseology. Suffice it to say, that there were several counts in his indictment.

I was first accused of having endeavoured to instigate to mutiny and revolt the slaves of the plantation Besançon, by having interfered to prevent one of their number from receiving his *just* punishment! Secondly, I had caused another of these to strike down his overseer; and afterwards had induced him to run away to the woods, and aided him in so doing! This was the slave Gabriel, who had just that day been captured in my company. Thirdly and Gayarre now came to the cream of his accusation.

"Thirdly," continued he, "I accuse this person of having entered my house on the night of October the 18th, and having stolen therefrom the female slave Aurore Besançon."

"It is false!" cried a voice, interrupting him. "It is false! *Aurore Besançon is not a slave!*"

Gayarre started, as though some one had thrust a knife into him.

"Who says that?" he demanded, though with a voice that evidently faltered.

"I!" replied the voice; and at the same instant a young man leaped upon one of the benches, and stood with his head overtopping the crowd. It was D'Hauteville!

"I say it!" he repeated, in the same firm tone. "*Aurore Besançon is no slave, but a free Quadroon*! Here, Justice Claiborne," continued D'Hauteville, "do me the favour to read this document!" At the same time the speaker handed a folded parchment across the room.

The sheriff passed it to the magistrate, who opened it and read aloud.

It proved to be the "free papers" of Aurore the Quadroon—the certificate of her manumission—regularly signed and attested by her master, Auguste Besançon, and left by him in his will.

The astonishment was extreme—so much so that the crowd seemed petrified, and preserved silence. Their feelings were on the turn.

The effect produced upon Gayarre was visible to all. He seemed covered with confusion. In his embarrassment he faltered out—

"I protest against this—that paper has been stolen from my bureau, and—"

"So much the better, Monsieur Gayarre!" said D'Hauteville, again interrupting him; "so much the better! You confess to its being stolen, and therefore you confess to its being genuine. Now, sir, having this document in your possession, and knowing its contents, how could you claim Aurore Besançon as your slave?"

Gayarre was confounded. His cadaverous face became of a white, sickly hue; and his habitual look of malice rapidly gave way to an expression of terror. He appeared as if he wanted to be gone; and already crouched behind the taller men who stood around him.

"Stop, Monsieur Gayarre!" continued the inexorable D'Hauteville, "I have not done with you yet. Here, Justice Claiborne! I have another document that may interest you. Will you have the goodness to give it your attention?"

Saying this, the speaker held out a second folded parchment, which was handed to the magistrate—who, as before, opened the document and read it aloud.

This was a codicil to the will of Auguste Besançon, by which the sum of fifty thousand dollars in bank stock was bequeathed to his daughter, Eugénie Besançon, to be paid to her upon the day on which she should be of age by the joint executors of the estate—Monsieur Dominique Gayarre and Antoine Lereux—and these executors were instructed not to make known to the recipient the existence of this sum in her favour, until the very day of its payment.

"Now, Monsieur Dominique Gayarre!" continued D'Hauteville, as soon as the reading was finished, "I charge you with the embezzlement of this fifty thousand dollars, with various other sums—of which more hereafter. I charge you with having concealed the existence of this money—of having withheld it from the assets of the estate Besançon—of having appropriated it to your own use!"

"This is a serious charge," said Justice Claiborne, evidently impressed with its truth, and prepared to entertain it. "Your name, sir, if you please?" continued he, interrogating D'Hauteville, in a mild tone of voice.

It was the first time I had seen D'Hauteville in the full light of day. All that had yet passed between us had taken place either in the darkness of night or by the light of lamps. That morning alone had we been together for a few minutes by daylight; but even then it was under the sombre shadow of the woods—where I could have but a faint view of his features.

Now that he stood in the light of the open window, I had a full, clear view of his face. The resemblance to some one I had seen before again impressed me. It grew stronger as I gazed; and before the magistrate's interrogatory had received its reply, the shock of my astonishment had passed.

"Your name, sir, if you please?" repeated the justice.

"*Eugénie Besançon!*"

At the same instant the hat was pulled off—the black curls were drawn aside—and the fair, golden tresses of the beautiful Creole exhibited to the view.

A loud huzza broke out—in which all joined, excepting Gayarre and his two or three ruffian adherents. I felt that I was free.

The conditions had suddenly changed, and the plaintiff had taken the place of the defendant. Even before the excitement had quieted down, I saw the sheriff, at the instigation of Reigart and others, stride forward to Gayarre, and placing his hand upon the shoulder of the latter, arrest him as his prisoner.

"It is false!" cried Gayarre; "a plot—a damnable plot! These documents are forgeries! the signatures are false—false!"

"Not so, Monsieur Gayarre," said the justice, interrupting him. "Those documents are not forgeries. This is the handwriting of Auguste Besançon. I knew him well. This is his signature—I could myself swear to it."

"And I!" responded a voice, in a deep solemn tone, which drew the attention of all.

The transformation of Eugène D'Hauteville to Eugénie Besançon had astonished the crowd; but a greater surprise awaited them in the resurrection of the *steward Antoine*!

Reader! my story is ended. Here upon our little drama must the curtain drop. I might offer you other tableaux to illustrate the after history of our characters, but a slight summary must suffice. Your fancy will supply the details.

It will glad you to know, then, that Eugénie Besançon recovered the whole of her property—which was soon restored to its flourishing condition under the faithful stewardship of Antoine.

Alas! there was that that could never be restored—the young cheerful heart—the buoyant spirit—the virgin love!

But do not imagine that Eugénie Besançon yielded to despair—that she was ever after the victim of that unhappy passion. No—hers was a mighty will; and all its energies were employed to pluck the fatal arrow from her heart.

Time and a virtuous life have much power; but far more effective was that sympathy of the object beloved—that *pity for love*—which to her was fully accorded.

Her heart's young hope was crushed—her gay spirit shrouded—but there are other joys in life besides the play of the passions; and, it may be, the path of love is not the true road to happiness. Oh! that I could believe this! Oh! that I could reason myself into the belief, that that calm and unruffled mien—that soft sweet smile were the tokens of a heart at rest. Alas! I cannot. Fate will have its victims. Poor Eugénie! God be merciful to thee! Oh, that I could steep thy heart in the waters of Lethe!

And Reigart? You, reader, will be glad to know that the good doctor prospered—prospered until he was enabled to lay aside his lancet, and become a grandee planter—nay more, a distinguished legislator,—one of those to whom belongs the credit of having modelled the present system of Louisiana law—the most advanced code in the civilised world.

You will be glad to learn that Scipio, with his Chloe and the "leetle Chloe," were brought back to their old and now happy home—that the snake-charmer still retained his brawny arms, and never afterwards had occasion to seek refuge in his tree-cavern.

You will not be grieved to know, that Gayarre passed several years of his after-life in the palace-prison of Baton Rouge, and then disappeared altogether from the scene. It was said that under a changed name he returned to France, his native country. His conviction was easy. Antoine had long suspected him of a design to plunder their joint ward, and had determined to put him to the proof. The raft of chairs had floated after all; and by the help of these the faithful steward had gained the shore, far down the river. No one knew of his escape; and the idea occurred to this strange old man to remain for a while *en perdu*—a silent spectator of the conduct of Monsieur Dominique. No sooner did Gayarre believe him gone, than the latter advanced boldly upon his purpose, and hurried events to the described crisis. It was just what Antoine had expected; and acting himself as the accuser, the conviction of the avocat was easy and certain. A sentence of five years to the State Penitentiary wound up Gayarre's connexion with the characters of our story.

It will scarce grieve you to know that "Bully Bill" experienced a somewhat similar fate—that Ruffin, the man-hunter, was drowned by a sudden rising of the swamp—and that the "nigger-trader" afterwards became a "nigger-stealer;" and for that crime was sentenced at the court of Judge Lynch to the punishment of "tar and feathers."

The "sportsmen," Chorley and Hatcher, I never saw again—though their future is not unknown to me. Chorley—the brave and accomplished, but wicked Chorley—was killed in a duel by a Creole of New Orleans, with whom he had quarrelled at play.

Hatcher's bank "got broke" soon after, and a series of ill-fortune at length reduced him to the condition of a race-course thimble-rig, and small sharper in general.

The pork-merchant I met many years afterward, as a successful *monte* dealer in the "Halls of the Montezumas." Thither he had gone,—a camp-follower of the American army—and had accumulated an enormous fortune by keeping a gambling-table for the officers. He did not live long to enjoy his evil gains. The *"vomito prieto"* caught him at Vera Cruz; and his dust is now mingled with the sands of that dreary shore.

Thus, reader, it has been my happy fortune to record *poetical justice* to the various characters that have figured in the pages of our history.

I hear you exclaim, that two have been forgotten, the hero and heroine?

Ah! no—not forgotten. Would you have me paint the ceremony—the pomp and splendour—the ribbons and rosettes—the after-scenes of perfect bliss?

Hymen, forbid! All these must be left to your fancy, if your fancy deign to act. But the interest of a "lover's adventures" usually ends with the consummation of his hopes—not even always extending to the altar—and you, reader, will scarce be curious to lift the curtain, that veils the tranquil after-life of myself and my beautiful Quadroon.

Note to the Preface

After what has been stated in the Preface, it will scarce be necessary to say that the *names* and some of the *places* mentioned in this book are fictitious. Some of the scenes, and many of the characters that figure in these pages, are *real*, and there are those living who will recognise them.

The book is "founded" upon an actual experience. It was written many years ago, and would have been then published, but for the interference of a well-known work, which treated of similar scenes and subjects. That work appeared just as the "Quadroon" was about to be put to press; and the author of the the latter, not willing to risk the chances of being considered an imitator had determined on keeping the "Quadroon" from the public.

Circumstances have ruled it otherwise; and having re-written some parts of the work, he now presents it to the reader as a painting—somewhat coarse and crude, perhaps—of life in Louisiana.

The author disclaims all "intention." The book has been written neither to aid the Abolitionist nor glorify the planter. The author does not believe that by such means he could benefit the slave, else he would not fear to avow it. On the other hand, he is too true a Republican, to be the instrument that would add one drop to the "bad blood" which, unfortunately for the cause of human freedom, has already arisen between "North" and "South." No; he will be the last man to aid European despots in this, their dearest wish and desperate hope.

London, July, 1856.